"But...but I don't even like you..."

"I know," his husky voice rasped out. "Damn curious to me, too." His strong hands ran slowly down her back as if he couldn't stop touching her. "You're a puzzle to me, Josephine, and I love a good puzzle."

"I'm not—" She inhaled sharply as his hands cupped against her bottom, gently pulling her hips tight to his and molding her against him. "I'm not a puzzle."

"A mystery, then, one begging to be solved."

"I'm not begging for anything."

At that, he gave a wicked laugh. "Not yet." His stare turned dark and predatory. "But you will."

Her lips parted with a soft breath. There was no mistaking his meaning, and a wave of heat rippled through her, gathering into a burning flame low in her belly.

"You *are* a puzzle, Josephine, one I desperately want to solve." He slowly unfastened the top two buttons of her jacket and pulled open the collar. "And I'm going to peel back the layers of you, one at a time." He lowered his head to place his hot mouth against the bare flesh of her exposed neck, and goose bumps raced down her arms...

Praise for Anna Harrington and
DUKES ARE FOREVER

"A touching and tempestuous romance, with all the ingredients Regency fans adore."
  —Gaelen Foley, *New York Times* bestselling author

"Harrington's emotionally gripping Regency-era debut, which launches the Secret Life of Scoundrels series, is ripe with drama and sizzling romance...The complex relationship between Edward and Katherine is intense and skillfully written, complete with plenty of romantic angst that propels the novel swiftly forward. This new author is definitely one to watch."
  —*Publishers Weekly* (starred review)

"As steamy as it is sweet as it is luscious. My favorite kind of historical!"
  —Grace Burrowes, *New York Times* bestselling author

"Pits strong-willed characters against one another, and as the sparks ignite, passion is sure to follow. There is a depth of emotion that will leave readers breathless. The pages fly."
  —*RT Book Reviews*

HOW I MARRIED A MARQUESS

Anna Harrington

FOREVER

NEW YORK   BOSTON

Forever
Hachette Book Group
1290 Avenue of the Americas
New York, NY 10104

forever-romance.com
twitter.com/foreverromance
HachetteBookGroup.com

First Edition: April 2016

Forever is an imprint of Grand Central Publishing.
The Forever name and logo are trademarks of Hachette Book Group, Inc.

The publisher is not responsible for websites (or their content) that are not owned by the publisher.

The Hachette Speakers Bureau provides a wide range of authors for speaking events. To find out more, go to www.hachettespeakersbureau.com or call (866) 376-6591.

ISBN 978-1-4555-3407-4 (mass market); 978-1-4555-3406-7 (ebook)

Printed in the United States of America

OPM

10 9 8 7 6 5 4 3 2 1

ATTENTION CORPORATIONS AND ORGANIZATIONS:
Most Hachette Book Group books are available at quantity discounts with bulk purchase for educational, business, or sales promotional use. For information, please call or write:

Special Markets Department, Hachette Book Group
1290 Avenue of the Americas, New York, NY 10104
Telephone: 1-800-222-6747 Fax: 1-800-477-5925

Dedicated to the real Josie.
Love, Mom

And as always, a very special thank-you
to Michele Bidelspach, Sarah Younger,
Jessica Pierce, and Mari Okuda

CHAPTER ONE

Mayfair, London
October 1817

"Lord Chesney?" Jensen's voice cut through the midmorning stillness of the stables. "Are you here, sir?"

Inside the end stall box, Thomas Matteson stilled, hoping the butler would simply leave and not interrupt his morning. The same morning he'd so carefully arranged by giving the grooms time off to attend Tattersall's. He let the silence of the stables answer for him, broken only by the restless shifting of horses in their stalls and a pawing of hooves.

But Jensen persisted in his hunt. "Sir?"

Stifling a curse, knowing he had no choice but to face whatever calamity had sent the man after him, Thomas stepped into the aisle and firmly closed the stall door behind him. He brushed pieces of straw from the sleeves of his maroon redingote. "What is it, Jensen?"

"A visitor, sir." The portly butler hurried forward, silver salver in hand.

Thomas fought to keep from rolling his eyes at the man's formality. An employee of the Matteson household for nearly twenty years, Jensen took his position seriously, even during times like these when the duke and duchess were at their country estate and Thomas was the only family member in residence.

And he was in residence precisely *because* his mother and father were not, needing the distractions of London and the freedom of turning Chatham House into bachelor's quarters until his parents returned in January. Yet Jensen and the rest of the staff continued to serve with the precision of a military regiment, taking pride in their positions within a duke's household even while the duke was away.

And while the old lord was away, the young lord would play...or at least that had been his plan. To fill his daylight hours with as many frivolous activities as possible and his nights however—and with whomever—he could. But it was deuced hard when the staff followed his every move. For heaven's sake, yesterday morning he'd caught Cook spying on him to make certain he ate breakfast!

Most likely their close attention came at his mother's orders. He would have found her concern endearing if it didn't aggravate the hell out of him. And it was damned grating that nearly everyone he interacted with these days—including the household staff—still thought of him as fragile. Still not fully recovered. *Broken.*

"My lord." Jensen presented the card with as much flourish as if he stood in the gilded front hall rather than in the stable with his shoes dangerously close to a pile of manure.

Irritated at being interrupted, Thomas snatched up the card and read the embossed name. The Earl Royston? *Odd.* Why the devil was he here? Royston was an old family friend and always welcome at Chatham House. But surely Royston knew that his father was in the country, and Thomas couldn't imagine what the earl would want with him.

"I've put his lordship in the drawing room, sir." Then Jensen hesitated and cleared his throat as if he dreaded telling him, "And Lady Emily is taking tea in the morning room."

"My sister is, is she?" His lips curled grimly. Yet another person set on ruining his morning, apparently. "Tell Royston I'll join him in a moment." He arched a brow. "And tell my sister that she has her own town house and should bloody well stop haunting mine."

"Yes, sir." Despite his curt nod, Thomas knew the portly butler had no intention of passing along *that* message.

Straw rustled inside the stall behind him. Jensen furrowed his bushy brows. "Should I call for a footman to help you with your horse, sir?"

"No need." At the sound of more rustling, he added, "Just a filly I've been attempting to break."

With a shallow bow, and careful to miss the manure, Jensen turned smartly on his heels and retreated toward the house. Thomas waited until the butler was out of sight before opening the stall door. Folding his arms across his chest, he leaned lazily against the post and looked at the woman standing inside.

"Just a filly you've been attempting to break, am I?" Helene Humphrey, the young widow of the late Charles Humphrey, pouted with mock peevishness as she brushed at the straw clinging to her riding habit. The same habit that moments ago had been pulled down to her waist and bunched up around her hips as she'd straddled him in the hay. "How positively uncomplimentary of you, Chesney."

He shrugged away her scolding, not caring if she was offended. After all, he allowed her into his stables in the mornings only because he wanted to chase away any lingering anxieties from the nights before. And he wasn't naïve enough to believe she visited him for any reason other than sex.

Having settled into wealthy widowhood with all the restraint of an opera diva, Helene thrilled at indulging in a string of dalliances, including those she'd risked before Humphrey died. Which was one of the main reasons Thomas had selected her to be one of his lovers. With Helene a man got exactly what he saw. No secrets, no surprises...just a beautiful and eager woman with a hot mouth and a cold heart.

"You're the one visiting *my* stables, Helene," he reminded her.

"And where else am I supposed to take such a fine morning ride?" She turned her back to him so he could fasten up her dress.

He obliged—of course he did. He was a gentleman, after all, and a gentleman always helped his lover freshen her appearance after a tryst, even if she made assignations with half of London society and had just ridden him off six feet from a pile of horse shit.

"One of these mornings, we really should put you onto a horse." As he fastened the last button, he lowered his head to brush his mouth against the side of her neck for one last taste of her. "I've got a new gelding you might like."

With a wicked smile, she turned in his arms and cupped his cock in her palm. "Why would I want a gelding," she purred, fondling him through his breeches more in possessiveness than in desire, "when I've got a stallion?"

Dragging in a breath through clenched teeth, he reached down to grasp her wrist and pull her hand away as fresh irritation surged inside him. The last way he wanted to think of himself was as providing stud service. Even if the implication was true.

"At least your guests have good timing." She stepped back and tugged at her gloves. As with her hat and its beaded half veil, she'd kept her gloves and boots on the entire time he'd been inside her. Mercifully, though, she'd discarded the riding crop. "Ten minutes earlier and I would have been extremely put out."

Ten minutes earlier. He would have been annoyed, but would he have truly cared?

His chest tightened with the bitter ache of self-recrimination. Good Lord, had his life really come to this? Pre-appointed tumbles in a horse stall with a woman he didn't even like, partaking of her pleasures more to release the acute uneasiness that pounded relentlessly at him than for physical satisfaction?

Only one year ago, his life had still possessed meaning. He'd felt alive and happy, and he never would have sought out the company of such a shallow woman as Helene. In public he'd moved in the inner circle of English society, taking advantage of all the benefits life within the *ton* afforded, for all outward appearances seemingly concerned with nothing more than fast horses, faster women, and the odds in the book at White's. But in private he'd served as a War Office operative, his skills highly valued and his work important. His life had been filled with purpose.

Until everything had gone so horribly wrong one Sunday evening, right in Mayfair. That was the evening when he'd learned the difference between being alive and truly living. The evening when his life had become a living hell.

Unconsciously he reached for his side, for that spot just above his hip where the bullet hole still hideously pocked his skin. His fingers trembled. *Goddammit!* Even now, even in the safety of his own home in broad daylight, he couldn't keep himself from shaking.

"Next Thursday morning, then, for our usual ride?" Oblivious to the darkness once more closing in around him, she trailed the end of her riding crop suggestively along his shoulder as she stepped past him into the aisle. "Although I have *so* been wanting to try a private ride in the park."

At the thought of her leaving, a sudden desperation swept through him. He grabbed her around the waist and pulled her back against him, eliciting a soft gasp of surprise from her.

He'd found release with her just minutes ago, but a dark restlessness still pulsed inside him, one that now shifted toward panic. His heart began to pound hard as the familiar metallic taste of anxiety formed on his tongue, and he recklessly sought one last moment of distraction with her.

"When it comes to riding, Helene," he murmured as he nipped at her earlobe, hoping to arouse her enough to convince her to stay, at least for a few more minutes, "I suspect there's nothing you haven't already tried."

He coaxed a soft moan from her as his still-shaking hand fondled her breast through her riding habit, and his cock flexed at the feminine sound. Did he have time to take her again? Nothing more than a desperate diversion, certainly, yet one that would keep at bay the rising anxiety for a little while longer and perhaps let him get through the rest of the morning without falling into the darkness that preyed on him.

Giving a throaty laugh, she slipped out of his arms.

He clenched his empty hands into fists. Physical pain speared his chest as he knew he had to let her go, because if he made another grab for her, then he'd look like a damned fool.

"Insatiable," she scolded with a teasing smile, and smacked him playfully on the shoulder with the riding crop. "But I'm due for breakfast, and you have guests waiting."

She sauntered from the stable with a wide sashay of her hips toward her waiting carriage in the alley, completely unaware that the darkness was circling him again, ready to tear at him with its claws. After all, he'd become so very clever during the past year at hiding his distress. Even from the people who loved him.

As he stared after her, he forced himself to breathe deeply and steadily, to push down the panic nipping at his heels and pounding the blood through his body so hard that the rush of it in his ears was deafening. A tight knot like hot lead burned low in his gut now, and he wiped the back of his hand across his lips as if he could easily brush clean the taste of fear from his mouth. As if he could wipe away the living nightmare his life had become.

He looked down at his hands, now shaking uncontrollably, then squeezed his eyes shut and fought against the demons rising inside him. Not this morning— Dear God, *not* with Royston and his sister waiting inside.

He knew what came next once the shaking started, and he willed it back with every ounce of his being. All the memories would come rushing back until he relived the shooting and its aftermath...the pain radiating from his side so searing that he couldn't breathe, the fear that he would die and slip forever into the blackness. And worst of all, the sheer terror of waking in the dark, screaming in confusion and panic, unable to move.

Squeezing his eyes shut and concentrating instead on the stable around him, on the sounds of the horses, the smells of the hay and manure, and the chilly morning air against his hot cheeks, he forced himself to slowly count to ten. Then twenty. Then one hundred...By the time he reached three hundred, he'd managed to subdue the shaking enough that it was no longer visible and to stop the itching at his wrists, even if his heart continued to pound like a hammer in his chest. He took a moment longer to gather himself enough that no one would notice the agitated state that Helene's departure had thrown him into, then left the stable.

Blowing out a harsh breath, he stalked toward the house

with his hands clenched in frustration so intense that his eyes burned with it. He knew he should be grateful for still being alive, that he still possessed a beating heart that could be sent racing and breath that could turn into anxious pants at even the slightest provocation. Because it meant he was still alive. But *damnation*, at what cost? How much more could he tolerate before it drove him completely mad?

And how much longer before he accepted that his life would never again be what it had once been? Before he realized that he would never have that life back, no matter how desperately he craved it?

He ran his fingers through his hair, cursing them for trembling. His work as a spy was finished. The War Office wouldn't give him another field assignment now, no matter how good his skills. The shooting had made him too conspicuous for espionage work. Too *wounded*. And because of both the shooting and his position as the duke's heir, he couldn't get any sort of military commission now. Even the damned admiralty had rejected him.

Apparently he wasn't even good enough to drown anymore.

Yet he couldn't bear the thought of returning to the life he'd led before he'd joined the War Office, when he'd had nothing to do but wait for his father to die so he could become duke and then…well, then do nothing all over again until he died and his heir replaced him. After fighting against Napoleon on the Peninsula as part of the Scarlet Scoundrels of the First Dragoons, he found little meaning in being a society gentleman. In only a few months after he'd returned from the war, he'd worked his way through all the pursuits enjoyed by the quality—cards, horses, women, more cards, even more women—until nothing was left. But he'd still felt empty.

No wonder so many men gambled away their fortunes, became drunkards, or turned into rakes who sported in ruining young women. They were bored out of their blasted minds.

When he thought about how little life as a peer held for him, the darkness now edging his existence, and both the increasing frequency of the attacks and their severity, he doubted he could survive. In the past year, he'd managed to hang on to his sanity only by clinging to the hope that he still had connections in the government who could get him back into fieldwork. But so far he'd had no luck. No one had been willing to recommend him.

Jensen opened the front door as he bounded up the steps and stalked inside the town house. He paused at the foyer table to sort quickly through the morning mail, searching for one particular message, one specific—

He saw the letter. His heart faltered with a desperate hope.

Earl Bathurst.

With a nervous breath—and damn his shaking fingers that he could barely get to work—he broke the wax seal to scan the message from the Secretary of State for War and the Colonies, the man responsible for overseeing the War Office, and his last hope at returning to the life he'd known before the shooting. But each sentence he read caused the demons inside him to reach out for him again, and his heartbeat raced as the blackness crept in around him, strangling the air from him. He sucked in a deep breath to steady himself as Bathurst's refusal to help fell through him. *I remain unconvinced that you will be able to provide the kind of assistance we need…*

The ghost pain pierced him. Leaning against the table on one hand for support, he protectively covered his side with the other, even knowing full well that the wound was completely healed by now, no matter how raw and sharp the pain. He pressed his eyes closed to concentrate on his breathing. Slow, steady, controlled— *One, two, three, four*—

"Sir?" Jensen arrived at his side. "Is there a problem?"

Opening his eyes and pulling himself instantly to his full height, he turned to face the butler as he covered his humiliation with a shake of his head and an irritated scowl. "Only an annoying piece of correspondence," he lied.

Just as with Helene, he'd become an expert at hiding his distress from the servants. From everyone who cared about him, in fact. And he was good at it. After all, he had years of practice as a spy, when he'd been forced to make himself look as if he belonged in the middle of groups where he never felt completely comfortable. Especially amid London society where his birthright declared he should belong.

He blew out a tired breath and thanked God that the shaking hadn't overcome him completely this time. The very last thing he needed was for the servants to think him ill. Or mad. "Put this in the study, will you?"

He tossed the letter onto the pile and turned away. He would deal with it later when he was alone and could fully absorb the refusal of this last, desperate attempt at life. When he could let the darkness smother him and fall helpless to it. But now the Earl Royston waited in the drawing room and his sister in the morning room, and he had to appear normal in front of them, no matter how agonizing the engulfing blackness searing his chest.

Taking a moment to gather himself and pull his jacket sleeves down to cover his scratched wrists, he paused to lean his shoulder against the doorway of the morning room and looked in at his sister as she sat on the sofa, her feet curled up beneath her and an open book on her lap. He'd brought Emily such worry over the past year. Guilt for the hell he'd put her through only added to the tightening remorse that ate at his gut.

But for now she was relaxed, happily humming to herself, and absolutely glowing. He took solace in the sight of her, and the darkness slowly retreated until his heartbeat stopped pounding and his breath slowed. Until he appeared normal.

"Do you have a valid reason for being here, Mrs. Grey," he drawled, hoping his voice sounded steadier than he actually felt, "or are you simply spying on me again?"

"The latter, of course." Emily smiled as she set the book aside and reached toward the tray on the low table to pour a cup of tea. His sister moved with an inherent gracefulness that turned women green with envy, and the sharpness of her mind only served to distinguish her more from those society ladies who could bore a man to death with their chatter about fashions and balls. "I know you have a visitor waiting for you— Royston wished me good morning when he arrived. But when you're finished with him, I expect you to join me for tea."

Not a request, he noticed. "You know, as a marquess, I outrank you."

"Only a courtesy title, brother dear," she reminded him, falling easily into the teasing jabs and barbs that were their wont. "Although it wouldn't hurt to put that title to good use and consider calling on some of the young ladies who—"

"No."

She shot him a peevish glare over the rim of her teacup, which he ignored. He would have to marry someday and produce an heir, but there was no hurry. No need to punish some poor girl unduly by bringing her into the madness of the Matteson family sooner than necessary.

"You came to check on me again," he accused gently, although in truth he was glad to see her. The darkness never disappeared completely these days, but when he was with Emily, it receded.

"I came because I had the day to myself for once, and I

wanted to spend time with my loving brother." Despite that obvious lie, she scolded lightly, "Shame on you for insinuating otherwise."

He arched a blatantly disbelieving brow. Emily was beautiful, charming, and elegant, and an absolute pain in the arse whenever she meddled in his business, which was most of the time. But he loved her, and he would gladly lay down his life for her—when he wasn't set on throttling her himself. "Where has Grey gone off to, then?"

"He and the colonel went to Tattersall's to look at a hunter that Jackson Shaw has up for auction," she answered far too smoothly, clearly having practiced her response in anticipation of the question. She never could lie well, not even as a child. "Kate and the twins are away at Brambly House. And I couldn't bear the thought of being all alone at home, so I came here."

"You couldn't bear the thought of *me* being all alone, you mean," he countered, knowing full well that she had her son, his nanny, and a dozen servants to keep her company. "So you came here to torture me."

With a shrug she lifted the teacup to her lips. "If you can't torture family, well, then, whom can you torture?"

"And that," he pointed out earnestly, "sums up every Matteson family dinner since we were five."

She choked on her tea. Laughing, she cleared her throat. "Go on, then. See to Royston. I'll be here when you return."

"Dear God," he grumbled painfully, "truly?"

He saw the devilish smile she tried to hide behind the teacup, then turned into the hallway.

"And give my regards to Lady Humphrey the next time you...*see* her."

He froze. *Damnation.*

Rolling his eyes, he glared at her over his shoulder.

"You've become as much of a spy as that husband of yours."

"Torture, spying—" With a wave of her hand, she dismissed him. "It's all Matteson family business."

Yes, he conceded as he took the stairs three at a time, he supposed it was.

Except not for him. Not any longer.

Pushing the black thoughts from his mind, he forced a smile as he strode into the drawing room. "Royston."

"Chesney." Simon Royston, Earl Royston, clasped his hand. "Good to see you again."

His chest lightened at the warm familiarity with which the earl greeted him. It was always good to see someone he could trust, especially these days. "And you."

Royston had been a family friend since the days when Thomas's father first returned from India and took a government post in London. Since then the two families had grown even closer. The two ladies often co-hosted soirees and elaborate parties that were the talk of the season, and the two men worked closely together in the Lords, with Royston an ardent supporter of several of Thomas's father's initiatives.

In comparison to the Matteson family, with its duchy going back nine generations, the Roystons were recently titled, the current earl only the third in the line. But the earl's grandfather had been well admired among his peers, and Simon Royston carried on that legacy, having become a rising star in Parliament and a trusted advisor at the ear of the prime minister. Thomas liked the man and his family. Royston had been one of the few peers to welcome his father to London long before inheriting had ever been a consideration, and Thomas personally felt a certain loyalty to the man that rose from Royston's help in securing his captain's commission with the Scarlet Scoundrels. Because of all that—and a niggling curiosity about what brought the earl to Chatham House during the off-season, a curiosity that just might distract him for the remainder of the morning—he warmly welcomed the earl.

Thomas gestured to the liquor cabinet. "Whiskey?" Not yet noon, the hour was still early, but he noticed with concern the tension in the older man's body, the dark circles beneath his eyes. The earl could use a drink. And truth be told, so could he.

Royston nodded. "Please."

Thomas poured two glasses and handed one over, then motioned for Royston to sit. He settled into his chair and watched as the earl tossed back nearly half the whiskey in a single swallow.

"I haven't seen you since August," Thomas commented. "I hope you're well."

"As fine as one can be in England in October."

But the forced jocularity to his voice raised Thomas's concerns. "And your wife and son?"

"The countess is happily fussing over the affairs of running Blackwood Hall, and Charles is finishing his last year at Oxford. I expect him to claim a first in mathematics."

He heard the tension edging the man's voice and forced himself not to frown. "Good to hear."

"And you?" Royston's eyes narrowed on him, and Thomas felt the peculiar suspicion that he was being scrutinized. Although, knowing the close relationship the earl had with his parents, his mother had most likely put the man up to checking in on him while he was in town. "It's been a year since the shooting. Is everything back to normal for you?"

If anyone else had asked him that question, Thomas would have told the man to go to hell. But he knew the deep regard in which Royston held him and his family, and he knew the question was asked with nothing less than true concern.

"Yes," he lied, raising the glass to his lips to cover any errant expressions that might flit across his face. "Back to my old self and doing my best to lay waste to whatever pleasures London can provide." Then, purposefully turning the conversation away from himself, he commented, "Although this morning's visit is a surprise, I must admit. I thought you'd be in the country until January."

"I had unexpected business in London," he answered vaguely with a polite smile.

Thomas respected the man's privacy and didn't press. "Of course you're always welcome at Chatham House." Over the years, Thomas and his father had spent more hours playing cards and shooting billiards with the earl than he could count, not to mention all the dinners and political talk at various *ton* affairs. A visit from Royston wasn't unusual, except... "But Father is in the country for the hunting season. Surely you know that." As should be every other man of landed property who had the good sense to avoid London this time of year. Including Royston.

"I came looking for you, actually." The earl paused. "May we speak in confidence?"

He nodded, holding back a puzzled frown. Whatever could Royston want with him?

The man leaned forward, elbows on his knees, and rolled the crystal tumbler between his palms. "There's been trouble at Blackwood Hall."

Thomas had never been to the Roystons' country estate, but he knew of the place, which had been granted to the earl's grandfather when he received the title. Located in the heart of Lincolnshire, the estate was two days' hard ride on horseback from London under the best of conditions; at this time of year, with the increasing cold and fall rains, a coach would be lucky to reach the estate in four. So whatever had sent the earl scurrying to London must have been serious. And it clearly wasn't a social call at his mother's behest.

He studied Royston with concern over the rim of his glass. If there was anything he could do to help, he owed it to the earl for the years of friendship between their two families. And the earl's troubles might just provide a distraction for him as well. "What kind of trouble?"

"Highwaymen."

"Highwaymen," Thomas repeated, and carefully kept his face stoic, not letting his disappointment at the mundane answer register.

Royston grimaced. "I know what you're thinking. What road in Lincolnshire doesn't have highwaymen?"

He had been thinking *exactly* that, but to ease the man's pride, he instead offered, "Actually, I was wondering why you didn't go to the constabulary."

"I have, but to no avail." He finished his whiskey, then stared down at the empty glass. "It's a damnable mystery."

With that odd comment pricking his interest, Thomas stood to refill his glass. "How so?"

"There appears to be no pattern, except that there is." When Thomas frowned at his contradictory words, he continued, "The only robberies have been of guests returning home from Blackwood Hall, and then, not all the guests and not all the time." Royston grimaced. "We're being targeted. My guests. *Me.*"

"I wouldn't go that far." Thomas tried to keep the patronizing tone from his voice, but truly, the description of the robberies struck him as simple paranoia. Yet Royston's distress over it concerned him, and he frowned as he fetched the decanter. "You're a wealthy landowner in Lincolnshire, so surely more of your guests than—"

"I'm one of the wealthy men in the area, true, but not the

only one." He held up his glass to let Thomas pour more whiskey. "*Only* my guests have been robbed by this particular highwayman. No one else's."

Well, that *was* odd. He set the decanter aside and sank back into his chair. "Nevertheless, it doesn't mean you, specifically, are being targeted. Could just be a run of coincidence and bad luck."

Royston shook his head. "When the carriages are stopped, only the men are asked to hand over their valuables. One man in each coach, no matter how many others are present. And never anything from the women, not even when openly displaying their jewels."

Thomas leaned forward. A highwayman who robbed only one man per coach and left jewels? Finally he was intrigued. "How long has this been happening?"

"On and off for the past two years."

A faint needling of suspicion, one he hadn't felt since he stopped being a spy, tickled at the backs of his knees and made his heart skitter. "You're just now noticing the pattern?"

"I had noticed before, I'm ashamed to say. But it never needed to be addressed until now."

"What changed?"

"I have grand hopes for the Lords next session. Some important positions will be opening, and I want to make my mark." His eyes met Thomas's intently. "With your help."

Shaking his head, Thomas set his glass aside. "I'm afraid you're wasting your time. I'm not involved in anything of importance in the government." *Not anymore.*

Royston leveled his shrewd gaze on him. "I know things about you, Thomas," he answered quietly, all polite pretense gone. "I know what you've done since you returned from Spain, and I have connections in the War Office who have vouched for your special skills."

Despite the electric jolt that pulsed through him at the earl's words, Thomas remained silent and stoic, unwilling to either deny or validate Royston's assumptions about him. Only a handful of people knew the truth about what he'd done for his country once he left the army, once his real fight against the French had begun. Despite the close friendship their two families shared, he wouldn't endanger Royston unnecessarily. No matter how much he wanted to help.

Besides, those special skills the War Office had assured the earl he possessed were the same ones they no longer wanted.

"I want you to come to Blackwood Hall and investigate." Asking for help from someone twenty years his junior was clearly difficult for the proud man, but judging from the exasperated look in his eyes, he'd found no other solution. "I want these robberies stopped, no matter the cost." His gaze dropped back to his drink. "And if it goes well, I see no reason why I shouldn't put in a good word for you with Lord Bathurst, assuring him that you have my full support and confidence. That you are truly back to being your old self."

Bathurst. Thomas froze even as his chest squeezed hard. This could very well be the opportunity he'd been seeking, his very last hope of returning to the life he'd led before the shooting. When he'd had purpose and meaning. When he'd last felt *alive*.

"Do we have an agreement, then, Chesney?"

Thomas nodded slowly, outwardly calm despite his racing heart. Stopping a highwayman was a far cry from the type of work he'd done as a spy, but it would also serve as a test to prove to Bathurst—and to himself—that his skills hadn't deteriorated.

"I'm hosting a house party at Blackwood Hall next week." The earl set aside his glass and stood. "A chance for friends and associates in the area to gather for a sennight and break up the boredom of the country season. An irresistible target for the highwayman, I presume."

Thomas rose to his feet, his mind already whirling with this new assignment. "Make certain the guest list is common knowledge to your household staff."

Incredulity flashed over Royston's face. "You think the highwayman could be someone within my own home?"

"I think he could be anyone." Fighting down the excitement that coursed through his blood and replaced the anxiety that had clawed at him less than half an hour earlier, Thomas slapped him on the shoulder and walked him downstairs. "See you next week, then."

With a grateful expression, Royston took his hat and gloves from Jensen and headed out the front door. "My thanks, Chesney."

And mine to you. More than the earl would ever know. His chest pulsed with the first real hope he'd had in a year. A highwayman in Lincolnshire...not exactly an enemy to the crown. But at this point, with all other avenues blocked, he would claim whatever small victories he could.

Small victory? He laughed. Whom was he trying to fool? He knew the truth, no matter how reluctant he was to admit it.

A week at a boring Lincolnshire house party might just save his life.

Emily looked up from her book as he sauntered into the morning room and slumped down next to her on the sofa. "Business concluded, then?"

"Not business." He grinned, feeling like the cat who'd gotten into the cream and the closest he'd been to his old self since the shooting. "Pleasure."

Her lips twitched mischievously. "Hmm," she commented with mock innocence, "and here I'd thought Helene had already departed."

He shot her an icy look that made grown men quake in their boots but seemed only to amuse her. *Brat.* "Royston invited me to a house party at Blackwood Hall."

"Oh?" Her single bewildered word spoke volumes. She blinked, incredulity visible on her face that he would so eagerly gallop off to a party certain to be filled with dull dandies and old gossips.

He dissembled by adding, "The earl has political aspirations and wants counsel on some recent matters which have been troubling him."

"And he picked *you*?" Astonishment rang in her voice. "He wants to succeed at these aspirations, does he not?"

He grimaced at the teasing insult. She was needling him, trying in her own fashion to get the truth from him, but he would keep this investigation to himself. If the trip to Lincolnshire went as well as he hoped, it just might prove his salvation, and he would tell her afterward when all was set to rights again.

And if not...well, there would be little she could do to help fight back the demons that would come for him, the suffocating blackness that would eventually devour him whole.

"Getting away from London might do you good after all," she added thoughtfully. "You might be introduced to a whole new group of potential wives."

Stifling an exasperated groan, he kicked his boots onto the tea table. "You know, brat, when you were a child, I sold you to the Gypsies," he told her bluntly. "I'm still waiting for them to take you away."

Emily laughed, her blue eyes shining, and offered him a cup of tea.

CHAPTER TWO

The following week
Islingham Village, Lincolnshire

*J*osephine!" Elizabeth Carlisle waved her fan high in the air to catch her daughter's attention across the crowded ballroom at Blackwood Hall. Every inhabitant of every household in Lincolnshire seemed packed into the room for the opening night soiree of the Roystons' annual house party. "Over here!"

With a smile Josie squeezed her way through the crush.

Countess Royston had topped herself this year. Complete with orchestra, free-flowing wine, and sugared fruits at the refreshments table, the evening would be the center of gossip for months to come. Even the dancing would be wonderful. Although it was a country dance and not a grand London ball, Josie had it under good authority from the second violinist that at least two waltzes were scheduled for the evening. And she did so love to waltz! In fact, waltzing was the only thing that had made the past five seasons bearable.

Five seasons. *Good God.*

Her shoulders sagged. At twenty-three, without any suitors or prospects, she supposed she would soon be officially on the shelf, and then she wouldn't have to worry anymore about seasons or finding waltz partners who didn't step on her toes.

Truly, though, she wasn't surprised. On paper, as the daughter of a baron, she rivaled most of the young ladies of England. But naturally, she was an adopted orphan who had been surrendered by her mother when she was three months old, a castoff of unknown lineage. Perhaps the child of a washerwoman or maid. Or worse. And no proper gentleman wanted to pursue a woman whose ancestry would only soil his progeny.

Oh, she'd had a few suitors over the years. There'd been a few young gentlemen who'd visited Blackwood Hall for previous parties and taken an interest in her, but in the end their interest had lasted only as long as their stay. Local sons of squires and merchants had called on her over the years, brought her posies, taken her for picnics, and even had the daring to request a few kisses before offering for other young ladies. Occasionally a soldier or a vicar had been bold enough to pursue her. *Those* she chased away herself, knowing they were willing to overlook her past only to gain her dowry and a familial connection to a peer.

Given all that, then, was it any wonder that she was still unmarried?

But truly, wasn't it for the best? While other young ladies focused on hunting husbands from the right families—with the right fortunes, of course—Josie had found purpose in working with the local orphanage and in doing everything she could to give the best lives possible to the children who hadn't been as fortunate as she'd been. Which was why she'd never asked her parents for a London season. Here, in Lincolnshire, what did it matter if anyone knew her true past? Those people who really mattered to her knew who she was and cared about her anyway. But the London ladies would ostracize her if her past became common gossip, and no gentleman would dare to court her then. And even if she found a man who loved her and was willing to overlook her soiled ancestry, he most likely wouldn't allow her to continue the work she did for the Good Hope Home. Certainly not *all* she did.

And she couldn't stop because she knew firsthand the horrors of that orphanage...cold winter nights sleeping three to a bed to keep warm, days when the only food was weak broth, and clothes worn until they fell away in rags, never washed and filled with lice and fleas. Mrs. Potter, the manageress whom Simon Royston had hired into the position, constantly stole from the supply stores and beat the children, locked them into the coal bin with no food or chamber pot, and often passed out drunk from gin.

But Josie had been lucky. Just six years old when Richard and Elizabeth Carlisle adopted her, she'd been picked by them because she was the toughest little girl in the orphanage, afraid of nothing, and more than able to hold her own against three older brothers. Even as a child she'd vowed that she would never forget the other children, that she would do whatever she could to help.

So if remaining unwed meant she could continue to care for the orphans, then it was more than a fair price to pay, she supposed. Yet her foolish heart still longed to meet a man who would fall in love with her. But with each passing season, that dream became more and more just that. Only a dream.

And so she was still unwed and most likely always would be. Her family had never pressured her to marry, leaving the choice entirely up to her, and at this point, she was accepting of her impending spinsterhood.

Impending? She stifled a laugh. Goodness! Hadn't it already arrived?

Finally reaching her mother's side, Josie kissed her cheek. Seventeen years after the moment when she'd first seen her, Elizabeth Carlisle still reigned as the most beautiful woman Josie had ever seen, even after raising four children to adulthood.

"I need your help tonight." Mama peered frantically over the top of her flitting fan to scan the ballroom for her three sons, all lost somewhere in the crush. "Keep a keen eye on your brothers, will you?"

As if on cue, Josie's middle brother, Robert, sauntered into the ballroom and headed straight toward the refreshments table and a glass of Madeira.

"Keep Robert away from Miranda Hodgkins at all costs," Mama warned.

"But Miranda's a lovely girl." The niece of the neighboring farmer, Miranda had practically grown up in their nursery at Chestnut Hill and, thankfully, had given her brothers someone other than her to torment.

"Yes, and someday she will make a wonderful wife. But right now she is only eighteen and easily influenced." She squeezed Josie's hand and lowered her voice as if sharing a secret. "She needs to hang a while longer on the vine."

Josie frowned at her mother, perplexed.

She arched a knowing brow. "She's not yet ripe."

"Mama!" Josie's mouth fell open in astonishment.

"As for Sebastian," she continued about the oldest of her sons, "I'm certain he's lurking in a corner, talking politics and farming techniques. Do make him have some fun tonight, will you? I swear he was born an old man."

Josie smiled at her mother's perfect description of Seb. "And Quinton?"

She watched as the youngest of her three brothers approached Robert and slapped him on the back just as he was about to take a sip of wine, spilling it onto his boots. If her mother was lucky, the two men wouldn't come to blows right there.

She heaved a sigh of frustration. "Don't let *him* do anything!"

Josie bit her bottom lip to keep from laughing. Her brothers had never been manageable, even as little boys, and how they hadn't killed each other long before now God only knew. But she dearly loved them, as much as if they were truly her own flesh and blood.

Interacting with them had been difficult when she was first adopted, not knowing her place as an outsider among the boys who had an established home and sense of security within the family. And of course, she'd been bitterly jealous of their golden looks and charm, while it seemed that with her uncontrollable chestnut hair and petite frame she was seldom noticed. Of course, years later she'd realized that if people hadn't paid as much attention to her as to the boys it was mostly because they were watching her brothers like hawks, as the three seemed to always be rigging traps for unsuspecting persons. Or setting things on fire. Including each other.

She'd grown to love them all, although even now an irrational part of her sometimes worried that she might never truly belong to the family as much as her brothers did. And the fact that no man wanted to marry her once he'd discovered her past only emphasized her difference from other society daughters.

But then, all three of her brothers were still bachelors, and none of them fretted about avoiding spinsterhood, as if such a thing existed for men.

Not that her brothers needed to worry about remaining

unmarried. The strappingly handsome, golden-blond Carlisle men stood at the center of female attention wherever they went. Her parents would have gladly seen them settled by now into homes of their own, although Josie also knew her mother was very cautious about choosing the ladies with whom her sons associated. Not because she worried that some social upstart would trap one of them into marriage but rather that the Carlisle boys would trap some poor unsuspecting girl who had no idea what she was getting herself into by leg-shackling herself to one of them for life.

"Where *is* Sebastian?" Josie swept her eyes across the room. "I don't see—"

She stopped, the words catching in her throat as a pair of blue eyes stared back. Dark eyes more sapphire than simply blue. Deep, brooding, a bit dangerous. And bold. Oh, *definitely* bold as they held her own gaze captive. And below those eyes was a full, sensuous mouth that quirked up in amusement. At her.

Oh.

She was staring at the man, and *he* knew she was staring, and *she* knew *he* knew…and when he raised his glass slowly in a rakish toast to her, that dark, brooding, dangerous, and bold stare curled hotly down her spine and straight to her toes, stealing her breath away.

Oh. My.

"Which devil are you?" she mumbled.

Because her family lived on the neighboring estate, Josie had assumed she would know all the guests at the dance, every last boring, elderly blue blood. But she certainly didn't know *him*. Whoever he was, blue blood or not, he certainly wasn't elderly, and from what she'd seen so far, he wasn't the least bit boring.

"What, dear?" her mother asked absently.

She tore her gaze away from the stranger to glance at her mother. "Nothing."

When she looked back, he'd turned away to join in conversation with Lady Agnes Sinclair and her niece. Disappointment washed over her that she should lose his attention so quickly, and before she'd even had the chance to meet him, for heaven's sake. And yet, never being one to let an opportunity pass by, she shamelessly seized the moment to study him.

Dressed impeccably in a dark blue superfine jacket over a gray brocade waistcoat and snow-white silk cravat, black breeches, and boots polished to an impossible shine, he was tall, dark, and—to her chagrin—handsome. *Very* handsome, right down to the wide breadth of his shoulders and the black hair that curled in thick waves against his collar. And undeniably charismatic. Even from this far away she saw how the two women hung on his every word. Yet Josie was struck at how he seemed to be aware of everyone around him, even while deep in conversation, just as much as she was struck by the keen jealousy pulsing through her that his attention no longer focused exclusively on her.

Jealousy? Good heavens, what on earth was wrong with her tonight?

Shaking herself, she cleared that ridiculous notion from her mind and tried to concentrate on keeping watch over her brothers. Which was the only place her attention should have been. She had no business making a cake of herself over a man when she knew from past experience that her curiosity about him would come to nothing as soon as he found out who she truly was.

"I'm going to find your father. Enjoy yourself, my dear." Elizabeth placed a kiss on Josie's cheek. "And don't let your brothers near the musicians. We certainly don't want a repeat of that cello incident from two years ago." She sighed heavily. "I don't think they ever found the bow."

With that parting warning, her mother slipped away. But Josie barely noticed, her interest still focused on the other side of the room.

Who are *you?* She'd never seen him before, of that she was certain, because she would have remembered a man like him, who filled the room with the intensity of an oncoming storm. A man who captured her interest the way no other man had in a long time. If ever. And who had her wondering if he found her just as intriguing.

Oh, she was fooling herself! A gentleman like that wouldn't pay her any attention once he discovered she was an orphan. Or worse, he would pay her the wrong kind of attention, thinking her past entitled him to take liberties with her that he'd never dare take with any other unmarried lady.

And yet…Oh, wouldn't it be lovely, for a few minutes at least, to be able to pretend she was someone else? To believe she could capture the attentions of a man like him?

So if all she had was a few minutes when she could be an ordinary young lady and pretend she had a normal future, why squander any of them?

With determination, she snatched a glass of punch from a passing footman and wove her way across the room, unable to tamp down her growing curiosity about him and the undeniable yearning to meet him that he roused inside her. Would those midnight-blue eyes be just as intriguing up close? Would that mouth be just as sensuous?

Sighing at her own foolishness, she slipped through the crowd like a moth drawn toward a flame. She should have been watching her brothers. At the very least, she should have been watching Miranda Hodgkins. Instead she was stalking a handsome stranger, lifting her glass ever so slightly as she glided toward him, bumping her arm against his—

And spilling punch across his jacket sleeve.

Bull's-eye!

"Oh, I'm so sorry!" she gasped as his hand immediately took her elbow to steady her...or to keep her from spilling the rest of the punch, she wasn't certain which. But when she glanced up at those sapphire eyes and a warmth stirred low in her belly, she simply didn't care.

Oh yes. Those eyes were just as intriguing up close.

With a shake, she collected herself. "How awful of me!" she exclaimed, and brushed her fingertips at the few droplets of punch still clinging to his sleeve.

The two Sinclair ladies excused themselves with a touch of embarrassment for her, which Josie didn't give one whit about. Especially when the corners of his mouth curled sensuously at her in amusement.

"No harm, I assure you." His voice came as a deep purr.

She cleared her throat at the responding shiver that scattered through her like warm rain. "I'm so terribly clumsy." She continued to brush at his sleeve long after the punch had been cleared away, inexplicably unable to stop herself from touching him. "Everyone's always saying, 'Josephine Carlisle, how absolutely clumsy you are!'"

She thought she saw knowing laughter sparkle in his eyes before he sketched her a shallow bow. "Miss Carlisle, something tells me you're not truly as clumsy as you protest."

His words were just cryptic enough to give her pause and make her wonder again who this man was and why he was at the earl's party when men of his caliber *never* came to Blackwood Hall. But at least they were now engaged in conversation, and she had managed to accomplish the meeting—albeit by the most wretched self-introduction in history—without having to seek out someone to do the honors for her. And she didn't feel the least bit guilty at her subterfuge. Just hearing that rumbling voice had been worth it, no matter how briefly the meeting might last.

Deep in her heart, she wished it would last a good long while.

She smiled apologetically. "I do hope I haven't ruined your jacket."

"It's fine." His eyes swept deliberately over her as he murmured, "Very fine."

Her heart skittered. Good Lord, was he flirting? With *her*? Despite her uncertainty, she blushed like a debutante at her first ball. *Goodness.*

"You're not dancing."

"Pardon?" she breathed, her foolish heart daring to hope that he might be asking…but no. His words were only an observation, not a request, and her stomach plummeted with disappointment.

Of course he wasn't asking her to dance. Why on earth would he make such a request of the clumsy woman who'd just doused him with punch? As if this man ever had to request a dance in the first place. Most likely the London ladies would have all sought out *his* dance card if men possessed such things. And then her pride sank even lower as she realized she'd done exactly that herself by approaching him with such a pathetic ruse.

He nodded past her toward the dance floor, where couples twirled in the roiling knots of a quadrille. "You're not dancing," he repeated.

"I'm saving my toes for the waltzes," she offered, curious to see how he would respond to that.

"Ah, toe preservation," he replied with mock gravity, his eyes gleaming. "A noble cause."

She smiled, strangely satisfied at his answer. Truly, she would have been disappointed had his response been anything less entertaining. "Indeed, sir, but perhaps I'm biased since I have a personal interest in the matter." She gave a small laugh. "Ten, to be exact."

When he followed the dart of her eyes to her slippers, which she wiggled beneath the hem of her gown, he slid her a charming grin that trickled its way down her spine with a languid warmth.

The laughter caught in her throat. *Entertaining?* Well, *that* was the understatement of the year. This man was utterly captivating. And for one shameless moment, bewildered at how he could draw such an unusual reaction from her so immediately, she wanted very much to become his captive.

"And you?" She cleared her suddenly tight throat and hoped her voice sounded much steadier than she felt. "Why are you not dancing?"

"I prefer the side of the room." Then he leaned in slightly as he admitted in a low voice, a faint smile tugging at the corners of his mouth, "So much easier that way for beautiful ladies to purposefully spill punch on my sleeve to gain my attention."

Her mouth fell open, and she gaped at him. Speechless. At his audacity both in calling her out for her ruse and in claiming she was beautiful. And at her reckless desire to hear him say it again.

"I suppose I should offer to fetch you another glass of punch," he continued, rocking back onto his heels. From the teasing gleam in his eyes, he was obviously enjoying her embarrassment. "But I'm wary about where that one might land."

Her mouth snapped shut. Yes, he *should* be worried. He might be tall, dark, and handsome, but now that she'd met him, he was clearly no gentleman. A man with manners wouldn't have called her out so blatantly on her trick...although the compliment about being beautiful she was willing to forgive. Still, as an embarrassed blush rose from the back of her neck, the undeniable desire she'd felt to meet him evaporated beneath a cold dose of reality. She'd suspected the meeting wouldn't end well, given her past encounters with eligible male guests at Blackwood, but she hadn't expected it to sour so quickly. It was a new record, even for her.

"As I told you, only clumsiness on my part." She feigned an innocent expression rather than let him see her true disappointment that he should have proven a cad after all, then retreated a step to put distance between them while she thought of a polite way to excuse herself. "No need to assume more."

"Then I should be greatly disappointed," he murmured, and advanced slowly to close the gap she'd created.

The tiny hairs on her arms tingled in warning. Was he...pursuing her?

Impossible. Not someone like him. Yet he matched her step for step as she slowly backed away. She couldn't decide if he wanted to flirt with her or drive her away, but whatever his goal, he definitely set her off-balance.

Drawing a breath for courage, she stood her ground and tilted her head in challenge. "Perhaps you should fetch me that punch after all."

That stopped him. He quirked a questioning brow.

"Then we could reenact the spill and know for certain whether it was an ill-conceived attempt on my part to get your attention or an ill-executed attempt on yours to move out of the way." She forced a saccharine smile meant to send him scurrying away. "After all, I wouldn't want you to be unnecessarily disappointed."

At her sassiness he laughed—the devil had the nerve to *laugh* at her! And not just any laugh, but a low and rich rumble that sank through her and filled her up. Yet something rusty resonated in the sound, as if he hadn't laughed in a very long time.

She trembled. Her attempt at pushing him away was failing miserably. And now she didn't know what to do with him. Heavens, she was in over her head, and a quick glance at her preoccupied brothers across the ballroom told her there would be no help from shore.

He dared to take another step until they stood shoulder to shoulder, facing in opposite directions. When he lowered his head to bring his mouth close to her ear, anyone watching would have assumed he did so only to be heard over the music. Yet the sudden realization struck her of how expert he was at creating a sense of privacy and physical closeness in the midst of a crowded room. And what a smooth rakehell existed behind those sultry eyes. She shivered at the heat he spiked inside her, this man who seemed nothing like the sort she should associate with yet who enigmatically drew her more than any she'd ever met before in her life.

"Be honest, then, Miss Carlisle," he drawled, amusement lacing that masculine purr of a voice. As if he knew exactly what effect he had on her. "Clumsiness or a bid for attention?" His fingers brushed unseen against hers at her side as they dangled hidden against the fullness of her skirt. He teasingly accused, "I don't like deception."

Deception. Stifling a surprised gasp, she yanked her hand away.

As she stared up at him, sudden fear sped through her. Her heart thudded so hard that the rush of blood through her ears drowned out the orchestra, and she thought her knees might buckle and send her to the floor right there at his feet. But somehow she remained standing, and with every ounce of willpower she possessed, she forced herself not to pale. Not in front of those remarkable eyes that seemed to notice everything.

But how could he possibly know about her? And how much, *exactly*, did he know? He was a stranger here. For God's sake, he hadn't even known her name until she'd walked up to him and told him! Unease knotted sickeningly in her stomach. However much she'd wanted to meet him just a few minutes before, she now knew it was time to take her leave before he learned even more that he shouldn't. Yet the thought of saying good-bye when she'd only barely met him inexplicably ripped a small tear into her heart.

"A misplaced attempt to garner your attention, then," she answered tightly, admitting to her folly and stepping away from him with a curt nod. "My apologies."

His hand closed around her elbow and stopped her. "Don't go," he entreated quietly, his face suddenly somber. "Please. I was merely teasing. I didn't mean to offend—"

"Josie." A large hand clamped down on his shoulder. "Is this man bothering you?"

*   *   *

Thomas tensed, every muscle in his body tightening as two mountains of men appeared beside him, flanking either side. But he gave no outward reaction to their presence except to release her arm as she stepped away. He looked at the intriguing woman in front of him and waited breathlessly for her answer, knowing it could mean the difference between being pummeled and being allowed to remain standing on two unbroken legs.

Yet she hesitated to answer, and indecision flickered in her green eyes as she bit her bottom lip.

From her body language, she clearly wanted away from him, but she also didn't want to cause the scene the two men would undoubtedly unleash when they beat him senseless. He had no idea what thoughts played through that sharp mind of hers as she searched his face for answers, but he desperately hoped she found them, both to appease the two men and because he found himself not wanting to part from her. Something about her put him at ease. Something he couldn't put his finger on but that he wasn't willing to let go so soon.

Her shoulders lowered as she made her decision. "He isn't bothering me."

But the way she crossed her arms and hardened her eyes told him he'd won a grudging victory.

"Good," the mountain at his left shoulder drawled, "because I'd hate to think someone was bothering my baby sister."

"Me, too," the right mountain affirmed.

Baby sister. Bloody hell. *This* was why he detested house parties. Far too easy to be killed at one.

"My brothers." Rolling her eyes, now as annoyed at them as she was at him, she waved her hand toward the mountain on the left. "Robert Carlisle." Then she gestured at the other hulking man. "Quinton. And somewhere in this crush is my eldest brother Sebastian."

Three brothers. He *was* going to be killed. And sadly, before he'd gotten even a single taste of her.

"Gentlemen, a pleasure to meet you," he commented to neither brother in particular, his eyes never leaving Josephine's face. She resembled her brothers not at all, who were twice her pixie size and golden to her chestnut hair. Not in the slightly upturned tip of her pert nose, the set of her green eyes, the fullness of her lips that now pressed into a tight line…*Interesting.* "I was just escorting your sister to the floor for our dance."

He noticed the surprised flare of her eyes and wondered if her brothers had seen it, too. At that moment he was literally flirting with danger. And enjoying it immensely.

In the past year, he'd attended too many soirees to count and had met all kinds of women, but not one had captured his attention the way this little bit of a country gel had. Not one of them had looked at him with such hope and expectation, with a combination of bemusement and daring that left his head spinning. They certainly hadn't challenged him in conversation the way she had. Good Lord, she'd even made him laugh! He couldn't remember the last time he'd actually *laughed*. And while that was a damnable surprise, even more stunning was the lightness that had filled his chest during the past few minutes since he looked up and caught her staring at him. For the first time in a year, the shooting and its aftermath hadn't been foremost in his mind.

Why *her* he had no idea. But he knew for certain that he wasn't willing to part with her just yet. Hulking brothers or no.

"Well." Robert removed his hand from Thomas's shoulder with a friendly pat. "While we're glad a man is taking an interest in Josie—"

"I don't think we can allow her to dance with you—" Quinton interrupted.

"A man to whom she hasn't been formally introduced," Robert finished.

Quinton nodded in confirmation. "Certainly not."

Both brothers ignored the ice-cold daggers she stared at them, and Thomas suspected she was already plotting her revenge. Emily certainly would have been.

"Oh, but we have been introduced," Thomas smoothly informed them. "How else would I know that your sister, the lovely Miss Josephine Carlisle, loves to dance, although her friends consider her a bit too clumsy for the quadrilles, so she prefers to waltz despite a sorely small pool of men in Lincolnshire who don't step on her toes?"

Her brothers stared at him curiously, clearly not knowing how to respond to that. And neither did Josephine, who stared at him as if he'd just admitted to stealing the crown jewels.

Dancing with her had been only an excuse for her brothers, to explain why he was holding her elbow, but now he wanted to do exactly that. "I believe our waltz is starting. Miss Carlisle, may I?"

Josie blinked, then gave a stunned nod of permission. As if knowing a refusal would draw even more attention to herself from the curious crowd around them.

He took her gloved hand and rested it delicately on his sleeve, the same one she'd doused with punch just moments before in that adorable but obvious scheme to meet him. "Gentlemen, if you'll excuse us."

As he led her onto the dance floor, she murmured in a soft voice, "That was smoothly done."

"Self-preservation," he replied in the same low tone as he drew her into position, "isn't just for toes."

Despite her earlier annoyance at him, she gave a small laugh. The soft, melodic sound flitted through his chest, easing even more the year-old weight he carried inside him. He couldn't help but smile at her.

Whatever he'd done earlier to offend her dissipated as he twirled her into the waltz, and she fell gracefully into step with him. "Robert and Quinn are quite protective of me," she explained.

He threw a pointed glance at her brothers. "So I noticed."

"Hmm," she replied knowingly. "And I could have sworn you noticed far more than just that."

His gut clenched in warning at her implication that he was more than he seemed, the reaction a remnant of a survival instinct honed sharply during his years as an army officer and agent. And yet... well, she wasn't wrong. He supposed he should be alarmed that she was the only woman save his sister who suspected he led a double life. What he actually was, however, was intrigued.

He shrugged as he twirled her into a circle, and she followed naturally, not missing a step. "Whatever do you mean?"

"Oh, come now. We've already established that you don't like deception, so don't dissemble with me," she chastised lightly even as she smiled, not at him but to appease her brothers who hovered on the edge of the dance floor like a pack of wolves. Interesting... she clearly didn't want to dance with him, yet she wanted a scene with her brothers even less. He'd never before been the lesser of two evils for a woman. His pride would have been pricked if she hadn't fascinated him so much. "I have a feeling those eyes of yours don't miss much."

His brow rose slightly. "Is that a compliment?"

"Would you like it to be?" she countered cheekily.

Yes, very much. He wasn't certain why, but from the moment they'd made eye contact, he'd wanted to make an impression on her. Perhaps because he'd caught her scanning the crowd just as he'd been doing, or because she'd held his gaze unflinchingly without an ounce of trepidation or self-consciousness. Such boldness in a young lady was decidedly rare.

But he knew one thing for certain—he would have made his way through the crowd himself to meet her if the Sinclair ladies hadn't trapped him into conversation. Instead she'd surprised him first with her ploy of spilled punch.

If he'd been in London and any of the ladies there had attempted such a maneuver, whether with aims to wed him or to bed him, he would have responded with a cutting remark that would have sent her scurrying for safety. But Josephine Carlisle was curious about him. Which made him curious. About her.

"You're an unusual woman, Miss Carlisle," he answered instead.

"Is that a compliment?" She tilted her head as if studying him.

He crooked a half grin. "Would you like it to be?"

She flashed a genuinely brilliant smile that made his heart skip as she played out her part. "And you're an unusual man, Mr...." She blinked, her face suddenly blank. Then, she gasped, "Good heavens, we *haven't* been introduced!"

He bit back another laugh. "Matteson," he offered encouragingly, hoping she'd return the familiarity of the introduction. "Marquess of Chesney." Then he lowered his mouth close to her ear, close enough to feel her shiver when he murmured, "Thomas."

He pulled back to a proper distance before her brothers could pounce and pulp him, but even then he could still feel the rustle of her skirts around his legs as they danced together and the heat of her fingers lightly folded around his. He'd hoped the introduction would soften her more to him; instead it drew a faint flicker of suspicion and distrust in the emerald depths of her eyes.

The woman perplexed him. She'd made the first move, but now, every time he encouraged her to be flirtatious and increase the intimacy between them, she pulled back. Like a skittish foal exploring its new stable, she was afraid of the very thing that drew her curiosity.

She raised her chin primly. "And what have you noticed, then, Lord Chesney?"

He smiled, amused at her doggedness to maintain a sense of formality between them while at the same time unduly pleased that she'd noticed him enough to know he'd been watching—and watching not just her but everyone in the room. Few people paid close attention to their surroundings the way he did, let alone society ladies, and in her he found the trait fascinating.

"Well, Miss Carlisle," he murmured hotly, holding her gaze, "I certainly noticed you."

She swallowed nervously, and as he watched the soft undulation of her elegant throat, a ripple of pleasure sped through him. "And what did you notice?"

His voice sounded unexpectedly husky, even to his own ears. "Beyond how alluring you are, you mean?"

That comment drew a soft pink to her cheeks, exactly as he'd hoped. She was even more beautiful when she blushed.

She followed his lead effortlessly as he twirled her through the circle, not missing a step. More proof that she wasn't nearly as clumsy as she'd led him to believe. Which immediately had him wondering what else about herself she'd hidden from him. And that mysteriousness intrigued him even more.

"What have you noticed about me, Lord Chesney?" she urged gently, and he was struck by the peculiar suspicion that she wasn't fishing for compliments as much as trying to learn about him from what he was able to reveal about her.

"Well, your brothers are constantly at the center of attention, but you prefer not to be." He admitted honestly, his voice lowering, "Although I'm very glad that you decided to spill punch on me tonight despite that."

"*That* was an easy guess," she countered skeptically, but her blush deepened, proof that she liked the comment despite her determination not to let it show. Hmm...how dark could he make that blush grow before her brothers pounced?

"Not as easy as you think," he muttered, flicking a glance at her brothers, who still watched the two of them like hawks. Then he looked down at her dress, noting both the style and the delectable way it draped over her curves. "Well, then, I also noticed that you travel to London once a year but never for the entire season."

That got her attention, and her green eyes widened. "How," she asked in an astonished whisper, shifting away from him, "can you possibly know that?"

He gently pulled her closer, unwilling to let her go. "Because your dress is last year's fashion," he explained, "so you were in London for the fitting, but you weren't there for the entire season."

"How do you know that?" she whispered, her pink lips parting delicately in surprise.

"Because I was there," he told her honestly, unable to prevent his gaze from dropping to her succulent mouth. "And I certainly would have remembered a woman like you."

At his unbidden confession, she stared up at him with eyes as dark as a storm-tossed sea, and he felt the pull of her. And the equally undeniable pull of her toward him. At that moment, despite being surrounded by the crush of the ballroom, he wanted to wrap her in his arms and shamelessly wipe away that teasing smile at her lips that had him longing to smother her mouth with his. How sweet it would be to hear her moan, to feel the warmth of that soft little body pressed eagerly against his as she kissed him back...When he stroked his thumb against her palm, she shivered, and he knew she wanted to do exactly that.

His heart pounding, he murmured, "Josephine—"

"Is that all you know about me, then?" she asked suddenly, the words coming out in a breathless rush. "Nothing else?"

"I know I'd like to learn more about you." He dared to stroke the small of her back in a slow circle as he stared down into her eyes. "A great deal more."

She missed a step and would have tumbled to the floor if not for his arm at her back catching her. As he drew her back into position, she dragged in a breath so deep, so hard that she shook. In fact, *all* of her trembled now. As if she were...afraid.

"Miss Carlisle?" Concern instantly gripped him as he stared down at her, his hand tightening around hers. "Josephine?"

She refused to look up at him now, her gaze trained at his chest and her body stiff in his arms. That wonderful blush he'd stirred in her cheeks had vanished, her pretty face gone pale.

He frowned with bewilderment. Good Lord, he'd only flirted with her, and an incredibly mild flirtation at that, compared to those scandalous whisperings the London ladies liked to hear so they could pretend to be shocked even as the words titillated them. With the way those brothers of hers guarded her, she was most likely still a country innocent, and yet what on earth had he done to cause *fear*? Surely nothing to make her shake, for God's sake.

And *damnation*, he was chasing her away again!

"If I overstepped..." He apologetically squeezed her hand. "I didn't mean to offend you."

"You didn't offend me," she protested, but as the waltz ended she pulled away quickly. She retreated a step and gave him a shallow curtsy. "It was a pleasure meeting you, Lord Chesney. If you'll excuse me, I—I suddenly feel unwell."

Unwell? His eyes narrowed on her. A damned lie.

But she was gone before he could stop her, and he fought the urge to run after her as she hurried from the dance floor toward her brothers, already feeling the tightening in his chest and the darkness pressing in around him from the sudden loss of her. He forced himself to breathe steadily and deeply—and to let her go.

He watched as she pressed her hand against her forehead in feigned illness and quickly gave excuses to her brothers as to why she wanted to leave so abruptly when the dance had just begun. Surprisingly, the glances the men sent his way were curious ones, not any that had him fearing for his life, so whatever excuses she made were wholly believable. And not blaming him. Thank God for that, at least. But knowing she didn't place the blame squarely on his head was little consolation for her sudden departure and the solace she took away with her. What had he done to chase her away?

One of the brothers—Sebastian, the one he hadn't yet met—took her arm and led her toward the front entrance.

As she disappeared from sight, an unexpected stab of loss tore into his chest. Needing air, he stepped outside onto the terrace, where he took deep breaths to steady himself. Only a few minutes later he watched her leave as the coach disappeared down the moonlit drive, carrying the enigmatic woman away, along with the last peace he would feel tonight.

He ran a hand through his hair in aggravation, his fingers already shaking at the thought of the night ahead. One he knew would be spent sleepless and moving restlessly in his room, when pacing for hours was the only way to burn off the anxiety that descended upon him when the night was quiet and he had nothing to do but think. And remember.

Blowing out a breath, he leaned on his palms against the stone balustrade. Who *was* this woman, that she of all people had such a calming effect on him when no one else had been able to help him? For the first time since the shooting, he had been completely at ease with someone other than Emily, Edward, and Grey.

She wasn't the most beautiful woman he knew, nor the most sophisticated. Yet with nothing more than a dribble of punch and a waltz, Josephine Carlisle had distracted him more deeply than Helene or his other lovers had done with their naked bodies, more than Emily had done with all her pots of tea. The pleasant distraction of her smiles and her teasing wit had him thinking of her and not of everything he'd lost when that footpad shot him. Or how desperate he was to have that life back, no matter what he had to do to get it.

Including hunting down a highwayman.

But his investigation for Royston certainly wasn't proceeding as planned. He'd been at Blackwood Hall for over eight hours now, and instead of actively pursuing leads, he'd been wasting time trying to impress a woman like some starry-eyed green pup, only to end up driving her away. That was different, because he couldn't remember the last time a woman had fled from him before. If ever. And that was oddly bothersome, because he found himself wanting to see her again. Because tonight, for a precious few minutes, there had been only her. And peace.

And *that* was the oddest thing of all. That a sharp-tongued, too-bright-for-her-own-good gel from Lincolnshire had aroused him until even now he grew half-hard just thinking about her. But the release he wanted to find in her was far from only physical.

Why *her*, for Christ's sake?

He had no idea. But he was determined to find out.

CHAPTER THREE

Thomas turned his horse down the treelined lane leading to the Carlisle home at Chestnut Hill and cantered slowly beneath the overarching branches. Once more he repeated to himself the apology he'd been practicing all morning—all night, in fact—for whatever offenses he'd mistakenly leveled at Josephine Carlisle during last night's waltz. He'd come to apologize, but his visit wasn't entirely selfless. He also wanted to see her again and discover why she intrigued him so damned much.

He hadn't slept last night. Not even the welcome distraction that she'd provided at the dance had been enough to keep the memory of being shot from replaying through his mind once he'd reached his room, making his heart race and anxiety course through him. So after hours of restless pacing, he'd saddled his horse and galloped off at dawn from Blackwood Hall, with the excuse of wanting to explore the spots where the robberies had taken place, when in reality he simply needed to get away from the smothering darkness of his room and the memory of being helplessly lashed to his sickbed.

Once the morning reached a decent hour and the village awakened, he'd checked with the constable and learned that despite nearly two dozen robberies during the past two years, no one had been hurt except for rope burns where the bound drivers had struggled to free themselves. The robbers knew the countryside well enough to stop a carriage without being seen, then disappear without a trace. Which meant they were likely local men and still in the area. Which meant he had a chance of—

Gunshots split the quiet morning.

Christ! He flinched, his hand reflexively darting toward his side. His heart leapt into his throat and began pounding brutally like a hammer against his ribs as the familiar metallic taste of anxiety and fear formed instantly in his mouth. His hands gripped the reins tight, but even that firm grip didn't stop the uncontrollable shaking that spread up his arms.

His horse skittered beneath him, sensing his sudden unease, and pranced nervously as they approached the stables.

"Calm down," Thomas murmured to the horse, reaching to brush a trembling hand against the animal's neck. "It's all right, just calm down now..." Although he could have been talking to himself.

A young groom trotted forward from the stables, and he seemed about as bothered by the ruckus as if gunshots at Chestnut Hill were nothing more unusual than the ringing of church bells. Taking comfort in that, Thomas sucked in a deep breath, straightened in the saddle, and successfully ignored the itching burning at his wrists. For now, anyway.

Pulling at the brim of his cap in welcome, the groom reached to hold the horse. "Welcome to Chestnut Hill, sir."

He mumbled his thanks and rolled his shoulders as he dismounted, trying to push the tension from the taut muscles in his back.

The groom nodded toward the rear of the house. "The shooting match is in the gardens, sir."

Well, that explained the gunfire. As the pounding of his pulse gradually slowed and his breathing grew normal, curiosity sparked inside him. True, he was here to call on Josephine, but a shooting match in a country manor house's formal gardens was simply too unusual to pass up, although judging from the groom's calm demeanor gunshots were a common occurrence here. Something Thomas could readily believe, given what he'd seen of the Carlisle brothers so far.

Besides, he wanted time to collect himself before he approached Josephine. The last thing he needed was for her to see him shaking like a green recruit in his first skirmish.

He tugged off his riding gloves as he strolled toward the rear of the pretty redbrick house, following the sound of random gunfire. When he rounded the corner of the house, he hesitated in his stride. A shooting match stretched before him, all right, but with what seemed to be all the men from Royston's party gathered around, waiting their turns. Targets backed by bales of straw sat on a gentle rise of the sweeping lawn about twenty yards away, with a row of pistols lined up on a table on the opposite end. Supervising the competition, the three Carlisle brothers shouted orders and laughed loudly when their conflicting commands only caused confusion.

"Chesney!" Robert motioned him over to the weapons table. "Thought we'd ease the boredom of Royston's party and hold ourselves a shooting match."

"So I see." Grimly, he also realized that Josephine had identified him to her brothers, right down to his title, but since they hadn't yet turned any of the pistols on him, she'd obviously not shared her version of last night's encounter. That much was a good sign, at least. The woman knew how to keep her silence.

"Glad you arrived," Sebastian interjected. "We rode over this morning to Blackwood after breakfast to invite everyone but didn't see you there." He loaded one of the pistols and handed it over to Lord Gantry, who moved away to line himself up at the target. "Greaves said you'd already gone out."

Thomas watched disinterestedly as Gantry aimed, squeezed the trigger, and missed widely, nearly taking off the ear of an inattentive footman marking the hits. "I was up early and took a ride. Thought I'd see the village." Technically that was a lie. He'd gone for a ride, but he hadn't been up early because he'd never been asleep.

Quinton laughed loudly and slapped him on the back. "And then what did you do after the minute it took you to ride from one end of the village to the other?"

"There's not a lot of village to the village," Robert explained.

"So I discovered," Thomas mumbled as another gunshot echoed across the garden. Then, as casually as if commenting about the weather, he added, "I did run into the local constable, though. Said there'd been some trouble around here recently with a highwayman."

Sebastian snorted. "A rotten highwayman by all accounts who—"

"Strikes only a few times a year," Robert interrupted.

"Never fires his gun," Quinton put in.

"And steals barely any loot to speak of," Sebastian added without so much as a pause, as if the three brothers regularly finished each other's sentences.

"But the clodpole doesn't even attempt to kiss the ladies—" Robert continued.

"Or stick his hands up their skirts," Quinton finished.

Sebastian smacked his palm lightly against the back of his youngest brother's head. "Mind your manners."

Duly chastised and rubbing his scalp, Quinton slumped away to join the rest of the men gathered on the makeshift firing range.

"I suppose, though," Robert continued, "we should be grateful to have even that nick-ninny of a highwayman to spice things up around here."

"Islingham isn't the most exciting place to live," Sebastian clarified.

Thomas swung his gaze between the two men. "So you're not worried about the robberies, then?"

"Islingham's safe, if that's what you're asking," Sebastian answered.

"Josie goes for rides and walks at all hours," Robert added, "and we've never had to worry about her."

That stopped Thomas cold, seizing his full attention. Although why he should be so concerned about Josephine Carlisle, a woman he'd seen only once and to whom he'd barely spoken—even then, more arguing than actually speaking—he had no idea. Still, inexplicably, Robert's casual comment made his heart skip with worry. "Not alone, surely."

"You try stopping her." Robert gave a grimace of fraternal aggravation. "At least she doesn't go out often, and she never strays far. If she didn't get to wander off by herself every now and then, she'd most likely have run away by now. She's always gone off alone, ever since—" A sharp look from Sebastian stopped him cold. "She likes to spend time by herself," he finished instead.

Thomas's eyes narrowed. Definitely more going on here than what the two revealed.

"Mostly she likes to walk in the woods and read books," Sebastian explained. "Pick flowers, take baskets to the orphans and the poor...that sort of thing."

"Says she likes the peace and quiet away from the house. I don't understand it myself." A round of gunfire blasted up from the guests, and Robert shrugged. "Always too quiet around here for my tastes."

Sebastian nodded. "But that's Josie for you. Always been one to do as she pleases."

As a second round of gunfire blasted behind them, Thomas forced himself not to flinch. He drew a steadying breath. "You don't worry about her?"

"She's capable of taking care of herself. No one bothers her."

Not with those brothers skulking about, Thomas decided, all three of them ready to pounce at a moment's notice if anyone even looked at her askance. If the highwayman was local—and there was no doubt in his mind that he was—then the man most likely knew the green-eyed woman personally, as well as her large and menacing older brothers. Even an opportunistic criminal wouldn't be so foolish as to threaten Josephine Carlisle. Not unless he had a death wish.

"Has anyone in your family ever seen the highwayman?" Thomas asked casually.

In unison the two brothers shook their heads.

"As I said, nothing exciting ever happens in Islingham," Sebastian commented.

"We make our own fun around here." Robert grinned. "Any good with a gun, Chesney?"

"Fair." Thomas shrugged, his attempt at learning more about the robberies over. For now.

"A pound a round, then, winner takes all."

His gaze darted to the men lining up to shoot. "That's rather steep."

Robert's grin deepened. "That's what makes our match more interesting than whatever dull drawing room entertainments Royston planned for this morning."

Two more men stepped up to the mark, fired their pistols, and lost their money.

"Speaking of drawing rooms…" Thomas feigned indifference as he selected a pistol from the half dozen laid out across the table and inspected it. "Is your sister accepting visitors this morning? Or is she at Blackwood with the rest of the ladies?"

"She's at home." Suspiciously Sebastian arched a brow. "Is that why you came here, then? To call on Josie?"

Hiding any traces of his interest in their sister by making a show of checking the gun, he lifted the pistol to his eye and squinted past the hammer and along the barrel. "I wanted to inquire if she was feeling better this morning."

"She is." Sebastian folded his arms across his broad chest in a very good impression of a giant Hessian. However, he was apparently too self-restrained to demand to know if Thomas had been the cause of his sister's sudden illness. "I don't know if she's receiving visitors."

In other words, Sebastian didn't know if she would receive *him*. Perhaps the Carlisle brothers were more astute than he credited them for. "I'll take my chances."

"Hmm."

The half-disapproving, half-curious grunt couldn't go ignored, despite the potential for bodily harm. Thomas leveled his gaze on Sebastian. "Is there a problem with me speaking to your sister?"

"Speaking with her, no." Sebastian paused meaningfully.

"I just wonder what else you have in mind in addition to speaking."

Well. *That* was refreshingly direct, something Thomas wasn't used to amid all the posturing from the blowhards in London. And he certainly didn't blame the brothers for being protective of her, because he'd been just as protective of Emily.

Still, the wrong answer here could get him killed. "Only gentlemanly concerns, I assure you."

The look Sebastian sent him pinned him for a rake, yet he answered, "Good, because it would be a shame if we had to hurt you, wouldn't it, Robert?"

"A damned shame." His brother nodded solemnly and reached for one of the pistols.

Thomas blinked. A *very* damned shame. "You have no worries there."

Sebastian gave a curt nod of permission. "Then keep your hands to yourself and *don't* make her any promises you aren't prepared to keep."

For a moment the two men held each other's gaze, man to man, brother to brother, then Thomas assured him solemnly, "You have my word."

"When she refuses to see you, come on back here," Robert interjected with a jaunty grin. "We'll gladly welcome your company ... and your money."

In response Thomas stepped up to the line, quickly raised the pistol, and hit the target dead center. Everyone stared in stunned silence.

Robert's grin faded. "No need to hurry back."

Thomas returned the pistol to the table and collected his winnings, then sauntered toward the house. He was beginning to like the Carlisle men. When they weren't terrifying the daylights out of him.

A flash of maroon near the stables caught his attention,

just in time for him to see the swooshing full skirt of a riding habit duck inside the stone building.

A slow grin curled at his lips. *Josephine.* So she *was* feeling better this morning, well enough to go for a ride. And if he wasn't mistaken, he'd just caught her spying on him.

The day was proving very interesting.

He changed direction and headed toward the stables.

*   *   *

Josie leaned back against the tack room door and tightly closed her eyes. *Blast it!* Thomas Matteson was the last person she wanted to see today. The *very* last person.

She'd been certain she'd gotten rid of him last night at the dance, along with those blue eyes that noticed far too much. Oh, he'd been just as alluring and intriguing up close as she'd imagined when she first caught him staring at her, and for a few moments, she'd even allowed herself the fantasy that he might find her just as appealing, that she was capable of attracting the attentions of a man like him. Good Lord, he'd *waltzed* with her! And what an amazing waltz it had been, too.

But then, all those things he'd learned about her—if she'd continued to talk with him, it would only have been a matter of time until he learned the truth.

No. However intriguing she found him, Thomas Matteson epitomized trouble for her, and the best way to stay out of trouble was to avoid it. So that was exactly what she'd planned to do. Simply keep away from him. After all, Blackwood Hall was a grand house on a large estate, and she should have easily been able to attend the party yet still keep distance between them without offending Lord and Lady Royston.

But now, for him to appear at her home, and looking so dashing in his riding clothes, too...surely fate couldn't be that spiteful.

Maybe he hadn't seen her or didn't *want* to see her after the way she'd fled from him last night. Maybe he was just there because of her brothers and that silly shooting match. Maybe—

"Hello, Josephine."

Her shoulders sagged. Maybe fate was simply out to get her.

She opened her eyes at the sound of the velvety voice. The same one that had found its way unbidden into her sleep last night and given her such dreams—*oh my*. Her cheeks heated. "Lord Chesney."

"Thomas," he corrected smoothly.

"*Lord Chesney*," she emphasized with a tight smile, to push down the yearning inside her to answer the siren call of those eyes. How wonderful it would be to be able to call him by his given name...and with that, she knew, send herself straight into a pit of troubles. No, best to keep her distance, no matter how disappointing that was. "My brothers are in the garden."

With a glance over his shoulder to make certain they were alone in the stables and the grooms were occupied elsewhere, he placed his hand against the doorway at her shoulder and leaned toward her, trapping her between the door and his body. "I just came from the shooting match, actually."

He stood so close now that she could smell the masculine scent of him, that wonderful combination of leather and soap, and despite herself she deeply breathed him in. "Good," she sighed.

His brows rose. "Good?"

Oh God! Had she said that aloud? Seizing on a false bravado she certainly didn't feel, she lifted her chin. "Because then you'll be able to find your way back."

Instead of leaving as she'd hoped, the frustrating man only grinned at her. That same slow, sensuous smile she remembered so vividly from last night curled at his very kissable lips. And just as it had last night, warmth spread inside her, right down to her toes.

She shivered. Oh, this man was dangerous!

"I think you should join them," she prodded as strongly as she could without being rude and demanding he leave.

"I don't like guns," he murmured, sending her heart racing when his gaze dropped to her mouth. "Besides, I came to see you."

"Me?" Instead of the squeak she expected, her voice emerged as a throaty, breathless rasp that made his smile deepen. Which made her heart pound faster. Oh no, this was *not* good!

"You left so suddenly last night." He reached to touch one of the loose tendrils of her hair that her maid had left hanging delicately from her chignon to frame her face and neck. "I wanted to know if you were all right."

With each twist of her curl around his finger, she wished he would stop touching her like that, while shamelessly wishing at the same time that he would unpin the knot and shove his hand into her locks, sift them through his fingers, tilt her head back to kiss her—heavens, she was in trouble!

She cleared her throat. "How very kind of you to be concerned, Lord Chesney."

"Thomas," he insisted.

She ignored that, although she certainly could never ignore *him*. He was too tall, too muscular and broad-shouldered, and far too masculine to be disregarded. And the expert way he flirted, making her feel as if she was the most beautiful woman in the room—she swallowed. Hard. "I'm feeling much better today, thank you." Although she felt feverish all of a sudden. And oddly achy.

"I apologize if I overstepped last night," he murmured.

He hadn't simply overstepped. He had effectively stripped her naked right in the middle of a crowded ballroom by telling her things about herself no stranger could ever have known, and she'd felt completely exposed beneath those sapphire eyes, vulnerable, and wholly at risk.

"No apology necessary." When he twined the curl around his fingers, heat shivered through her until she couldn't bear it any longer and forced out, "Please stop touching my hair."

"All right." He released the curl . . . only to trail his fingertips along the side of her neck.

Her breath caught in her throat. Devil take him! He was doing this just to bother her. And frustratingly, it was working. He *was* bothering her all right, in all kinds of ways that left her tingling down to her toes and praying he couldn't feel her racing pulse or see the heat rising in her cheeks.

"As I said, I wasn't feeling well, that was all." Then she repeated in a pathetic whisper that held no resolve whatsoever, "Please stop touching me. It—it isn't at all proper."

The only response she gained was an amused twitch of his lips . . . and an ever-widening pattern of caresses against her neck and throat. "I see your maid is feeling better this morning as well."

"Yes, Mary's bett—" She halted as his words registered, and panic rose in her belly. If he knew something as personal about her as that, what would stop him from deciphering all her secrets? She demanded, "How do you know that?"

"Last night your coiffure was uneven, but this morning not a curl's out of place." To punctuate his point, he stroked the back of his knuckles across her cheek, drawing a heated flush in the wake of his touch that she was unable to tamp down. "Beautiful, in fact."

Her heart thumped so hard she suspected he could hear it even from a foot away. She knew she should bat his hand away, shove him back, and leave. For goodness' sake, someone might stumble across them! She'd never be able to explain why she'd let him put his hand on her. She wasn't certain herself, except that it felt so very good.

But she found no will to do any of that. Instead she let him remain dangerously close, let him trail his fingers down to her jawline, then slowly forward to her lips. She trembled.

When he brushed his thumb over her bottom lip, she sighed and shamelessly parted her lips beneath his caress. His dark eyes stared down into hers so boldly, so intensely that his gaze heated straight through her, swirling low in her belly and landing between her legs with a throbbing ache.

Oh, sweet heavens! She had to get away from him. *Now.*

So she jutted up her chin, smacked away his hand, and attacked. "So last night I was uneven?"

His eyes narrowed at her unexpected reaction. *Good.* Let him be angry. Let him focus on anything but the truth about her.

"Lord Chesney," she scolded, summoning all the primness of a governess. "I refuse to stand here and let you insult me. Or ruin my reputation with your rakish ad—"

In one swift motion, he grabbed her arm and pulled her with him as his shoulder shoved open the tack room door behind her. Propelling them inside, he lowered his mouth hungrily against hers, capturing her in a hot kiss before she could regain her wits and stop him. And when he kicked the door closed behind them, sealing them together inside the small room, his mouth molded against hers, and she didn't want him to stop.

Her soft gasp of surprise turned into a moan of submission against his lips as he leaned back against the door and drew her toward him, tugging her off-balance until she had no choice but to wrap her arms around his shoulders to keep from falling.

"You know damned well that wasn't an insult," he growled as he tore his mouth away from hers to sweep back along her jaw. Each caress of his lips sent a hot shudder of aching arousal swirling through her. "Just as you know I'm not here to find out if you're feeling better."

Unable to find the willpower to push him away, she tilted back her head to give his seeking mouth access to her bare neck and to allow him to dance hot kisses across the same place where his fingertips had tormented her just moments ago. "Then—" She breathed raggedly. "Why are you here?"

"For this." His teeth nipped at her throat. "And this." The tip of his tongue circled the curve of her ear. "And especially this."

With his thumb he pulled down her chin and parted her lips so that this time when his mouth captured hers, his tongue shoved inside to plunder her kiss completely.

With a whimper of half pleasure, half need, she dug her fingertips deeper into the hard muscles of his shoulders and surrendered helplessly to the strength and power of him, to the heat he pulsed tantalizingly down her spine. Her body trembled and her mind blanked until all she knew was the insistent pressure of his mouth, the teasing strokes of his tongue along hers. She'd never been kissed like this before. *Good Lord*, she'd never known such a kiss was even possible!

And oh, what a delicious kiss it was, too, one that left her quivering and craving the tangy taste of him.

Forcing back a soft moan, she tentatively touched the tip of her tongue against his. He inhaled sharply, and she thrilled at his reaction. Lost in the heady sensations that his kisses poured through her, she rose up on tiptoe to boldly return the kiss, run her fingertips through the silky softness of his thick black hair, and lick brazenly into his mouth.

"Josephine," he groaned. He captured her tongue between his lips, sucking hard and drawing it deep into his mouth until he stole her breath away, until fingers of liquid flame rose up from her toes and tickled at that private place between her legs. And then she did moan, long and loud and shamelessly.

She tore her mouth away from his, panting and fighting for breath. She buried her face in his chest and halted the wild ride he was giving her before she completely lost control to him.

As she clung to him, her weakened knees shaking so hard beneath her she had to lean against him to keep from falling away, she wrapped her arm around his neck and rested her forehead against his hard shoulder. Her body pulsed hot. Trembling. Aching. And traitorously wanting more.

"Good God," he breathed, incredulous, his mouth buried against her hair.

Good God indeed. How was it possible that he could make her so uncontrolled and reckless with only a kiss? "But...but I don't even like you," she protested in a confused whisper.

"I know," his husky voice rasped out. "Damn curious to me, too."

His hands ran down her back in slow, gentle caresses as if he couldn't stop touching her. Although, truth be told, she didn't want him to stop. Which made him more dangerous than she'd ever imagined. Because not only would he eventually prove no different from all the other men before him, *this* one held the power to learn more about her than she could ever reveal.

"But you have such an effect on me, Josephine, you don't even realize…and I have no idea why." His large hands cupped her bottom and gently pulled her hips tight to his, to mold her wantonly against him. And God help her, she let him do just that. "You're a puzzle to me, holding all kinds of secrets. And I love a good puzzle."

Secrets. Her heart raced impossibly faster. "I'm not—" She inhaled sharply as he squeezed her bottom in his hands. "I'm not a puzzle."

"A mystery, then." His warm lips brushed against her temple. "One begging to be solved."

Shamelessly delighting in the scandalous way he held her, she protested weakly, "I'm not begging for anything."

He gave a wicked laugh and tipped up her face. "Not yet." His stare turned predatory as he lowered his gaze to her mouth. "But you will."

There was no mistaking his meaning, and an unexpected wave of longing rippled through her so intensely that it gathered into a burning flame in her belly and ached to be extinguished. "I'm just—" She shivered as his hands slid up her sides, his thumbs pressing over each rib as he moved higher. "A normal woman."

"Oh no, you're not." He lowered his head to kiss teasingly at the corner of her mouth, the tip of his tongue darting out to taste her. "Not with the way you've intrigued me since the moment I first saw you." He gently took her bottom lip between his and sucked, eliciting a soft whimper of pleasure from her. "There's something about you, Josephine," he murmured hotly against her mouth. "Something only you do to me. And I need to figure out why."

She turned her head away before she begged him to kiss

her breathless the way he'd done before, when he flamed that delicious throbbing that heated wickedly between her legs. But she managed only to bring his mouth against her ear, where he devilishly traced the outer curl with his tongue. She trembled.

"No, I *am* normal. I like dances and gowns, playing the pianoforte...I like to buy lace and try on gloves and bonnets." She swallowed nervously as his fingers played at the buttons of her collar, as if he were contemplating undressing her right there in the stable. "I—I like dances..."

"You already said that," he breathed hotly against her ear, making her shudder.

"Well, you are making it difficult to think straight!" She groaned in frustration and somehow found the will to slap her hand against his shoulder to capture his attention and make him stop kissing her ear like that. He was so scandalously delicious, too dangerously close.

He shifted back far enough to look down at her, and the burning heat in his eyes stole her breath away. "Good," he purred.

Velvet. Dear God, his voice was *velvet*...

Her stomach knotted. Could he feel the hammering of her heart, the humming of her blood through her veins? All of her shook now, worked up to the point of bursting from a combination of nervousness at not knowing what to do and fear that he would uncover her secrets just as he claimed he would. And from a craving she didn't know how to satisfy, one that left her aching and frustrated because she was certain that he did.

Oh, how dangerous he was for her! Did he have any idea what wanton sensations he swirled through her with just a kiss and a caress of his hands? Or, God help her, how much she enjoyed it?

She looked into his eyes, and the heated desire she saw there...Oh, he certainly knew, all right.

"You *are* a mystery to me, Josephine." He slowly unfastened the top two buttons of her jacket. "You're beautiful, with a sharp mind that keeps me wondering what you'll do or say next." Another button slipped free. "Although if that's all it was, I'd be able to stay away. But you're so much more than just that."

His fingers gently pulled open her collar, and her breath hitched in her throat. No man before had ever come this close to discovering—

His fingertips fluttered over her throat, and a soft gasp tore from her. She closed her eyes against the temptation of him. Futile resistance, because instead of shoving him away her traitorous body leaned toward his heat. Her hands clutched at his shoulders, and her heart, certain to be broken, pounded a fierce tattoo.

"Which means you've compelled me to discover why you of all women, Josephine, are the one to invade my thoughts and capture my attention so completely. So I'm going to peel back the layers of you, one at a time." He lowered his head to place his lips against the bare flesh of her exposed neck. Goose bumps raced down her arms, and she shivered. "Until I figure out exactly what spell you've cast over me."

She stifled a whimper with a bite to her bottom lip. "Lord Chesney, please! You—"

"Thomas," he insisted as he brushed his lips tantalizingly against her throat. "My name is Thomas. Say it."

She sucked in a ragged breath, somehow praying she could find the strength to make him stop before he did exactly as he'd warned and discovered who she truly was. "You have to leave."

"Say my name, Josephine." He lifted his head to stare into

her eyes, and she immediately missed the heat of his very capable mouth on her body. And wantonly wanted it on her again.

In helpless capitulation she breathed, "Thomas."

"Thank you."

In reward his mouth lowered to touch hers, the tip of his tongue slowly tracing along her bottom lip, as if savoring her. Then he pulled away and gazed at her in wonder, as if he couldn't quite believe...

"My God," he murmured. "You taste like peaches."

She blinked, lost in the fog of arousal. "I... what?"

A barrage of gunfire erupted from the gardens. Flinching violently, he shoved her away, and his hand flew to his side.

She staggered backward from the unexpected force of the shove and stared at him. *What on earth...?* Stunned, she pressed the back of her hand against her lips and caught the unexpected wildness in his eyes, the sudden panic that seized him.

Her throat tightened with panic of her own. "Thomas?"

Forcing deep breaths of air into his lungs, he squeezed his eyes shut as if physically pained. His pale face darkened, and he muttered a sharp curse as he raked a trembling hand through his hair, the other one still pressed against his side. His entire body shook. Violently.

"That was just my brothers," she explained quietly, feeling the need to say something—*anything*—to fill the awkward space between them. "The shooting match, remember? You said you'd been there."

"I know," he bit out, then cursed again.

She stared, unable to slow the frightened pounding of her heart. His reaction was so unexpected, so *odd*. He'd seen the shooting match himself and knew they'd be firing off pistols all day. But he'd reacted like a man terrified. And trapped.

"Are you all right?" Her gaze lowered to his side and the hand still pressed there. With a concerned frown, she reached for his arm—

"Don't!" He jerked away with a scowl, then savagely rubbed at his wrists even as he continued to take deep, harsh breaths. "I'm fine," he snapped.

Rawness edged his voice, and the icy blue eyes, which just moments before had looked on her with heated desire, now flashed a warning to leave him alone and keep her distance.

Even as her own heart raced, she forced herself to breathe slowly and stand there calmly. For his sake. But if she'd had any sense, she would have fled. Just hitched up her skirts and run toward the house, not giving him any lingering thoughts except to wonder how much distance she could put between them. He was dangerous, far too keen for her safety, and oh so magnetic—*everything* about him screamed frantically at her that she should leave him be.

Except that she knew he needed her.

She slowly reached for him again.

This time he didn't stop her. With her eyes steadily holding his gaze, she closed her fingers over his, careful to avoid his wrists. She moved toward him, one deliberate step at a time, and closed the distance he'd created when he shoved her away. Her hand slid down into his palm, their fingers interlocking in a caress that was somehow even more intimate than the press of his mouth on her bare throat had been just moments before. The fierce beat of his pulse coursed through him and pounded into her. After a few minutes, his shaking ebbed.

She lifted her free hand to brush a lock of black hair from his forehead. Slowly she rose up on tiptoe to touch her lips reassuringly to his, the entire time holding his hand, his fingers laced tightly through hers.

"Thomas," she whispered, attempting to chase away the wildness in him and pull him back to the moment. "It's all right. We're safe."

"I'm fine," he insisted again, but this time much less harshly and much more like the confident man she'd met last night. The same man who'd pulled her into the tack room this morning and kissed her so ferociously before the gunfire shook him. "Your brothers startled me, that's all."

"They do that quite often to people," she acknowledged quietly, and somehow kept her disbelief of his words from registering on her face. Oh, his reaction had been so much more than simply being startled! He had panicked. Even now she sensed the hesitation in him, an anxious unease as if he didn't trust himself not to fall into another fit. But she respected his unspoken desire that she not press and stepped back.

"Whose idea was it to give loaded weapons to those three?" he grumbled.

She relaxed, knowing then that he would be all right. "Well, it was either guns or swords," she informed him, finally feeling certain he was calm enough that she could release his hand and button up her coat. "At least with pistols they have to stop to reload occasionally."

When she looked up at him, he seemed perfectly normal again, perfectly at ease. Yet she was stunned by how quickly he'd recovered, how his breathing was now once again steady, his blue eyes clear, and the wild fear she'd seen in him gone. Almost as if he were used to hiding the panic. As if these terrible fits happened so often that he'd grown used to them. But she suspected that beneath his calm façade he was just as uneasy as before, that she'd find his heart still pounding fiercely if she touched his chest.

She frowned. He'd said she was a mystery, but clearly so was he. "If there's something you—"

"We should go," he interrupted, and grabbed for the door handle behind him. "I've kept you here too long already."

With a glance over his shoulder at her to check that her riding habit was properly straightened, he opened the door and peered cautiously into the stable. Then, certain they were alone, he held the door open and motioned for her to follow him from the room.

"Wait here ten minutes," he advised, once again in control of both himself and the situation as he put a respectable distance between them in case anyone happened to discover them together. "Then do whatever you'd planned before I found you."

Whatever she'd planned before he found her? She blinked, bewildered. Was that all? Was this how the morning's encounter would end? He'd kissed her so heatedly that her toes curled, told her that she was beautiful and that he had an attraction for her unlike any other—then he'd startled, nearly terrified until she soothed him. Now he expected them to simply say pleasant good-byes and leave as if nothing had happened?

Her throat tightened with humiliation. Obviously he hadn't been nearly as affected by the embrace as she had. She'd melted moaning in his arms, for goodness' sake, while he had been more bothered by her brothers' silly shooting match.

Her eyes stung. Oh, she felt so utterly foolish! He'd proven to be no better than the other gentlemen who'd visited Blackwood Hall in the past, those men who'd thought she'd make for a pleasant flirtation and distraction. Some had dared to presume even more.

But she'd so desperately wanted Thomas to be different, even though she knew she had to push him away before he discovered too much about her, no matter how wonderful his kisses and how strong his arms. Her foolish heart still dared to dream, while her head knew the harsh realities of her life.

"Well, then." She forced a tight smile despite the embarrassment pinching inside her chest. "I'm very glad that you found me this morning."

His eyes flickered warily. "Are you?"

"Yes." She forced her smile to widen, although she certainly didn't feel at all like smiling. "And now that you've satisfied your curiosity about me—" She paused, not letting the words choke around the knot in her throat. "You needn't bother with me again."

Instead of heeding her warning, he smiled at her, his sapphire eyes gleaming as if she'd thrown down a challenge rather than an insult. "You're mistaken," he corrected in a husky voice that slithered dangerously like a serpent around her spine. "I very much want to bother you again, Josephine."

Her lips parted in a soft gasp at the blatant innuendo. During that moment's shocked reaction, he took a half step toward her before catching himself and stopping suddenly. Sharp annoyance flashed across his face that he couldn't reach for her again for fear of someone seeing now that they were back outside in the aisle. But the corners of his mouth curled into a slow, predatory smile.

"And trust me," he assured her rakishly in a low, amused voice, "you'll know when I'm satisfied."

"Oh," she whispered breathlessly, her cheeks burning and her foolish brain too stunned to form the put-down he deserved.

"Tomorrow afternoon, two o'clock," he announced, folding his arms across his chest, as if he were afraid he might just toss all propriety aside and reach for her anyway. "We're going driving so you can show me the village and countryside." His voice lowered clandestinely. "And we can bother each other all we want."

Oh no. That was a bad idea. A *very* bad idea. But her silly heart leapt at the suggestion, even though her sensible mind knew he was nothing but a rake. And pure trouble.

"I'm sorry," she refused, unwilling to acknowledge to herself how her stomach sank with disappointment. And to think that just last night when she first saw him at the dance she'd have been thrilled beyond words to be offered such an invitation by him. But already he'd gotten too close. She couldn't risk another encounter. "I'm afraid I've already made plans."

He crooked a disbelieving brow.

"I've…" Her mind whirled to find an excuse. "I've promised to visit the orphanage."

"Then I'd be happy to accompany you there. Two o'clock," he repeated firmly. "Don't keep me waiting."

Trailing his fingers against her skirt as he stepped past her, he strode off, while Josie stood there in the middle of the stable, gaping after him.

She touched her lips, which still tingled hot and moist from his kisses. Oh, this man was dangerous! Impossibly perilous for her. And she should *never* have let him kiss her like that or responded so eagerly. With Thomas Matteson she knew she was playing with fire, but she was helpless to stop.

Closing her eyes, she shook herself. Oh, what a silly, silly cake she'd been to let him unsettle her like that. Worse, to let him get that close. Why did this man chase all rational, self-preserving thought from her mind every time he smiled at her? But this time, oh, he'd done so much more than just smile. And Good Lord, she'd let him! She'd *wanted* him to kiss her, in fact, to touch her…shamefully, to let him do even more. Never had she been kissed with such heat, never with such raw need. Thomas left her shivering and craving to be closer, so close she'd wanted to crawl beneath his skin.

She groaned in miserable frustration. He was a rake, and she'd fallen for his charms as if she'd never encountered a man before. As if she didn't know what destruction such creatures were capable of wreaking on a heart.

And she simply could *not* let him get that close again.

CHAPTER FOUR

❧

*W*ell." Josie ducked out from beneath the fireplace in the first-floor common room of the Good Hope Orphanage, where she'd practically wedged herself to stare up into the chimney, and wiped her soot-blackened hands on her apron. "If there *was* a family of bats living in there, they have since vacated and moved on to tenant elsewhere."

"Are you sure?" a skittish voice asked from behind the settle on the far side of the room. A blond head peeped cautiously around the side and stared with uncertain three-year-old eyes.

"Absolutely, Clara." Josie smiled to reassure her.

Which didn't seem to comfort the little girl at all, based on the worried way her young brow furrowed. "Will they come back?"

"I'll ask Mr. Cooper to fix a grate across the chimney so they can't. Will that make you feel better?"

Clara nodded. Satisfied no bats would come winging out of the fireplace to attack her, she slowly approached with one of the cloth dolls Josie had donated to the orphanage last Christmas gripped securely against her chest. Her big eyes wide with curiosity, she tilted her head to the side to examine the cleaning Josie and the older girls were giving the rooms, with all the windows shoved open wide to let in the sunshine and fresh air of the mild fall day, surely one of the last of the season.

Clara pointed a finger at the buckets of water and scrub brushes. "I wanna help."

"She can't," interjected Alice, one of the older orphans, who put down her brush and rocked back on her heels. "She's too small."

"Am not!" An angry foot stomped on the floor.

"Are too!"

"Am not!"

"Are—"

"Stop!" Heavens, it was like listening to Robert and Quinn! Laughing, Josie held up her hands to interrupt the exchange, which she knew could easily go on for at least a quarter of an hour. "Clara, you can help by running down to the kitchen and fetching up another bucket of warm water, all right?" She turned the child's shoulders toward the door and gave her a gentle push forward. "Scoot!"

Giggling, Clara skipped bouncily across the floor and dangled the cloth doll from its arm behind her.

Josie returned to the spot where she'd been working until Clara interrupted her and insisted she check the chimney for bats, and then she made a mental note to ask John Cooper to fix the chimney, adding that repair to her already long list. She hadn't seen any trace of bats, but the bricks were starting to crumble and the mortar between them cracking, and it would surely have to be fixed soon.

She dunked her brush into the water, knelt beneath the

skirt of her dirty work dress, and scrubbed at the plank floor. A frown darkened her dirt-smeared brow. "Alice, were there really bats in the chimney?"

"Yes, miss. Three nights ago, one of 'em swooped down the chimney and into the room, flying all about 'til Benny opened the windows an' all of us chased it out." She laughed, her smile wide. "Quite a bit o' fun, that!"

At sixteen, with unruly red hair and apple cheeks, Alice was boisterous and bright, old enough to mother the smaller children and protect them as best she could. If she wasn't an orphan, she'd be at the age to start attending country dances and catch the eye of a good number of local farmers' sons. In her current circumstance, however, she'd be lucky to be noticed at all.

Josie's chest squeezed tight with guilt, the way it always did when she thought about the fate of the orphans. If fortune hadn't interfered in her life, she very well might have ended up like Alice, with few prospects and a dim future. She was so *very* lucky to have been adopted and removed from the horrors of the orphanage and the fate that had most likely awaited her as a washerwoman or a scullery maid. Or worse, as a prostitute forced to sell her body to buy bread. No, most likely she'd already be dead from disease or starvation.

Instead she had a safe and kind home where she never wanted for anything. For all that, and so much more, she'd come to love the Carlisles with all her heart. But she wasn't truly one of them, not their flesh and blood. She was reminded of that each time she stepped through the orphanage door.

Even now, after seventeen years with the Carlisles, she sometimes felt as if her life were a dream she didn't deserve. And in darker moments, she felt a dread that perhaps the adoption hadn't been real, an unreasonable fear that this life could be snatched away at any moment. In the dark recesses of her mind, she still heard whispers of doubt that Papa and Mama might yet realize that she could never belong to them the way a real daughter would and turn her out. She knew those thoughts were wholly irrational, that not once had her parents ever shown so much as a hint of not wanting her, but she'd never been able to completely shake away her fears. Because she knew that if they did ever change their minds and cast her from the family, she might as well truly be dead.

Which was why she still worked at the orphanage and would do anything—*anything* she had to do—to make a better life for the children.

Alice grinned at her. "I think that bitty bat was just as scared of us as we were of it."

"I'm certain." She frowned as she attacked the floorboards hard with the brush, as if she could physically scrub clean each child's future as easily as she could the floor. "But I've never heard of a bat flying down a lit chimney before."

"'Tweren't lit, miss," she whispered, shifting to lean closer to Josie so no one who might be outside on the stairs or landing could overhear. "None of the fires have been lit lately, not even the ones upstairs."

Upstairs. The old converted attic space where the boys and girls slept in separate dormitory rooms on short, narrow beds. Josie made certain there were mattresses and blankets up there, enough so each child had a place to spend the night off the floor. But the rooms cooled drastically by dawn, and only the coal fires Mrs. Potter was supposed to stoke between sleeps kept the rooms from being unbearably cold.

Her hand stilled on the scrub brush. She glanced up, dreading the answer even as she asked, "Why not?"

"There's no more coal."

Impossible. Josie had made certain herself just last month that enough money remained in the home's accounts to purchase plenty of coal to see the children through to spring, and she had strongly insisted to Mrs. Potter—coming near to full-out threatening the woman, in fact—that the funds be spent for nothing other than that. *Nothing.* The delivery should have been made a fortnight ago, and the bin in the basement should have been full. "What happened?"

Alice shrugged, as if the answer was obvious. "Mrs. Potter."

With a sharp curse, Josie slammed the brush into the bucket with a loud splash. Fury churned inside her, so white-hot as to be almost blinding. Mrs. Potter had stolen the money once again from the home's coffers and left nothing to purchase more coal for the winter.

Damn her! And damn Royston for hiring her in the first place, because the woman did exactly as the earl wanted and cowardly kept her silence. As long as she did that, Royston would overlook everything else she did, including stealing. Including starving and beating the children. And nothing would change as long as Royston was involved with the orphanage.

Josie sat back on her heels and wiped an exhausted hand across her forehead. Helpless tears stung at her eyes as bitter frustration burned hollow in her chest. Royston would never fire Mrs. Potter, nor would he replace the stolen money. And Josie couldn't go to her parents or brothers again for donations. They'd already provided more for the orphans than anyone would have expected, including by helping her purchase new coats and shoes last May.

No. She would have to come up with the money herself yet again. And somehow find a way to purchase and deliver a ton of coal before the first snow.

Her slender shoulders sagged under the enormous weight of the responsibility as she folded her trembling hands in her lap. She blinked away the hot tears of frustration and fatigue. *Dear God*, would it never end?

Alice frowned at her. "Are you all right, miss?"

Josie exhaled heavily and gave a determined nod. "I'll find a way to replace the coal."

"How?"

How indeed. "Never you worry." She forced a smile to reassure the girl and hide the uncertainty eating inside her. "I'll think of something."

A clamor sounded from the street below. The noise of running feet was punctuated by slamming doors and the echo of horses' hooves against the cobblestones. A shrill whistle split the quiet afternoon.

"What on earth...?" Josie mumbled as she swiped her hand at her eyes and climbed to her feet.

"Miss Josephine Carlisle!"

She froze, and the little hairs on her arms stood on end. She knew that voice, the smooth way it soaked through her like a warm summer rain, how it made her heart pound and her stomach flutter...

Thomas Matteson.

"Miss Carlisle!" he shouted again, and Josie cringed. Blasted man! He'd have the attention of the entire village drawn to them if he kept up like that. He probably knew it, too, and simply didn't care. Or more likely, he knew she wouldn't let him go on like that and would feel compelled to answer him just to silence him. Devil take him!

Alice ran to the open window and peered out at the street below. Her eyes widened, and she waved excitedly to Josie. "Oh, miss! You've got to see this!"

Not knowing whether to be curious or terrified, Josie

crossed to the window with trepidation, leaned over the sill, and peered down—straight into the sapphire eyes of the Marquess of Chesney on the street below.

A slow grin spread across his handsome face. "Miss Carlisle, there you are!" he called out as he stood at the seat of a high-perched phaeton, holding the reins wrapped around one hand. "Like fair Juliet at her balcony window."

"Stop that!" she hissed, her face flushing hot as a crowd of villagers gathered around his team and stared at the curious spectacle of this gentleman, rig, and dirt-covered woman. Good Lord, the last thing she needed was for him to make a scene!

Unperturbed, he doffed his hat. "I've come to take you for our drive."

Fearing he would come for her at Chestnut Hill as promised, she'd fled early that morning so she wouldn't be there when he arrived to collect her. She'd hoped he would understand that she wanted nothing to do with him when he found her gone.

She grimaced. Apparently not.

"I told you." She glared mutinously. "I have other plans."

"But my plans for us are more interesting," he assured her.

At that, several of the men laughed at the insinuation, and she reddened even more. Did the irritating man have no sense of propriety? "I am busy *here*!"

"Then I'll wait for you to finish." Turning away from her, the determined devil sat on the seat and kicked his boots onto the footrest, clearly settling in for a long wait. "But I thought the children might enjoy the treats I've brought for them."

"Treats?" Alice piped up, and leaned farther out the window.

Josie grabbed the girl's dress and pulled her back into the room. "Lord Chesney, you cannot—"

Too late. The children heard his pronouncement and poured out of the building and into the street, to crowd eagerly around the phaeton and the man whose expression had now turned into one of smug triumph. He *knew* he'd won, drat him!

"Oh, just go away!" she cried in exasperation.

"Come down, and I will," he challenged smoothly.

With no other choice but to do as he wanted—not unless she wanted to create a spectacle in the middle of High Street for the rest of the afternoon and disappoint an entire orphanage of children—she snapped out, "Fine!" and spun away from the window on her heel.

What nerve he had to show up here like this! Worse yet, to create a scene that would have village tongues wagging for weeks, when she spent most of her life trying not to call attention to herself. Little good that did her when this man was determined to thrust it upon her.

Although, to be completely honest with herself, part of her found his attentions flattering. No other gentleman had ever pursued her with such determination before, not after she'd given them the kinds of setdowns she'd given to him since they'd met, and why he, of all people—a marquess, for heaven's sake!—should be the one to do so utterly bewildered her. Even though she knew his attentions would prove just as temporary as those of past visitors to Blackwood Hall, her belly fluttered with foolish hope. She couldn't help herself. She was still as attracted to him as she'd been from the first moment she saw him, and how wonderful to fantasize that his interest might be something more than just passing entertainment for a bored rake at a dull house party.

But she had to stay away from him. Especially if he continued to call attention to her like this. *That* she could not allow, handsome marquess or not.

She stomped downstairs and out the front door, the rest of the children flocking out with her. Their eyes grew wide as they stared at the team of horses and smart racing phaeton that Thomas had borrowed from Royston's stable, while Josie's eyes narrowed into slits at the man perched on top.

"You said treats, sir." Jasper, one of the older boys, pushed forward from the crowd of children. "What kind o' treats?"

Thomas jerked his thumb toward the back of the phaeton. "Untie that basket back there and find out."

Jasper and Benny rushed forward as excited chatter rose up from the crowd of children. They rarely received treats, and for them to be delivered like this made it an event just short of Christmas morning. Despite feeling a stir of excitement inside her own chest, which probably had nothing to do with the basket and everything to do with the dashing man who'd brought it, Josie irritably scowled as she watched the boys take down the basket, which was almost as large as little Clara, who peered skittishly at Thomas from behind Josie's skirts.

Jasper lifted the lid, and happy oohs and ahhs went up from the children pressing around.

She glanced over their heads to find Thomas's blue eyes staring back at her. "What did you bring them?"

"I asked Blackwood's cook to put together a basket of meat pies and lemon biscuits," he explained, his eyes never leaving hers. "I knew you wouldn't refuse them such a surprise."

"Blackmail, Lord Chesney?" she scolded, although she admired his cunning. It was exactly what she would have done herself. "You would stoop so low as to curry favor with children in order to force me to do your bidding?"

"Of course." Holding back the stopped team with the reins wrapped around one hand, he held out his other hand toward her. "So please thank me for my thoughtfulness by showing me the countryside."

She glimpsed the glint in his eyes and knew he was daring her. Just as she knew she was caught. She couldn't be so rude as to curtly decline his invitation in front of the crowd of curious villagers, especially when he'd brought the children such a wonderful surprise.

But she also refused to take the bait. Instead she gave him a sickeningly saccharine smile. "I've been working inside. I'm too mussed and dirty, I'm afraid."

"I think you look lovely."

Warmth seeped through her like morning sunshine, and her heart skipped. Did he really think she was lovely?

But there would be time later to contemplate that remark, when half the village wasn't staring at her and waiting for her reply. "Unfortunately, my maid isn't here, and I see no groom with you to accompany us."

"I'll accompany you," Alice offered.

Josie kicked at the girl's foot to quiet her. "Without a *proper* chaperone," she continued, aiming a scowl at Alice to make her keep quiet, "I simply cannot go anywhere."

At that, several villagers scoffed in amusement, and some in nodding approval. But her firm refusal on the grounds of propriety was enough to disperse the crowd now that there was little left of interest to witness in the street, especially since they knew her well enough to know she wouldn't concede. And especially now that the children had absconded with the meat pies and biscuits into the orphanage, basket and all.

"But you can." He leaned down to bring his eyes level with hers. "That's why I asked Royston to borrow the phaeton, specifically."

She blinked, completely uncomprehending. What did a phaeton have to do with the lack of a chaperone?

"You honestly don't know?" he murmured with surprise. "Surely suitors have taken you driving—"

"Lord Chesney," she interrupted irritably, and put up a hand to stop him. Previous suitors—or a decided lack of them—had nothing to do with her present unease. It was *this* man, with his charms and melting kisses and his determination to uncover her secrets, who left her shaking in her shoes with trepidation. "I don't have time for your games."

"No games. I'm serious." He leaned closer to explain. "The driver of a racing phaeton cannot take his hands off the ribbons, so you're perfectly safe without a chaperone. Gentlemen in London often drive phaetons so they can have private time alone with their ladies."

Her heart leapt into her throat. "You—" She lowered her voice to a breathless whisper no one could overhear. "You want private time...with me?"

"Very much." Then his eyes filled with an earnestness that tugged at her heart. "Spend the afternoon driving with me, Josephine. Please."

She wanted that, too. Even now her toes curled at the tempting thought of being alone with him. Perhaps he'd kiss her again with that head-spinning, delicious need that had kept her awake all last night and sent her stomach flip-flopping whenever she remembered how good being in his arms felt. Which was nearly constantly. Because it *had* felt good. So very good.

But she knew better. *Not* with this man, no matter how tempting he was.

So she sniffed as haughtily as possible despite her dirty appearance in an attempt to drive him away. "We are not in London, my lord."

"No, we're not," he acquiesced. "But we do have a phaeton." He whistled. "Boys!"

Without warning three pairs of hands went around her waist and lifted her up toward the seat. She gasped in surprise at Jasper and the two boys behind her, then Thomas grabbed her arm and pulled, tugging her up the rest of the way onto the seat beside him.

Just as her bottom touched the bench, Thomas flicked the ribbons and the team moved down the street. He tossed three coins behind to the boys, who must have been in on the plan all along, then turned forward, wrapped both ribbons around his hands to control the horses, and sent them into a quick trot.

"What are you doing?" she fumed. Her hands tightly gripped the seat beneath her as she settled against the leather cushion, with no choice now but to hang on for dear life.

"I thought that was rather obvious." He expertly set the team into a smooth, fast pace and grinned. "I've kidnapped you."

She looked down at the spinning wheels and at the ground speeding by beneath them as they raced from the village toward the river road and the fields beyond. Oh, she had definitely been kidnapped! And with no means of escape short of breaking her neck.

"Stop this instant!" she ordered, using the same disapproving voice she used on the children when they misbehaved. "You do not have my father's permission to take me driving."

He slid an amused glance at her and crooked a brow. As if she'd just said the silliest thing in the world. "Do you really want me to explain to your father how we met and what we were doing when I asked you to go driving?"

Her mouth slapped shut, and the heat of a new blush spread up from the back of her neck. Blast him for using propriety against her! With a heavy sigh, knowing she was defeated, she shot him her deadliest glare. "You do this sort of thing often?"

"Take ladies driving?"

She'd meant kidnapping. But now that he'd voiced the question, she found herself oddly curious about exactly that, although there was no good reason to be. He would prove just like the other gentlemen before him—interested in her only as long as he needed to be entertained, then forgetting her as soon as the party was over.

Still, since he'd asked... "Yes. Do you?"

He shrugged. "Occasionally." She wasn't prepared for the flash of jealousy in her chest at that single word, or the tingle that pulsed through her and landed shamelessly between her legs when he drawled, "But never with a woman as intriguing as you, Josephine."

She didn't have time to contemplate what he meant, because with a flick of the ribbons he easily set the team into a slow canter when they passed the edge of the village, where the cobblestones gave way to dirt and the road curved slowly away toward the river. She sat back on the bench, one hand grasping the seat edge, the other one latching tightly on to his arm for lack of anything else to hold on to.

He glanced down at her, his gaze deliberately drifting over her. Her cheeks heated beneath his scrutiny. She knew she looked a fright, and perched high up on the seat next to him, she had nowhere to hide from those sapphire eyes that saw far too much. Her pulse raced, partly because of the sudden nervousness that he roused inside her and partly because she felt as if she'd stumbled into a trap. And desperately needed to find her way out.

She shifted away from him. "Why are you doing this?" she demanded bluntly. "What could you possibly want with me?"

He slowed the horses, finally bringing the team to a walk as they turned off the main road and down a dirt lane angling away toward the fields and behind the cover of a tall hedgerow. He faced her on the seat, the walking team needing less of his attention.

Which meant he could focus more of it on her. "I told you—"

"Yes, that I'm a mystery to be solved," she threw back. Which was *exactly* what she feared, why she'd tried so hard to dissuade his attentions. Because he was getting too close now, with a curiosity about her that could lead nowhere but to trouble. Yet every time she tried to chase him away, she seemed only to raise his interest more. And that had to stop. *Now.* "And as I told *you*, there is nothing to solve."

"You're lying," he accused evenly.

She gaped at his audacity. "Really, Lord Chesney, you make—"

"Thomas," he corrected.

Blowing out an aggravated sigh, refusing to use his Christian name, she began again, "You make carrying on a proper conversation impossible. Ladies do not like to be called liars."

"Then ladies shouldn't lie," he admonished softly. "You *are* a mystery, Josephine. You're not like any other woman I've ever met."

Her heart skittered at the flirtation. Clearly nothing but a lie itself, the compliment he'd given was obviously meant only to soften her to his pursuit, yet the words warmed her insides as much as if he'd declared her the most beautiful woman in the world. And oh, what a dangerous warmth that was!

With determination to withstand his charms, she sniffed as if offended at the compliment. "I'm not special."

"Oh yes, you are," he murmured, and his deep voice curled around her like caressing fingers. "Deny it all you want to, but there's something different about you. And I need to find out what it is."

She swallowed nervously. Her secret was still safe from him, although she wasn't completely certain *she* was. Not with the way he kept looking at her as if he were contemplating taking a bite of her. And certainly not with the inexplicable longing that crept up inside her to let him do exactly that.

Yet suspicion pulsed through her. "Why?" she demanded, but drat him, the word emerged as a throaty purr.

He hesitated and looked away. "Yesterday morning when we were in the stable…" His gaze remained fixed on the horses' ears in front of him. "How did you know how to comfort me like that?"

She blinked. *That* was the big secret he wanted from her? Well, that wasn't at all what she'd expected. But she also didn't know how to answer. She bit her lip. What could she say? That she'd known how to soothe him because she'd calmed the orphans through harsh beatings, freezing days without food or blankets, and nights locked in the cellar with the rats? But she couldn't tell him what life had been like for her before she met the Carlisles, because then he truly would pity her. And he would never look at her with those heated eyes again, as if she were a woman a man like him would truly desire.

She had no future with him; she was neither naïve nor foolish enough to expect more with him. But she wasn't quite ready to surrender all hope, either, and end the fantasy before she had to.

Dropping her gaze to her hands in her lap, she shrugged and evaded, "What does it matter?"

"Because sometimes," he admitted with a touch of embarrassment underlying his voice, "I startle like that. A loud sound or a quick movement, and I become...nervous."

Nervous? What she'd witnessed yesterday hadn't been nervousness but a full-out panicked fit, and clearly, with the quick way he'd recovered, he hadn't been surprised. Which meant the fits happened often.

Apparently Thomas Matteson was guarding his own secrets.

"When I'm around you, Josephine, there's none of—" He stopped, censoring whatever quiet admission he'd been about to make. When he continued, he said instead, "No one's been able to help like that before. I need to know what you did, how you knew to do that." He paused. "I need to know why *you*."

He needed to know, just as much as she needed to keep her silence. Yet for one moment she considered revealing everything, to find relief in finally being able to share with someone the part of her life that isolated her so much from the people she loved. Even from her family.

No. No good would come of that. She had to make him leave her alone before he discovered all her secrets. And there was no other way to do it than by revealing the most painful one of all.

Ignoring the stabs of equal parts dread and panic plunging into her, she drew a deep breath and said softly, "That night at the dance, you met my brothers." She ignored the tight clenching of her chest as she confessed, "But they're not my true brothers."

"Ah, stepbrothers." He nodded knowingly. "Which explains why you don't look a thing—"

"I was adopted."

* * *

Thomas pulled back sharply on the reins and brought the team to a prancing stop. He turned in the seat to stare at her as stunned surprise flashed through him. *Adopted?* He'd known she was keeping secrets, but good Lord, he hadn't expected that.

His eyes narrowing, he took in every bit of her, from the sea-green eyes to the dirt smear on her forehead. Since the moment she'd stuck her head out the window of the orphanage to glare down at him, he'd seen a hundred different emotions flit across her pretty face, but always the unguarded moments were fleeting, as if a veil had come down across her features.

But this expression now...well, that was pure feminine vulnerability, and it took his breath away.

She glanced down at her hands, as if unable to look at him for fear that he gazed on her with shock. Or worse, with pity. "Mama wanted another child—a girl—but she'd had complications with Quinn and the doctors advised her against getting with child again. So they adopted me." Her gaze fixed on her fingers as they plucked nervously at her skirt. "I was six and a hellion, the most impossible child to be the daughter of a baron, truly. But they wanted a girl who could hold her own against the boys, and they raised me as if I were their natural-born daughter."

"You're very fortunate," he mumbled, not knowing what else to say.

But a sad, self-deprecating smile tugged faintly at her lips. "I suppose."

That certainly wasn't the response he'd expected. "Josephine, if I—"

"Now that you know who I really am," she interrupted, her spine straightening as she pulled herself up tall on the seat beside him, "I'm certain you'll want to apologize for kissing me yesterday in the stables and return me to the orphanage."

"Not for the world," he murmured, letting his eyes drift down to stare tantalizingly at the top swells of her breasts just visible over her lace-edged neckline. He thought he saw her tremble. "The way you look and taste, what you do to me—" She swallowed nervously at that, and the gentle undulation of her throat made his gut clench, so hard that it stopped him in mid-sentence. *Sweet Lucifer*, this woman was a poisonous cure.

He shifted slightly to brush his thigh against hers on the narrow seat, and now there was no doubt she was trembling. Such a strong and confident woman, yet still so vulnerable, still so unaware of the effect she had on him. Frustration roared inside him that he couldn't take her into his arms and kiss her again, just to prove to her how right kissing her had been. The same phaeton that allowed them to be alone and unchaperoned also prevented all the pleasures of being unchaperoned. And alone.

"Did you enjoy it, Josephine?" he asked gently, not wanting to frighten her with the intensity of his desire to hear her answer.

Her hands tightened in the fabric of her skirt, as if she was fighting back the urge to either slap him or grab him and pull him closer. And the little hellcat could very well have been contemplating either option. But he knew which one he wanted from her, although he feared she didn't want the same. *Good Lord*. This had never happened to him before, not knowing if a woman wanted him or not. His kisses usually left women begging to be taken to his bed, but then, Josephine Carlisle was no ordinary woman. She was an intriguing, sharp, and independent creature, the likes of which he'd never met before. One who made him feel whole again when he was with her. And he wasn't ready to let go of that sensation just yet.

When she didn't answer, he pressed forward. "Well, *I* certainly enjoyed kissing you." He slowly brushed his leg against hers, the leather of his boot sliding against the softness of her stocking beneath the hem of her skirt. She shivered with blossoming arousal, her sensuous lips parting delicately, and his heart thudded against his ribs in response. "Tell me you enjoyed it, too," he urged softly, praying she couldn't hear the desperation edging his voice. "Come on, Jo. Don't make me feel like a cad for wanting you."

Her eyes widened as they found his, the green seas in their depths turning dark and stormy. She murmured incredulously, "You *wanted* me?"

The unintended sultriness of her words cascaded down to the tip of his cock, and he hardened instantly. *Jesus.* Thank God he was sitting down, or she would have had a clear view of exactly how much he wanted her.

"I still do," he answered, in the same sultry tone. She continued to stare at him with a look of confounded disbelief, but there was desire there as well, mirrored back at him. His chest soared like some green boy's who was alone with his first woman. "But what do you want from me, Josephine?"

At that moment he would have given her anything she asked as long as she remained with him, keeping the darkness at bay and making him feel alive again. And if she dared to whisper that she wanted him as badly as he wanted her—

A grim sobriety darkened her pretty face, and she answered so softly he barely heard her, "Coal."

"Pardon?" He couldn't have possibly heard correctly...*coal*?

Instead of repeating her words, she stared at him curiously, her head tilting slightly to the side as she studied him. "It doesn't bother you to know that I'm an orphan?" Disbelief flooded through her soft voice. "It doesn't make you want to race back to the orphanage to return me?"

"Absolutely not." He didn't give a damn that she was adopted. His best friend and brother-in-law had been an orphan, and he loved Nathaniel Grey like a true brother and thought nothing less of him for it. In fact, he admired him for surviving that horrible childhood and raising himself up to become one of England's most powerful men.

But the dubious expression that flitted over her face told him she didn't believe him. No matter, as long as she let him remain in her presence. As long as he could figure out what it was about her that gave him the only peace he'd experienced since the shooting, so he could take that same peace with him when he found Royston's highwayman and returned to the War Office.

She arched a challenging brow. "Then don't move."

Well, *that* was an unexpected response. The drive had suddenly turned very interesting, and his gut burned with curiosity to discover what thoughts were speeding through her nimble little mind. "All right."

Drawing a deep breath, as if gathering her courage, she slowly reached her hand toward his as he held the reins between his knees. Her fingers were gentle and soft as they touched him, and even through his gloves he could feel the heat of her, the tenderness of her fingertips as she explored him curiously. Her hand trembled in its inexperienced innocence despite the sophisticated façade she presented. He would have laughed at her pretense except that an electric shiver that was anything but innocent raced through him, and his cock jumped at the tantalizing thought of her hands exploring lower down his body.

"There have been previous gentlemen at Blackwood Hall who wanted to catch my attention the way you have," she admitted quietly as her hand continued along his forearm to the bend at his elbow, then up toward his shoulder, feeling the hard muscle beneath his sleeve.

A stab of jealousy pierced his chest, but he'd be damned if he'd let her see it. "I don't blame them."

"Hmm. They spent the week giving me posies and compliments, maneuvering their way into being seated next to me at dinner, flattering me with their attentions and invitations for strolls through the gardens, drives in the countryside…"

Beneath her careful explorations, he remained perfectly still, not daring to say a single word for fear she'd stop touching him. He couldn't remember the last time any woman had so leisurely discovered him like this. The women he associated with were experienced and worldweary, so much so that feeling a man's muscles held no fascination for them. But Josie's touch was curious and unpracticed, most likely driven on by the heat of the encounter they'd shared in the stables, and the last thing he wanted to do was stop her.

Yet he found her innocent touch more than just sexually intoxicating. He found it healing. Because when she rested her other hand lightly on his arm, her fingertips touching that spot on his wrist just above the end of his glove where the bindings still held him prisoner in his nightmares, the itching ebbed away until only the warmth of her touch remained.

"One or two of them went so far as to take me shopping for ribbons at the mercantile." She laughed faintly at the ludicrousness of that. "Can you imagine—*ribbons*?"

"They must not have known you very well." His voice came ragged with arousal, his lips thick from craving the taste of her.

"Oh, they thought they knew me well enough. After all, they'd found out that I was an orphan."

Her hand trailed along the collar of his redingote to his lapels and down his chest. Inwardly cursing the phaeton now and his inability to remove his hands from the reins to put them on her, he forced himself to breathe slowly and steadily, only to give a shuddering pant when her hand slipped beneath his jacket to fondle the buttons of his waistcoat.

"Which meant they thought they could enjoy the pleasures of ruining me—those who didn't presume that I'd already been bedded, that is. They thought they could put their hands on me however they pleased."

He sharply sucked in a mouthful of air beneath clenched teeth at the thought of doing just that... of his hands exploring beneath her skirt and finding her damp and hot for him, of his mouth suckling at her breasts. Of having her touch on him, her hands running across the muscles of his chest and that ripe mouth of hers closed around his cock. There would certainly be no fear of the darkness beneath *that* distraction, and when they'd finished taking their pleasure in each other, he would sleep. Without nightmares, without the terror of waking alone in the darkness. With Josephine still lying in his arms.

"You see, they believed they wouldn't be forced to take responsibility for it. After all, I might be a baron's adopted daughter, but underneath all the silk and lace, I'm still just an orphan." In the green pools of her eyes, he saw arousal and desire; there was no denying that. But he also saw something else—suspicion. "The *ton* would never cut one of their own for refusing to marry someone like me. And they knew it. *You* know it."

"I'm not one of those men," he ground out, anger mixing with his arousal. "I would never dare to presume that about you."

His hands tightened around the ribbons. He was furious at those men for thinking they could ruin her and simply walk away, as if she were nothing more than another party entertainment. And then his fury turned on himself when he realized that was exactly what he wanted to do, too—take selfish pleasures in her, then somehow keep the peace she brought him after he returned to his old life. A life that didn't allow for the distractions she'd bring.

Her fingers slipped the top button free, and his breath hitched. She was playing a dangerous game now. "Josephine—"

She placed her lips near his ear and whispered, "So I'm to believe that you're paying me attention, kidnapping me for drives, and kissing me only because you enjoy spending time with me?"

Her fingertips slipped beneath his waistcoat and cravat to caress the bare skin of his neck...so soft and delicate, so tantalizingly erotic in their featherlight touches. The irony wasn't lost on him that she was purposefully mimicking the same way he'd touched her yesterday morning in the stable, the same way he'd tugged open her collar to feel her soft skin beneath. She was using his own seduction against him.

"And for no other reason than that?" Her soft words tickled against his ear like a dare.

With arousal and anger speeding his heartbeat in equal

measure, he refused to answer. He couldn't deny wanting to seduce her, and more with each passing moment. The damned woman knew it, too. But he wanted her for more than just physical release, and how could he explain that without frightening her away?

"Be honest with me, Thomas." Each word came as a hot, shivering breath. "Do you have intentions of courting me after the party ends?"

It would have been so easy to lie to her and get exactly what he wanted—her company for the next four days, the delicious distraction of her keeping away the darkness, perhaps additional kisses and even more shared intimacies. But he wanted his old life back more, and there wasn't a place in it for a woman. Even one as special as her.

"No," he bit out honestly, the frustration pounding achingly through him.

"Then you're no different from those other men after all." Having proved her point, she dropped her hands away from him, then folded her arms tightly across her chest to erect as much of a barrier between them as she could. Her eyes glowed hard with recrimination. "And I think it best if we stay away from each other from now on."

He clenched his jaw. Stubborn, willful, challenging... She was lucky he couldn't take his hands off the reins or he would have throttled her right there for that damned object lesson she'd just delivered. *Stay away from her?* He nearly laughed. He was too close to gaining back the life he'd lost, both in Royston's recommendation for arresting the highwayman and in the receding darkness he'd felt since he met her, to dare to stop now.

"The devil I will," he muttered, then gave the ribbons a hard flip and sent the team into a fast gallop to reluctantly return her to the village.

CHAPTER FIVE

⁓ ❧ ⁓

*T*homas sat unmoving on his gelding beneath the black cover of the dark woods and tried not to shiver against the cold.

At well past midnight, he had been here for over two hours, unmoving, waiting at the spot where most of the robberies had taken place. He didn't mind. What was one more night without sleeping after the year he'd had, especially when tonight might very well put an end to all his nightmares?

He glanced down at his hands holding the reins, and a crooked smile pulled at his lips. Not one visible tremor.

But then, since he'd arrived in Lincolnshire, he'd felt better than he had in months. This mission for Royston kept him too busy to dwell on the shooting, and even being out here in the cold night, surrounded by darkness, didn't raise the panic and anxiety he'd come to expect whenever he ventured from the safety of home and light.

The frigid night bit into his bones, but after his encounter with Josephine Carlisle in the phaeton yesterday afternoon, he welcomed the cold. The chill kept his blood from boiling in anger at the memory of how unbelievably tempting he'd found her before she gave him that calculated setdown. And at how the blasted woman had been avoiding him since, which he suspected wasn't completely because she'd told him that she was an orphan or that she considered him no different from the men before him who had tried to use that to their advantage.

Bloody hell.

He was losing his mind. Why else would he be thinking of a woman when his chance to prove himself had finally arrived? *This* was his opportunity, the one he'd wanted for a year. The one that would finally bring back the life he'd had before the shooting. And no woman, not even an extremely intriguing, inexplicably alluring one with big green eyes, a kind heart so generous that she scrubbed orphanage floors, and a stubborn streak the size of London, would interfere with that.

He rolled his shoulders in an attempt to shake out the tension but failed. The damned woman was going to haunt him all night with her haughty little sniffs and sharp tongue, that thick chestnut hair, and those full lips that tasted of peaches and had him wondering what other delicious flavors she might—

A sudden movement caught his eye.

He narrowed his gaze and stilled as shadows shifted below him in the woods along the edge of the road. Every muscle in his body tensed. More shadows moved silently through the trees. In the darkness he could discern a handful of men on horseback, all dressed from head to toe in black, and all wearing masks and tricornered hats. A spike of tension licked at the backs of his knees as electricity crackled in the air.

A robbery was about to occur.

His intuition about tonight had proved correct. As the riders stopped moving to blend themselves into the black shadows exactly as he had, he knew his old instincts were still sharp, his skills as an agent still valuable. And tonight he would be vindicated.

As an approaching coach rumbled down the narrow road, a small man with a build not bigger than a boy rose up from the shadows at the bottom of the hill and waved his arm over his head. A large tree crashed down and blocked the road. The riders in the woods waited unseen in the darkness while two men on foot moved to crouch low in the bushes near the fallen tree, one on either side of the road.

A moment later the carriage skidded to a stop. The driver drew up the reins and motioned to the two liveried tigers to jump down from their seats and remove the log. In the silence of the woods, Thomas heard the grumbles of the two men, followed by muscled grunts as they struggled to push the fallen tree to the side of the road.

A shrill whistle tore through the night. The robbers jumped from the bushes to grab the two tigers and wrestle them to the ground as the riders swooped down from the trees, shouting and waving their pistols in the air. Thomas remained right where he was, unmoving, keenly watching it all unfold around him. Within seconds the driver and tigers were bound at the side of the road.

The masked leader jumped down from his black horse. He threw open the carriage door, pointed a pistol inside, and held up a sack. A moment passed while the mounted men circled the coach and tonight's selected passenger filled the bag. Then the highwayman closed the carriage door and swung easily up onto his horse. Another whistle followed, and the robbers scattered in all different directions while the highwayman galloped away into the woods.

And Thomas set off after him.

An expert rider familiar with the countryside, the high-wayman charged through the black woods, while Thomas stayed carefully behind in the shadows, close enough not to lose sight of him yet far enough away to not be noticed. The highwayman slowed his horse to a loping canter and crossed into an open clearing beside a pond. Pulling up, Thomas watched as the man slowed his black horse to a trot and shoved the sack into a hollow tree as he passed, then spun the horse on its hindquarters with a rear and plunged back into the woods.

Thomas followed cautiously, his senses alert to the shadows around him, his muscles tense. No one had been hurt in any of the previous robberies, but he would never risk his life unnecessarily. The highwayman carried at least one pistol, and Thomas couldn't be certain that the man wasn't riding to meet the rest of his gang or leading him straight into a trap.

Tucked inside a small clearing in the woods, the black silhouette of a cottage emerged from the darkness of the trees. Thomas silently reined his horse to a stop and leaned forward in his saddle to watch as the highwayman trotted easily up to the tiny stone house, swung down from the saddle, and led the horse into a small lean-to stall attached to the building. Moments later the man left the stall and entered the cottage.

Careful not to be seen or heard, Thomas slipped from his horse, tied it to a tree, and silently approached the cottage. Slowly he withdrew a pistol from beneath his coat, leaving the second one tucked in its holster. He hadn't lied to Josie. Since the shooting he'd disliked guns, but he dreaded being vulnerable even more. And tonight he would take no unnecessary chances.

The front door stood ajar, the faint light from a single

candle slanting out into the darkness. As Thomas reached for the door, he considered sneaking around to the rear of the cottage to hunt for a back entry or open window, but from this vantage point, he could clearly see that the cottage was shuttered tight, not even a hint of light shining through any cracks around the windows. The highwayman didn't know he was there, which gave him the advantage, but if he started prying open shutters and picking locks, the noise would give him away. Coming in through the doorway was dangerous, but there was no other choice. If he waited for a better opportunity, the man might slip away, taking with him Thomas's best chance at arresting him. No, better to come through the front door with the element of surprise than lose this opportunity by cowardly waiting.

Standing carefully to the side, he slowly nudged open the door with his foot just far enough to slip through. He paused, listening carefully. No sounds, no rustle of movement— nothing. Keeping his back against the wall, he stepped further inside the cottage.

"Stop where you are." The click of a pistol broke the silence. "Or I'll shoot."

For a beat he froze, frustration flooding through him for falling for such an easy trick. *Damnation!* Inwardly cursing himself and raising his hands slowly, he turned to face the end of a pistol.

And the woman behind it.

Josephine Carlisle stood across the room in the dim glow of the candle and pointed the pistol directly at his chest. Dressed in solid black from head to toe, she blended well into the shadows, the boy's clothing covering her lithe figure from the oversized coat hiding her feminine curves right down to the boots on her feet. Her hair fell loose in a wild mass of chestnut curls around her slender shoulders, the tricornered hat tossed away to the floor, and from her left hand dangled a black mask.

"You?" he murmured as he stared at her, unable to hide his disbelief. "Impossible."

For a moment she did nothing but stare back, as if just as stunned as he. Then, her voice husky with surprise, she answered, "Well, you're the one who said I was a puzzle." Despite the brave tone of her words, her hands trembled. "Puzzle solved, then."

"Not even close," he muttered with a scowl, then angrily slammed the door closed with a shove of his hand.

A curse snapped from his lips, and ignoring the threat of the pistol still pointed at him, he crossed the room and stopped directly in front of her. She wouldn't shoot him, he knew that; she would have pulled the trigger the moment he slipped through the door if she'd truly wanted him dead, and as the highwayman, she'd never before fired a shot. He was willing to bet his life she wouldn't start tonight.

She raised her chin as he approached but didn't step back or cower. He had to give her credit for that, although he wasn't certain if she was brave for standing up to him or just plain mad.

"You followed me," she accused, her voice slightly unsteady. "Why?"

"There was a robbery tonight." He slowly bent down to set his pistol on the floor at his feet, then removed the second one from beneath his coat and did the same with it. One raised gun was more than enough, in his opinion. "A coach leaving Blackwood Hall."

Then he stood to his full height and stared down at her, forcing her to look up at him as he towered over her. His heart raced at the sight of her, although he didn't know how much of that was because of the pistol still pointed at his chest and how much because of the untamed way she looked, with her wild eyes flaring and her face flushing, standing so close he could stroke her cheek if he only raised his hand.

And if he did that, then the blasted chit *would* pull the trigger.

So he folded his arms across his chest in irritation and tried not to do anything that would get him shot. "But you know about that, don't you? Because you were there."

"Yes."

"Then you know why I'm here."

Her head tilted slightly as she studied him. "You mean to arrest me?"

"Yes." He'd meant to arrest the highwayman. But Josephine Carlisle, of all people— *Christ!*

"You can't, you know."

She said that so matter-of-factly that he blinked. "Actually, I can."

"No one would believe you." With a shake of her head, she lowered the pistol and slowly released the hammer. "You can hardly believe it yourself, and you saw the robbery with your own eyes."

His jaw tightened. The surprise he'd experienced at entering the cottage and finding her instead of the man he thought he'd been chasing turned into anger for being played a fool. Her admission in the phaeton of being an orphan, that comparison of him to the other men who'd pursued her—all of it had been done only to throw him off her scent. And it had worked. Because he never would have guessed she hid a secret this big behind those stormy green eyes.

"I'm placing you under arrest," he told her as she crossed to the stone fireplace and set the gun on the mantel.

"You can't," she repeated, confident in her assertion.

"The well-respected daughter of a baron, one who can't ride well and doesn't know how to use a pistol, arrested as a highwayman? You'd be laughed out of England to even suggest such a thing."

"You're an expert rider," he scoffed.

"I fell off my mare just last week on High Street in front of several witnesses."

He clenched his teeth. She was right, damn her. No one would believe him. Even at that moment, he didn't know for certain himself what he'd seen tonight in the woods—or was still seeing in front of him.

His chest tightened as the full realization of the situation washed over him. Of all the people to stand between him and solving this investigation for Royston...the pretty woman with the proclivity for spilling punch, the one who led everyone to believe she was clumsy, unassuming to a fault, and so fragile that her simply declaring a headache had her brothers stumbling over themselves to care for her. The same one who successfully distracted him from the darkness that had surrounded him since the bullet ripped into his side a year ago. And whose skills of subterfuge and deception matched his own.

The irony was almost laughable. He would have admired her machinations, if his life didn't depend on arresting her.

"In fact," she added softly, "you have no proof of anything."

At that he arched a brow and deliberately swept his gaze over her from head to toe in silent accusation at the way she was dressed. She wore breeches...*breeches*, for God's sake, and as his mouth went dry, he suddenly understood why women weren't allowed to wear them in public. Because breeches made men aware that they had legs, which made them think about that warm, tight space between their legs, which made them think about how much they wanted to sink themselves inside—

Good God. He really *had* lost his mind.

"My clothing?" She shrugged with feigned innocence. "I wanted to try riding astride because I thought it might be easier than sidesaddle, but riding astride in skirts is impossible."

"At night?" he drawled mockingly.

She clucked her tongue like a disapproving governess. "Far too scandalous during the day. I do have my reputation to uphold." She retreated toward a doorway at the side of the room and into what he assumed was a bedroom. "Start a fire, will you?"

Cursing beneath his breath at her flippant request, he crossed back to the door and slid the bolt home. The last thing he needed right now was for her gang of men to come charging through the door to her rescue. Or worse, for the constable to arrive and arrest her before he could sort through this mess himself.

If this mess could be straightened out at all.

Gritting his teeth in aggravation, he grabbed the tinderbox from the hearth and knelt to start a fire. He had to arrest her, he had no choice. As the daughter of a baron, she'd most likely face prison or deportation rather than the gallows, but he found little consolation in the difference. And yet, however repulsive the thought of her rotting behind bars, she'd broken the law, and he wasn't going to surrender his future so a criminal could go free. Even such a beautiful and admirably daring one.

When the flames finally licked at the tinder, he tossed in a couple of logs and sat back on his heels, then glanced around the cottage and grimaced. The place was dry, secure, and perfect for hiding in comfort after a busy night of separating noblemen from their blunt.

He turned away from the fire and muttered wryly, "Quite a little hideout you've got here."

"It's an old hunting cottage," she called out from the bedroom. "Been in the Carlisle family for years."

He circled the room, his eyes taking in the comfortable pieces of furniture. There was even a basket of food on the table, for Christ's sake. "Seems like you've planned for everything."

"Not everything," she corrected. "I certainly didn't plan on you."

As he approached the bedroom door, he noticed that she'd accidentally left it cracked open, and he could hear the rustling of fabric and movement beyond. He stopped, his attention irresistibly drawn inside.

Peering through the gap, he saw her in the dim shadows cast by the flickering candlelight. She was changing, facing away from the door, and he watched shamelessly as she pulled the shirt off over her head and tossed it aside, baring her back.

Sweet Lucifer. His gaze swept over her, from her bare shoulders down the smooth stretch of back disappearing under the waistband of the breeches, which were the only things that kept her from being completely naked. His cock hardened instantly, and he somehow restrained the nearly overwhelming urge to step inside the room and join her, to place his mouth between her shoulder blades and lick his way down her spine.

"Christ," he mumbled as he blew out a breath and turned away before she could see him staring at her like some lecherous old fop. Or worse, before he peeled off her breeches himself.

"Did you say something?"

"No." He ran a frustrated hand through his hair. He was

shaking again, but this time it wasn't because of the darkness.

"Is the fire lit?"

He rolled his eyes at the throbbing erection beneath his breeches. "Bloody well blazing," he muttered.

The bedroom door opened, and she stepped into the firelight, tugging the sleeves of a pink muslin dress into their proper places. "Pardon?"

"Nothing." He grimaced, thankful that his long coat hid the bulge between his legs.

He watched her pull up her hair and secure it quickly into a twisted knot with two long pins as she crossed to a cabinet in the corner, although a part of him—a very interested and now aching part—wished she had left it down. He liked her hair better that way, falling free across her shoulders, all wanton and wild. He'd spent far more time than he should have during the past few days imagining himself digging his hands through those dark-chestnut waves, sifting the softness between his fingers, and letting her hair spill across his chest as she collapsed with moaning release on top of him.

He'd been a damned fool.

"Please, have a seat." Gesturing at the sofa, she pulled open the cabinet doors. "Would you like a drink?"

"Josephine—"

"Whiskey or brandy?" She ignored the warning in his voice.

He bit back his irritation. "I don't want a drink."

"No, you want to arrest me. But since that's not going to happen," she called over her shoulder as she selected a bottle and two tumblers, "you might as well settle in and enjoy the benefits of being in a hunting cottage while we answer each other's questions." She tucked the bottle beneath her arm and returned to him, then gave him the two glasses to hold so she could pour brandy into the first glass. "Why I'm the highwayman." She poured the second. "And why you want to arrest me." She capped the bottle and looked boldly into his eyes. "If you leave now, we'll never learn the truth."

He glared down at her, his frustration mixing with the growing distrust of her now pulsing through him. He had no proof that she'd just robbed a coach, and as she stood there in that pink dress that brought out the color in her cheeks and the rich darkness of her hair, she appeared for all the world like an innocent young lady. She was right. If he tried to arrest her, no one would believe him, and he could forget ever being reinstated to the War Office.

"And you'll be honest with me?" he challenged.

For a moment she said nothing and simply held his gaze as she considered the question, then she slid him a sly smile, one that coiled heat low in his gut. "Of course."

Not believing her for a second, he grudgingly handed her one of the glasses and watched as she set the bottle on the end table beside the sofa, then sat delicately, tucking her legs beneath her. He thought he saw her tremble. But surely he was mistaken. This infuriatingly bold, reckless woman didn't appear to have an uncertain bone in that delectable little body of hers.

Maddeningly, with no piece of furniture to sit on but the sofa, and right next to her, he scowled as he sank down and forced himself to keep his hands off her, not so he wouldn't kiss her but so he wouldn't shake her. Hard. The most infuriating, challenging, stubborn woman he'd ever met—with no idea how dangerous a game she was playing, how deadly the consequences if she misstepped. Or what it meant that she, of all people, now stood between him and his old life. The irony was biting.

He steadied his cold gaze on her, no longer seeing her as the innocent woman who put him at ease but as the opponent she was. "Tell me, Josephine, do you even like brandy, or is this just another ploy to confuse the truth about you?"

* * *

Tightening her fingers around her glass so he couldn't see them trembling, Josie did her best to hide the nervousness boiling inside her, the same worry and fear that had been there since the moment he'd walked through the door tonight and surprised her. No—since long before that. Since the moment she'd glanced up at the dance and found those sapphire eyes watching her. From that first glimpse of him, she'd feared this moment, somehow knowing that he would eventually discover her deepest secrets.

She struggled with how to answer that simple question, her mind so befuddled by his presence here that she couldn't think straight, let alone figure a way out of this mess. So she'd delayed the questioning—and most likely her arrest— first by changing her clothes and then by pouring drinks that neither of them wanted. Now, with no way left to put off the inevitable, she offered a silent prayer that she could appear bold and confident, when in reality she wanted to melt into a puddle on the floor and beg for mercy.

But she couldn't risk a glimpse of uncertainty or weakness in front of him. So she raised the glass to her lips to drink a large swallow. The liquid burned down into her chest, and a choke tickled her throat. With tears gathering in her eyes, she fought back a cough.

"I like brandy," she lied hoarsely, having never taken a sip of the stuff in her life and, now that she had, finding it utterly disgusting.

The amused flicker in his eyes told her that he knew she was lying. And more—it also sent a wave of silky warmth through her, curling her bare toes beneath her. Lifting an eyebrow in challenge, he downed his own drink in two gulps, and she watched as his throat pulsated tantalizingly with each swallow, stirring within her the inexplicable urge to place her lips right there at his neck and experience the soft motion for herself.

Lord help her, she was in trouble.

"You said you hadn't planned for me." He reached past her to set down his empty glass, and his arm brushed against hers.

She shuddered. As if jolted with electricity, her skin tingled where he'd touched her. She took a deep breath to steady herself. "I hadn't," she admitted honestly. "You were definitely a surprise."

With a curse he shoved himself off the sofa and stalked away from her. "Because you found me so easy to play for a fool?"

"Because you were so easily learning all my secrets." Ones she'd kept for years, that no one else had ever come close to discovering. Not even her own family.

He faced her, his expression stormy and furious. The anger seething inside him was palpable even from several feet away, so strong he pulsed with it and made her shiver with fear. And with something else equally as unsettling.

"When I left the orphanage," she explained, trying to calm her skittering heart, "I promised the children that I would never forget them, and I kept that promise. That's what I was doing tonight."

"By committing highway robbery?" he drawled with disbelief.

"By making the families pay for what they'd done, for

casting away their unwanted babies into that place and washing their hands of them. They gave their children no chance at a decent life, not caring if they were starved or beaten or…" The emotions swelled inside her, and to keep from becoming overwrought, she took another sip of the brandy, this time welcoming the burn in her throat. A cough sputtered at her lips, and she swiped at them with the back of her hand in a gesture of grim determination. "I decided to even the odds, that's all."

"Robin Hood," he scoffed. "Is that who you think you are?"

She raised her eyes unflinchingly to meet his. "I *think* that I'm the only one who cares about those children."

She set the brandy aside. The stuff was making her sick! This whole situation made her nauseous, in fact. The only relief came from finally being able to share the full truth of her life with someone other than the men in her little gang. She'd never dared to tell her parents, knowing she already lived tenuously within the Carlisle family because she wasn't their own flesh and blood and fearing this secret would be the impetus for them to cast her out the way a dark part of her heart had always expected them to do. And her father—how would she bear the look of disappointment on Papa's face if he ever discovered the truth about her? So she'd hidden it, until tonight, when she took some solace in finally admitting what she'd done rather than keeping it bottled up inside. Even if the man she told was the same one set on arresting her.

"You're a criminal."

She flinched at his accusation. His stinging words dredged up all the guilt and self-loathing that had eaten at her for the past two years. The moment she'd decided to make the families pay for their unwanted children, she'd known what she was turning herself into, just as she'd known the consequences she might someday face. She'd been able to justify her actions only by taking no more than the exact amount each child needed for care and a proper education. Not one penny more. But there was no other way. They would never pay for their illegitimate children unless forced.

Even then, when she allowed herself to contemplate what she was doing, how she was no better than a thief—

She looked away from the harsh indictment on his face and whispered, "I know what I am, and sometimes—" The words choked in her tightening throat. "Sometimes I hate myself for committing the robberies."

"Then stop."

"And who will take care of the children then? Where will the food come from, the clothing and bedding, the medicines?" And all the other day-to-day expenses that seemed so large sometimes as to overwhelm her. *Dear Lord!* Even now she trembled from the enormity of all the responsibility that rested on her slender shoulders. Whenever she considered stopping this madness, she was compelled to continue in order to provide all the basic necessities that the orphans needed, the same ones she took for granted in her own life.

"The coal," he put in knowingly. "That's what you meant in the phaeton. You wanted coal for the children."

"Yes," she admitted. "And tonight's robbery will pay for it."

He shook his head. "You don't need to do this to take care of them." His voice was quiet now, strangely sympathetic, and when she glanced at him, compassion for her situation touched his face. But the steely determination to arrest her was still there as well, flashing deep in his eyes. "I'm certain Royston would gladly become a benefactor and donate—"

"Royston is the reason that place exists!" She shot to her feet, her hands clenched into fists at her sides. "That home is a dumping ground for the unwanted children of English society, a place where they can rid themselves of their accidents without any chance of scandal, far from the attention of anyone in London who might be watching. They leave them there in poverty and filth, to be beaten and abused, and Royston makes certain no one knows."

He took her shoulders in his hands to make her listen to him. "Orphanages all over England are filled with the castoffs of peers." Sympathy softened his eyes. "It isn't right, but that's how it is."

"No, you don't understand!" She tried to pull away, but his grip was too strong. "He doesn't take the children of the peers—he takes the illegitimate babies of their sisters and daughters."

Thomas froze, momentarily stunned speechless.

"Don't you see?" she pressed. "If knowledge of those pregnancies is ever made public, those women and their families will be completely ruined. Their social standing will be immediately destroyed, right along with the men's political aspirations. With an ordinary orphanage, there's always a chance that the children's real identities will be discovered, that the families will be blackmailed. But because Royston controls the Good Hope Home, he can assure them that he can hide away their accidents so no one ever discovers the truth."

"Why rob only the men, then? Why not also collect from the women?"

"Because men control the money. A woman possesses only what a man allows her to have," she said quietly, "including her children." She desperately wanted him to believe her as she added, "And because it's the men who contact

Royston, and it's Royston who secretly places the babies at the orphanage in exchange for political favors."

At her accusation, the surprise that had flitted across his face changed to disbelief. "My father has known Royston for years. Our families are close. He's earned an upstanding reputation among his peers, and I know what a good man he is. He would never do what you're accusing."

Josie stared at him as her heart tore. His loyalty to the earl was clear in every inch of him. Oh, she'd made a terrible mistake in thinking she could trust him! She paused to draw a steadying breath and blink away the hot tears of fury threatening at her lashes. "Yes, he would."

He shook his head. "What proof do you have?"

"Information from the servants. Servants see a family's most personal moments and have access to their most private belongings. They know the secrets inside every house, including what the men do while working for the government or sitting in Parliament. It isn't difficult to get servants to share, especially if they were orphans themselves."

"Only hearsay and coincidence." His expression melted into one of pity and roused the white-hot anger inside her. "You are mistaken about Royston."

"I'm not! Those children, all of them, sick and hungry, cold…beaten with belts, locked into the cellar at night with the rats—" Her voice choked with fury and pain as she twisted his coat lapels into her frustrated fists. "I was *there*, Thomas." A hot tear slid down her cheek. "I *know* what he's—"

"Stop it," he growled, grabbing her wrists to tear her hands from his chest.

Josie gaped at him as she staggered back. She'd never told anyone before what life was like for her in the orphanage, not even her parents or her brothers. Until now. From the way Thomas had reacted when she'd told him she was adopted, she'd thought that perhaps he of all people would understand where she came from and why she felt compelled to help the children, but now the furious glare he gave her stripped her breath away.

"You don't believe me," she whispered, her suddenly hollow chest aching so hard that each heartbeat was agony.

"I don't know what to believe about you." His jaw clenched. "You've deceived me since the moment we met. The *very* moment we met."

"I didn't mean—"

"Oh yes, you did." He took her chin and forced her to look at him. "The spilled punch, the headache, pretending you're too clumsy to dance or ride a horse—even tonight with the damned brandy. And now you think I should just take your word and trust you about Royston? A man who has been a good friend to my family for years, the man who helped me get a position with the First Dragoons?"

Her stomach knotted at the contempt she saw on his face, and with a ragged breath, she pulled away from him.

He was right. She *had* deceived him, just as she had been forced to deceive everyone in her life. And now, when she needed him to believe in her, she'd cried wolf too many times to earn his trust. The irony wrenched at her heart. In her weakness tonight, with her guard down and her secrets exposed, she'd wanted him to trust her. Worse, she'd wanted him to put his arms around her and tell her everything would be fine for her and the orphans.

What a fool she'd been for wanting that! And for thinking she could confide in him.

She lifted her chin. "Quite frankly, I couldn't care less what you think." With as haughty a sniff as she could muster, she stepped away. "But I do want you to leave. Now."

She picked up the two pistols he'd placed on the floor and handed them to him, then moved toward the door. Her hands shook as she slid back the bolt—

"Stop this game, Josephine." His deep voice was suddenly close at her shoulder, his breath warm against her neck. "Before someone gets hurt."

She tensed at the nearness of his body, the heat of him seeping through her muslin dress and setting her blood humming. He'd moved so quickly, so quietly she'd not noticed him approach until he was behind her. But his closeness, and her unbidden reaction to him, wasn't enough to calm the anger and humiliation churning inside her.

"Do whatever you need to do, Thomas, but I won't stop." Her voice was just as low as his and held just as much conviction. "I won't turn my back on those children."

Muttering a curse beneath his breath, he took her elbow and turned her to face him. As her hands went instinctively to his chest to push him away, the hard muscles rippled beneath her fingertips. The sensation sent an electric tingle up her arms and down into her breasts, and she knew she didn't stand a chance at keeping him away. Nor did she want to. A very traitorous part of her longed to have his hands and mouth on her, his body pressing hard against hers. And one glance at the heat blazing in his eyes as he stared at her mouth told her he wanted that, too.

He was dangerous, both to her life and to her heart, and she should have been running away from him as fast as she could. Instead she was drawn to his fire, and even though she knew she was going to get burned, she craved his heat.

She couldn't fight back the soft moan of need that tore from her throat or the way her arms slipped around his shoulders to tug her against him as she breathlessly whispered, "Thomas, please—"

With a growl he grabbed her with both hands and shoved her back against the wall, his mouth capturing hers.

*   *   *

Thomas pinned her between the wall and his body, a willing prisoner who returned his hungry kiss with just as much ferocity as he gave. But he couldn't kiss her fiercely enough to quench the fires of passion and anger flaming inside him. She tasted delicious, an intoxicating flavor of peaches and brandy that spun his head as if he were drunk and made him wonder if other parts of her tasted just as sweet.

A groan of frustration escaped him. He couldn't get enough of her, of her soft body beneath his seeking hands, the sweet taste of her as his tongue thrust deep into the moist, warm recesses of her mouth, or her soft mewlings of arousal and pleasure. He gasped as she closed her lips over his tongue to suckle gently at him in an unpracticed but impulsive kiss that instantly hardened his cock.

Sweet Lucifer, the things this woman did to him! She'd lied and deceived him until he didn't trust a word she said, and he should have been shoving her away. Instead his hands encircled her hips and tugged her forward against his erection, shamelessly pressing his hard length into her soft belly. She was completely wrong for him, this woman who had now placed him in the impossible situation of having to arrest her in order to secure his own future. Who was an exquisite, inexplicable release from the haunting darkness. And who would only cause problems for him.

Yet he still wanted her. Desperately.

Shifting back just far enough to caress his hands up her arms, he slipped his thumbs beneath the shoulders of her dress and tugged, pulling both sleeves down her arms to the elbows and baring her breasts to the firelight. She gasped in surprise against his mouth but didn't try to stop him.

"The second layer," he explained, nibbling at the corner of her lips and thanking God she hadn't bothered to put on a stay when she changed. "I'm peeling it back now."

"Thomas—"

"I told you I would, Jo." She shivered tantalizingly when he cupped her fullness against his palms and began to tease his thumbs over her nipples in slow circles. "That I'd peel back one layer at a time until I'd revealed all of you."

With a whimper of surrender, she instinctively arched her back against the wall, to bring his hands harder against her. In response he scraped his thumbnails across her nipples, and a shudder of pleasure-pain swept through her as they pebbled temptingly into taut buds.

"And I always keep my promises." Unable to resist, he ducked his head to lave his tongue over her nipple.

"Thomas!" she gasped. Her hands clutched at his shoulders not to push him away but to keep his body close and his mouth at her breast.

Laughter rumbled from deep in his chest over her reaction to so simple a caress. So, his pistol-wielding highwayman was still innocent of a man's mouth on her body, and knowing he was the first to kiss her like this pleased him immensely. More than he had a right to be. Yet he couldn't make himself stop, not yet. Shamelessly he closed his lips around her nipple and sucked.

She quivered with need and dug her fingers into his hair, and he thrilled at her response. As he suckled at her, drawing her deep into his mouth, his hand gently caressed her other breast. The featherlight strokes of his fingertips against her nipple contrasted against the hard pulls of his lips until she shuddered.

Beneath his mouth and hands, he felt her resistance slipping away. She was a criminal, and he should have been arresting her and hauling her away to face the constable, yet he wanted nothing more at that moment than to seduce her, to bury himself between her thighs and thrust into her warmth until she shattered around him, then hold her close until dawn, when the nightmares and darkness had all passed.

He groaned and fought to hold on to what little self-restraint he still possessed. A small taste of her he could excuse, but anything more…*madness*. And not only because he'd prove himself no better than those other men who'd thought they had a right to bed her without consequence, but because he now wanted her for more than just her body, more than the way she calmed his racing heart and put him at ease. He found himself now wanting *her*.

But at what cost?

Even as the highwayman, she was a distraction from the darkness. Yet he knew exactly how dangerous distractions could be, how they could easily claim a man's life.

"You have to stop the robberies," he murmured against her soft skin, placing delicate kisses against her nipple.

Her fingers tensed as they traced against the nape of his neck. "I told you, I can't."

"You'll make a mistake eventually." He shifted his mouth to the other breast to take another taste of her, one so sweet yet torturous because he knew he could never claim more from her, no matter how much he longed for it. "And you won't have an easy explanation to save you."

"And then"—she panted for breath, arching herself into him—"you'll arrest me?"

"Yes."

"You won't."

"I will."

"No, you—" Her fingernails scratched into his neck as he took her nipple deep into his mouth and suckled hard, so hard she moaned. "You won't."

He released her breast and slid back up her body, kissing her throat before nipping at her earlobe in warning, both to stop the robberies and to put an end to the impossible dilemma she posed for him. "You shouldn't tempt fate."

"Fate shouldn't tempt me," she whispered.

He lifted his head to gaze down at her, her eyes and face dark with arousal, her lips moist and trembling. *Dear God*, she was frustrating, stubborn...every inch of her screamed trouble. And he'd never wanted a woman more in his life.

"Stop this now." Best he heed that warning himself, so he dropped his hands away from her and stepped back.

"Or what?" Her chin lifted slightly, although he couldn't tell if in defiance or with a longing to be kissed again.

Regretting that he couldn't stay to discover which, and knowing he'd enjoy either far too much, he pulled up the sleeves of her dress to cover her and smoothed the fabric back into its proper place. "Or there won't be anything I can do to protect you."

He reached past her to jerk open the door and stalked outside into the night.

CHAPTER SIX

I'd heard he killed a man."

Josie stabbed herself through her embroidery. "Ouch!"

She stuck her finger in her mouth and scowled. Sitting in Blackwood Hall and listening to the dozen or so female guests discuss Thomas Matteson was the last way she wanted to spend her afternoon, but the ladies' drawing room had seemed the safest place to avoid the rake in question. Unfortunately, all the ladies in the room had heard the rumors floating through London about the young marquess and his roguish reputation and so had made him the center of their gossip.

"Because he saved the Prince Regent's life," Mrs. Peterson corrected Lady Denton's accusation. "That assassination attempt, you remember? That was the man he shot."

Josie blinked. Thomas had . . . killed someone?

"Right there at the Stanhope ball!" Mrs. Peterson spoke with such conviction that no one in the room doubted her. "Absolutely ruined Penelope Stanhope's debut. The poor girl was completely unnerved. Couldn't waltz for weeks."

If that story was true, Josie decided, then the Prince Regent had more of a reason to be unnerved than Lady Penelope.

"And then, last year," she continued in hushed tones, "when he was nearly killed by that robber in Hyde Park—so dreadful!"

Josie's head jerked up, her breath catching in her throat.

Lady Denton snorted. "I'd heard it was really a French spy who shot him."

Shot Thomas? Her face paling, Josie leaned forward.

"No, *he* was in France during the war," Lady Agnes interjected.

"It was Spain," Mrs. Peterson corrected.

"It was Mayfair," someone else put in.

"Why would anyone be spying in Mayfair?"

"No, no! He was *shot* in Mayfair."

"I'd heard it was because he was on a secret assignment to protect the prime minister."

"Well," Miranda Hodgkins piped up, "I'd certainly let him protect *me*!"

At that a round of muffled giggles sounded throughout the room.

Elizabeth Carlisle leaned toward Josie and whispered knowingly into her ear, "Not long enough on the vine."

Josie forced a tight smile at her mother, but her attention focused on the gossip, on what the ladies had said about Thomas. Killing? *Shot?* Although she'd long ago learned that most of the gossip women shared in drawing rooms was exaggerated in order to titillate and shock, she'd stared into those gossiped-about sapphire eyes herself and experienced the undeniable allure of him. It was possible, *very* possible, that he was both England's hero and someone capable of taking a life.

Either way, she needed to be careful. She'd been so stupidly careless in letting him follow her back to the cottage last night, then so foolishly weak in letting him kiss her, touch her—oh good heavens, he'd *licked* her! And God help her, she desperately wanted him to do it again.

"Well, I can tell you this much. He's certainly the darling of the London social set these days," Lady Tinsdale interjected, flipping through the pages of the gardening book she'd been pretending to read. "Apparently quite the catch. He's heir to a duchy, you know."

"Oh?" That got Miranda's attention again.

A mischievous smile tugged at Lady Tinsdale's lips as she glanced at Miranda. "Best to stay clear of him, my dear. He's turning into quite the scapegrace, and rather quickly, too. The things he's rumored to have done—well, they're not fit for ladies' ears."

"Do tell us anyway," Lady Denton urged, her seventy-two years of age letting her get away with such scandalous suggestions. When the ladies glanced at her, feigning shock, she snorted. "Oh, come now! You all want to know just as much as I do."

No. Josie certainly did *not* want to know anything about Thomas's amorous exploits. The last thing she needed was more fodder for her imagination, which already kept her awake at night with all kinds of wicked thoughts and fantasies about him. Oh, definitely better to concentrate on her embroidery like a proper young lady. Even if she wasn't one.

"I heard he keeps a mistress in Notting Hill."

Ouch! She sucked at her thumb. *Blast it!*

"An opera singer."

"Not a singer," someone else corrected. "An actress. Parisian."

As a chorus of *ooh*s sounded beneath their collective

breaths, Josie grimaced. No, she definitely did *not* need to know these things, not when she could still feel the pressure of his mouth on hers, when she was certain she could still taste the brandy flavor of his lips and remember the heat of his hands caressing her breasts. Beneath her muslin bodice, her nipples puckered achingly at the memory of his mouth on them.

She frowned down at the misshapen pattern in her hoop. How, exactly, she was supposed to concentrate on her embroidery when all the talk of Lord Chesney only served to remind her of how wonderfully he kissed? And only made her want even more from him?

"Why is he here?" Miranda asked. "This party doesn't seem his sort."

Josie paused in mid-stitch. *That* was a very good question.

A moment of silence fell over the gaggle of women, and all eyes drifted to Lady Royston for an explanation of why the marquess had been asked to attend when the Roystons had never invited anyone of his roguish reputation to one of their parties before.

"Royston and I know his family well." Her answer was stilted, not as if she was trying to hide anything but rather as if she was just as puzzled as the other women and didn't quite believe the explanation herself. "The earl's on a committee with Chesney's father in the Lords."

Several *I see*s sounded in time to nodding heads. A political connection. Of course. Which satisfied their curiosity.

Until Miranda Hodgkins chirped, "I heard he left Blackwood Hall last night after dinner and went out riding all by himself. *All* night."

And *that* made him seem suddenly even more mysterious, brooding, and dashing to this group of hens. A clack and clatter of whispers rose up.

Josie's heart leapt into her throat in panic. If they started asking questions about why he'd been out last night, how long until someone realized that she, too, had been missing?

Miranda nodded with authority. "Tom, the groom, said he didn't return until after dawn."

"Really?" Lady Agnes Sinclair frowned. "I wonder what he was doing—"

Lady Tinsdale interrupted, "Or *whom* he was sneaking out to see."

"Which could explain his sudden arrival in Lincolnshire."

"And why he's been so frequently absent when—"

"I'd heard he'd killed a lion with his bare hands."

That brought the conversation to a skidding halt.

All the women turned in their seats to stare curiously at Josie for making the unusual comment, as if she were on exhibit at the British Museum. Or in a carnival. Their curiosity was pricked even further by the fact that she so rarely said anything that called undue attention to herself.

Now she'd done it. In her rush to distract them, she'd brought trouble straight down onto her own head. She cleared her throat. "I only meant—"

"Truly, with his bare hands?" a familiar and oh-so-masculine voice drawled with amusement from across the room. "That's quite a feat."

Her face reddening with mortification, she glanced up and caught her breath as dark-blue eyes found hers. Those same eyes that now haunted her dreams.

Thomas Matteson leaned against the doorway and grinned charmingly, his arms folded across his broad chest and looking for all the world like the rakehell, war hero, or royal savior—or even lion-killer—they'd just declared him to be.

But Josie knew better. Behind that handsome façade lay a snake. And if she wasn't careful, he might just bite.

"And who is this fierce hunter?" he pressed, much to the delight of the tittering women and much to Josie's chagrin. "Do I know him?"

"Lord Chesney." Lady Agnes Sinclair smiled, genuinely pleased at the perfect timing of his arrival. "I'd thought you'd gone fishing."

He returned the woman's warm greeting with a nod. "I changed my mind when I saw the Carlisle brothers heading toward the river with crossbows."

Elizabeth Carlisle gave a long-suffering sigh.

"So you decided to join us women instead." Lady Denton waved her hand. "Do come in then and have some tea."

"Actually, I thought to go riding and wondered if any of you ladies wanted to join me."

"I'll go with you!" Miranda glowed with excitement.

Thomas's cool smile stated clearly that the invitation was not meant for her, his gaze sliding from the overeager girl to Josie. Along with every other curious pair of eyes in the room. *Oh no.*

"And how about you, Miss Carlisle?" he offered casually. "Will you join us?"

Drat him for causing a scene! He was focusing the unwanted attention of every gossipy hen in the room right on her, and the devil knew it, too. Most likely he'd issued the invitation just to watch her squirm. Reparations for last night's encounter.

When she didn't answer, he persisted annoyingly, "You gave me the honor of a waltz at the dance and didn't complain when I stepped on your toes." More giggles went up from the ladies. "I thought I'd repay the kindness with a ride."

Lady Denton let out a loud chortle as Josie's cheeks flushed a hot scarlet color that no one in the room could possibly have missed.

"Her?" Miranda's face fell. "Why, she can't even ride! She fell off her horse just last week, right in the middle of High Street. Everyone saw her!"

"Did she?" Thomas's mouth curled into a self-pleased grin. "Well, then today seems a perfect opportunity for a riding lesson."

The collective weight of the women's eyes landed on her to catch her response. Her spine stiffened. "I'm sorry, my lord, but I'm not dressed for riding today."

"Perhaps"—their gazes swung to him—"a walk in the garden."

Back to her—"I wore the wrong shoes, too, I'm afraid."

Then to him—"A drive in the phaeton, then. I insist."

Back to her—*Goodness!* She felt like a player in a tennis match. Her head was beginning to spin. "I really couldn't possibly." When he began to open his mouth again, she had no choice but to declare firmly, "*No.*"

The room froze, all the ladies holding their breaths to see what his reaction would be to such a blunt refusal, although none of them would have dared presume she'd ever have accepted such an invitation from a noted rake in the first place. Especially not when sitting by her mother, who watched the entire exchange with a curious expression.

"Well, then." No one else seemed to notice the mischievous gleam in his eyes, but of course Josie did. She couldn't help but notice everything about this man. Drat him. "Perhaps another time. Enjoy your afternoon."

And with that he ended the tennis match, although Josie couldn't have said which one of them had emerged the winner.

"Ladies." He gave them a smile as if completely unaffected by her cut. "If you'll excuse me, I think I'll grab a pole and join the men after all."

Sketching a shallow bow to the room at large, he turned and left.

"Well, *that* was certainly interesting," Lady Denton exclaimed, her old but sharp eyes settling on Josie from across the room.

Knowing the ladies expected some sort of comment from her and that they wouldn't turn their attentions away until she'd given one, Josie waved her hand dismissively in the air. "He only wanted to avoid my brothers while they're armed with crossbows." Faint chuckles rose at that, all of them knowing well the antics of the Carlisle brothers. "You can't blame a man for wanting to keep himself from bodily harm."

"I don't think it was *harm* which concerned him *bodily*," Lady Denton muttered with scathing wit.

Oh, Josie wanted to die! She felt the burn as her cheeks turned scarlet. But the other women only laughed halfheartedly at the innuendo, too stunned—or too jealous—that the focus of Thomas's attention had been on her.

Beside her, though, her mother stiffened with embarrassment. A pang of guilt struck Josie's chest because the game of cat and mouse that had sprung up between her and Thomas was now affecting her family. She doubted she would ever be completely sure of her true place among the Carlisles, but she loved them all with every ounce of her heart and never wanted them to be hurt.

"Best to avoid him, my dears," Lady Denton warned, her now serious gaze passing between Josie and Miranda, all her previous teasing gone.

A wave of frustration poured through Josie. Heavens, hadn't she been trying to do exactly that since he arrived? But fate—and Thomas—clearly had other plans. Yet she had to hold out only for another three days until the party ended and he returned to London, and she would never·have to be bothered by the infuriating rascal ever again. Although even as she reminded herself of that, it wasn't relief she felt but inexplicable sadness that he should be leaving so soon.

"As Lord Chesney said, he was simply attempting to return a kindness," she insisted, hoping to diffuse the unwanted attention he'd poured squarely onto her head. "I assure you that there was no other purpose behind his invitation."

A lie. He believed she'd played him for a fool as the highwayman, so he'd returned the embarrassment. In spades. But she didn't let her expression show one bit of annoyance with the infuriating man.

"Knowing me—and the size of my brothers," she added to bolster her point, which earned her several chuckles from the group, "he never truly expected me to accept."

And certainly he hadn't. Not after the last conversation they'd shared, when he'd threatened to arrest her.

Yet everyone continued to stare at her as if suddenly seeing her in a new light. A light that would draw the attention of someone like Thomas Matteson. Although an attraction to her might have been the furthest thing from the truth— a marquess and an orphan? Hardly!—she couldn't let the ladies continue to believe in any kind of connection between them. Her secret life as a highwayman couldn't stand close scrutiny, and she still had one more father to make pay his share before the end of the party, which was coming more quickly than she'd realized.

"I'm not certain that Chesney is the sort who takes no for an answer," Lady Tinsdale commented wryly, and her innuendo sent up a new round of giggles.

"Well, then, he isn't *my* sort," Josie retorted, fussing with her embroidery to hide any trace of the lie in her expression. Thomas was *exactly* the kind of man she'd always dreamt about capturing her heart...well, except for the fact that he wanted to arrest her. "Unfortunately," she declared in a loud, prim voice, "*his* reputation is dangerous to *my* reputation."

Based on the ladies' titillated whispers and laughs, that cutting remark had put an end to their embarrassing teasing and assured them that she possessed no interest whatsoever in the dashing marquess...except for her mother, who continued to stare at her as if she didn't quite believe her.

When the talk turned to the latest fashions, however, Elizabeth Carlisle's attention returned to the conversation.

Josie released a silent breath, feeling as if she'd just escaped a trap. But when she returned to her embroidery, her hands shook as she pulled through the needle. She remembered the feel of Thomas's hard shoulders beneath her hands, the softness of his black hair between her fingers, and his mouth—oh, that sensuous, wicked mouth! It had been somehow both demanding and coaxing at the same time, kissing her in delightfully scandalous ways until she'd melted against him like some shameless wanton. God help her, she'd thought of little else since last night's encounter but of letting him do that to her again.

Her mother leaned toward her with a concerned frown. "Are you all right, dear? You're flushed."

Josie's shoulders sagged in defeat. Whom was she fooling? Thomas was far more to her than a dance partner and a bored rake who'd focused his attention on her. And if she didn't remove herself from the drawing room soon, every lady at Blackwood Hall would discover that as well.

"I need some air," she mumbled, and set the embroidery aside. "Excuse me."

She was on her feet and through the door before her

mother could stop her, and before Thomas could come back and make her another offer she couldn't refuse so easily.

When she reached the hallway, she turned and fled in the opposite direction from the one he would have taken toward the front door. A quiet room, that's what she needed. A place where she could sit, collect herself, and hide away like a coward for the rest of the afternoon.

With a soft groan, she pressed the heel of her hand against her forehead. She was insane to let this man affect her like this, the same man who wanted to arrest her. She would simply have to find a way to avoid him, or hide whenever possible, or...perhaps a kiss every now and then couldn't hurt *too* badly, could it?

No, she thought, sighing heavily, not even that. She couldn't be weak and off guard around him again, no matter how much she craved his kisses, no matter the aching thrill that blossomed inside her with even the smallest touch from him. Good Lord, if he could do all that with a just a kiss, what would it feel like if he—

"Josephine."

She froze in her steps. As she slowly faced him, she narrowed her eyes to slits despite the sudden racing of her pulse. "You."

"Me." Thomas leaned casually against the doorway of the morning room. He'd been waiting there for her, devil take him! He'd known she would flee the drawing room after he left, to escape him. Just as he'd known she would turn around and come back when he called out to her. And she had done exactly that. Like a moth to a flame.

Her shoulders sagged. A very pathetic moth.

He gave her a smug grin. "Changed your mind about that ride after all?"

"You know I haven't." Her lips pressed into an irritated

line although she wasn't certain who raised her irritation more—he for trapping her or she for so foolishly walking straight into his snare. "Why did you embarrass me like that in front of the ladies?"

His smile faded. "My apologies. That wasn't my intention."

Despite the sincerity on his face, she didn't believe him. "Then what was it?"

"An attempt to get you alone. You've been avoiding me all day."

And she would keep right on avoiding him for the next three days, too, until the party ended and he rode home to London. No matter how difficult staying away from him would prove.

His lips twitched. "Something told me that unless I issued a direct invitation in front of the others that you'd find a way to be conveniently elsewhere when I came to call."

She sniffed haughtily. "You were correct."

When her cutting remark garnered her only an amused half grin from him, fresh aggravation rose inside her. To think that she'd once been worried he'd prove nothing more than a cad, like all the gentlemen before him—she would have laughed at the absurdity of it all, if her heart hadn't been aching so badly.

She glared at him. "Unless you plan on sending for the constable right now, I would prefer if—"

In a quick movement, he stepped from the doorway and placed his fingers against her lips to silence her as he glanced over her shoulder. "Someone's coming," he said quietly, taking her elbow. "In here."

He pulled her into the room and out of sight just as a footman entered the hallway. As he began to close the door, she stopped him.

"Blackwood Hall isn't the stables or a hunting cottage," she reminded him, backing away to remain by the open door. "I have my reputation to protect." Although *he* seemed to be set on destroying it.

His brow jutted upward with amusement. "You mean your alibi?"

She ignored his barb, if not the swift stab of distrust in her chest, which upset her more than she wanted to admit. A part of her—an utterly mad part of her—was still attracted to him. But she might as well be shooting arrows at the moon for all the hope an orphan had with the son of a duke. Especially one set on arresting her.

"Someone will see us," she scolded, aggravated that he was proving to be as devious as all the men before him who'd pricked her interest. "And I just left a roomful of women gossiping about what a rakehell you are."

Giving in to her nod to propriety—and thankfully not bringing up how much more being arrested would ruin her reputation than being caught with him—he retreated to the far side of the room and sat on the edge of the deep windowsill.

"A rakehell?" His eyes gleamed devilishly. "Why, thank you."

She scowled. "That was not a compliment."

"Well, we rakes take our compliments however we can get them."

Instead of being angry that he'd turned her words against her, she couldn't help her admiration of his quick mind, nor the pull of him. Unable to stop herself, she took a step farther into the room.

"So," he drawled, "you were talking about me."

"Speak of the devil," she muttered, which only seemed to amuse him more. "*They* were talking about you," she corrected pointedly. "*I* was listening and trying to sort fact from fiction."

"And what did you decide?"

"That killing a lion might not be so far from the truth."

A slow grin crossed his face, and despite her anger at him, she felt an answering flutter deep inside her. Pathetic moth that she was, she took another step closer.

"And what did the ladies say about me?" He leaned forward, fixing his dark gaze on hers like a siren song and drawing her forward another step.

"Lots of things." Another hesitant step, until she stood close enough to touch him simply by raising her hand. Her heart thumped, and she knew she'd stumbled right into his trap. But at least now she knew why the cat fell prey to its curiosity. Because it simply couldn't help itself.

He smiled impishly. "Anything interesting?"

She hesitated, because a proper lady would never utter the words—but since when had she ever been a proper lady? "That you keep a mistress," she said quietly, more to hide the unbidden jealousy in her voice than for secrecy. "An opera singer."

"Baseless rumor," he replied in the same secretive tone.

With a forced shrug, feigning disinterest, she raised her hand and plucked the heavy drape framing the window where he sat, just inches from his shoulder. "Then she's a Parisian actress."

"Another baseless rumor...regrettably."

Her hand stilled for just a beat as she flinched at the tightening in her chest. Oh no—*that* was definitely jealousy. Immediately she was aggravated with herself. With whom he spent his time or wished to spend it was absolutely none of her concern...except that she inexplicably wanted him to spend that time with her.

She shrugged again as if his comment meant nothing. And truly, didn't it? Why should she be jealous over him, of all people? "They said you saved Prinny's life."

"Also a rumor." His eyes sparkled mischievously. "But I started that one."

Despite herself she smiled at that, then waved her hand idly in the air to indicate the foolishness of the next bit of *on-dit*. "The silly hens also said that you'd killed a man."

When he said nothing, remaining darkly silent and still, her eyes snapped to his. All traces of the amusement from just seconds before were gone. Dread clenched around her heart.

"I've killed lots of men, actually," he admitted quietly, his blue eyes solemn.

"They said you were a soldier in the wars." She swallowed to clear the knot from her throat and find her voice. "Is that what you mean?"

"Yes." He paused, searching her face. "But you don't believe them."

"No."

"Why not? I'm very good with guns."

"Yes, and you carry them with you. In fact, if I were to reach beneath your jacket right now, I bet I'd find one."

"By all means, don't let me stop you from searching," he murmured rakishly.

She ignored his words, but not the heat spreading through her at his invitation to put her hands on him. And traitorously, her fingers itched to do just that. She quickly twisted them in her skirt. "But you don't like them, and the sound of gunfire unsettles you. What kind of soldier doesn't like guns?"

He leaned toward her, his face even with hers. "The kind who was also a spy."

A spy. Her breath strangled in her throat, her body flashing numb. Was anything she knew about him the truth? "Ours or theirs?"

"Ours, chit." He laughed, the rich sound rumbling into her, and stroked his knuckles across her cheek.

The tenderness of his unexpected but reassuring touch warmed into her, and despite herself she didn't pull away even as her breath came ragged and the rush of blood pounded through her ears.

She drew a deep breath that did nothing to settle the butterflies in her stomach. In fact, it only pulled his gaze to her mouth and increased her uneasiness. "You want me to believe that an heir to a duchy is a spy who goes scampering across the countryside to arrest a common highwayman?"

"Of course not." He arched a haughty brow. "I never scamper."

She pushed at his shoulder in irritation. "Thomas, be serious! I'm not daft enough to believe you're a spy."

He leaned toward her again, closer than before, so close now that the soft warmth of his breath whispered against her lips as he corrected, "*Was* a spy."

Something about the somber way he said that, with an intense flash of regret deep in his blue eyes, made her shiver, and she instinctively knew deep down in her bones that he was telling the truth. Her heart pounded like a drum, so hard that the rush of blood through her ears was deafening.

"Why tell me? I'm a criminal, remember?" She would have been a fool to think she was special enough to him to warrant disclosure of such a secret. No, if anything, he'd admitted it only to set her off-balance and make arresting her easier. "Aren't you afraid I'll tell everyone?"

Answering her challenge, he leaned forward one inch more, to brush his lips against the corner of her mouth in passing as he brought his mouth to her ear. "No one would believe you."

With an exasperated scowl, she shoved him away. *No one would believe you.* The same words she'd flung at him so confidently after the robbery. Apparently she and Thomas Matteson were two of a kind.

He rocked back, folded his arms, and smoothly resumed his original position perched on the windowsill. His gleaming eyes reminded her of a panther's . . . right before it pounced. "I spent all last night thinking about you, Josephine."

Her foolish heart skipped. He'd thought about her?

But she wasn't naïve enough to think he meant he'd thought about *her.* No, he meant the robberies, although she couldn't deny the stab of disappointment in her chest. Because she'd certainly spent all night thinking about him.

She shifted onto her heels, just out of the reach of his hands should he decide to touch her again, because she wasn't certain she'd be able to find the strength to push him away next time. "And what did you conclude?"

His dark gaze turned grave. For all the raw attraction between them, they were still adversaries, still caught up in a dangerous game of cat and mouse. "That there's no way out of this mess for you. The best you can do is stop and pray no one else ever discovers you. Rather than arresting you, I'll convince the earl that the highwayman has stopped targeting his guests and moved on."

"And let Royston and the families get away with what they've done to those children?" *Never.* She'd rather be behind bars than let the earl continue to exploit the orphanage and leave the children to suffer alone. "I won't stop."

Thomas shook his head, and she saw irritation equal to

her own rise inside him. "And you think it's all because of political favors?"

"Yes."

He scoffed at that. "Royston's an important man in Parliament, has been for years. What kind of favors could a man of his rank and reputation gain from an orphanage in Lincolnshire?"

"I don't know. Whatever he needs, I suppose."

His dubious expression deepened. "But you have no hard evidence, do you? Or you would have already gone to the authorities yourself."

Frustration clenched in her belly. "What kind of evidence would I—"

The words choked in her throat, and she shook her head, the pent-up frustration roiling inside her at this argument waged in hushed tones and whispers so no one would overhear when what she wanted to do was *scream*! Instead of dragging her down to the local gaol, Thomas was giving her a chance to prove herself. She should have taken hope from that, but she didn't have the proof he wanted. And he knew it, too.

"He *is* guilty!" she insisted.

"You have no proof of your accusations. No letters, no notes—nothing to prove his guilt."

"Of course I don't have anything like that. Why would I?" Damn him for not believing her! And damn those sapphire eyes that noticed far too much about her but refused to see the truth about Royston. "How could I?"

"Then how do you know whom to target?"

"The orphanage records." Her chest tightened hollowly with sharp disappointment that he would so readily doubt her and so easily trust Royston. "They list the details of each baby, including the names of the men who surrendered them to the orphanage."

"The fathers' names?" Incredulity edged his voice.

"No, of course not. Grooms or footmen, men employed by the babies' families. Once I have their names, it's easy to connect them to the estates where they work. It only takes a bit more digging among the servants to learn about the pregnancies. And if I dig deep enough, I can usually discover that Royston was given a favor in return."

"But nothing you can hand over to the authorities." Not a question. An accusation.

She clenched her hands into angry fists. "You still don't believe me."

"Royston is a longtime family friend and my father's ally in Parliament, and I have never witnessed him doing anything remotely scandalous or illegal. While you…" His words trailed off.

"While you saw me holding up a coach," she finished for him.

He said nothing to contradict her. He didn't have to; the expression on his face spoke volumes.

Her frustration rose to the breaking point. *Enough!* She'd had enough of living with fear and guilt during the past two years since the robberies began, and during the past four days, she'd had enough of fate dangling him in front of her, toying with her—the man with whom she could never have a future. "Then arrest me and get it over—"

"Damnation!" He ran a hand through his hair, his fingers shaking violently. "I don't want to arrest you, but *Christ*, Jo, you broke the law. It's a hanging offense!" Each whispered word came ground out through clenched teeth, and all of him shook now, as violently as he had that morning in the stables. "I want to help you, but—"

"But you can't without proof." The man sent her head

spinning! Her eyes blurred with angry tears. "Then perhaps you should have spent the night sleeping instead of thinking of me." She turned to leave. "Good-bye."

Launching himself off the sill, he chased after her and reached her just as her fingers touched the door. He grabbed her arm and pulled her back, her body falling against his. She was immediately aware of his hardness against her softness, the heat of his hand seeping into her arm through the cotton sleeve of her dress, the strength of his fingers refusing to let her go. She trembled, and her breath came in shallow pants that matched his own.

"I don't spend my nights sleeping," he confessed quietly, his eyes focusing heatedly on her mouth.

She stared at him, speechless, even as her heart began to race so hard she feared he might feel it. Was that an invitation to share his bed? *Good Lord*, it couldn't be! Not from a rake like him, not to an innocent like her. And yet, as the predatory gleam in his eyes ripped her breath away, a part of her very much longed for it to be.

"I want to help you," he repeated, his mouth so close to hers that the warmth of his breath shivered across her lips. "But without proof of wrongdoing by Royston—"

"Which you don't believe," she forced out.

Anger flared in his eyes. "Or *any* proof to show that you were acting in good faith, I have to arrest you. I have no choice, not if you continue with the robberies."

"Of course you do," she protested, hating the pleading she heard laced through her voice. "You can choose to forget you ever saw me last night."

"No," he corrected solemnly, anguished desolation flashing across his face. "I can't."

Her lips parted as she stared at him, stunned. The desperation inside him was palpable. So was the pain.

"That's the choice, Josephine." He briefly squeezed his eyes shut. "You or me, your life or mine."

"What?" she breathed, the anger inside her replaced by sudden fear. For him. "What do you—"

"If you're right, I will help you and protect you. But without proof…" He shook his head. "I have no choice but to believe Royston."

And arrest you. The silent words hung between them as loudly as if he'd shouted them.

"Then I'll find proof," she whispered, unable to shake the peculiar suspicion that the proof she needed to save herself would also end up saving him. "Somehow."

"No more robberies," he ordered firmly.

"I won't promise that."

He cursed beneath his breath. "If you get caught—"

"I won't."

Impulsively she rose onto her tiptoes and touched her lips to his. A quick kiss, chaste and prim, meant only to silence his argument.

But as she lowered herself away, he groaned and clutched her tightly to him. Unwilling to let her go, he kicked the door closed behind them, sealing them together in the room.

His mouth descended hungrily against hers and ignited the innocent kiss into a full-out plunder as his tongue shoved between her lips and ravished her mouth. Each thrust of his tongue claimed another bit of her resistance, until with a soft whimper she wilted against his hard chest.

His trembling hands skimmed down her back to cup her bottom and lift her against him. "Thomas," she moaned against his mouth.

"You're the most frustrating woman I've ever met, Josephine." His voice was a throaty rasp as he tore his mouth away from hers to bite at her shoulder, each sharp nip of his teeth making her shudder. "The most challenging, the most infuriating…" He rested his palm against her cheek and lifted his head to stare into her eyes. "And the most beautiful."

Then he kissed her again, his mouth molding against hers, possessive and hot, and with so much yearning that he stole her breath away. The tidal wave of emotions he crashed through her sent her reeling until she could do nothing more than cling to him, her arms wrapped tight around his neck, not wanting to let him go.

Pressing her back against the door, he roughly fisted her skirt and tugged it up, bunching it and the thin stay beneath between their bodies. She shivered, not with cold or nervousness but with an aching need that flared low in her belly, a need that crept lower between her thighs as her skirt rose higher.

"I've wanted to touch you since the first moment I laid eyes on you," he murmured hotly against her ear, each word a breath that swirled through her and caressed her from the inside out.

He slipped his hand beneath her skirt and brushed his fingers across the lace-hemmed tops of her stockings just above her knees, not daring to move closer to the tingling ache throbbing between her legs. Goose bumps sprouted across her flesh in the wake of his warm caresses, and a shiver of longing rushed through her.

The tip of his tongue traced the outer curve of her ear, eliciting a shudder from her as he enticed temptingly, "You want that, too, don't you? To be caressed the way a beautiful woman like you deserves." He placed a soft kiss against the tender flesh behind her ear. "And touched just a bit wickedly."

Sweet heavens, how much she wanted that! "Yes," she confessed, the word barely a sound on her trembling lips.

His finger slipped teasingly beneath her stocking and claimed a caress against her bare thigh. "Then let me touch you, Jo."

She should have stopped him, knowing how dangerous he was for her, this man who could end her life with just a word to the constable, but her body ached for him with a primal need she'd never known before. As a pulsing heat swelled between her thighs, she couldn't find the strength to push him away.

"Yes," she whispered her surrender. "Please."

His body relaxed with a sigh of relief against her temple, and her heart stuttered. Had he been worried she might refuse? As if she could have possibly rejected the waves of pleasure lapping at her toes from each of his kisses or the flutters of electricity fanning out from his hands wherever they touched her.

"How do you do this to me?" he murmured as he trailed his mouth across her throat. She was certain he could feel her racing pulse beneath his lips, knew what the anticipation of his touch was doing to her. His fingers combed teasingly through the curly triangle between her legs, so close yet still so frustratingly far from touching her where she longed to be caressed. "Both calming and exciting me at the same time, the way no other woman ever has."

Sucking in a ragged breath, she closed her eyes and lost herself in the delicious humming of her blood through her body, in the heat seeping out from beneath his fingertips and radiating down her legs. His hand was scandalously close to the moist heat at her center, and God help her, she longed for him to touch her there, right where she throbbed wantonly with each beat of her pounding heart.

"You make me ache to be inside you, Josephine." He tenderly touched his lips to hers. "Right here."

His fingers slid down into her cleft, burying gently in her folds.

Gasping against his mouth, she grabbed on to the hard muscles of his shoulders to keep her knees from buckling beneath her. He teased against her, making her shiver deliciously as he fondled her with both tenderness and arousal, making her feel absolutely wicked and wanton and wonderful, all at the same time. *Oh sweet heavens!* His touch felt so good, and she wasn't the least bit ashamed as she shifted to open her legs wider. Judging from the masculine groans coming from his throat, he enjoyed caressing her just as much as she did, taking pleasure in the way her body had grown hot and wet beneath his fingers.

"You have no idea how much I want you, Josephine." He lowered his head and licked the tip of his tongue into the valley between her breasts. "How much I want to touch and taste every inch of you."

With a throaty moan, her head rolled back at the sweet torture of his fingers playing across the slick folds between her thighs and at the boldness of his words. His finger slid down along her folds, then slipped smoothly inside her.

Her heart leapt into her throat. Heavens, he was *inside* her!

"What are you doing?" she asked, suddenly nervous, her lips thick with arousal. Those clever fingers of his were doing all kinds of wonderfully wanton things as he plunged and swirled and retreated in a steady but demanding rhythm until the throbbing ache inside her matched his tempo.

"Pleasing you." He kissed his way up her throat and claimed her mouth in a blistering kiss that once more left her clinging helplessly to him. "You do like that, don't you?"

"That's..." A second finger joined the first, and she

moaned at the delicious fullness inside her as she buried her face against his shoulder. "Oh, that's lovely!"

He chuckled, his lips tickling her ear. She should have been ashamed at what she was letting him do to her. At the very least been embarrassed. But all she felt was the tantalizing ache he tingled through her, from her hot core straight up through her to her nipples puckering beneath her dress. Surely something this wonderful couldn't be wicked.

He delved his thumb down to flick teasingly across her aching nub, and a whimper tore from her. Oh, if this was wicked, she simply didn't care!

"If I could," he confessed, his fingers not slowing in their intimate rhythm, "I would take you to my bed right now, Josephine, and make love to you until you cried out my name, until I felt you shatter around me."

"Thomas," she breathed, so softly his name was barely a sound on her lips. If he kept whispering such words to her, kept stroking her so deliciously, then heaven help her, because she might beg him to do exactly that.

"I would keep you right there in my arms until dawn." He stared into her eyes, punctuating his words with a deep plunge of his fingers that made her gasp as the tiny muscles inside her clenched down so tightly around him that he groaned. "Until all the darkness was gone."

She suspected so much more behind his soft words than merely a description of a bedding. But her arousal-fogged mind couldn't think as he expertly ground the heel of his hand against her now, and her body responded in kind, thrusting shamelessly against his hand. She could do nothing more than cling to him as the flames licked at her toes, then worked their way up her trembling body. When they reached the unbearable tightening at her core, a fuse lit inside her, and exquisite release exploded through her.

His mouth smothered the soft cry at her lips as she fell limp against him. Undulating waves of pleasure sped out from where his fingers lay buried inside her, all the way to her fingertips and toes. She clung to him as he slowly pulled his hand from between her legs, then encircled her in his strong arms and held her close, so tight that she could barely catch back the breath he'd stolen. As if he didn't want to let her go.

He tenderly kissed her temple. "But you're an impossible choice for me, Josephine. Because your capture means my freedom."

Her heart lurched painfully even as pleasure still pulsed dully through her. How could she reconcile it, that the same man who made her enjoy laughing and waltzing with him and who had just made her blood boil with such primal need was the same man who held the power to destroy her? "Thomas, I don't under—"

"Shh," he warned quickly. He froze as he listened, but all she could hear was the pounding of her heartbeat and the rush of blood through her ears, the shallow panting of her breath.

She trembled. "What is it?"

"Someone's coming."

Just as suddenly as he'd grabbed her into his arms, he released her and stepped away, flipping down her skirt to cover her legs before putting the distance of the room between them. She shivered at the loss of his heat as he turned his back to her with apparent disinterest, leaving no visible trace that she'd just shattered so scandalously against his palm beneath her dress.

Too stunned to speak, she could only stare at him, blinking with confusion, and trying unsuccessfully to process all that had just happened as the back of her hand pressed against her lips, still hot and wet from his kisses. Instinctively she knew the intimate caresses he'd given her were only the beginning of what he was capable of doing, that there could be so much more pleasure with him just waiting to be enjoyed.

If she was brave enough to let herself take it.

"Thomas?" she whispered breathlessly, her face growing hot with humiliation and rejection, tears stinging at her eyes. She didn't want him on the other side of the room. She wanted to be back in his arms.

Without warning the door opened behind her. Turning, she gasped.

Simon Royston.

Oh God. If he'd heard what they'd just discussed, if he knew what they'd done—her reputation ruined at the very least, her life ended at the gallows at the very worst. Her hand went to her throat as her breath strangled with fear.

Across the room Thomas lounged casually against the windowsill, as if they'd done nothing more scandalous than discuss the weather. Yet despite the cool, calm exterior he showed the earl, Josie could see the heat of desire still burning in his eyes.

"Royston," Thomas called out jovially, claiming the earl's attention before he could see Josie and giving her a precious few moments to collect herself. "Thought you were out fishing with the men."

"God no. I despise fishing." Royston's voice was clipped as he muttered, "I've been hunting for you." Then his gaze flicked across the room to Josie. "Miss Carlisle."

"Your lordship." Her legs trembled as she gave a quick curtsy.

But with a dismissive glance, he quickly passed over her presence as unimportant. From his irritated expression as his eyes narrowed once more on Thomas, he obviously couldn't have cared less that he'd found her in the compromising position of being alone with the marquess.

Yet somehow Thomas had known the earl was coming, which was why he'd released her as quickly as if she'd scalded him with her body. Now that he sat there, so cool and collected, his calm presence worked only to make her even more aware of the embarrassment and arousal that must be showing so clearly on her flushed face.

"Well, it seems you've found me." He grinned at the earl, but Josie knew him well enough now to know that the smile was forced. He was no happier to see Royston than she was, but he hid his irritation with the ease of the spy he was. "What can I do for you?"

Royston nodded toward the hallway. "A game of billiards, if you don't mind." Not a request but an order.

Josie knew Royston wasn't interested in playing billiards. From the way his body stiffened, Thomas knew that, too. Still, he nodded his acquiescence, and with a parting glance in her direction that she couldn't decipher, he trailed out of the room behind the earl.

Groaning softly, Josie sank into a nearby chair, her head hanging in her hands and her body still trembling and aching. Thomas swore he would arrest her if he had to, yet she still wanted him, and not just for the remainder of the party. And not just for the way he made her body shiver with pleasure. She wanted so much more than that, so much that hot tears formed on her lashes as she ached with bittersweet longing for that impossible dream...the dream of having him with her always, this man who made her feel so beautiful and wanted, who made her feel safe and secure in his arms, and to whom she'd entrusted her deepest secrets.

But he was also the same man who would never trust her. Not without the proof she didn't have. And it was that lack of trust in her that had just sent him running after Royston.

Yet she knew the larger truth. Even if she somehow found her proof and he believed her, nothing would change between them. In only three days, he would leave, most likely never to give her another thought. After all, he was destined to be a duke, while she—

A choking sob tore from her. She squeezed shut her eyes and gulped in mouthfuls of air to keep back the tears.

While she had already lost her heart.

* * *

Thomas kept his face stoic as he followed Royston into the billiards room, with no trace in his expression of how his chest burned with self-recrimination at having to leave Josie like that. But perhaps it was better that they had been interrupted. His anger that she was so foolishly endangering her life had led to arousal, and that pulsing arousal still had him half-hard even now. A few more minutes alone with her, hearing those soft sounds of pleasure on her lips, feeling her body shatter around his fingers like that, and he would have done exactly as he'd warned—carried her to his room and seduced away her innocence, this woman who made his blood boil with equal parts frustration and desire.

And whom he didn't trust.

Ludicrous, that she would believe Royston capable of using an orphanage to gain political favors. An earl, for God's sake. Yet she believed it, and to the point that she risked her life to secure retribution.

One of them was lying, and his return to the War Office now hung in the balance. Which one was he supposed to believe—the man who had been loyal to his family or the woman who brightened the darkness?

Royston turned on him. "Well?" he demanded impatiently, clearly agitated, as his hands clenched and unclenched at his sides. "What have you learned about the robbery last night?"

"I've been talking with the constable and investigating the robbery site." He carefully dodged the real answer. The one that would send Josephine Carlisle swinging by her pretty little neck.

"Has the highwayman been found?"

"He got away." *For the moment.* Until he could figure out a way to stop Josie from committing any more robberies and convince Royston to give him that recommendation without his actually having to produce the highwayman in the flesh.

"Damnation, Chesney," Royston bit out beneath his breath, his fingers pulling at his cravat, as if the knots choked him. "I invite guests here to my home, only for them to be robbed. What the devil is going on here?"

Thomas shrugged out of his jacket and tossed it over one of the chairs, then reached for a cue stick from the collection hanging on the wall rack. "What's going on, Royston, is that you're being targeted." He held the cue in his hands as if judging its weight and balance. "What we need to figure out is why."

"We know why. Money."

"I'm not so certain." Treading carefully, knowing he had to prove Josie wrong without tipping his hand, Thomas circled the table and scattered a few balls across the red felt. "According to the constable, the highwaymen made off with less than one hundred pounds, and all the robberies have been similar." He lined up his shot, but even as he judged the alignment of the cue stick, he kept a close watch on Royston from the corner of his eye. "Whoever is responsible isn't interested in money."

"So why is he robbing my guests, then?"

"You tell me." He slid the stick forward smoothly and connected with the cue ball to send it spinning across the table. The object ball dropped into the corner pocket with a quiet thud. "Who are your enemies?"

"I don't have enemies."

"Everyone has enemies," he corrected casually. The old axiom was true. If you wanted to know a man, know his enemies. Josephine Carlisle was this man's enemy. And Thomas certainly wanted to know a great deal more about her.

In frustration Royston snatched up the cue ball from the table. "Have you made any headway at all? Do you know anything about who's behind this?"

"I know how the robberies are being committed," he evaded skillfully.

"With horses and guns," Royston scoffed. "I knew that much myself."

Thomas ignored that. The man was too agitated over the most recent holdup to realize that every robbery had a signature as distinctive as the criminal who committed it. Even a thoroughly aggravating, impossibly alluring criminal with stormy green eyes and thick chestnut hair.

At least Royston didn't suspect Josie, that much was clear from his comments. But then, why on earth would he? A baron's daughter who kept falling off her horse? The damn woman really had covered her tracks amazingly well. His chest would have warmed in admiration at her cunning if he didn't want to shake her for so recklessly risking her life.

"Who are your enemies, Royston?" he pressed, circling casually back to the only lead Josie had given him. If it was true that Royston was using the orphanage for political favors—and he couldn't bring himself to believe it, knowing the man as well as he did—then perhaps the earl was being blackmailed into it by someone else. He foolishly hoped against hope for that, because it would mean he'd be able to both save Josie and get his recommendation, after all. He could stop whoever was blackmailing Royston, and then Josie would no longer have any reason to keep being the highwayman.

"I told you. I don't have any," Royston ground out, his irritation flaring to the surface. "And why are you playing games? My reputation is at stake, and you're plunking balls around the damned table!" He threw the cue ball down onto the felt.

Thomas calmly met Royston's gaze. "We're standing in a billiards room." A spy always had to blend into his surroundings, no matter how out of place he felt. And Thomas felt damnably out of place at that moment as uncertainty tore at his insides. "If anyone should happen to observe us, we should look as if we're playing."

Royston blanched. "You think the robbers are among my guests or servants?"

"I don't know what to think," he answered, which was certainly the truth. Which one of them did he believe? Thomas had known Royston for years. He was an earl of the realm who had always been a loyal friend to the Matteson family, while Josie was a criminal. She'd broken the law, no matter how altruistic her motivations, and she deserved to be arrested. And damnation, he deserved to have his life back. But at what cost—Josie's life or his?

He had no choice but to keep prying at both of them until he found answers. Although he suspected deep in his gut that by the end of this conversation he'd have proven Royston innocent of the implausible allegations of which Josie had accused him.

"A man doesn't reach your standing in Parliament without angering people for not supporting their causes." Thomas set his cue aside and leaned back against the wall, watching Royston closely. "Or their political appointments."

Royston's face darkened. "What are you talking about?"

"Political appointments," he repeated calmly. "And favors." Those were the reasons Josie gave for the orphanage's existence. But he wanted to hear Royston's version, compare the two, and try to sort fact from fiction. "Now that the wars are over, there are new opportunities for ambitious men in Parliament."

"Yes, there are," Royston agreed. "I need friends if I'm going to build influence and power. You of all people should understand that."

You of all people. Royston was sadly mistaken about that. Thomas had never wanted power or influence; he didn't care if he never received any credit for the service he'd given his country from the Englishmen whose lives he'd undoubtedly saved by risking his own. He'd been an agent because he wanted his life to matter, because he wanted to be more than just a placeholder in the long line of Chatham dukes. He wanted purpose. Meaning.

"But at what cost?" he asked quietly, giving voice to his worst fears.

"I've done nothing illegal," Royston replied confidently. "Lord Liverpool is aware of all my actions."

"There's a fine line between illegal and unethical." Thomas calmly stepped to the table, took only a moment to line up the shot, and sank the last ball. "Especially if you haven't been entirely transparent in your ambitions."

"Are you accusing me of committing criminal misdeeds?" Royston demanded coolly.

"Of course not." Then, coming too close to Josie's secret

for comfort, yet having no choice but to dance on the razor's edge, he explained, "I am suggesting that whoever is targeting your guests might be doing so because *he* suspects you are."

"Absurd." Royston laughed with an assured smile. "I've never done anything that would be considered unethical or illegal."

Or anything that would cause someone to blackmail him into using the orphanage for favors. Thomas's last hope for an easy solution vanished like smoke. "I didn't think so," he replied, forcing out a smile he certainly didn't feel.

"You know how your father is," Royston assured him. "Honorable beyond measure. Would Chatham take me as a political ally, or a friend, if he suspected I had done anything even remotely questionable?"

"No, he certainly wouldn't," Thomas agreed, conceding the point. But his chest didn't lighten with relief at knowing Royston was innocent of the crimes of which Josie accused him. Because it meant that she was entangled in an even bigger mess than before. One from which he might not be able to free her.

Turning his back to the earl to return his cue to the wall rack, Thomas rested his hand on the handle of the cue and drew a deep breath. *This* was the decision point. The moment when he would have to choose between Royston and Josie, between a respected member of the peerage who had never been anything but proper and dignified in all his public dealings and a woman for whom deceit and distrust were second nature. Between securing a recommendation to the War Office that would effectively erase the past year and give him his life back and saving the woman who had captured him the way no other woman ever had.

Christ! He didn't want to arrest her. He *couldn't* bring

himself to arrest her, in fact, now that he'd experienced the contradictory calm she brought to him at the same time that she made his blood boil with desire. Yet his future didn't lie with her; it lay in his past, with a brilliant career as a spy still ahead of him, a sense of purpose instead of nightmares and fear. The last thing he needed—the *very* last thing, damn it!—was a woman in his head and heart to distract him from the life he had always been meant to live.

He closed his eyes briefly, silently cursing his own self-ishness. "I'll stop your highwayman, I promise you."

"Thank you." Royston clapped him affectionately on the back. "I want this matter settled by the time the party ends."

In only three days. "It will be," he answered grimly, remembering Josie's refusal to stop the robberies. He was left with no choice now but to force her to stop. "One way or another."

Royston nodded, satisfied with Thomas's answers and oblivious to the guilt churning inside him. As the earl turned toward the door, Thomas sucked in a deep, shaky breath and scratched at his wrists.

They left the room and walked down the hall toward the stairs, but Thomas wasn't breathing any easier. His progress report was done, and his evasions and delay tactics had bought Josie a brief reprieve. But he'd only delayed the in-evitable. He would have to make a final decision soon, and God help them both when he did.

In the meantime he needed to find a way to keep the frustrating woman from committing any more robberies. He'd lied to Royston. The highwayman robbed coaches precisely for the money, risking her neck to keep the orphans in the best home possible.

If only the orphanage had enough money, then the robberies would be unnecessary, and perhaps she'd stop. If she could have the money all at once, instead of one purse at a time—

The idea hit him like a lightning bolt. There *was* a way to get her the money, and if Royston himself provided the blunt, perhaps she'd even let go of her accusations against him. *If* he could talk the earl into increasing his patronage.

"When I was in the village," he commented offhandedly, yet very carefully approaching the topic, "I saw a little orphanage there."

"The Good Hope Home." Royston nodded as they reached the top of the stairs. "And?"

Thomas noted the sudden coldness in the earl's voice. "I know that you and the countess are patrons."

"We help however we can," he replied dismissively.

"I'd like to help myself. Would you mind if I visited to see if there was anything I could do for the children while I'm here? Perhaps look through its accounts and books?"

Royston hesitated, pausing at the top of the landing. Then he forced a smile and continued down the stairs. "Of course not. But I'd rather you found the highwayman first."

Thomas's heart skipped. *Royston hesitated.* So briefly that it had barely been perceptible, yet he'd noticed—the pause taken in mid-step, the silence as loud as a canon shot.

Suspicion jolted through him, sending his heart into his throat and spinning confusion through his mind. Yet he forced himself to keep his face impossibly blank even as an instinctive sickening clenched in the pit of his stomach. Good God…could Josie be right after all? Was Royston truly using the orphanage for his own gain?

And which one of them was he supposed to trust now?

Maintaining a calm façade, despite the rising anxiety stirring inside him, he descended the stairs beside Royston and walked through the entry hall to the front door, passing a group of women on the stone portico who had made their way outside from the drawing room to take in the fresh air. They chattered as the two men approached, matching the chirping sounds of the songbirds from the gardens.

Thomas felt her before he saw her. Josie stood apart from the group and did her best to pretend not to see the two men while at the same time noticing every move they made.

En masse the women turned to greet their host, and in that brief moment when everyone's attention was focused on Royston and his on them, Thomas crossed behind her and brushed his hand against her skirt as he passed.

"Get me your proof," he warned, his voice low. "*Now.*"

Then he forced a charming smile at the women and nodded his greetings before bouncing down the stone steps to the drive and sauntering off toward the stables, as if he didn't have a care in the world.

CHAPTER SEVEN

❧ ❧

Thomas nodded as he tried to concentrate on what Lady Agnes Sinclair was telling him about the Earl of St. James, his new wife, and some tragic accident involving kippers at Vauxhall—no, that couldn't be right. He couldn't imagine anything involving kippers that could possibly be considered tragic.

But then, neither did he care. Not when the focus of his attention stood on the other side of the drawing room, beautifully draped in a yellow satin gown that brought out the auburn highlights in her chestnut hair. And completely ignoring him.

He hadn't had the opportunity to speak with her in private since their encounter that afternoon in the morning room, but he'd hoped to get her alone for a few minutes tonight. After all, he couldn't very well kidnap her again—twice in one week would certainly set tongues wagging, phaeton or not. And if he simply showed up at Chestnut Hill, asking to call on her when she was so obviously agitated with him...Well, he doubted he'd survive the pulping her brothers would give him.

Irritatingly, she was avoiding him, having ignored him during dinner and now lingering on the opposite side of the room. She was trying so hard to avoid him, in fact, that she now kept her attention riveted to Lord Gantry as if the paunchy old fop were the most interesting man in the world. She probably believed all his boasting, too, those made-up stories about his adventures in the Colonies. While here *he* stood, capable of providing true stories of daring for king and country, but he found himself unable to garner her attention for even a few minutes.

Instead he was trapped in kipper hell.

"Don't you agree, Chesney?"

"Pardon?" His attention snapped back to Lady Agnes, her bright-red turban impossible to ignore. "Oh—yes, quite."

Pleased by his response, she continued with her story. The great kipper caper…or something. Occasionally he nodded when she paused, but his eyes never strayed far from Josie.

She'd captured his imagination in a way no other woman ever had. Even now his hands itched not from the memories of the ropes binding him to his sickbed but from the desire to run his fingers through her chestnut waves. In less than a sennight, she'd changed him just as much as the hell of the past year.

But he wasn't green enough to think there was more to the spell she'd cast over him than allure and intrigue. Even the initial effect she'd had on him, which puzzled him so deeply that he'd been preoccupied to distraction, could be attributed to the challenge she presented as the only woman he'd ever met who was his equal in craftiness and attention to detail. If he'd slept better since meeting her than he had in the past year, then sleep came simply because the dreams he kept having about her left him too aroused and aching at night to be bothered with panicked fits at the silence and darkness.

What he felt for her was certainly desire, and the small taste he'd had of her passion had only whetted his appetite. He'd even admit that perhaps he also felt a growing affection for her, spurred on by what he'd seen of her bravery, her brilliance, and her devotion to the orphans.

But he also didn't trust her. And the most important lesson he'd learned during the past year was that trust meant everything…in his own survival, in his abilities, and in the people he loved.

As if on cue, her gaze wandered over Lord Gantry's shoulder toward him. For a moment their eyes met across the room.

Then she angrily stiffened her shoulders and tore her gaze away. But even in the dim glow of the beeswax candles, he saw her cheeks pinken in a faint blush and knew she was just as affected by his presence as he was by hers.

"Lord Chesney?"

He looked back at Lady Agnes, who stared at him expectantly. "Yes?"

"I asked what you thought about this whole mess."

He frowned as he watched Josie excuse herself and cross to the buffet where Greaves, the butler, stood attending the silver coffeepots. "I think kippers should be considered a most dangerous food."

"Kippers?" Lady Agnes blinked, bewilderment settling on her round face. "I don't know what—"

"Excuse me."

Without waiting for her to respond, he strolled to the buffet and arrived at Josie's side just as she smiled at Greaves in a friendly enough way that the normally stoic butler twitched his lips almost pleasantly. And Thomas knew then exactly who within the earl's household had been passing information to her about the guests.

"Miss Carlisle." Thomas inclined his head.

Her back stiffened, and she sniffed disdainfully. "Lord Chesney."

Oh, she was definitely angry at him. *Wonderful.* "I trust you're having a pleasant evening."

"I was." She smiled tightly, aware that Greaves stood near enough to overhear their conversation. "Good evening."

With her head held regally high, she walked away toward the fireplace. In her hurry to cut him, she'd completely forgotten why she'd gone to the buffet.

"Coffee, Greaves," Thomas requested. Then, watching her put half a room between them, he added, "With lots of liqueur."

"Certainly, sir." The butler fixed a cup and presented it on a saucer.

Thomas accepted it and strolled after her.

When he stepped up behind her, he gently took her elbow to keep her from walking away again. She caught her breath at his touch, the little inhalation of surprise tingling his fingertips.

"You forgot your coffee," he murmured in a voice low enough that even surrounded by houseguests he wouldn't be overheard, then held the cup and saucer out to her.

"I no longer want any, thank you." She glanced icily down at his hand at her elbow. "Please release me."

He arched a brow. "Please don't walk away."

"Fine," she agreed irritably. He eased his hold on her elbow, and she slowly pulled her arm free as she faced him.

"You've been avoiding me," he commented in a low voice

with a forced smile, cautiously aware of the roomful of guests around them. During the past week, the two of them had become quite adept at having intimate conversations in the middle of crowded rooms.

"How keen of you to notice, my lord."

His lips twitched. *Cheeky chit.* He had half a mind to tell her she was beautiful when she was angry, but he wasn't certain she wouldn't slap him. "Why?" He lowered his voice to a murmur. "Because I dared to touch you?"

He refused to apologize for what happened between them in the morning room. They'd both enjoyed it. Very much, in fact. He certainly didn't regret caressing her or watching the desire on her face as she'd quivered against him, her body warm, tight, and soft like silk. And he knew that she didn't regret letting him. Because she might be scowling at him as irritably as a governess, but her breath had grown shallow, her cheeks faintly pinkening. The memory of that encounter aroused her even now.

"It has nothing to do with that." She glanced away in embarrassment, then grudgingly admitted in a soft voice, "That was...nice."

His chest warmed at the small victory, and he longed to show her all the other ways he could be *nice.* "Then what's wrong?"

"How can I trust you?" she ground out, a sense of betrayal lacing her voice. "Royston rang a bell, and you went running to his side!"

He straightened. So *that* was what fanned her anger tonight. Not that he'd pleasured her but that he'd shown loyalty to the earl. "I wanted to learn what he knew about the highwayman," he explained, raising the cup to his lips to continue the pretense of a normal after-dinner conversation. "If he knew enough to have you arrested."

"So you can arrest me yourself instead?" she scoffed angrily. "You still don't believe me about Royston, do you?"

He didn't know what to believe, and he cursed beneath his breath, frustration flaring inside him. Yet he calmly returned the cup to its saucer and pressed, "Where is your proof?" He was willing to give her the benefit of the doubt based on nothing more than a gut hunch about Royston, one his logical head told him couldn't possibly be true. But he couldn't prove her innocence by himself. "For me to simply take your word against his—"

"And you would never do that, would you?" She searched his face, doing her best to read him. Or find anything on which to pin her hopes. "Simply trust your instincts instead of your observations?"

"No," he admitted grudgingly. When it came to this woman, his instincts flew right out the window. He didn't know which one to trust, her or Royston, but he damned well knew that when he was around her he certainly couldn't trust himself.

"So that's it, then. Nothing's changed." Her eyes flared like storm-tossed seas. "Royston gets away with what he's done, you'll still leave when the party's over—"

His eyes narrowed. "That doesn't have any—"

"And the orphans still have no one to help them but me."

If he had his way, they wouldn't even have her. Not in the manner she meant. "You have to forget this madness now," he warned, lowering his voice as Lord Gantry walked past and acknowledging the baron with a slight nod. "Royston's sworn to stop the robberies, which makes him dangerous. Because he won't arrest you, Jo."

"Well, thank goodness," she drawled. "Then you still have a chance to—"

"He'll just shoot you and leave you for dead on the side of the road."

Her breath strangled in her throat, and she paled. Fear blazed in her eyes even as she resolved, "I won't let that happen."

He gritted his teeth. The *most* frustrating woman! "For God's sake, I am trying to keep you from getting hurt!"

She raised her chin only slightly, but he noticed. He noticed everything about her. "I don't need your protection."

"You need me more than you realize." His voice dropped to a throaty murmur. "You need me to keep you unharmed and out of gaol." And if they hadn't been standing in the middle of a drawing room, surrounded by women playing cards and men arguing about horses, he would have pulled her to the floor right there, ripped off her dress, and shown her exactly how much *he* needed *her*. Damnation, how was it possible to want a woman this badly when he didn't know if he could trust a word that came out of her succulent mouth?

"But you don't believe me," she answered sadly, her eyes glistening. "And you'd still arrest me, wouldn't you?"

"If I had to," he answered quietly, the honest admission ripping a hole in his chest. Arresting her was still the best way for him to regain his old life, and the last thing he wanted to do to her. He was still hoping he could find a way out of this mess for her. "Stop the robberies before you get hurt."

"I'm sorry." Despite the tremor in her soft voice, she forced a smile for anyone who might have been watching. "But I can't do that."

Taking a deep breath, as if collecting her resolve, she walked away, leaving him standing there alone like an idiot, the coffee he'd fetched for her still in his hand.

He raised the now-tepid coffee to his lips and took a sip, wishing mightily that he had a whiskey instead and having half a mind to bribe the footman to sneak him some.

The coffee splashed in his cup, and he scowled. For God's sake, even now she had his hands shaking from wanting her so badly, from remembering how responsive her body was to his touch, and from craving to taste again the flavor of peaches that clung to her like an erotic spice.

He was a fool for letting her get beneath his skin, this woman of all women, the one who held his future in her scheming little hands. Because that same tantalizing woman who came draped in yellow satin also came wrapped in a giant ribbon of mistrust. One he had no idea how to untie to get to the truth beneath.

"Chesney."

Thomas glanced at the distinguished man who stopped at his side. "Althorpe."

Richard Carlisle, Baron Althorpe, extended his hand. In his early fifties, with a touch of gray at his temples, yet still possessing the strong frame of his youth, the baron held himself with dignity, and Thomas could easily see where the three Carlisle brothers got their mountainous builds. And where Josie had learned that cutting, no-nonsense stare of hers. From the ends of his well-trimmed moustache to the tips of his polished boots, every inch proved him the respectable country gentleman he was.

"I trust you're enjoying your stay at Blackwood Hall," Althorpe commented casually.

Thomas shook his hand, unable to stop the pulse of nervousness in his gut at meeting Josie's father. *Good Lord!* When had he ever been nervous about meeting a lady's father before? "Very much." He cleared his throat. "Sir."

The two men hadn't spoken since the start of the house party, with the baron leaving the outings to his sons and the domestic activities to the ladies while he remained at Chestnut Hill, overseeing the small estate himself. Even though the baron was in attendance this evening, Thomas suspected that his pressence was only due to the insistence of his wife and that Althorpe was more comfortable among hired workers and tenant farmers than mixing with the *ton*.

Thomas certainly understood that. Even as heir to a duchy, he seldom felt as if he belonged among society, and he rarely was at ease in social gatherings, although anyone looking at him would never have suspected. Perhaps he and Richard Carlisle had more in common than his constantly surprising daughter after all.

"I'm disappointed that your father isn't in attendance for the party," Althorpe remarked. "How is Chatham these days?"

"Father's well, thank you."

He nodded. "Glad to hear it. I've had the pleasure of working with him in the Lords, although my involvement is decidedly limited compared to his."

"He enjoys the political intrigue, I'm afraid." His eyes strayed toward Josie as she lingered on the far side of the room, and the corners of his lips curled in amusement. Her unease at finding him in conversation with her father was palpable as she watched the two of them, with nervous curiosity and dread passing in turns across her face.

"She's quite wonderful, isn't she?"

"Pardon?" Thomas tore his gaze back to the baron, feeling like a fool for being caught staring at the man's daughter.

"Josephine," Althorpe commented, now drawing Thomas's attention openly to her, although it had never strayed far from her all evening. "She's a wonder."

"Remarkable," he offered evenly. Although *incomparable* was more exact. He'd never before known a woman who seemed so much his equal. "I've never met anyone quite like her."

A look of fatherly pride crossed Althorpe's face. "When

she was eight, she rode her pony right up the front steps of Chestnut Hill, through the doors, and straight into the entry hall. Seems she had a craving for one of Cook's biscuits and couldn't find a groom in the stables to hold the pony for her while she ran inside." He chuckled at the memory. "She would have gotten away with it, too, except that the butler noticed hoofprints on the rug."

Thomas easily imagined her doing just that. "I hope she wasn't too badly punished for it."

Althorpe shook his head, a smile tugging at his lips. "How do you punish your child for being independent and determined? Aren't those qualities we all pray our children acquire?"

"Especially in your household," Thomas quipped wryly, "with those brothers." But even as the baron chuckled at that, Thomas knew better. Her independence resulted from a keenly honed survival instinct, a courage borne of a childhood spent in the horrors of an orphanage.

Althorpe continued thoughtfully, "She'll never be part of the *ton*, and you would never find her at a society event."

Her father was right, Thomas conceded, the two men now standing shoulder to shoulder and gazing openly together across the room at her, which made her so nervous that he could see her trembling even from so far away. He never would have found a woman like her anywhere in the drawing rooms of the quality. And he was glad of it.

"She's not one of those London ladies, Chesney."

Thomas stiffened at the tone of Althorpe's voice, the comment a very subtle apology for any slight she'd given him tonight.

But his words were also a warning to remember that she was not as urbane as the women with whom Thomas was known to associate, both publicly and privately. And an order that he should immediately forget any rakish designs he might have on her.

"No, sir," Thomas agreed quietly. He watched her for a moment over the rim of his cup, then said earnestly, "I would never make the mistake of confusing Josephine for one of those women."

"Good." Satisfied at Thomas's answer, Althorpe lightly slapped him on the shoulder. "Enjoy your evening, then."

Althorpe finished his coffee and handed the empty cup to a nearby footman, then walked away. He approached Josie and said something that drew a relieved smile from her. Then he affectionately leaned over to place a kiss on her cheek before taking her arm to escort her across the room to join his wife at the pianoforte.

Thomas stared after them, the look of love Josie gave her father taking his breath away. Althorpe was right. She was nothing like Helene or the other ladies he associated with. She was so much more beautiful and special than those women could ever be. Every moment he spent with her only confirmed it.

Always before, he'd bedded women for nothing more than sexual satisfaction. But with Josie, the primary desire he longed to satisfy wasn't physical. He felt a yearning for her that set his soul on fire, and he craved the comfort and solace he knew she'd bring to him merely from being with him in the darkness. Oh, the thought of having her naked beneath him was certainly appealing, but so was the thought of simply holding her close, of falling asleep knowing he'd still be in her arms when he woke.

Yet he couldn't purge his doubts about her, even as he couldn't stop the churning of desire and frustration battling inside him.

He set down his half-finished coffee and left the room

in search of whiskey. The night was going to be damnably long.

* * *

In the dark shadows of the silent woods two hours later, Josie cinched the black mask tighter around her head and tried to ignore the terrified pounding of her heart. The robbery would happen at any minute.

She'd done this nearly two dozen times in the past, every move perfectly choreographed and expertly anticipated, every man there entrusted with her life. Yet still she couldn't escape the absolute terror that would cascade through her at the moment when the rumbling noise from the approaching carriage finally echoed through the dark woods, the sickening dread in the pit of her stomach when she had to give the signal to her men to swarm. Perhaps she never would grow used to it. Perhaps that meant she hadn't yet become the cold-hearted criminal Thomas accused her of being.

But at that moment, with the carriage rolling into sight and only seconds from another holdup, that was exactly what she was. A criminal. But one without a choice.

The carriage rolled to a sudden stop, the team of horses nearly skidding into the felled tree blocking the road.

Now.

She placed two fingers to her lips and let loose a shrill whistle.

The woods came alive as men on horseback plunged down the hill toward the coach, and two men leapt out from the bushes to pull down the driver and tiger. She raced her horse toward the carriage, dropped to the ground, and pulled out her pistol as she grasped for the door to fling it open.

From out of the darkness, shouts split the night as the

pounding of horses' hooves sped toward them on the hard-packed road. A gunshot cracked through the trees. Her horse reared onto its hind legs, and she fought to hold on to the reins while around her the small band of robbers panicked. The shouts and gunfire came closer now. One of her men fired into the darkness.

"Hold your fire!" she shouted.

But a barrage of guns erupted from everywhere around her.

Her horse jerked back its head and spun on its hindquarters, ripping the reins from her hands and bolting down the road, leaping the felled tree and disappearing into the black night. She stared after it. Terror paralyzed her. Without her horse, she was as good as dead.

A horse crashed out of the dark woods to her left and galloped straight toward her. The tall, broad rider rode with his hat pulled low over his face, his thighs clenched tightly to keep him in the saddle even as he held the leather reins clenched between his teeth and a pistol in each large hand. He fired a pistol into the top of the coach, splintering the empty driver's seat with a loud crack. Dropping the first pistol, he fired off the next shot behind him toward the on-rushing outriders, scattering them into the trees, then flung the spent pistol to the ground and shoved his hand down toward her.

"Take hold!" he snarled.

His long fingers grabbed her wrist and jerked her off the ground. She was barely off her feet and not yet on the horse when he dug his heels into the animal's sides and sent it charging back into the black woods. A tree limb just missed her head, but he never slowed the horse to give her time to find her seat behind him. Instead he urged the horse faster.

Her arms went around his waist as she finally got her leg

across the horse's back and sat astride behind the saddle, then clung to him for dear life. She couldn't see her rescuer's face with the hat forced down low on his head, but she knew...the solidity of his body as she pressed against him, the hard panes of his chest beneath her palms as her arms encircled him and held tight, that familiar scent of leather and soap—

"Thomas," she sighed with relief, her eyes stinging as she squeezed them shut against the hot tears.

"Are you hurt?" he asked.

"No."

A fierce curse exploded from him, and she flinched, more startled than she'd been at the gunfire.

He spun the horse in a circle and charged back in the same direction they'd just traveled for a dozen or so yards, then pointed the large gelding downhill toward the river. Without hesitating the well-trained mount plunged into the cold water and galloped on in the knee-deep current for several minutes before finally turning up the bank and out of the water, straight toward a small stone fence. The horse took the jump as easily as if the wall weren't there at all, and they galloped on along the edge of the dark meadow, circling slowly back toward the woods.

"Where are we—"

"They're hunting us down," he snapped. "I'm confusing our tracks."

Once again she was reminded that he was no ordinary man, and if she'd doubted him when he told her that he was a spy and a soldier, she was certain now. Just as she was certain that barely controlled fury burned white-hot inside him.

"Which way to the cottage?" he demanded.

She pointed to the right, past the clearing with the hollow tree where she usually dropped the burlap sack.

"Give me your gun."

She unbuckled the strap at her shoulder and handed over the holster and pistol. He flung them away into the trees.

She gasped, stunned. "What are you doing—"

"If they find us, I'm not giving them an excuse to kill us," he snapped at her over his shoulder. "I won't die for you, Josephine. Not tonight in the woods, nor on the gallows."

Her heart thudded painfully. Of course he wouldn't—she would never ask that of him—but dying... *Oh God!* Thomas could have been killed tonight, and she couldn't bear the thought that he might have been hurt while trying to save her.

"I'm sorry," she mumbled, her words muffled by the rough wool of his greatcoat as her cheek rested against his back. "Thomas, I'm so sorry—"

"Stop apologizing," he growled. "We're not out of this yet."

As if on cue, more shouts and gunshots echoed from the woods behind them, distant but clear, and close enough that she pressed herself even closer to him, her arms tightening around his waist.

He leaned forward and urged the horse dangerously faster through the black night. No moon, no stars, not even shadows. Only darkness so deep she could barely see a few feet ahead of them. But she closed her eyes and placed her trust and her life completely in his hands.

They arrived at the cottage and rode the horse into the lean-to stall. As Thomas jumped to the ground and tied the horse, she slipped down from its back. Her feet had barely touched the ground before he grabbed her wrist and yanked her away, pulling her through the darkness toward the cottage door.

Stumbling to keep up with his long strides, she followed

him inside the dark cottage. He closed the door and slid the bolt home, locking them inside. Instead of releasing her, he pressed her back against the door and covered her mouth with his hand to keep her quiet.

Frozen in place, she listened to the night around them but heard nothing except the rush of blood pounding in her ears and the fast, shallow sound of his breathing, so close to her in the darkness that each exhalation fanned hot against her cheek. Outside, the woods were silent, the men no longer chasing after them, and inside, the cottage was cool and dark. So dark that for a moment she didn't know if her eyes were open or closed. So dark she couldn't see Thomas as he stood less than a foot away from her.

And then his fingers weren't covering her mouth to keep her quiet anymore. They were caressing her lips, tracing their fullness, seeking her out in the darkness.

"Thomas," she breathed achingly against his fingertips.

His thumb tugged at her bottom lip, and then his mouth was on hers, ravaging her lips in a hot, openmouthed kiss. In the blackness she couldn't see him, but oh God, how she could feel him—the insistent thrusting of his tongue between her lips, the rough strokes of his hands down her body. And when he pressed against her, pinning her between his body and the door, his erection jutted hard into her belly.

He wanted to possess her, and *oh heavens*, she desperately wanted to let him! Giving herself to him would be wrong, sinful, dangerous. She would be ruined. But she didn't care. Deep in her heart, she knew there would never be a more wonderful man with whom to share this night than Thomas. She had long ago resigned herself to never having a husband to share her life, to never being loved, but she could have tonight. And even this one night with such a special man was more than she'd ever let herself dare to dream of having.

One night with him would be enough. It *had* to be. Because she couldn't bear not having him at all.

When she shifted her hips against his to declare her decision, she heard his answering groan from the blackness.

"We shouldn't do this," he half growled, half whispered against her neck in weak protest.

"I need you, Thomas," she breathed into the darkness, unable to find her voice. "As much as you need me."

A shudder swept through him, and his hands tightened their hold on her, as if he were determined not to let her go even as he argued, "I am *not* one of those men, Josephine, those bastards who thought they could use you for their own pleasures."

"I know. You're—"

Interrupting her, he cupped her face between his palms and kissed her deeply and tenderly, stirring a yearning inside her that she knew only he could satisfy.

"I want you so much, so much more than you realize." He rested his forehead against hers and took deep, steadying breaths. "But I won't marry you." Anguish laced his voice as he murmured into the darkness, the sound cutting deep into her heart, "I *can't* marry you."

"I know." Her chest panged at the raw honesty in his quiet admission, and she thanked God that he couldn't see the pain on her face. They had no future. She'd known the truth of that all along, yet knowing it hadn't stopped her from dreaming that a man like him might want her after all, just as it didn't stop the sharp rejection knotting agonizingly in her belly. Or dull her need for him.

But they had this night, the one they'd been destined to share since the moment their eyes met across the ballroom. Fate had cheated her out of so much because of her birth; she refused to be cheated out of this, too.

Her body ached for his, throbbing and trembling to have him impossibly close to her, to have him inside her and his arms around her, making her feel wanted and safe. And yet—

"You can prevent...I mean..." She swallowed, hard, then stumbled over the words as they tumbled out in a rush, even now thinking of the orphans. "I've heard there are ways to prevent getting a child—because if we—if *I* were to—"

He silenced her with a soft touch of his lips to hers. "There are," he assured her quietly.

"Then give me tonight." She nuzzled her cheek against his palm, wanting the comfort she knew she'd find with him. "That's all I ask."

"Josephine," he murmured softly, then kissed her with such tenderness and longing that she shivered from the intensity of it. From the promise of what was to come.

Her hands grasped his caped greatcoat and pulled it over his shoulders, down his arms and back, to cast it away into the darkness. And then she hunted for the buttons on his waistcoat, fumbling as she struggled in the darkness.

"Let me." His raspy voice floated down to her from unseen lips. His hands closed over her trembling fingers to remove them from his chest, and quickly he unbuttoned his waistcoat and shrugged it away onto the stone floor at their feet.

She reached blindly for him in the darkness, and sudden panic swelled inside her when she couldn't find him. "Thomas?"

"Yes?" he murmured. His mouth brushed along the side of her face as he lowered his head toward her and found her lips to kiss her again, heated and urgent.

She sighed with relief. "Don't lose me to the darkness."

He froze for a heartbeat, one instant when every muscle in his body seemed to tighten. Then just as quickly he relaxed, and his lips smiled against hers. "I won't lose you, Jo. Don't you dare lose me."

"Keep your hands on me, then." She grasped his shirt in her fists and yanked it free of his breeches. With one palm resting against the warm skin beneath, she pulled it up over his head with the other hand and tossed it off into the darkness. "Keep touching me."

He groaned. "Absolutely."

His hand covered hers as it rested against his hard stomach, the muscles rippling as she flexed her fingertips against him, then he shifted away from her and bent down. She heard the soft thump of a boot hitting the floor, followed by its mate. A hot shiver slipped through her, like a silk ribbon unraveling from lace. He was undressing, and soon his attentions would turn to undressing her.

As he straightened, he brushed up along the length of her body, his mouth trailing up her throat to claim her mouth again, to mold her lips against his and steal another moan from her.

Emboldened by the darkness, her nervousness hidden from his experienced eyes, she stroked her hands down his bare chest, then leaned forward to trace her mouth after her fingers. When her seeking fingertips found one of his flat nipples, she dipped her head forward to flick her tongue over it before closing her lips around it and sucking gently. He inhaled through clenched teeth, and she thrilled at the reaction she stirred in him, wondering what else she could do to cause such a response, where else she could trail her mouth...

She lowered her head to lick down his chest to the rippled muscles in his abdomen. Her tongue flicked over each hard ridge, slowly moving lower—

With a sharp gasp, he shoved her backward and pinned her shoulder against the door with one hand to keep hold of her in the darkness while with the other he reached between them and worked at the buttons of his breeches. She heard the rustle of material sliding across flesh as he shed them from his legs, and heat washed down her body, all the way to the tips of her curling toes.

He stood in the darkness with her, now completely naked. And she desperately wanted to touch him. Biting her lip to keep from losing her courage, she brushed her fingertips over his warm, bare body. Down his chest, lower to the muscular ridges of his flat stomach, then lower still...

When her seeking fingers found him, large and erect, he flinched against her touch but didn't stop her or shift away. So she traced her fingertips curiously up and down his hard length, making him shudder by gently rubbing her thumb across his tip. Her fingers trembled. So this was what a man felt like...*Amazing.* He was incredibly smooth, with soft skin belying the steely hardness beneath, and when her hand closed around him, his entire body stiffened as much as the thick shaft she now stroked within her palm.

Her mouth went dry. She licked her lips, asking more huskily than she'd intended, "Is this...all right?"

He groaned softly, and the hand he'd held pressed openpalmed against her shoulder curled slowly around her arm, gripping her as if to hold her in place, as if he were afraid she might slip away into the darkness out of his reach. "It feels..." The words tore from him as she found a drop of wetness clinging to his tip and smeared it gently across his skin with her fingertip, and he had to draw in a deep breath to continue. "God, that feels so wonderful. You have no idea..."

"Good," she purred as warmth filled her at giving him this pleasure when he'd already given her so many.

Although she thrilled at the way his breathing now came in labored pants, she was unprepared for the reaction that surged through her own body as the wet heat rose between her legs and her nipples tightened achingly. After their encounter in the morning room, she knew how wonderful he could make her feel, and she shamelessly wanted him to do that to her again.

"Thomas," she begged breathlessly, "please."

Answering with a groan, he grasped her in his arms, pressing her tightly against him as he turned with her in the darkness and backed her across the room. His lips were on her mouth, her jaw, her neck. His hands swept up and down her back, pausing to cup her buttocks though her breeches and squeeze in time with the plunging of his tongue inside her mouth. As if he couldn't touch her enough, taste her enough—

The backs of her knees hit something in the darkness. With a gasp she tumbled onto the sofa, flinging her arms around his neck to pull him down with her. As he leaned over to kiss her, his hands found the collar of her jacket, pushed it down from her shoulders and off her arms, then made equally quick work of unbuttoning her waistcoat.

She tensed, unable to prevent the hard stab of jealousy at the thought of all the other women he must have undressed to have become such an expert at blindly undoing buttons in the dark. A stinging burned behind her eyes, and she trembled, suddenly realizing how far out of her depth she was with him. She didn't even know where to place her hands or if the untrained caresses she'd just given him had been pleasurable enough.

"Thomas, I've never…" She swallowed, nervousness at her lack of experience overwhelming her, and she trembled. "I've never been…undressed by a man before."

He paused for just a heartbeat at her confession, undoubtedly knowing what she really meant. But she heard the warm affection in his voice when he murmured softly, "Then it's a night of firsts for both of us because I've never undressed a woman in men's clothing before." As if reading her thoughts in her hesitation, he added, "But I undress myself quite often, and I think I can manage it."

The last button slid free, and he slipped the waistcoat from her shoulders. He gently lowered her onto her back, then removed her boots and unfastened the breeches, peeling them slowly down her legs and off.

"It doesn't bother you," she whispered as his hands encircled her waist and moved slowly upward beneath her shirt, his thumbs tracing along her ribs toward her breasts, "that I've never before...been with a man?"

He laughed as if she'd said something amusing. The deep sound rumbled through her and blossomed a throbbing heat between her thighs. "It pleases me more than you know," he murmured as he gently lifted her shirt over her head and cast it away. "There now, completely undressed. As for the rest"—he stretched himself over her and kissed her tenderly—"we'll figure it out together."

She lay naked on the sofa beneath him, warmed by the heat of his body over hers. Cool air wafted over her hot skin, and she shivered at the exhilarating mix of heat and cold, longing and anticipation. Nervousness swelled inside her from not knowing exactly what to expect, but she knew with certainty that this was right. And good. With him.

Then his hands swept over her to capture her breasts against his palms and circle his thumbs around her puckered nipples, and her mind blanked. Her worry and nervousness vanished beneath his warm caresses, and all she knew was the delicious, aching sensation he sent tumbling through her.

She was lost beneath his rough, warm hands massaging her fullness, teasing and pinching at her nipples. In the darkness she had no idea if her eyes were open or closed, nor did she care as long as he kept touching her like this, because everywhere his hands wandered, he set her skin afire.

"You are perfect, Josephine," he whispered, his soft words swirling around her and caressing her as heatedly as his hands on her body. "Tonight we'll find pleasure together. And it will be good." With a soft sigh, she arched her back against him as his mouth found her nipple, and he murmured hotly against her bare flesh, "So *very* good."

She gasped as he suckled hard at her and dug her fingernails into the muscles of his back, but he didn't relent in his gentle assault against her and instead took her nipple between his teeth and bit down gently. He was an expert at this, she realized as the delicious sensation of pleasure-pain jolted through her. He knew exactly when to be tender, when to be rough, and how to drive her out of her mind.

She writhed beneath him, the moist heat of his mouth nearly unbearable as his teeth worried at one nipple while his palm fluttered teasingly against the other. Prickling heat gathered beneath her bare skin, and all the blood in her body pooled between her legs, right at that private spot that now throbbed achingly, burning and begging to be touched as deliciously as he'd touched her before.

When his mouth moved to her other breast, to start the sweet torture all over again, she whimpered with aching need.

"I want you, Jo," he whispered as he laved his tongue against her nipple, as if he understood and shared the ache he created inside her that demanded release. "More than I've ever wanted a woman in my life."

"You... truly?" Her suddenly thick lips struggled to form the words.

"I've wanted you since the moment I caught you staring at me across the ballroom." His mouth left her breast and planted a trail of kisses down her stomach. "And I have been very patient since then. Very, very patient."

That had been Thomas being patient? *Goodness.* She'd be terrified, then, to know how he behaved when he set his focus on immediate possession.

The tip of his tongue swirled into her belly button, and she bit back a scream of pleasure. "But I need to know you want me, too."

His words enveloped her in the darkness and heated her from her toes to the top of her head. No man had ever said those words to her before, had ever touched her or kissed her the way Thomas did. No one had ever stared at her with such longing and need the way he did, nor made her feel this warm and alive. Thomas did all that to her. And more. He'd filled an emptiness in her life she hadn't even known existed until he was there and the void was gone, and all she could do was surrender to the overwhelming yearnings and emotions he churned inside her.

"Tell me." As he nudged her legs apart with his shoulder, he kissed his way down her body toward the triangle of curls between her legs. "Tell me you need me inside you, filling you, pleasing you... as much as I want to do all that to you."

"Yes, I want that." She took a deep breath, fighting for any control or sanity that hadn't been robbed from her by his caressing hands or the moist heat of his lips slowly moving toward her own moist heat between her legs. Surely he didn't mean to kiss her *there*. "Thomas, I think—"

He licked her.

She gasped, the erotic sensation tearing the words from her throat. His hands grasped her hips and kept her pushed down against the cushion, to hold her open wide beneath the onslaught of his mouth against her sex. He slid his tongue along the length of her cleft, swirling against her wet folds and delving deep into the hollow at her aching core. Oh, sweet heavens, she'd never imagined that his mouth could be this pleasurable, or that a kiss could ever be this exquisitely wicked. Her fingernails dug into his bared shoulders, and she moaned into the darkness, her thighs quivering around him.

"Tell me, Josephine," he murmured hotly against her, his breath tickling her intimately and sending a delicious tingle pulsing deep into her belly.

His wicked mouth stole away her breath. In the darkness she heard the soft, wet sounds as his lips sucked gently at her, the most erotic sounds she'd ever heard. She writhed beneath him, and her hands sought out his head as he lay between her thighs, to grasp his hair in her fingers and hold him tightly against her even as she lifted her hips from the sofa to grind herself harder against him.

"Yes," she cried, "I want you!"

"You want me to do what to you?" With one hand on her thigh, he gently pressed her back down onto the sofa and lowered his lips against her. "This?"

She groaned and rolled back her head. Oh, wicked, wicked man! He was teasing her on purpose, intentionally torturing her as he licked harder against her now, making her breath come in fast pants. She trembled helplessly beneath him.

"Or this?" The tip of his tongue flicked against the pulsing nub buried in her feminine folds.

Her hips bucked beneath him. "Thomas!"

But he only chuckled and continued the delicious torture. Burning her up from the inside out, the aching heat between her legs threatened to consume her. She whimpered and wrapped her arms tightly around his shoulders. She wanted him inside her skin, filling her, dominating her, possessing her.

"I want—I want...*you*," she panted out. "Right there, right where you're kissing." A low moan of frustrated arousal escaped her. "Oh, Thomas, please!"

"Gladly." He whispered the single word into the darkness and settled himself in the cradle of her spread thighs.

He rose up on his left forearm to poise himself in the darkness over her while he reached down to gently caress between her legs. His fingers parted her intimate folds, already wet and ready for him, and as he lowered himself, the tip of his erection pressed gently but firmly against her as he held her body open to his. Then he slowly pushed inside.

As she held her breath, he slipped deeper into her. Her body yielded to his hardness and expanded to accommodate him, and he filled her, so warm and tingling...*so good*. And she wanted more, craving him even deeper.

She squirmed beneath him and whined with frustration because he was holding back, keeping his hard body in reserve when she wanted him to keep nothing from her, surrendering all of himself, pouring all his strength and courage into her.

"Slower now," he cautioned as he sank another inch inside her, then retreated.

Frustratingly, maddeningly, each carefully controlled stroke took him only slightly farther and not nearly deep enough to satisfy the craving her body held for his, not nearly deep enough to touch the throbbing desire at her core. "I don't want to go slowly. I want you, *all* of you. Now."

He shook with restraint as he held himself over her on his forearms. "It will hurt—"

With a fierce groan of exertion, she thrust her hips up

against his, pushing him fully inside her and ripping through the thin barrier of resistance. A gasp tore from her throat at the sharp pinch of pain, her body stiffening around his.

He grasped her hips to keep her from moving away and held her pressed tightly against him. "Stay still," he ordered gently. "Just for a moment. Trust me, Jo."

Breathing deeply, her eyes closed and her arms wrapped tightly around his neck, she did as he told her. The pain ebbed away quickly, replaced by something warm and deep, something...*wonderful*. He filled her completely now, the delicious heat and strength of him radiating out from her middle and cascading all the way down to the tips of her toes and fingers.

Then he began to move the way she'd longed for him to do, gently stroking inside her with each rise and plunge of his hips.

"Dear God, Jo." His voice shook. "I can't believe how hot you are...how tight." He gave a testing swirl of his hips, and in response she shuddered, her body clenching impossibly tighter around his. He groaned. "You feel incredible." He swirled his hips again, this time withdrawing from her until just the tip of him remained inside her before plunging deep inside. "So delicious."

Delicious. She moaned her response, unable to put into words the exquisite pleasure he gave her. How special he made her feel. As if she truly was the woman he wanted most in the world.

Her fingers dug into the hard muscles of his bare back in an attempt to bring him even closer, and her heart raced. How could being with a man be so breathtaking, so thrilling? Because *this* man and only this special man made this first intimacy so wonderful. He was her hero who knew her deepest secrets and greatest vulnerabilities, yet who was still so careful with her heart, still so tender with her body as he continued to rock into her.

Each retreat of his hips brought a whimper of loss to her lips, each return thrust an answering moan. The heat drew deeper and hotter and tighter inside her until it pulled up from the very bottom of her being and gathered into an ever-tightening knot of fire between her thighs. Right where the base of his manhood ground against her as he slipped in and out of her sex.

"Thomas," she whimpered, burying her face in his neck. She tasted the salt of his sweat on her lips from equal amounts of restraint and exertion, and the pounding of his pulse was a fierce tattoo beneath her lips.

Leaning onto one arm, he wiggled his hand between their bellies and down to work his fingers against her aching nub, flicking rapidly against her even as he continued to stroke into her. A spasm gripped her and she gasped, panting hard beneath him. She was running straight for a cliff, helpless to stop and wanting to plunge over the edge, wrapping her arms as tightly around him as possible to take him with her—

She broke around him and splintered into a thousand pieces in his arms. His name sounded her cry of pleasure in the darkness, and she collapsed beneath him, every inch of her body pulsating with exquisite pleasure.

He shifted her hips beneath him, hitching himself up higher against her, then groaned as he dropped into her, grinding his pelvis against hers before retreating and doing it again, to satisfy a ferocious need inside him she'd never imagined a man could possess. A need for *her*. There was no gentleness now, just a driving desperation punctuated by low, throaty groans at each deep thrust.

Without warning he suddenly pulled out of her and pressed himself tightly against her stomach. As he shuddered against her, a warm, wet tickle spread across her belly, then he collapsed against her, spent and satiated, his forehead resting against her bare shoulder.

Neither moved. Gradually their shared breaths slowed. His racing heartbeat calmed, and the shaking that had gripped his body when he climaxed slowly ebbed away. Goose bumps still dotted his arms and legs, but those weren't from the cool air but from the heat they'd created between them, the same fire that had flamed out and consumed her.

Exhaling a long, trembling sigh, she tightened her hold around him. Her life would be completely different now, and she would never be the same again. Because of him. And she did not regret a moment.

"You were right," she whispered into the darkness, finally breaking the spell cocooning them.

He tenderly touched his lips to her temple. "About what?"

"That I would know when you're satisfied."

A soft laugh rumbled from his chest, and she tingled as the sound passed into her. His arms were still wound tightly around her as if he was afraid she would leave. But leaving was the last thing she wanted to do. With her body still entangled with his, the delicious weight of him still pressing down upon her, she wanted to stay like this forever.

"You are so beautiful, Josephine Carlisle," he murmured.

Tears gathered in her eyes. "But you can't see me in the darkness."

"I don't need to. You're the most beautiful woman I've ever met," he whispered against her lips. "And I don't mean the way you look."

Then he kissed her, and the first tear of utter happiness slid down her cheek.

CHAPTER EIGHT

Thomas traced his finger lazily across Josie's bare back as she lay next to him on her stomach, the sheet still tangled around her legs on the bed where he'd carried her after they'd had sex on the sofa. Her skin glowed golden in the flickering light of the single candle, all warm and silky smooth, and he couldn't keep himself from touching her.

His lips pulled into a satisfied smile. *Sweet Lucifer*, she was exquisite. If he hadn't taken her virginity, he'd never have suspected an innocent could be so passionate, so responsive to his touch. But she was all that. And more.

For the first night since the shooting, he felt completely at ease. His heart didn't pound with anxiety, and he didn't taste the familiar metallic tang of fear on his tongue. And for once he didn't dread the darkness or wish for the dawn. If she was in his arms, he was certain he would even be able to sleep without having nightmares or waking in the darkness, shaking and panicked. Except that the last thing he wanted to do tonight was sleep.

Her long hair spilled around her slender shoulders, and he tucked a strand of the silky softness behind her ear.

She smiled lazily over her shoulder at him. "I can't believe you're real," she whispered, her voice filled with wonder, "or that tonight actually happened."

"Oh, it happened." He placed a kiss on her bare shoulder, then gave an animal-like growl. "But I can prove it to you again if you'd like."

With a soft laugh, she playfully swatted him away.

"Tell me." He eased back down beside her and continued to let his fingertips explore her tantalizing body. "At your age, someone as beautiful as you"—and completely unlike any other woman he'd ever known—"how did you manage to keep your innocence so long?"

Her green eyes sparkled. "You mean, how did I escape the evil clutches of some sinister man bent on seducing me?"

He chuckled despite the unintended pricking of that teasing barb. He might as well have been that sinister man, what with the way he'd single-mindedly ruined her tonight.

She shrugged. "You've met my brothers."

"So I'm the only man foolish enough to pursue you with those three hovering about?"

"No." She smiled sweetly. "You were the only one brave enough."

His heart thudded. She thought he was brave. His chest tightened, the unexpected compliment curling delightfully through him. "But you said there were other gentlemen visitors to Blackwood who attempted to seduce you." In other words...*why me?*

She shyly lowered her gaze until she stared at him through half-lowered lashes, unaware of the desire that innocent look stirred inside him. "They were...different from you." Her naked shoulder gave a small shrug as she admitted, "I like you."

For a moment all he could do was stare into her eyes. Surprised as hell by her soft words. And not knowing exactly how he should feel about her, not when he didn't know for certain if he could even trust her. Except…

He lowered his head to kiss her shoulder again, this time letting his lips linger against her skin as he mumbled honestly, "I like you, too."

A soft sigh escaped her. "Thomas, what do we—"

"Brandy?" he offered, interrupting her, then slid off the bed and quickly headed into the darkness of the main room. He knew what she was going to ask, and he didn't think he could bear it right then. Not a discussion about how they had no chance at a future together, not when his skin still smelled of hers and the taste of her still lingered on his lips. Further, at least two hours stood between them and dawn, and he needed sustenance. Because he didn't plan on wasting a minute of time with her tonight.

"It's in the little cabinet—"

"I was asking if you wanted any," he clarified, calling out from the other room as he grabbed the bottle by its neck and two glasses. "I noticed where you kept it the last time I was here."

"Is there anything you don't notice?"

He could almost hear her rolling her eyes, and his lips twitched with amusement.

"Very little. Details keep a spy alive," he commented as he returned to the candlelit bedroom. "Ignore them and you die."

Sitting up, she raised the sheet to cover herself. "Is that what happened to you?" she asked solemnly. Her gaze drifted to his waist. "Did you ignore the details?"

He paused at the edge of the bed, freezing in his steps as she stared at the scar that extended along his side. He'd much rather she'd been staring lower, distracted by his cock instead of the scar. But oh no, not this woman. Her eyes were on the wound. Ugly. Jagged. Deep. Even with the flesh fully healed, the scar showed conspicuously discolored from the rest of his skin. And even now he had to physically fight back the urge to place his hand over it and hide it from her sight.

"That wasn't the French," he answered, setting the glasses down on the bedside table and joining her on the mattress, the bottle of brandy still in his hand. "That happened in Mayfair, at half past seven on a Sunday evening."

Her gaze flicked silently between his eyes and the scar, as if she could somehow read the answers she sought in the marks on his flesh.

"Lie down," he ordered gently, uncertain how long he would be able to tolerate her stare on him like that.

She hesitated. "The ladies said you were shot, but I—"

"Lie down, and I'll explain."

Reluctantly, but doing as he ordered, she shifted onto her back.

"Roll over."

With a wary look—at least not one of pity, which was why he wanted her facedown on the mattress, because he didn't think he could bear that, not from her—she did as he asked, then rested her cheek on her folded arms as she turned her head to gaze at him.

"I was walking home from visiting friends, a route I'd taken dozens of times." With his finger he peeled the sheet off her body, baring her slender back and round buttocks to the candlelight. "I'd planned on spending the night at home. For once I was going to do nothing more than read a book."

He opened the bottle of brandy and dribbled the golden

liquid slowly down her back, watching it bead and pool against her skin. She flinched at the wet sensation but didn't protest, and despite the macabre memories he stirred up by recounting the events of that evening, he smiled with private pride at her. The woman was fearless. If she wasn't, she wouldn't be there with him tonight. And he wouldn't be sharing this story with her, the first person he'd ever told. Others had found out—London thrived on gossip, after all—and his dearest friends knew within minutes after the attack happened, his family shortly after that. But he'd never *told* anyone before.

"I was in Mayfair, two streets from my home." He set the bottle aside and leaned over her. "I should have been safe," he murmured, pausing to draw a finger down her spine and through the puddles of brandy. "The streetlamps weren't even lit yet."

She shivered. "Thomas—"

"And then a footpad stepped out from behind a wall and shot me."

His mouth plunged down against her, to drink up the brandy pooling at the small of her back, and a gasp tore from her—whether from the story or from his eager lips on her, he would never know. Which was exactly why he'd done it. Because he didn't want to hear the shock in her voice or see the pity on her face. Instead he turned her gasp into a soft moan as his tongue licked across her body, drinking her up, relishing in the delicious mix of brandy and flesh. And the faint flavor of peaches.

"He rifled through my pockets," he mumbled against her skin as he continued, both with the story and in sucking up the brandy as his tongue licked over her buttocks and down the backs of her legs, "took whatever was valuable, and left me there to bleed out."

She shivered beneath his lips, her soft inhalation shaking as goose bumps formed on her skin. She fisted the sheet into her hands as she struggled to lie still, as if knowing he'd stop with his story if she moved.

"I was gutshot," he murmured against her, "and gutshot men always die. But for some reason I didn't."

As much to distract himself as her, he greedily drank up the brandy, shamelessly taking sweeping licks and bold sucks across her luscious body. Anything to distract himself as he shared this last, most terrible secret. She was heavenly...just as the memory of what he described was pure hell.

"The pain was unbearable," he whispered. "Each breath I took felt like a knife stabbing into my stomach. Darkness pressed in on me, like a demon sitting on my chest, and the silence—that god-awful silence..."

She didn't move, didn't say a word, but he felt her tremble, and he knew it wasn't from the cold.

"I couldn't open my eyes, couldn't tell if it was day or night, if I was asleep or awake, alive or dead..." He gave up on the brandy and rested his cheek against her bare back, finding comfort there as her heartbeat pulsed faintly against his cheek. "Although I was certain I must have died and gone to hell because of the pain." He had to squeeze his eyes shut and inhale a deep, shaky breath to continue. "And all of it was made worse because I couldn't move, not even when I'd wake screaming from the nightmares, because they'd tied me down to keep me from ripping open the sutures and bleeding to death in my own bed. All I could do was lie there and let the demons take me."

"Thomas," she whispered, a world of heartache and pain in her voice. "I'm so oh...sorry my darling."

She turned over and gathered him into her arms, cradling

him close as she pressed tender kisses across his forehead
and cheeks, whispering his name repeatedly. Her hands
moved over him in soothing caresses so soft and gentle that
he trembled beneath their tenderness, and everywhere she
touched, warmth and calm flowed into him.

When she cupped his face in her hands and tenderly
kissed him, he tasted the salt of her tears on his lips.

His arms wrapped around her and held her pressed
against him, now comforting her as she wept for him. He had
no idea how long they lay there like that, wrapped tightly together in the glow of the candlelight, but it was long enough
that she cried out all her sobs for him, and he kissed away
the tears on her cheeks.

He'd told her everything about the living nightmare he'd
gone through, but instead of the darkness closing back over
him and the uncontrollable shaking he'd experienced every
other time he thought of that evening and the weeks afterward, there was peace. Quiet. Finally his heart pounded not
from terror but with affection and hope. And he knew it was
all because of Josie.

"I wish I had been there with you, my darling," she
breathed. "I would have found a way somehow to keep the
darkness away."

She'd spoken so softly that her lips made no sound. But
his heart heard.

His eyes burning, he turned his head to nuzzle his cheek
against her shoulder, overcome by sudden emotion for her.
Dear God, how would he be able to go on without her?

* * *

Hours later Thomas opened his eyes. He blinked, trying to
clear the sleep from his head as he looked around the room

and slowly remembered where he was and how he'd gotten there. It was still dark, not yet dawn. The candle beside the bed had burned out, but a soft glow came faintly from the hearth in the other room. And beside him, lying quiet and still on her side with one arm folded beneath her head as she watched him and her other lying possessively over his chest…

"Josephine," he whispered, his hand sliding up to cover hers. She was truly there with him; the night hadn't been a dream. "What happened?"

A faint smile teased at her lips. "You fell asleep."

Asleep? *Impossible.* He didn't sleep like that, not any-more. Not without nightmares that left him shaking and covered with sweat. Not without his heart racing and his breath coming in gasping pants.

But he had done just that tonight. Slept deep and carefree, like a normal man. For the first time in a year, he'd woken rested and at peace. And it was all because of her.

"I'm sorry," he apologized softly as he reached out to brush her hair over her shoulder, feeling like a damned fool to fall asleep with such a beautiful woman sharing the bed. Although she was a breathtaking sight to awaken to, he'd ad-mit. Lying there all warm and naked, covered only partially by the sheet and with her hair wild and loose across the pil-low, she looked like one of those Italian paintings of Venus. A perfect, beautiful goddess. "You should have woken me."

She stretched like a cat, as if waking from her own sleep. "I thought you needed the rest, so I didn't want to wake you."

He'd certainly needed that rest. Dear God, how much he'd needed this night! And her. And not just the physical pleasures of being in her arms, but being able to unburden himself to her about the shooting and the hell he'd gone through.

"Thank you." Feeling energized, as if he'd woken from a long nightmare into peace, he rolled over on top of her and kissed her. Softly and sweetly, with all the affection and longing he carried inside himself for her, all the emotions he wasn't yet willing to name.

When he lifted his head and she opened her eyes, meeting his gaze in the soft shadows, he knew she understood. That he meant far more than gratitude for a few hours of restful sleep.

"I'm glad you told me about the shooting," she admitted softly. "I think I understand you better now."

He lowered his head to place a kiss on her shoulder, unable to bear the confidence and faith in him that he saw in her eyes. How could she understand him when he was as confused as hell about himself? How could she hold such trust in him when he still didn't trust himself to make the right decision regarding the highwayman and his future? Even if that highwayman was Venus herself.

"You mean now that you know how I ended up here chasing a highwayman instead of French spies," he murmured against her shoulder. He shifted himself completely away from her to lie beside her. Still close but no longer touching. "How I'd survived against Napoleon, French enemies, Spanish allies...only to have my life ended by a common thief."

She reached for him. "Your life didn't end."

"Yes, it did." He pulled back, just far enough to avoid the touch of her fingertips. Embarrassment heated through him now as he had to share how his life had been ripped away. The wound had been painful, but the aftermath was humiliating.

She leaned closer, this time not letting him shift away as she rested her palm against his chest, right over his pounding heart. "Your life did *not* end," she insisted, curling her fingertips possessively into his muscles.

"It might as well have ended because I lost everything worth living for—my career, my identity, my purpose. *Everything*. All gone in a heartbeat."

Bewilderment flashed over her face. "But lots of spies must get wounded. Surely the War Office doesn't dismiss every man who—"

"I lost my nerve, Jo."

Her expression darkened, and in her eyes he finally saw comprehension dawn of how a single bullet had irreparably changed his life. Her gaze flickered down his front to settle once more on the scar at this side.

Sucking in a ragged breath, he shook his head. "The wound took months to heal, and even then I wasn't...right. I haven't been right since."

"I don't believe you." She laced her fingers through his, and he let her, unwilling to let go just yet of the closeness they'd shared. "You're the bravest man—"

"Who jumps at his own shadow," he snapped from the anger stirring inside him at what his life had become. "An anxious insomniac who's afraid of the dark."

"You weren't afraid in the dark tonight with me. And you slept—"

"Well, then the War Office can just send me onto missions with a naked woman," he bit out sarcastically. "Problem solved."

He hadn't meant to be cruel, but when he saw the wounded look flash across her face, he knew he'd been exactly that. A cruel bastard. To someone who didn't deserve it.

His shoulders sank as he murmured regretfully, "I didn't mean that." He apologetically touched his lips to hers, but he

sensed a hesitation in her, this woman who had taken pleasures so freely from him and cradled him so lovingly in her
arms. Who had cried tears for him and then watched over
him while he slept. *Damnation.* He drew a deep breath and
tried again. "But you didn't know me before."

"What I know," she said with conviction, "is that you rode
straight into the fight tonight to save me. That wasn't the ac-
tion of a man afraid."

His chest warmed unexpectedly at her words. She made
him sound like a hero, and he hadn't been one of those
in a very long time. "I didn't have a choice," he answered
honestly. "I wanted to keep you from being arrested."

She hesitated a moment, then whispered tentatively,
"And…this?" She waved her hand, indicating the rumpled
bed around them, the musky scent of sex and sweat lingering
in the air.

He stared into her eyes, all the hot desire and passion he
held for her boring into her. "I also wanted to spend the night
with you."

She said nothing for a long while, but her eyes dulled
and sadness once more marred her beautiful face. A niggling
worry knotted in his gut that he'd somehow said the exact
wrong thing. At the exact wrong moment. *Christ.*

"And now you've had me," she whispered, then glanced
away self-consciously, but not before he saw a wretched desolation sweep across her face.

She twisted the sheet between her fingers, as if she was
afraid he'd tell her that tonight had been a mistake. Her worries couldn't have been further from the truth. True, the night
hadn't started out with making love to her in the forefront of
his mind, and he certainly hadn't intended to tell her about
the shooting, but he'd wanted her since the moment he'd first
laid eyes on her across the ballroom.

Trying to soothe her worries about him, he placed a tender kiss on her shoulder. "I don't regret a moment of tonight."

She trembled and shifted away.

A stab of worry pierced his gut. "Jo—"

"But you're still leaving when the party ends," she whispered softly, barely making any sound at all. "And everything will go on exactly the same as before, with Royston taking advantage of the orphanage. You still don't believe me about him, do you?" A pained expression passed briefly over her face. "Not even now, after we shared so much tonight, after we…" She drew a tremulous breath. "Made love."

His heart jumped in his chest. *Made love?* He'd never considered… With all the women before her, he would have laughed at the naïveté to describe what they'd shared in such emotional terms. Yet that was exactly what they'd done tonight. For the first time in his life, he'd not simply taken a woman for sexual pleasure—he'd made love to her, with affection and caring behind every caress and touch. A coming together of equals, a melding of bodies and a meeting of hearts… Her pleasures and feelings had been more important than his, and the sweetest part of the entire night had been simply lying in her arms, letting her caresses soothe him into sweet sleep. She'd healed him more in these few hours with her soft touches and tears than he'd been healed in an entire year.

But she was right. Doubts about her still lingered in his mind, even now. He'd built his life around trust. First with Edward and Grey during the wars, when all three men trusted each other with their lives. Then during his spy work, when he'd had to trust his instincts. And last year, during that horrible and dark year, when he'd trusted his sister Emily to help him survive.

Could he trust Josie, knowing the lies, schemes, and secrets she kept to be the highwayman? A woman to whom deception was second nature…could he ever trust her with his heart?

And if he chose her over Royston, if he let the highwayman get away and lost his last chance at returning to the War Office, only to learn that she couldn't be trusted after all—Good God, what would become of him then?

His chest sank painfully, and he shook his head. "Royston is an old family friend."

"While I'm just a woman who shared her bed."

Her soft accusation sliced at his heart. She was so much more than that, so much he could never bring himself to admit. "I didn't mean that, and you know it."

"Didn't you?" The expression on her face grew unreadable, and she lifted the sheet to cover herself in a thin barrier between them. "I'm not some naïve girl, Thomas. I never expected for you to care or—" She cut off her words with a far-too-casual shrug, and he saw her fingers tremble as she pulled the sheet farther up her body to hide even more of herself from him. "But I'd thought you'd realize that if I trusted you enough to make myself vulnerable to you that you could trust me, too."

"I do trust you." For Christ's sake, he'd told her everything about the hell he'd gone through with the shooting, and he'd never told anyone. Not even Emily.

"But not about this," she whispered sadly. "When it comes to this, you still don't know what to believe, do you?"

His gut clenched into a burning knot. "Josephine." He reached for her shoulder, but she shrank away from him, turning her head so he couldn't see her expression. "Please listen—"

"We should get dressed now." Her back straightened with

resolve as she slipped from the bed. "I need to go home, and you should—"

He grabbed her hand and pulled her back, bringing her down across his lap. Her hands pushed against his chest as she tried to break free.

"Let go of me!" She twisted her body to pull away from him, but he only tightened his hold. He refused to release her. Not until she'd heard him out.

"This isn't about you," he said adamantly. When her green eyes narrowed dubiously, he explained, "It started a year ago, long before I ever knew about the highwayman."

His hands tightened on her shoulders to keep her still, because if she kept wiggling her bottom against him like that he'd end up tossing her onto her back and taking her again. And if he did that, he might very well end up losing his mind and his heart, after all.

Which he could never let happen. Because once the party ended in just two days and he'd secured Royston's recommendation—no matter how he managed to do that—he would return to his old life, and that life certainly didn't include a lady bandit, no matter how beautiful. Not when he had to focus on regaining all the ground he'd lost as a spy, when Bathurst and the entire War Office would be scrutinizing his every move for any sign of weakness. She would be a distraction. And the last time he'd been distracted, he'd nearly lost his life.

"This is about proving my worth as a spy," he admitted. "And getting that life back."

She raised her chin defiantly when she couldn't free herself from his grip. "But you're not a spy anymore. You're—"

She froze, suddenly stopping her struggling. Her green eyes flashed knowingly with a hundred emotions—and a thousand accusations.

"That's it, isn't it?" she whispered. "Why you want to arrest me...so you *can* be a spy again."

The earth dropped away beneath him at her words. The terrifying burn flared up beneath his skin again, the same anxiety and desperation that being in her presence had held at bay. Until now. When he was losing her even as she sat perched on his lap.

He took a deep breath to steady himself. "It's not—"

"That's why you rode into the fight tonight to rescue me. It wasn't that you didn't want me arrested"—she swallowed hard, the words choking her—"but that you wanted to arrest me yourself. Wasn't it?"

"Josephine, please listen—"

She pounded her fists against him. "Damn you! All this time you were lying to me, and I trusted you. You bastard!"

"Listen to me!" He grabbed her wrists and held her hands still. "This is my last opportunity to be a spy again, so I took it."

"And what was tonight, then, Thomas? An opportunity for you *personally*?" She glared at him in betrayal, furious tears glistening accusingly in her eyes as she whispered, "You used me..."

"I didn't use you, damn it!" He tightened his grip around her wrists. "Yes, I came here because Royston promised to recommend me to the War Office if I stopped the highwayman. But then it all changed." He dragged in a harsh breath. "And you, Josephine—I never expected to find you."

With a scowl he released her and set her away from him, letting her bottom bounce on the mattress as he dropped her, then stood and began to pace beside the bed, suddenly unable to stand still as anxiety and agitation rose inside him. But the unease wasn't due to the demons and the darkness that had plagued him during the past year. This time it was desperation to keep from losing her.

Her gaze followed him silently, glaring at him, but now more wary than furious, more confused than wounded.

"And I certainly didn't expect...*this*!" He gestured toward the bed in frustration. "You've changed everything for me."

He ran a hand through his hair and resisted the urge to punch the wall. She was angry at him, deservedly so, but her anger ate at him. He couldn't ignore it, not after being so close to her. Not when he still wore the scent of her on his skin and still held the sweet taste of her on his lips.

"I don't believe you," she said reservedly, her voice even. She was clearly not fishing for empty compliments as she added, "Actresses, opera singers, the darlings of London society—you must have been with lots of women, and I don't presume to be special compared to them."

"Go ahead and presume it, chit." He placed his hands on the mattress on either side of her and leaned in menacingly. "Because you are. I've never come across another woman as stubborn, self-confident, challenging, and downright aggravating as you." When she scowled at the insults and tried to push him away, he leaned in even farther, so close he could feel the warmth of her breath on his lips. "Or one so beautiful, captivating, interesting...Half the time I don't know whether to kiss you or throttle you, and I don't care which as long as I get to have my hands on you."

Her lips parted silently in surprise.

"And tonight, when I watched you ride toward that carriage and heard the gunshots, I was terrified. *That's* why I rode into the fight to save you. Because I was terrified you might be hurt." He shut his eyes tightly for a moment, "That I would lose you before I ever had you."

"Thomas," she whispered.

"And it stops *now*, understand? All this highwayman

madness, all the robberies and the deceit. You nearly got caught tonight, and sooner or later you will misstep." He roughly grabbed her shoulders and ignored her soft gasp. "Then I won't have any choice but to arrest you, and no one will be able to save you. Do you understand?"

He pushed her down onto the bed, his body sliding over hers and trapping her beneath him as his eyes bore into hers. They were lovers now, but also adversaries, and she was still the obstacle standing between him and his old life. Only now she was much more than just the highwayman he needed to arrest. Now she was also the damsel he needed to save, only this damsel kept putting herself into distress, and he worried he might not be able to save her if she kept on.

Worse, his attraction for her went far beyond just a physical need to possess her, and even the hours he'd spent with her tonight had only whetted his appetite, not satiated it. The way she smiled and laughed, the unexpected comments that left him wondering what she'd do next, the fearless way she held her own against him...the woman cleaned orphanages on her hands and knees, for God's sake! And all while somehow making him feel comforted. If he kept feeling this way about her, he might just be tempted to forget about returning to his old life and begin a new one. With her.

His mouth swept down to capture hers, molding against hers and demanding a response until she moaned against his kiss.

"Stop this business now," he ordered, nipping his way down her jaw to her neck. Desire sprang up instantly between them again, but the cold warning in his voice was clear. "Or I'll make certain you do."

"You can't—"

"I will arrest you if I have to in order to keep you safe."

He grabbed her arms and shoved them up over her head,

pinning her against the mattress. When she tried to struggle, she could do little more than wiggle helplessly beneath him. *Sweet Lucifer.* His cock stiffened instantly.

"No one will believe you," she panted out her protest.

"I don't have to make them believe me. I just have to raise suspicions. The daughter of a baron accused of highway robbery? Your every move will be watched so closely you'll never escape notice again."

"They'll think you're mad."

"Then I'll tell them I know for a fact you aren't the highwayman because you spent tonight in my arms." He lowered his head and bit possessively at her throat. "*All* night."

The blood drained from her face. "That would ruin me...you wouldn't dare!"

"To keep you safe and alive?" He threatened, "Just try me."

Holding her breath, she stared up at him, and he could see her searching his face, attempting to discern how resolute he was. And when her shoulders sagged with a heavy sigh, although one still filled with anger and irritation, he knew she'd given up any attempt to defy him. Which was a good thing, too. Because when it came to protecting her, he wasn't bluffing.

"All right," she agreed reluctantly through gritted teeth, as if every word pained her, "I won't hold up any more coaches. Now let me go!"

With a wave of relief so deep it surprised him, he released her. "At least you've come to your senses and will leave Royston alone—"

Catching him off guard with a fierce shove, she flipped him onto his back, bringing her body over on top of his. It was her turn to trap him beneath her, yet if he'd wanted, he could have easily sent her flying across the bed with just a toss. But at that moment, with her legs straddling his waist, his hardening cock brushing tantalizingly against her inner thigh, escaping was the last thing he wanted to do.

"To be clear, I never agreed to stop going after Royston," she explained, leaning over him to pin his arms to the mattress above his head as he had done to her. Her bare breasts dangled deliciously in front of him.

His lips twitched. She had no idea of the temptation she posed.

"I agreed not to rob coaches." She smiled slyly, and he wondered, again, exactly what he had gotten himself into with this woman. "I never agreed to stop robbing Royston and his cronies in other ways."

"Josephine." Her name was a growled warning. "You will leave Royston alone, do you hear me? He's dangerous. He sent men with guns after you tonight, and if he thinks he has nothing to lose, there will be nothing to stop him from hurting you."

She lifted her chin. "Maybe I have nothing to lose by going after him."

You have me to lose, but he bit his tongue. "You have a lot to lose," he said instead. "Your family and friends, your home…" *Your life.*

Her chestnut hair fell forward across her breasts as she leaned over him, as if waiting for him to continue and admit his feelings for her. But he couldn't. He wasn't ready to acknowledge those, not to her, nor even to himself. Not when he was too confused to know exactly what to feel about her.

But he could offer her a piece of himself. "Let me do it, then, and not you." He easily slipped his hand free from her grasp and brushed her hair over her shoulder and down her bare back. "Spying is what I do best." His fingers curled around her shoulder to gently tug her toward him. "I'll find your proof against Royston."

"How?"

"I don't know yet." He pulled her down to his chest and raised his head to touch his lips to hers.

"But you will?"

"I will."

"Promise?" she pressed.

"Dear God, woman, you are difficult!" he muttered. In response her mouth curved into an amused smile.

She shifted as she moved to slide off him, unwittingly brushing against his erection. Sucking in a mouthful of air between his teeth, he grabbed her hips and stopped her, to hold her still until he could recover.

"Don't move," he ordered in a voice that sounded strained even to his own ears.

But of course, she wasn't about to do anything he asked of her. Instead the frustrating woman wiggled her bottom and sent an electric jolt pulsing through him.

When she wiggled again, he knew she was toying with him. Purposely trying to drive him out of his mind. And succeeding. Because he was steel-hard now, throbbing painfully, and longing to bury himself between her legs.

His breathing came shallow and ragged as he fought for control. If she didn't stop rubbing against him like that, he was going to lose himself right there against her thigh before he was even inside her.

"I want you, Thomas," she whispered. "Just like this." Her words sent heat pulsing into him. "Can we... is that possible?"

His chest swelled. He felt impossibly more attracted to this woman who was so adventurous yet so inexperienced at the same time. He wanted to possess her. *All* of her. Every inch of her delectable body, every sigh and soft breath passing her lips, every misguided but kind and loyal thought stirring inside that sharp mind of hers.

"Very much possible," he answered with surprising tenderness.

"Show me."

He shook his head. He wanted her desperately, but he would never hurt her. "You're still sore from the first time."

"No, I'm not," she insisted.

He slid his hand between them to stroke his fingers against her damp heat. Already she was wet and quivering for him. "Are you sure?"

As his fingers teased against her, she briefly closed her eyes. An expression of delight crossed her face, and her tongue darted out to lick her lips. "Oh yes."

"Then lift up." He directed her with a hand on her hip as she rose onto her knees above him, her legs straddling his waist. His full erection pointed sinfully upward between her thighs like an arrow, large and long, and aching to strike its mark. "Now lower yourself."

As he guided her down slowly, a moan of pleasure sounded from the back of her throat as his cock slid smoothly inside her slick warmth, burying deep within her. Her full lips pulled into an O of silent surprise at the sensation of having him inside her at this angle as she sat perched on him, her sex fully sheathing his manhood. He held her unmoving against him for a moment to let her adjust, knowing she would be sore despite her protests to the contrary but unable to resist her siren song. Then he began to lead her in slowly raising and lowering herself, sliding so delectably up and down along his length in a steady rhythm.

"Thomas, that feels so…" She trailed off into a deep sigh of pleasure.

"Yes—yes, it does," he agreed in a husky groan, his body aching with the same desire now moving through hers, and he thrilled that he was able to give her such pleasure.

Letting her set their pace, he brushed his hands up her body to cup her breasts. He squeezed hard at the pebbled nipples between his thumbs and fingers in time with each rise and plunge of her body over his. Her eyes closed with a soft whimper, and she began to move faster as she ground her pelvis down against his with every rise of his hips beneath her.

Her unpracticed movements felt incredible, but he wanted more. Grabbing her shoulders he pulled her forward until she lay nearly horizontal across his chest even as he continued to thrust upward into her, her fingers digging into the muscles of his upper arms and hanging on as if for dear life.

"Like this," he rasped, his hands sweeping down to cup her bottom and press her down harder over him as he drove up into her. He groaned. "Sweet Jesus, yes…just like this."

With the new angle of her tilted hips allowing him to plunge even deeper inside her, he shivered from the intensity sweeping through him, from the pleasure that he found in someone so fierce yet so gentle at the same time. Taking this much raw satisfaction in a woman seemed impossible, yet she was giving him exactly that. She made his body shake, his mind swirl, and his soul weep.

She rocked forward and back over him now, her legs folded beneath her, her feet pushing for leverage against the mattress with each thrust. "It's like…Oh my!" She paused to catch her breath, finally panting out, "It's like riding a horse."

An unbidden memory stabbed into his chest of those mornings he'd spent with Helene in the stables, letting her bounce off on top of him. "It's nothing like riding a horse, damn it," he growled.

Before she could respond, he lifted his head to snatch one of her breasts into his mouth as they danced just above his face, his lips latching tightly onto the nipple and sucking hard. He heard her gasp, then she arched her back and drove her breast deeper into his mouth even as her hips bore down against his cock. All those little muscles inside her drew up deliciously tight around him at the same time her nipple puckered against his tongue, and his cock jumped inside her. He was ready to burst.

Her fingernails dug into his shoulders as she clenched her body around his. She was on the edge, ready to come at any moment. He took her nipple between his teeth and bit down.

Tossing back her head, she cried out his name, high and helplessly. Her body shuddered violently against him as her thighs convulsed around his waist. Then she collapsed against his chest, her limp body trembling with spent desire.

At the last possible moment, when he could barely hold back any longer and the first squirt started from his cock, he lifted her off him. He grabbed a pillow, placed it over his hips, and with a groan released himself into it, pulsating dully with exquisite satisfaction. He tossed the pillow onto the floor and gathered her into his arms, pressing her warm body into the tall curve of his. Then he kissed her with all the surprising tenderness swelling inside him and reached down between her legs. Even now he could still feel her orgasm throbbing dully against his fingertips and wished he could still be inside her, sharing that pleasure with her.

His gut clenched as he placed a kiss against her hair. There was a time when he hadn't cared about the consequences of bedding a woman, when he was younger and reckless and stupid. When he thought no harm would ever come to him. Now, though, he knew better. He was still willing to play with fire, he supposed, but the difference was that now he knew how devastating those flames could be.

And with the wildfire that was Josephine Carlisle, well, it was only a matter of time until he got burned.

Like riding a horse, she'd said. Never. *Never* something that base. Not with her.

He deserved that laugh from fate, he supposed, for the way he'd used Helene and let her use him. During all those mornings in his stable, he'd known he meant nothing to her and was simply an aristocratic cock servicing a bored widow. He'd thought she'd been fulfilling a need, but he'd had no idea how deep his need went until he met Josie. She did more than satisfy the need—she'd begun to heal him.

Holding her naked and trembling in his arms, the heat of lovemaking still warm between them, he knew now the answer to the question that had been plaguing him since he arrived at Blackwood Hall. Why she affected him with such a primal pull the way no other woman ever had. Because with Josephine, what he experienced was more than physical lust, more than distraction—within her arms she held the possibility of happiness.

The further irony was that Helene had never been up on a horse, not even for a slow amble through Hyde Park, while Josie was not only an expert rider who fearlessly charged into fights—

His heart froze as the realization sank sickeningly through him. The damned *horse*!

Scrambling to sit up, he grabbed her shoulders and pulled her up with him. "Your horse," he demanded, ignoring the sudden confusion flashing across her face. "Where do you stable it?"

She blinked. "What?"

"It ran away."

"The gunshots frightened him. Why—"

"Think!" He shook her, trying to drive into her the importance of this. *Christ!* A spy lived and died by the details, but in his desire to spend the night with her, this detail had completely slipped his mind. "The men who came after you tonight saw it run off and will track it. Where would it have gone?"

"I don't know."

"Chestnut Hill?"

"No, I've never had him there." The blood drained from her face. "But I've ridden him here."

He shook his head. "If your horse had come here, the constable would have arrived by now. Where is it stabled?"

"With John Cooper and his family on their farm." She pressed her hand to her mouth. "*Oh God!*"

He slid off the bed. "Do you keep an extra dress here?"

She nodded.

"Put it on. We have to leave. *Now.*"

* * *

Josie rushed to the armoire and grabbed her spare dress while Thomas quickly tugged on his clothes and then hurried into the main room. Still pinning up her hair as she left the bedroom, now wearing a blue muslin dress and matching pelisse, Josie paused in the doorway to watch as he scooped up the black clothes she'd worn for the robbery and flung them into the fireplace, where they caught fire on the dying embers. The same clothes he'd peeled from her body in the darkness. As the heat of that memory mixed with fear that she'd put them in danger tonight, her hands shook so hard she could barely slide the last hairpin into place.

He stood and brushed the ashes of her clothes from his hands. "I need your jacket."

Without protesting, she shrugged out of the pelisse and handed it over.

"Thank you." Twisting one sleeve inside out, he tossed it carelessly over the arm of the sofa.

Then, without explanation, he ripped two buttons from his waistcoat. She watched wide-eyed as he tossed them onto the floor.

"Come on." His hand clamped over her wrist, and he half dragged her from the cottage as she struggled to keep up with his long strides.

With Josie riding in front of him, sitting sideways across his lap as his arms held her tight, they cantered through the woods and hugged the dark edges of the fields so they wouldn't be seen. The night was silent and dark, but the hour was much later than she'd thought. Swept away in the pleasures of being with him tonight, she'd lost all track of time. Even now the first fingers of dawn's light stretched across the sky from the horizon.

"Aren't we going to the Cooper farm?" she asked as he turned the horse away from the village.

"*I'm* going to the farm," he corrected. "You're going home."

"I want to go with you. It's my fault—"

"And how do you explain why we're riding up together at dawn on my horse?" He glanced wryly down at her. "We'd both be leg-shackled at gunpoint, then, and not because of any robberies."

Her hollow heart thumped painfully, and she looked away, unable to answer. Because in the deepest, most hidden recesses of her heart, where she didn't dare admit it aloud, that was exactly what she wanted. To be married. And if she were to be married to him, how could that not be wonderful?

She'd never met another man like him. He was so incredibly special, the hero and protector she'd been waiting her entire life to find. She certainly didn't regret having given her innocence to him tonight. She would *never* regret that. Both tender and passionate, he'd made the experience so wonderful for her that she couldn't imagine how it could have been better. Or that she could have given herself so freely to any other man.

But she had no future with him; she'd known that from the moment they met. Even if she found a way to make him believe her and take her word over Royston's, he was still heir to a duchy, and she was...well, nothing a duke would ever want in a wife.

She might have desperately wanted the dream of a husband, home, and family, but Thomas didn't want her for a wife. He'd been very clear about that. He might not have been like the other men in the past, who cared nothing for her except for the possibility of bedding her and returning home once the house party ended, but in the end, that difference made none after all.

Blinking back hot tears, she rested her cheek against his chest and remained silent for the rest of the ride. For all she knew, this would be the last time he'd ever hold her in his arms. He'd never mentioned sharing another night, and now, with everything falling apart around them, not only would he leave her, he might just end up arresting her. She didn't think she could survive that. Not after being naked and trembling in his arms.

Thomas reined the horse to a stop at the edge of the property, carefully remaining out of sight behind the stone wall. He slipped from the gelding's back. "You can get inside?"

She nodded. The servants' entry would be unlocked, and

she'd sneak in that way, stealing up the rear stairs as she did every time she slipped out for the night.

"Go straight to your room," he ordered as he set her on the ground. "Then pretend to be ill, so seriously that you can't leave your bed."

She shook her head. "I want to know what's happening."

He cursed sharply, and she flinched, not because of the outburst but because she already felt the chasm opening between them, already sensed him pulling away from her.

"For once, Josephine, just do as I ask." He pulled his hands away from her and stepped back, then glanced up the drive toward the still-sleeping house. "I'll send word as soon as I can, but I need to know where you are. I can't help Cooper if I'm worried about keeping you safe. Do you understand?"

"Yes." But her agreement was a grudging one.

"The constable might come here after you." He stared down somberly at her, his eyes matching the dark blue of the predawn sky. "If you're accused of being at the robbery, explain that we met up secretly at the cottage and that we were together there all night." He paused pointedly. "Understand?"

Her breath strangled in her throat. Instantly, she knew...the pelisse made to look as if it had been pulled from her shoulders, the buttons he'd torn from his waistcoat, the two glasses of brandy sitting on the beside table—he'd staged the cottage so there would be no doubt about what had happened between them if she needed an alibi. Right down to the still-tangled sheets on the bed.

"If my parents find out, they'll force us to marry," she whispered, grimly serious.

"Better to be forced into marriage than swing from the gallows," he returned in the same grim tone.

He grabbed the front of her dress and pulled her against him as his mouth came down hungrily against hers. Despite herself, she moaned against the kiss and leaned into him.

Stepping away, he released her and swung up onto the horse. "Get to your room and stay there until you hear from me."

He set the large gelding into a gallop and rode away. Standing helplessly in the middle of the lane, pressing the back of her hand against her still-moist lips, she watched him leave until he was no longer visible in the blue darkness. An anguished sob escaped her. Good God, would she ever see him again?

CHAPTER NINE

$\mathscr{E}$lizabeth Carlisle stared down at her daughter as she lay in bed, the morning sunlight streaming into the room. "Ill?" She arched a disbelieving brow. "You were fine at dinner last night."

"It must have been something I ate," Josie mumbled, hating that she was lying to her mother. "Or perhaps the change in weather."

But she was certain she *did* look terrible from everything that had happened last night, from the foiled robbery to losing her innocence to her worry over John Cooper, all compounded by a lack of sleep. And parting so miserably from Thomas. Worse, her body now hurt in places she'd never before suspected it could hurt, and she knew the soreness wasn't from fleeing through the woods.

He had done that to her. Thomas's unquenchable need and desire for her had marked her, branding her on the inside, and she suspected his imprint on her would last forever.

"Or perhaps this sudden illness is due to a certain marquess."

Suppressing a gasp, Josie was unable to hide the blush of embarrassment heating up from her neck and the guilty look crossing her face. She swallowed nervously. "Whatever do you mean?"

"Don't dissemble with me, Josephine Grace," Mama chastised as she sat on the edge of the bed. "Don't pretend I'm so oblivious I've not noticed the way you and Lord Chesney behave around each other. You two have been sniping at each other since the first night of the party and cutting each other in front of the guests."

Her mouth fell open, and she gaped for a moment before remembering to close it. "So," she said carefully, "you think I'm pretending to be ill in order to avoid Lord Chesney because we've...fought?"

"Unless there's some other reason you've been behaving so oddly around him."

Josie stared at her mother, struck speechless. Did she suspect...Sweet heavens, had Mama noticed? *Impossible.* She and Thomas had been careful in front of the other guests, so careful, in fact, that her mother wasn't alone in thinking the two of them disliked each other. The ladies had teased her in the drawing room just yesterday afternoon about how many more of her cuts the marquess would accept before he gave up his interest in her.

"No, of course not," Josie lied quickly, doing her best to slow her racing heart and steady her breathing before she gave herself away. "I know well enough to avoid a man like him." *Knew* but hadn't managed to carry it off, much to her shameless pleasure.

"Well." Her mother narrowed her gaze dubiously. "If that's all it truly is—"

"It is." Josie leaned back against the pillows, doing her best to ignore the swelling of guilt inside her chest at lying to her mother. *Goodness.* Her life used to be so much simpler when she was only a highwayman. "And I promise to pay closer attention to how I speak to him. In the future I shall endeavor to always be ladylike with the marquess." Then, unable to fight away the devil on her shoulder compelling her, she added, "In public."

Her mother smiled and patted her hand. "Good. Because I think Miranda Hodgkins has developed an infatuation with him, and as long as she's mooning after him, then she's not chasing after Robert."

Josie smiled in private amusement. Miranda Hodgkins with Thomas Matteson? The silly goose wouldn't stand a chance with a man like him. He'd chew her up and spit her out as if she were nothing at all.

"I don't think Miranda is the kind of woman to catch the marquess's interest." Or at least she hoped not. Selfishly, she didn't want anyone catching his interest but her.

"Well, better his than your brother's." Elizabeth shook her head and moved away from the bed. "If I could just put Robert into storage for five years to let her catch up to him..." She exhaled a patient sigh. "Perhaps ten."

Josie hid a bubble of laughter by breaking into a coughing fit. She *was* supposed to be ill, after all.

"So stay in bed if you'd like." Mama leaned over and kissed her on the forehead, which Josie suspected was an attempt to check her temperature. "Sleep the day away and get your strength back for the farewell dinner tonight. The countess would never forgive us if we begged off."

The farewell dinner? Heavens, how had she forgotten about that? Her chest tightened painfully. No, that was impossible. The party couldn't be coming to an end so quickly, because when it ended Thomas would have no excuse for lingering at Blackwood Hall. He'd be gone from both Lincolnshire and her life.

"Yes, Mama," she whispered, suddenly truly ill.

"I shall be back to check on you later." Her mother gently squeezed her hand, then glided across the room.

Josie sat up. "Mama?"

"Yes?" She paused, her hand on the door.

"Thomas Matteson," she said quietly, focusing her attention on the coverlet as she plucked her fingers at the quilting. "Do you think— I mean, would it be so terrible to suppose…"

"To suppose what, dear?" her mother prompted gently.

She took a deep breath. "Would someone like me ever be able to…marry someone like him?"

She could feel her mother's curious gaze on her, but she couldn't bear to look at her, not even as she slowly returned to sit beside her on the bed. "That man should consider himself fortunate to ever have the attentions of someone like you, my darling."

Josie's shoulders sagged. Of course, her mother would say that. That was exactly what mothers were expected to say to their daughters. But Josie wasn't her daughter. Not her *real* daughter. She wasn't a true Carlisle, and that made all the difference. "He's a high-ranking gentleman from a well-respected family." She shook her head sadly, twisting her fingers into the coverlet. "And I am not."

"While your father was awarded his barony and not born to it, he *is* still a baron, and you *are* his daughter."

"But I am not," Josie repeated, so softly the words were barely more than a breath.

Her mother touched her chin and lifted her face until

Josie had no choice but to look at her. Quick anger hardened her features, reminding Josie of the fierceness of a lioness protecting her cubs. "Did Lord Chesney say something to you? Is that why you and the marquess are at odds? If he did, so help me, I will demand an apology, and that man will—"

"No, of course not!" Even though he knew the truth about her past, Thomas would *never* say anything like that to her. He was far too much of a gentleman.

Elizabeth sighed heavily, and her anger dissipated as she shook her head. "Then where is this doubt coming from?" She stroked her fingertips soothingly across Josie's cheek and frowned with concern. "You haven't spoken of the adoption in so long...I thought you'd finally put it all behind you and come to fully accept that you are part of this family and always will be."

"I know I'm accepted here, by you and Papa, and the boys—" Her voice choked. "But I'm not truly a Carlisle, and I never can be."

"You *are*." She lovingly brushed a curl from Josie's forehead. "When you arrived here for the first time, so small but feisty, you filled an emptiness in this house. We needed a girl's laughter echoing through the halls, her dolls left on the nursery floor, pink ribbons underfoot everywhere—" Her words caught in her throat, her eyes glistening. "I might not have given birth to you, but you belong to me, my darling. And I love you as much as any mother could ever love a daughter."

Her mother wrapped her arms around her and pulled her against her bosom, holding her close and cradling her in her arms just as she had when Josie first arrived at Chestnut Hill as a little girl.

She closed her eyes tightly against the embrace. No matter how much Mama insisted she was the same as a natural-born daughter, she knew better. As newly titled peers, her parents were still used to the country lifestyle and middle-class mannerisms into which they'd been born, and they were very different from other peers who never would have even considered adopting a child, who at most would have welcomed into their home a distant cousin or niece. That alone made her unlike every other society daughter in England.

"Do you feel unwelcome here?" her mother asked. "Has anyone in Islingham, any of our tenants or household staff, ever treated you as anything less than a member of our family?"

"No, but…" Would a gentleman? When someone from a well-respected family looked at her, someone with position and property, someone like Thomas, would he see her as the daughter of a baron, or as what she really was— "I'm nothing."

"Do not *ever* say that again!" Mama chastised sternly, shooting her the well-practiced scowl of displeasure whose force she'd spent the past thirty years perfecting on her boys. "You are beautiful, intelligent, loving, and kind. Any gentleman who cares more about blood lineage than all that does not deserve you."

Josie sadly shook her head. Those words were so simple for her mother to say, but she knew how harsh the world could be. Well-bred gentlemen married well-bred ladies to produce well-bred heirs; there was no changing that. "And if all they do care about is lineage, if none of them want their progeny soiled by marrying the natural daughter of God only knows whom? If no one ever offers for me…"

"Then it is their loss and our gain because you will always have a home here. Always." Her mother paused, her brows drawing together as she studied her closely. Then suddenly, knowingly, her lips parted, and her cheeks paled. "Is that why you declined seasons in London? Because you thought you wouldn't have any suitors, that no one would offer for you?"

She swallowed hard and looked away. That was exactly the reason. "That doesn't signify."

"Oh, my darling." Her shoulders slumped as she cupped her daughter's face in her hands and looked at her with deep regret and sadness. "If I had known... but you declined them, and your father and I never wanted to press you."

"I know." She'd never dared to hope for a London season, knowing what would happen as soon as the gossip of her past swirled through the *ton* and they learned that her real mother had been a maid or a prostitute. For heaven's sake, if she couldn't even catch the son of a Lincolnshire squire, what hope could she have had for a London gentleman? Her birth had put her on the shelf before she'd ever donned her first ball gown.

"It's not too late. If you want a London season, we'll still make it happen for you." She squeezed her hands. "A good man *will* eventually offer for you, I know it. Perhaps not one quite as prestigious as Lord Chesney, but a fine man nevertheless." She forced a reassuring smile, but to Josie her mother's expression was heartbreaking. "Do you understand?"

She nodded silently, unable to find her voice.

"I want you to be happy, darling, whether that means marrying a gentleman or a footman, or never marrying at all. Do you believe that?"

Josie nodded, blinking hard, and whispered, "Yes."

"Good," her mother said firmly. Then she paused, biting her bottom lip apprehensively. "But please don't marry the footman."

"Mama!" Josie choked out in surprise through unshed tears.

"Well, you cannot blame me! I already have enough trouble on my hands with your brothers, and if I live to see the three of them married without scandal, it will be a miracle." She gave a long, weary sigh, then kissed her cheek and stood. "As for Chesney," she added as she crossed to the door, "just do your best to avoid him and ignore whatever teasing he aims at you."

Avoid him? Oh, it was much too late for that. She'd already tried avoiding him and, well, look where that had gotten her—the furthest thing from avoided. She should have known all along that Thomas Matteson simply wasn't the kind of man a woman could ignore. And as for the teasing... *Oh my*. Her body heated feverishly just at the thought of how he'd teased her.

"After tonight's dinner, you'll never have to be bothered by him again."

Her chest sank. Because she liked being bothered by Thomas. Very much. Even now, sore and stiff, her body still tingled with arousal at the thought of him. And that was the problem, she thought, as she watched her mother close the door quietly after herself. *Not* being bothered by him was the last thing she wanted.

With a frown she tossed the coverlet aside and began to pace beside her bed, hoping the movement would keep back both the growing ball of unease in her belly and the tears. Thomas was simply the most wonderful man she'd ever met, and she knew she'd never cross paths with another like him. It was so easy now to imagine spending all her nights in his arms in that relaxed way they'd shared last night, teasing and laughing with each other once the physical need was satisfied. And oh, she could easily imagine satisfying that physical need with him again, and often.

She wanted quiet moments, too, when she would be

happy simply to have him sitting with her before a fire on a cold winter's night or to feed him strawberries on a spring picnic. She'd love for him to show her everything about his life in London.

She froze, and her heart skipped painfully. *Love?*

No, she hadn't meant that. Not love! There was absolutely no *love* between them.

Of course, she was indebted to him. He'd saved her life, and in keeping her secret, he'd proven himself an ally.

And of course, she found him attractive. With that thick black hair and those piercing blue eyes, he was dashing in a way that sucked the breath from her every time she watched him walk into a room. And each time he pulled her into his arms, she knew she belonged there in a way she'd never belonged anywhere before in her life. The feeling was inexplicable. Downright mad, in fact. So were the fantasies she'd let herself have of daring to hope she might someday marry...him.

But *love*? In her wildest dreams, she'd never dared to let herself—

Her knees gave out, and she sank onto the bed. Even as she heard the rush of blood in her ears from the pounding of her heart, she knew it was true. A groan escaped her lips. She *had* fallen in love with him, this man who was heir to a duchy, a spy, and a hero. The one man who was the most impossible choice for her in all of England, next to the Prince Regent himself. The same man who'd come into her life in the first place only because he'd planned on arresting her.

But none of what she felt mattered. Because he wasn't hers to have, and he never would be.

With a deep breath of resolve, she pushed herself away from the bed. She might never have a chance at a future with him, but at least she could help him now by ending the mess in which she'd entangled him and perhaps, just perhaps, also find a way for him to be seen as the hero in all this. A hero who deserved to be welcomed back by the War Office.

Twisting her hair into a knot and doing her best to pin it into place, she hurried to dress. She had retired as a highwayman, but she hadn't completely given up breaking the law. Not just yet. Because this morning she planned on sneaking into Blackwood Hall and stealing the proof she needed to stop Royston, once and for all.

*   *   *

An hour later, Josie walked down the upstairs hallway of Blackwood Hall as normally as possible…if *normally* meant holding her breath, wringing her hands, and creeping on tiptoe.

Word had spread among the guests about last night's foiled robbery attempt and that the constable now held the highwayman in custody, and the mood of the party had turned grim. The countess had taken to her suite of rooms, too overwrought to face her guests. And Royston waited in the village for more information, according to Greaves, who'd greeted her when she arrived.

With all the guests huddled inside the house, no one would suspect that she was up to anything if they saw her wandering from room to room. If anyone did ask why she was there, she would simply say she was going to the music room to look through the sheet music to find a song or two to play tonight after dinner. But she knew no one would give her subterfuge a second thought. No one ever had.

Until Thomas.

She groaned inwardly. Why *him*? Of all the men to fall for, the one who had to come sweeping in and capture her heart was the same man set on arresting her. The same one who made her feel so exquisitely beautiful and desired yet didn't believe a word she said.

Her heart lurched painfully. Such a fool! She'd been mad to ever let herself fantasize for a moment about the possibility of sharing a life with him, to keep alive even a mere sliver of hope that they might have more than a sennight together. Or to still believe in her silly childhood dream that someone might want to marry her after all. After all these years, she should have known better and let that foolish dream die. Even if he proved himself to be the one gentleman in all of England who didn't care that she was an orphan, Thomas didn't trust her. And to be honest, she'd not given him much reason to. In her desperate pursuit to help the orphans, she'd made him doubt everything about her.

Gathering her determination, she hurried faster down the hall. She might not be able to overcome her past, but she *would* find the proof that would finally make him believe her, even if she had to search through all two hundred rooms of Blackwood Hall inch by inch.

A door opened, and an arm shot out around her waist. Someone yanked her into the room and pushed her up against the wall. The door shut behind her, trapping her inside. She took a deep breath to scream—

A hand pressed against her mouth. "Quiet!"

Her eyes lifted, then widened. *Thomas.* If she'd known what was good for her, when she saw the cold fury on his face, she would have screamed anyway.

"What in the *hell* are you doing here?" he growled through gritted teeth, then pulled his hand away from her mouth to pin both of her shoulders against the wall.

"I came to help you."

"I don't need your help." The sting of his fresh rejection

stabbed into her heart like a stake. She'd been naked in his arms less than twelve hours ago, but already he felt a world away. "I told you to stay in your room."

"I wasn't going to stay there while you—"

He cursed, so vehemently she jumped. "I'll damn well tie you up with ropes next time."

Her chin jutted into the air. "I'd like to see you try!"

"*Don't* tempt me." His face hardened at the challenge, and his hands tightened their hold on her arms, the frustration inside him palpable. "I told you to stay at home. Now I find you prowling through Royston's house, right under the man's nose." The muscles in his shoulder flexed as his hand clenched, and she suspected that the need for silence was the only thing stopping him from slamming his fist into the wall. "Damnation!"

"Stop cursing at me," she scolded.

"I'm not cursing at you."

"You're supposed to be a spy."

"I am," he snarled.

"Then keep your calm." She rolled her shoulders, but his grip remained firm. "And let go of me!"

"And you'll go back home immediately and stay there until I send for you?"

"No."

"*Christ*, Jo!"

"Stop cursing at—"

"For God's sake, why won't you ever do what I ask you?" He leaned toward her until his warm breath fanned her cheek, his anger dark on his brow. "Are you trying to get yourself killed?"

"I'm trying to help," she defended.

But at that moment, as they faced off like two bulldogs in a fight, she knew that neither of them completely trusted the other. He didn't trust her enough to take her word over Royston's, and she didn't trust him not to arrest her to regain his old life. The life he'd claimed held no place for her. Already her heart ached at the thought of losing him. Any more rejection from him would break it completely.

As she turned around and reached for the door handle, praying she could escape before he saw the pain on her face, he slammed his hand against the door and held it closed.

Her heart plummeted. *Oh God* . . . why wouldn't he leave her alone so she could be miserable in peace? *Never* had she thought that loving someone could be so agonizing.

He stepped up behind her, and the heat of his body seeped into her back. Despite her anger and pain, a shiver of heat sped through her and sent her heart racing as his mouth lowered to her ear.

"I want you at home so I can keep you safe," he explained in a gentle tone that she knew he fought to control, because even now she could feel the anger and confusion burning inside him. He trailed his knuckles across her cheek and elicited a shuddering tremble from her. "I don't want you to be hurt, Jo. Please believe that."

But how could she? Even if he let her go without arresting her, having to leave him tomorrow when the party ended would be torture. No matter what happened now, she would be hurt.

With tears filling her eyes, she choked out, "Would you still arrest me if you had to?"

"Yes," he answered, the raw honesty shooting a spear of anguish into her.

She drew a shaking breath. "Then I hope you understand why I couldn't stay home."

"No, I can't." His deep voice was husky now, each word a

heated breath against her ear that had her longing to simply lean back and put herself once more into his arms. And if she did that...oh heavens, she truly would be lost forever! "I don't understand why you keep risking your life, first with the robberies and now by walking right beneath Royston's nose."

He slowly turned her to face him, and she somehow resisted the urge to wrap her arms around his neck even as her skin tingled from the nearness of him. "Because the orphans have no one to protect them but me."

"And your family, Josephine? Have you thought about what it will do to them if you're caught?"

Her chest clenched painfully. She *had* thought about them, from the very moment when she'd decided to become a highwayman. But she wasn't truly a Carlisle, and if she were caught, her family could distance themselves from her by reminding everyone that she was adopted and keep themselves away from the greatest part of the scandal that would fall onto their heads. They could place the blame solely on her, and society would understand, having expected disaster all along. After all, that was what came of adopting an orphan. Mama and Papa just hadn't realized it yet.

Her hot tears blurred his handsome face. "They're not my real family."

"Oh yes, they are." He caressed his thumb gently across her bottom lip, and her lips parted of their own volition with a trembling sigh. "The way they love you—you'd hurt them irreparably, Jo, and they'd blame themselves. Could you really bear it, knowing the hell your arrest would put them through?"

"If my only other choice is turning my back on the orphans, then yes," she answered, believing her words. "I could bear it." *Somehow.*

Disbelief darkened his eyes, turning their depths a sultry midnight blue. "No, you couldn't."

"You're wrong about me," she whispered, wishing he wouldn't look at her like that, as if he'd figured out everything about her. "You think you know me, Thomas, but you don't."

Stepping forward, he closed the distance between them. She fought back a soft cry of frustration and need as she closed her eyes against the sensation of his hard body pressed so tantalizingly against hers. The wonderful memories of last night pulsed through her, and her thighs clenched hard against the wanton throbbing between her legs. She ached to be with him again, to give herself over to the delicious pleasure only he could give her when he made her feel so beautiful, so desired and happy... only for the pain to be twice as agonizing when he left.

"After last night," he murmured, his mouth close to hers, "I know you *very* well, Josephine." His deep voice rumbled through her and set her heart pounding. "And I don't mean just your delectable body."

He lowered his head to kiss her. As his lips brushed over hers, she fought the temptation to beg him to pull her to the floor right there and make love to her again. There would be comfort in his arms, but the consolation would be fleeting. As fleeting as his presence in her life. By this time tomorrow, he would be gone forever.

She blinked hard to clear the stinging from her eyes and pulled away, breaking the kiss. Forcing her voice not to tremble, she challenged, "Yet you don't trust me."

He blew out a harsh breath of frustration, and she felt the tension clawing at him. "You know it isn't that simple."

"Because you want to be a spy..." *More than you want me.* She couldn't bring herself to finish the soft accusation that sliced a raw wound into her heart.

"Yes," he answered somberly.

Unable to bear looking at him, she turned her gaze away in dread of whatever emotions might be passing over his face. Guilt, pity, obligation... but certainly not love. The one emotion she wanted to see most of all.

"And that's why I'm here," she forced out, somehow making her words sound more resolved than she felt. "To make you a spy again."

Ignoring the pain of utter desolation that swept through her, she shoved him back with all her might, threw open the door, and hurried into the hallway.

She couldn't bear to be alone in the room with him for another moment longer, fighting the urge to wrap her arms around his shoulders and pull him close, because no good would come of that. He was thoroughly maddening and aggravating beyond belief, and made more so each time he was kind and tender to her. Like now. Parting from him would be so much easier if he truly were nothing more than a heartless rake, because then she would care nothing for him. And she wouldn't want anything more.

"Make me a spy again, huh?" he asked as he fell into step beside her. The anger inside him couldn't keep the pain and vulnerability from creeping into his voice. She knew him well now, too. "How do you plan on doing that, exactly?"

"I'm going to search Royston's study for proof that—"

"*I'm* going to break into his study." His fingers closed in warning over her elbow. "*You're* going back to Chestnut Hill."

She stopped so suddenly he almost crashed into her, and his expression hardened, as if he were readying himself for another fight with her, another biting comment or harsh accusation. Instead she murmured softly, "It's my fault, Thomas, all of it. The robberies, the fight last night, Mr.

Cooper's arrest...I have to be part of this." His eyes flickered at the intensity in her voice as she insisted, "I *have* to. Do not send me away, not now."

He stared at her silently as he clearly considered the ramifications of keeping her with him. Then, with a decisive nod, he took her elbow again and led her down the hallway at a sauntering pace. Anyone who happened upon them would think they were simply making their way to join the other guests in the downstairs drawing room.

"All right," he acquiesced with a hard sigh. "We'll do this together. But you'll do as I say without question. Understand?"

She nodded her compliance only because she didn't have a choice. "Do you think we'll find any evidence?"

"I don't know, but we have to hurry. Royston was still in the village with the constable when I left them. We'll have about an hour, maybe less."

They stopped outside Royston's study. Thomas casually tried the handle, but it didn't budge.

"Of course he wouldn't make this easy," he muttered. Then he slid a sideways glance at her and scrutinized her from head to toe.

"What is it?" A self-conscious blush rose in her cheeks.

"Give me one of your hairpins and your necklace."

"Why?"

"Don't question me, Jo." He held out his hand. "Just trust me."

She hesitated, then unfastened her necklace and removed one of her hairpins. When she handed both over, her fingers brushed against his. Only a fleeting contact, but it stirred the familiar warmth of arousal low in her belly.

He dropped the necklace onto the floor, then took her shoulders and positioned her at an angle to the door. "Stand here and keep watch. If anyone comes into the hall, even one of the servants, warn me."

Nodding, she watched as he crouched in front of the door and slid the long pin into the lock. His fingers worked expertly, and with a twist of the pin and a sly smile at her, he turned the handle and opened the door. As he rose to his feet, he snatched up the necklace and pulled her inside, closing and locking the door behind them.

He fastened the necklace around her neck and placed a quick kiss on her nape before stepping away. A warm tingle slithered down her spine.

"That was smoothly done," she murmured, nodding toward the door as she returned the hairpin to its place. "One would think you often broke into locked rooms that way."

He sent her an inscrutable glance as he hurried to the desk. "That skill comes in handy sometimes."

"I can imagine." Yet she tried very hard *not* to imagine as she watched him search through the desk drawers, her mind conjuring unbidden images of Thomas picking the locks of dozens of doors belonging to beautiful women.

He carefully turned over the contents of each drawer and left no visible evidence they'd been searched. "Have I picked the lock on your bedroom door?"

Her throat tightened. "No."

He looked up and steadied a piercing gaze on her. "Then don't assume I've done it to any other woman."

She glanced away, duly scolded. Thomas Matteson was not only a spy but apparently also a mind reader.

He searched the last drawer but came up empty.

"What can I do?" she asked as he methodically began to search through the cabinets and side tables.

"If Royston's locking the door, there's information in here he doesn't want found." He nodded toward the shelves.

"Look through the books, one by one, and check for anything which might be hidden behind them. But make certain to put them back *exactly* as you found them. And keep a close eye out for any threads, hairs, or the like that might be sitting on the shelf or the books. If you find one of those, don't touch it and call for me."

"Whyever not?" Standing on tiptoe, she reached for the first book on the top shelf.

"A stray thread or hair can be planted to show whether someone's been looking through your things." He swiftly searched the liquor tantalus in the corner. "It's an old spy trick."

"Hmm, then it's a good thing you're an old spy."

He glanced at her briefly over his shoulder, a half grin at his lips, before stepping to the next table and searching it. Her chest warmed at the thought that they were searching for the proof together. For once they weren't at odds, and it was wonderful.

"So why the necklace?" she asked as she made her way through the row of books and shook out the pages of each one.

"In case someone came upon us." He slid his hands under the table to search for any documents hidden beneath it. "An excuse to explain why I was on my knees in front of the door."

She gaped at him, remembering how he'd taken the same detailed care last night with the cottage. Apparently, noticing the details truly was central to a spy's life. "Because I'd dropped it, and you were picking it up?"

"Exactly." With narrowed eyes he surveyed the room. "This is taking too long. We'll never finish searching before Royston returns."

When he looked at her, she knew he wasn't seeing her as

the highwayman or even as the lover he'd taken last night. For once he looked at her as an equal partner, and that realization sent a wave of heated pleasure spilling through her.

"Think, Josie," he urged her. "You know him, you know this house. Where would he hide something he'd never want anyone to find?"

She replaced the last book on the shelf. "I don't know. Royston is a typical aristocrat, I suppose. He loves to ride and shoot and has no patience for parties or idle dinner conversation, but the countess adores that so he tolerates it for her sake. Spends every season in London. His son Charles studies at Oxford but rarely comes home." She shook her head in frustration. "But Royston isn't what he seems."

"So look around. What do you see that's out of character for him?"

She turned from the bookshelves and scanned the room. "His desk, the liquor cabinet, the side tables—"

"Already searched. *Think.*"

"I *am* thinking," she countered peevishly, her hands on her hips. "A plain desk, brown chairs, beige rugs... there's no personality here, nothing unusual." She pointed at the wall in frustration. "For goodness' sake! He even has the most boring painting of fishing gear imaginable—" Her breath strangled. "The painting! Royston hates to fish."

He rushed across the room and lifted the painting from the wall, then grinned over his shoulder at her in amazement. "It's a good thing you didn't side with the French."

Holding her breath, she watched him reach into a shallow niche in the wall behind the painting and pull out a small black book.

"That's it, then?" she asked as her excited heart raced. "The proof we need?"

"I'm not certain, but it's important enough for Royston to hide it."

"Let us hope it's—"

Metal scraped against metal as a key slid into the lock from the hallway. For a split second her eyes locked with his, then she flung herself at the door.

CHAPTER TEN

~ ⌒ ~

Thomas made a grab for her but missed, and with a loud cry, she pressed herself up against the door.

"No!" she called out. "Don't come inside!"

She braced herself to put all her weight against the door, but she was just a slip of a woman and wouldn't be able to hold Royston back for long.

"Who's there?" The earl shoved at the door. "I demand to know who you are and what you're doing in my study!"

"It's Josephine Carlisle, my lord."

Thomas bit back the curse at his lips.

"Miss Carlisle?" Royston paused. "What the devil!"

"I had an accident, and I tore my dress." She wedged herself hard against the doorframe. "So I had to duck in here to fix it."

She grasped her neckline and ripped the fabric, tearing both dress and shift low across her shoulder.

Thomas's heart leapt into his throat, fear and anger rising inside him even as he admired her cunning. Oh, she was brilliant! If Royston barged in on them together with her dress like that, he'd think he'd stumbled onto nothing more than a lover's tryst. And even if the earl suspected more, he'd never be able to accuse them of searching through his private study without raising an alarm throughout the entire house and raining scandal down upon all their heads.

But Thomas would be damned before he let her be disgraced in front of a houseful of guests who would all certainly come running at the first sound of uproar. With a furious glare and a warning finger to his lips, he ducked beneath the desk just as Royston forced the door open and sent her stumbling backward into the room. The last glimpse he caught of her before he hid was of her hand yanking the bellpull by the door.

"What are you doing in my study?" Royston demanded.

Hidden behind the desk, Thomas reached beneath his jacket, tucking the book into his waistband at the small of his back and withdrawing his pistol.

"I told you, sir," she answered with a nervous quiver in her voice. "I tore my dress. I was coming up the stairs, looking for my brothers. They said they were heading to the billiards room when they finished fishing."

Thomas drew a deep but silent breath. She'd made a mistake by adding so much to her story. Too many details always made a story sound like, well, a *story*. And right now he needed her to put on the best performance of her life if she wanted to save herself from the gallows, or both of them from the altar.

"I tripped on the stairs and ripped my dress. See?"

A long pause followed. In the silence Thomas could imagine Royston leering at her breasts. She was bringing the earl's attention to herself in order to help him, he knew, but knowing that didn't stop the jealousy from flooding through him.

"Are you all right?" Royston asked.

"I'm fine, thank you."

A deep chuckling. "Well, you've always been a clumsy one, haven't you?"

Thomas clenched his jaw, resisting the urge to jump up and plow his fist right into Royston's face, old family friend be damned. Josie wasn't clumsy. She was one of the most careful, most graceful women he'd ever known.

She forced a light laugh of self-deprecation. "You're right, my lord."

"And what are you doing in my study?"

"This was the first room I came to where I could fix my dress. Surely you don't think I could let someone see me? Not like this—just look at me, for heaven's sake!"

Thomas gritted his teeth. As soon as he finished smashing in Royston's face, he was going to throttle his little hellcat.

"The door was locked. How did you get inside?"

"But it wasn't locked," she answered smoothly.

"It *was* locked," Royston corrected, and Thomas could hear him moving across the room. Toward Josie. His hand tightened its grip on the pistol. "I locked it myself this morning. No one else has a key."

"It wasn't locked." She laughed, not a trace of nervousness in her. *Good girl.* Thomas pictured her placing her hands on her hips, scolding like a governess, as she added, "If it was locked, I wouldn't be inside, would I?"

But the shifting direction of her voice told him that Royston was backing her around the room. If the man laid a hand on her, Thomas would kill him. Without hesitation.

"Just look at me!" she gasped. "I'm so embarrassed."

Oh, he was definitely going to throttle her! But the distraction seemed to be working, because Royston stopped mentioning the locked door. If they were lucky, the earl would believe her, but Thomas had no idea how he was going to get out of the room without being seen. He could do nothing but wait and put his faith in her, the woman he was only now beginning to trust.

"Pity, though, to ruin such a pretty dress." Royston's voice was huskier now, and an ice-cold warning shot down Thomas's spine. "And one that looks so stunning on you, Josie, dear."

Josie. Thomas ground his teeth together. *Dear.* Royston was a dead man. Just one squeak from her, and he'd put a ball through the man's heart.

"Not nearly as stunning as your wife's dresses, though, don't you agree?"

In the awkward silence following her reply, his lips twitched in silent amusement. She'd swiftly reminded Royston that he was married and that she wouldn't tolerate his attempt to be unfaithful to the countess. Thomas smiled. His little hellcat was capable of taking care of herself.

His? His heart thudded. When had he started to think of her as belonging to him?

But that was exactly how he felt about her. She'd given herself to him last night, and now she was his. And truthfully, he didn't know anymore if he could part with her.

"My wife," Royston repeated stiffly. "Yes. Well."

A knock came at the door, and Josie gave a loud gasp of feigned surprise as Greaves called out for Royston. "Oh no! No one can see me like this!"

Her voice bordered on the hysterical as she played up the moment for all she was worth. Thomas smiled with pride. She'd have been a fabulous stage actress.

"Please calm down."

"Calm down? *Calm down!*" she angrily threw Royston's words back at him. "If anyone finds us like this—with my

dress torn—alone with you in your private study—I'll be ruined. Ruined!"

"There's no need to—"

"And so will *you*," she added pointedly.

Her words of warning crackled through the air like electricity. Thomas fought hard not to laugh aloud.

"If your wife finds out, if she thinks…Oh, I'm going to
faint!"

"No, don't do—"

"We can't be seen like this! Please, go downstairs and
take Greaves with you." Thomas heard the faint rustle of fabric, the scuff of shoes on the floor as Josie presumably took
Royston by the arm and pulled him toward the door. "While
you're distracting him, I'll sneak down the hall to the music
room and fix my dress there. Please, go!"

"All right," Royston agreed. But his voice was cold, and
Thomas heard the menacing tone in its depths. "But, Miss
Carlisle, stay to Blackwood's public rooms in the future. I
would hate for you to wander somewhere you didn't belong."

"Of course, sir."

The tread of feet across the floor, the sound of the door
being opened and Royston ordering Greaves downstairs
with him, then the soft click of the closing door and the
sound of footsteps in the hall retreating away—

She hesitated. "Thomas?"

He waited patiently for her to circle around the desk to
him as he sat on the floor, his hand holding the pistol resting
casually by his wrist over his bent knee. When she knelt in
front of him, he quirked a brow at her.

"Tore your dress, did you, Jo?" he murmured dryly, his eyes
straying to the deep rip and the exposed tops of her breasts,
noting how they nearly fell out of the wrecked bodice.

A guilty look flitted across her face. "It was the only excu—"

His hand shot out to wrap behind her neck and yank her forward, catching her off-balance and tumbling her down onto his lap. He seized her mouth greedily beneath his and kissed her with a possessive ferocity that burned in his gut. Unlike anything he'd experienced before.

"Don't ever do that again," he warned, and slid his lips back along her jaw.

She shuddered as the tip of his tongue darted against her ear. "I won't."

He knew she thought he meant putting herself in harm's way, but he also meant calling another man's attention to her breasts. The thought of Royston openly leering at her sent a stab of fury through him so piercing he shook from it. He hadn't been prepared for that.

He tugged gently at her stay and slipped it lower to reveal a single breast to his jealous gaze. Making her breath come in soft pants, he traced his fingertip around the dusky pink nipple. "If Royston had touched you, Jo," he murmured quietly, watching as her nipple drew taut into a hard point as he slowly circled it, like magic, "I would have killed him."

She trembled, although he couldn't tell if the shiver that sped through her was because of the possessive way he was touching her or because she believed the brutal honesty behind his words. "He didn't," she whispered. "He didn't even try."

Relief poured through him, and he trembled as he placed a delicate kiss on her breast, then pulled her bodice back into place as neatly as he could given its gaping tear. He took her hand and helped her to her feet.

He paused to gaze down at her face, upturned slightly toward his, with her wide, expressive green eyes and those sensuous lips that tasted of peaches. He almost gave over to the urge to assure her that everything would be fine. That she would always be able to trust in him, to depend upon him never to hurt her or cause her to doubt her faith in him...

"Thomas?" she whispered, her brow furrowing with bewilderment.

Blinking, he shook himself to clear his mind. Madness—it was madness to think of anything more with her than the few hours they had left together, no matter how tempting. Just as it was madness to think she could ever truly belong to him.

He led her toward the door, warning her with a finger to his lips to be silent. And warning himself as well. There would be time later to sort out all the confusion swirling through his head and come to terms with this inexplicable way she drew him. This insatiable way his body tingled with an awareness of hers as her warm fingers tangled securely in his, even now wanting her panting and eager beneath him again. And the growing desire to find a way to keep her with him, long after the party ended.

But the worst thing he could do was admit to feelings he couldn't even be certain he was capable of possessing. Later, when he was alone, when there was quiet and time and he could concentrate, he would finally figure out how he felt about Josephine Carlisle.

And then he'd have to find a way to forget her.

* * *

Half an hour later, Josie stretched lazily across the bed in his room and watched shamelessly as Thomas dressed, buttoning his breeches and pulling his shirt over his head, then letting it hang loose around his hips. She'd never realized before how arousing it could be to watch a man dress. *Goodness.* The muscles of his back and shoulders rippled as he pulled on his tan waistcoat and let it fall open over the white shirt beneath, the same waistcoat and shirt she'd practically ripped off him just minutes before.

She drew a deep breath, then exhaled slowly in a futile attempt to steady the rapid skittering of her heart. He was magnificent. Every inch of him was hard and sculpted, and oh, what an expert lover! Her body still pulsed deliciously from the way he'd taken her so hard and fast as soon as he'd pulled her through the door. *Against* the door, in fact. In scandalous, stand-up sex. As if he couldn't *not* have her. Simply...amazing.

His eyes met hers, sensuously holding her gaze as a languid smile played at his lips.

"Is this how spies spend their time?" she asked coyly. "Picking locks to steal information, then having their way with young ladies?"

"Just the very, very lucky ones," he drawled. His smile blossomed into a full-out grin, and it shivered through her in a cascade of heat that joined the dull ache still throbbing between her legs.

Sweet heavens. She wondered, not for the first time, how long they had to wait before he could be hard and inside her again.

He slumped down into a chair in front of the small blaze glowing in the fireplace, his elbow resting on the chair arm and his head tilted against his hand. With his long legs stretched out before him, he was the perfect picture of a man utterly at ease. For a moment she wondered if he might just fall asleep right there.

"We've ruined my dress," she sighed, trying her best to distract herself from how scrumptiously rumpled he looked before she launched herself onto his lap and begged to be taken. Again.

His gaze drifted lasciviously over her. She knew she looked a fright, with her hair tumbled in tangled curls over her shoulders and her dress ruined. He hadn't bothered to remove it, ripping the tear at her neckline even more to get to her breasts and bunching her skirts up around her waist before thrusting inside her. After the breathless way he'd taken her, she couldn't have cared less about the dress, yet she futilely attempted to smooth her skirt across her legs and adjust the battered sleeves into place on her shoulders.

He commented quietly, "And I've completely ruined *you*."

There was no guilt in his voice, no regret or remorse. She didn't think she would have been able to tolerate sitting there, holding his gaze so resolutely, if she'd heard even a trace of any of that. "Thank you."

His brow inched up. "That wasn't a compliment."

"Then you shouldn't make ruination so much fun."

And it *was* fun. More fun than she'd ever imagined being with a man could be, so much so that she now understood why fallen women let themselves, well, *fall* in the first place. Especially if they'd come across a man like Thomas Matteson, one who seemed tailor-made for both her body and her mind. How could any living, breathing female deny herself that?

And yet... She bit her lip, now studying him as curiously as his gaze did her. He was a marquess and heir to a duchy. How the thought had ever crossed his mind to put himself into danger for his country she simply couldn't fathom. But he'd not only been a spy, he wanted to be one again. If she would ever be able to go on breathing after he left her, she needed to know what had drawn him into that life. And why he insisted on leaving her to return to it.

She took a deep breath to summon her courage. "How did you become a spy?"

He said nothing for a moment, the only answer his silence as he returned her gaze. In that moment's hesitation, she knew he was considering how much he could trust her, how much of himself he was willing to share. She saw his eyes harden, his face set grim, and in that moment she knew she'd lost him. After all, now that she'd promised to stop the robberies, he could both assure Royston that his guests would never be held up again and receive the recommendation he'd been promised. He'd gotten exactly what he wanted from coming here.

Her cheeks heated shamefully as she glanced down at her ruined dress—and her ruined body beneath—and her heart panged hollowly in her chest. Oh, he'd gotten so much more than just that!

He nodded stiffly toward the armoire. "There's a greatcoat in there. You can take it with you when you leave," he told her evenly. "I would suggest you tell anyone who sees you that you took a shortcut through the woods and ruined your dress, and Greaves gave you the coat when he learned of your distress."

Her chest burned, and she could only return his stare as she waited for him to say more. But he didn't, and obviously didn't want to. The rejection stabbed into her heart. She'd overstepped the line where his confidentiality was concerned, and it was clear that he'd rather be rid of her than divulge any personal information about this part of his past. Even now, after all they'd shared, he still didn't completely trust her.

Turning her face away, not wanting him to see the agony inside her, she rose from the bed and crossed to the armoire. It was filled with his clothes and toiletries, and this glimpse into his everyday life made the ache inside her clench into a lead knot in her stomach. *This* was what she longed to have with him. A simple, ordinary, day-to-day existence in which they thought nothing of the familiarity of looking at each other's personal things, exemplified by a stack of folded cravats and the comfortable intimacy of shirts and waistcoats. Including the blue evening jacket hanging in the front, the same one on which she'd spilled punch nearly a sennight ago.

She pulled the coat from its hook and slipped into it, and in her sudden desperation to flee from the room—and from him, before he could see the disappointment on her face and the frustrated tears welling in her eyes—her mind barely registered that the coat hung over her like a tent. And that it smelled deliciously of him. Her fingers shook as they scrambled to button it closed and cover all traces of the ruined dress beneath.

Her eyes burned with fresh rejection. "You're right," she whispered, unable to breathe. "I shouldn't be here. I was a fool to ever think—" The words choked in her tightening throat, and a hot pain burned inside her chest. When a tear slipped from her eye and trailed down her cheek, she swiped angrily at it with her fingers and turned her head away, furious at herself for letting him see her pain. "I'm sorry."

As she hurried past his chair toward the door, his hand shot out and grabbed her arm. A groan of frustration rose from him as he capitulated. "Josie, stay."

She shook her head. "You've got Royston's book and—"

"Stay," he repeated, and she suspected from his bleak expression that relenting cost him a great deal.

"Let me go," she begged in a breathless whisper as another tear fell from her eyes. Oh, she was a silly cake for crying in front of him! And a complete fool for losing her heart.

Instead of releasing her, he slipped his hand down her forearm, twisted his fingers through hers, and asked quietly, "Are you certain you want to know?" When she began to answer, he interrupted her. "You can never share it with anyone. People's lives would be put in danger. They could be killed, their families destroyed. Including me and mine."

Josie saw a gravity in his expression that made her throat tighten, and she didn't doubt him. As a spy he must have seen and done things that would have earned him enemies across the Continent and beyond.

But she had to know the truth about him, as surely as she needed to keep breathing in order to live. "Yes," she whispered.

A somber expression pulled at his brow then, an odd mix of determination and worry. He tugged her gently toward him, settling her onto his lap and bringing his eyes level with hers.

"I was back from the wars and done with the army, but I wanted to do more than spend my days gambling and whoring." Absently he erased the tears on her cheek with a caress of his thumb. "The War Office had an ongoing mission hunting down foreign agents inside England. They wanted someone who could move within society without suspicion, and I fit perfectly into their scheme. So I agreed to join."

"Just like that?" It all seemed too simple, too innocuous for something as dangerous as espionage. And far too sudden a decision for someone as careful as Thomas.

He blew out a long breath, the admission coming hard. "My mother was half-Indian."

"Pardon?" She blinked, not understanding that unexpected piece of information.

"She was the daughter of a maharaja who met my father when he was stationed in India. They married and had me, then we lost her to fever. I was a year old. Father remarried to an Englishwoman when I was two, and we moved back to England."

She searched his face closely. Despite his black hair, he had fair skin and sapphire-blue eyes. Nothing about him signaled that he was anything more than the result of a long line of British aristocracy, bred and born to be an English peer.

"I take after my father," he explained, once again making her believe he could read minds. Or at least hers. This ability of his should have unsettled her. Instead it connected her to him in a way she'd never been to anyone else. "I have his height, his coloring, his eyes…I look English. If someone didn't know about my mother, they'd never suspect."

She certainly hadn't expected such an exotic background for him.

"Growing up, no one ever said anything directly to me, but I heard the rumblings, the accusations and gossip that I was a half-breed."

"Thomas," she whispered, appalled that anyone would dare say that.

He tenderly brushed his fingertips along her jaw, and she suspected he was attempting to soothe her rather than letting her comfort him. "That's why I joined the army, and later why I became a spy. I wanted to prove to everyone that I was just as English as every other blue blood strolling along St. James's Street. *More*, in fact. I would be more patriotic, more dedicated to my country than they would ever be because I was willing to kill and die for England, and the most any of them was willing to do was sit in the Lords."

Willing to kill and die. He made the sacrifice sound so casual that she shuddered, and her fingers tightened their grip on his.

"I was forced to give up the army when Father inherited,

but the fieldwork with the War Office gave me purpose and made my life important."

"Your life *is* important without you having to risk yourself as a spy." *You are important to me.* She rested her palm against his cheek and felt the strength and warmth radiating from him. "Someday you'll be responsible for a duchy."

"A duke is only a place-keeper." A faint mocking tinged his voice. "A name in a list of names from two hundred years in the past. Two hundred more years into the future, and I'll be nothing but another forgotten name. Nothing more significant than that." He grew solemn, and she sensed the change in him, having become so attuned to him that his every mood registered inside her. "I want more from my life. I want purpose. I want to know that I made a difference."

"You have," she whispered, and leaned forward to kiss him reassuringly. He'd changed her life in so many ways, the extent of which she could barely fathom. None of which she dare speak aloud. And he'd trusted her with this most private secret. Her heart somersaulted with hope. After all, if he was willing to share his past, then perhaps he might be willing to share his future.

"But there's always more to do." He reached behind him and pulled out the black book that they'd taken from Royston's study. "Starting with this."

He handed her the book, then placed his hands around her waist and lifted her from his lap to set her onto her feet.

"Go on," he urged. "Read it."

Trembling, she stared down at the small book. Her work for the past two years all came to this. The proof that would find Royston guilty of what he'd done to the orphans. And the proof that would rip away Thomas's last chance at returning to the War Office.

Suddenly unable to bear the enormity of it, she shoved

the book back at him. "No, I can't! Thomas, you read it. Please."

With a smile that didn't quite reach his eyes, he rose to his feet and gently closed his hands firmly around hers as they clutched the book. "It's yours, Jo."

He cupped her face and tenderly touched his lips to hers. In that kiss she tasted grief, and it tore at her heart.

He dropped his hands away and stepped back. "Go on. Read it."

*   *   *

As Thomas watched Josie's face, he saw a hundred different emotions register there. Uncertainty, dread, a touch of fear, trust...but most of all, there was love.

Suddenly everything was clear. The puzzle he'd found in her solved itself before his eyes, and he saw her, finally, without pretense or artifice. This woman standing barefoot in her ruined dress, his coat draped like a tent over her body, had tempted him since the moment he'd seen her across the crowded ballroom. Brilliant and quick, she possessed more character, kindness, and personal strength than all the women he'd ever met put together. She was warm and soft in his arms, and she made him laugh and smile in a way he hadn't done for months. If ever. And she had him longing for more than just fleeting moments of intimacy, contemplating instead how wonderful it would be to be able to pull her into his arms and fall asleep with her not just for a few hours but all night and every night, and to have her next to him in the morning when he woke.

But that dream was impossible. She deserved a lifetime of happiness, a real home, and children, and he couldn't give her that life. Not when he still needed to recapture his own, the one he was destined to have of meaning and purpose. And Josephine had no place in that life. He could never function as a spy if he was worried about her. The fight last night, when he'd been terrified that she'd be hurt, and the incident today in the study with Royston, both proved that to him. In those moments he hadn't been thinking like an agent. He'd been thinking only of her.

Someday he hoped he could tell her the truth, how he'd known at this moment that he was in love with her.

But that he'd been unable to do anything about it.

"Read it, Jo," he insisted quietly, then stepped away from her before he yielded to the temptation to pull her into his arms and admit how he felt about her.

A ragged breath tore from him as he leaned back against the windowsill and watched her read through the book. Of all the things to happen when he was finally so close to having his life back—to meet *her*. He'd been with more women than he could remember, and his desire for all of them combined didn't equal the longing he carried for this one. One who drove him so completely mad she couldn't help but be...Well, she was the one he didn't want to give up. But if he went back to the life he'd known before he'd become an agent, the emptiness would kill him completely.

He cleared his throat. "What did you find?"

"I don't know. A list of names and dates, some notes..." Her fingers flipped through the pages, her brow furrowing in a frown. "This is the oddest thing, but in the back, it looks like an account ledger of men's names."

"A ledger of names?" he repeated, puzzled.

"At the front of the book, each page has a name written at the top. I recognize these. They're the men connected to the orphans, and some of the notes make mention of Potter in Islingham."

He shrugged, not yet convinced that she'd found the proof she needed against Royston. "Every village has at least one potter."

"Not *a* potter," she corrected firmly. "Henrietta Potter. The woman who runs the orphanage." She ran her finger over one of the pages. "And I wasn't the only one making the families pay. Listen to this—'Jane Steadwell. October 1810—Potter accepted delivery. May 1812—John Steadwell argued favorably for Italian trade vote in Commons. Roberta Huntley. January 1811—Potter accepted delivery. November 1814—George Huntley introduced canal bill in Lords.'" She glanced up at him, her eyes shining with excitement. "Royston's been manipulating votes in Parliament. Thomas, we found it! Proof of what he's been doing."

He stared at her grimly as his insides churned in a riot of betrayal and anger. Josie had been right all along. Royston had been lying to him and his family for years, pretending to be the reputable peer he wasn't— *Christ*, he'd lied to all of England, manipulating and blackmailing for his own gains. And the bastard had used innocent children to do it.

He should have been relieved that the motivation behind Josie's crimes had been validated, that they'd found the evidence that would prevent her swinging from the gallows or being sent to gaol. Hell, he should have been tugging her into his arms with joy and carrying her back to the bed, to spend the rest of the afternoon making love to her, now that he knew she was vindicated.

Yet the tingling at the back of his neck told him that what she'd found was so much worse than evidence of political favors. He held his breath, forcing himself to ask calmly, "You said there was a list of men's names?"

"In the back. That's the part that made me think of a ledger." She flipped to the end of the book. "This part looks like an account book, with a column of dates, another of payments made, one of payments received. But instead of listing items in the center column, Royston's written names."

His heart thudded, skipping a fearful beat. Royston had deep connections within the War Office. That was how the earl had known to come to him for help with the highwayman. And if Royston was engaged in political blackmail, if he was making lists of names and recording prices next to them, then... *Oh Christ.*

"Jo," he said somberly, trying to ignore the chill of dread tickling at the base of his spine, "stop reading now."

She flipped back and forth between the pages. "Here's another list, with the same columns of dates and payments made and received—"

"Josephine, stop."

"But some of the names have been crossed out... James Fitch-Batten, Stephen Graves, Vincent Matthews—"

"*Stop.*"

She looked up, and he saw the blood drain from her face, the green pools of her eyes suddenly stormy and intense. "Thomas Matteson," she whispered, reading the last name. "You knew, didn't you? When I started describing the lists— you knew your name would be here." Her eyes narrowed as suspicion darkened her face. "How?"

"Because I was once one of those men." When he pushed himself away from the window and approached her, she stepped back as if suddenly afraid of him. He stopped, hating the trepidation he saw on her face. "Listen to me—"

"What connection do you have to Royston?" she demanded as she inched away from him. "You said he was just an old family friend."

"He is. Nothing more."

"Then why is your name here?"

His jaw tightened as he glanced at the book in her hands. "Because you're right. That *is* a ledger. It's Royston's account book. He's been working with the enemy and recording his transactions inside." He couldn't tell her the entire truth, that the listed names were of British secret agents, because then her life would be placed in as much jeopardy as those of the men listed inside that book.

Her lips parted warily, the color fading from them just as it had from the rest of her face, but she boldly held his gaze. Then her eyes flicked down to the page. "Your name's been crossed off. What does th—"

"That book is dangerous. Give it to me." He held out his hand. When she didn't move, he added softly, "Please."

But she was sharp and inherently distrustful, and she must have sensed why he now wanted the book when he'd practically forced it on her only moments ago, because instead of handing it over she clutched it tightly in her arms. With a sickening knot clenching in his gut, he knew he had a fight on his hands to get it away from her.

She took another step away, angling toward the door. If she made an attempt to run, he'd be on her before she reached the hallway.

"Josephine," he ordered calmly, "hand over the book."

"Why?" She tightened her grip around it, so hard her fingertips turned white against the black cover. "What are you going to do with it?"

"Destroy it."

"I won't let you." Another step backward, almost to the door now—"This holds the proof I need to free John Cooper and stop Royston from ever harming those children again." Another step. "It has all the names, all the dates, the favors he took in return..."

That book held so much more, and because of that, he

could never let her leave this room with it. "I'm sorry, Jo, but I need that book."

"Because your name is listed inside?" Her chin jutted into the air accusingly. "Who are you helping now, Thomas—Royston, the orphans...or yourself?"

That accusation pierced his chest, but he kept his face even, his expression blank, to hide the pain she so easily inflicted on him. Then he knew why the War Office didn't want its field agents to marry. Affection made them far too vulnerable, especially to the ones they loved. "Give me the—"

She bolted.

He caught her in a heartbeat, pouncing on her and pressing her against the back of the door, the same spot where he'd pinned her less than hour before when he'd been inside her and she'd fiercely returned his passion. Now, though, not desire but fury blazed in her eyes as he pivoted her around to face him and pressed her shoulders against the white-paneled wood.

The swirling suspicion and distrust on her beautiful face broke his heart. He'd proven himself no better than those men before him who'd thought they had a right to hurt her. But he had no choice.

"Let go of me," she demanded, her voice low and trembling.

He did as she asked, sliding his hands off her shoulders, but he placed them on either side of her to keep her trapped between the door and his body. "That book will not leave this room. I cannot allow that."

"Cannot *allow*?" The disbelief ringing in her icy voice was cutting. "You'd rather John Cooper remains in gaol, or that I take his place behind bars? Because that's the decision you're making, Thomas." She hesitated, as if afraid to put voice to her fears, then whispered, "This book or me."

"I know," he said soberly.

His quiet admission tore through her in a shudder, and she stared at him as if she couldn't believe...Her eyes glistened with unshed tears. "And the evidence you need to get back into the War Office? Without Royston's recommendation, this book is all you have. You'll be destroying that as well."

He heaved out a ragged breath, the burden of fighting against her weighing heavy on his shoulders. "I know that, too."

"I don't understand." Alarm crossed her face as she slowly held up the book. "What *is* this? What has Royston been doing, exactly?"

Ignoring her questions, he gently took the book from her trembling fingers, and his solemn gaze bore into hers. "You can never tell anyone you saw this book or read the names in it, understand?"

"What is it that you're trying to hide fr—"

He slapped his palm against the door, making her jump and stopping the question he could never answer without putting her life at risk. And he would never, *ever* endanger her. "Understand?"

Silently she studied his face as if he were a stranger and not the man who had been intimate with her, so familiar with her that he now knew every curve and blemish on her body. And she the same with him. Except that she now also distrusted him, and he regretted with every bit of his being the need to threaten her into keeping her silence.

Then her expression turned harsh. All the affection he'd seen in her during the past week vanished beneath a look of fierce betrayal. "I understand," she bit out.

He turned away from her and crossed to the fireplace, grabbed the poker to stir up the small fire until the exposed coals glowed red, then made a motion of tossing the book onto the fire.

"No!" She lunged forward.

He grabbed her around the waist and pulled her in a circle, snatching her back just before the coals burned her outstretched fingers.

"Don't do this, Thomas!" she pleaded, fighting against him. "Please!"

"Josephine, stop." He pulled her farther away from the fireplace, letting her struggle but not slip from his grasp. He lowered his mouth to her ear and wrapped his arms around her, holding her tightly against him. "Please, love...let it go."

An anguished cry tore from her as the flames rose higher in the fireplace, and in a matter of seconds, nothing could be seen but a pile of ash. She stopped struggling, and with a fierce shove, she jerked herself free of his arms. Her glare cut like ice at his betrayal.

"Tomorrow," she said firmly, her hands clenching into fists at her sides, "the party will end, and you can return to London. No one will ever know what happened between us. And we can forget we ever met or made the mistake of being intimate."

The pain that ripped through his chest was as blinding as that of the bullet that had pierced his side. "Josephine," he rasped out hoarsely, "listen to me—"

"You're good at keeping secrets," she choked out, the tears shining in her eyes only compounding the pain clawing inside him. "It's what spies do best, isn't it? Surely you can keep this one."

"Jo, please." He reached for her.

She put up her hand in warning and backed away. "Do *not* touch me—do not *ever* touch me again!"

He dropped his hand to his side. He deserved every bit of her anger for being weak enough to take her innocence when he could offer her no future, for making her distrust him when he could provide no answers. Yet he couldn't do what she wanted and simply ride away tomorrow, to leave her at the mercy of Royston when he discovered the ledger was gone and to leave John Cooper in the hands of the constable. He certainly would never be able to forget her or how it felt to hold her in his arms. And the very last thing he wanted was never to be able to touch her again. "What happens to you while I'm riding back to London?"

Her chin rose, daring him to challenge her. "I'll turn myself in for arrest."

"I won't let you do that," he assured her calmly.

"Just try to stop me!"

She turned on her heels, and as her hand swiped angrily at her eyes, the small movement of vulnerability sliced through him like a saber. Pausing only to glance into the hallway to make certain no one saw her leave, she fled the room without looking back.

The door slammed closed behind her.

Cursing at himself, Thomas reached beneath his waistcoat and withdrew the black book, the same one Josie had flipped through just moments before. He opened it and scanned through the list of names to confirm what he already knew to be the truth before he tossed it onto the bed in disgust.

Somehow Royston had gotten the names of the War Office's secret operatives, both here in England and on the Continent, and was selling their names to the enemy, one man at a time, with the audacity to keep an ongoing record of the prices on their heads. Like pigs sent to market for slaughter. His name had been crossed off only because he'd been released as an agent and so carried no more value. But many of the men whose names were marked with payments had been caught by the enemy, tortured, killed...and the same would happen to Josie if anyone ever discovered she'd seen that list.

He'd made the right decision just now, he *knew* that. The lives of the men listed in that book and Josie's safety were far more important than his own selfish wants. By letting her think he'd destroyed the book, though, and with it all her hopes of linking Royston to the orphans, he had also shattered whatever trust she'd placed in him.

But he now had exactly what he'd come to Lincolnshire to get—information he could trade for a foothold back inside the War Office. Information, in fact, that would make Bathurst welcome him back as an even bigger hero than when he'd left.

Except that he didn't feel like a hero. He felt like a ruthless bastard.

He ran a frustrated hand through his hair. The party ended tomorrow. Not only would he no longer have an excuse to linger at Blackwood Hall, especially now that Royston was convinced the highwayman had been caught, but thanks to him and that damned book, Josie was now determined to turn herself in.

One day. He had one day to put together a plan to rescue Cooper from gaol, arrest Royston for treason, help the orphans, and save both Josie and her reputation, all at the same time.

Good Lord. Defeating Napoleon had been easier.

CHAPTER ELEVEN

$\mathscr{L}$et me see if I understand correctly." Colonel Nathaniel Grey slid an inscrutable glance from Thomas to Edward Westover, former colonel of the Scarlet Scoundrels and current Duke of Strathmore, who sat beside him at the table in the Islingham Village posting inn.

Both men appeared bedraggled from riding straight through on horseback from London. In plain, dark clothes and sporting two days' growth of unshaven beard, they were unrecognizable, although Thomas also counted on the fact that no one in the tiny Lincolnshire village would ever suspect that among them sat two of the most important men in England.

"You came to Lincolnshire to stop a highwayman, only to discover that the highwayman is a baron's daughter who's been playing Robin Hood and robbing Royston's rich guests to give to poor orphans. The same woman who accidentally stumbled upon Royston's treason and who now wants to hand herself over to the authorities in order to free a local sheep farmer from gaol." Grey paused. "Do I have all that correct?"

"Yes," Thomas affirmed glumly.

"The same woman who is now his lover, don't forget," Edward put in dryly.

Thomas gritted his teeth. "Yes."

"Tell me." Grey leaned forward across the table and arched a brow. "How did you manage not to get yourself killed by the French?"

Thomas scowled at the two men. As his closest friends in the world, Edward and Grey were like brothers to him, and so they'd certainly never let him live this down. But he was in no mood today for their antics. Time was running out. "Will you help me or not?"

"Of course we'll help." Grey signaled for another round of ale. "We rode all the way here as soon as we received your message, didn't we?"

"I sent that message four days ago, before I knew about Royston's real motives." And before he'd fallen in love with Josie. But his feelings made no difference now. He knew what he had to do, and he needed Grey and Edward's help to carry out his plans. His shoulders sagged as he blew out a breath. "But I'm damnably glad you're here."

"You're certain that he's selling the identities of agents to the French?" Edward's expression softened with concern. "Accusing a peer of treason is no small charge."

"I recognized the names." Withdrawing the book from his inside jacket pocket and sliding it across the table toward Grey, he pinned his brother-in-law with a look. "Including mine."

Without a word the former army officer turned War Office agent took the book and thumbed through the pages. Thomas watched him closely for any trace of a reaction, but

Grey was one of the best spymasters the War Office had ever produced, and not a flicker of recognition of any of the names listed inside registered on his face, although Thomas was certain he knew every one.

"I've no idea how Royston came by it," Thomas told him quietly. "But someone inside the War Office is supplying him with information."

Closing it slowly, Grey passed back the book so Thomas could return it to the study before Royston realized it was missing. "That's enough to hang both the earl and whoever gave him the names. And the girl?"

"I'd rather she didn't swing," Thomas said quietly, avoiding his friends' gazes as he slipped the book inside his jacket pocket. "I've grown quite fond of her neck." And other parts of her as well. Parts he would most likely never again see.

"She did plan and lead the robberies," Edward stated in that deceptively smooth and aristocratic tone of his, the same one that belied all the horrors he'd witnessed in the heat of battle before he'd inherited. Anyone who looked at the duke now and thought he was just another dandy blue blood highly underestimated him. "Who else knows of her involvement?"

"A handful of men who help her, all of them former orphans. None of them will give her up."

"What makes you so certain?" Grey asked suspiciously.

"She's been robbing carriages for the past two years, and Royston's offered a reward since the first holdup. If they'd wanted blood money, they would have divulged her by now. Those men are loyal."

"And the farmer?"

"Cooper has refused to answer questions. The only evidence the constable has is the horse."

"Flimsy evidence to try him as a highwayman," Edward mumbled.

Thomas shook his head. "Royston's pressuring the constable. He wants this ended. Immediately."

Grey and Edward exchanged glances, but Thomas understood the silent communication. Cooper might swear that he'd go to the gallows before he gave up Josie, but the three men sitting around the table knew better. As spies and army officers, themselves trained in interrogation to get whatever answers they needed, they knew Cooper would break eventually, especially if Royston threatened his wife and children.

"Well, then," Grey said solemnly but with brotherly concern, "I suppose Edward and I need to get busy saving your arse."

Hiding his grim relief, Thomas reached for the ale. With Grey and Edward's help, he could put an end to this mess. They could stop Royston before any more agents died or went missing. No more unwanted children would be abandoned at the orphanage in exchange for political favors, and no one would ever know that Josie was behind the robberies. His recommendation to the War Office was secured in the evidence inside that book, and Bathurst would have no choice but to reinstate him. Of course, he would lose Josie But then, she never could have been his. He'd been right about that from the beginning. Yet he would have everything else he'd spent the past year so desperately trying to regain, and he'd once again have purpose.

So why did he feel dead inside, more lifeless and broken than he'd been since the bullet pierced his side?

"I have a question," Edward interjected quietly, watching as Thomas raised the tankard to his lips. "Does the girl know you're in love with her?"

Thomas choked. Coughing on the ale, he shot a piercing glare at his former colonel. "How I feel isn't important." The expressions of his two companions never changed, but he knew they'd both noticed that he hadn't denied the accusation. "We make certain she's safe, and we stop Royston. Then we all go back to London, and I return to the War Office. End of story."

The two men exchanged glances, then Grey nodded slowly. "All right, if that's what you want." He tossed a coin to the barmaid, who set down three more tankards of ale and smiled flirtatiously at the three men before sashaying away, not one of them paying her a second look. "When do we begin?"

"Tonight."

*   *   *

Thomas was staring at her.

Again.

Josie knew without having to glance down the long dining table at him as he sat at the opposite end, stuck between Mrs. Peterson and Miranda Hodgkins, that his eyes had once again drifted toward her, just as they'd done all through tonight's farewell dinner. She felt his gaze on her as surely as if he'd brushed his fingertips down her bare arm, and even from so far away, he made her tremble.

Blasted man!

Swallowing hard, she kept her gaze firmly on Admiral Wesson beside her as the gray-whiskered naval officer finished some story about facing down pirates in the West Indies. She refused to glance at Thomas. *Absolutely* refused! She would not give that man the pleasure of knowing she was doing anything other than ignoring him, as if she couldn't care less that he existed at all. And she didn't. And just as soon as she was able to stop thinking about him, she planned on telling him so.

"That was when the cannons fired on us," Admiral Wesson told her, and she forced a smile as if she were paying attention to him instead of the bothersome man at the other end of the room.

From the moment Thomas had sauntered into the farewell dinner—late, of course, which was why he'd ended up at the opposite end of the table, much to her relief and to Miranda Hodgkins's sheer delight—he'd been staring as if trying to catch her gaze. Whether in silent apology or condemnation, she didn't know, but neither signified. She was done with him now. True, he made her feel alive and special in ways no other man ever had, and she hadn't known until she met him what physical pleasures men and women shared together. Or what emotional mountains and valleys caring about someone could create.

Thomas Matteson, Marquess of Chesney, made her feel all that, and more.

But Thomas Matteson, War Office agent, had caused her to commit the biggest mistake of her life by trusting in him to make the morally right choice.

From the head of the table, Royston laughed easily, relaxed and confident now that he was certain he'd caught the highwayman, and she forced her eyes to stay glued to Admiral Wesson even as her chest squeezed so painfully with frustrated anger that she couldn't breathe.

Oh, she'd made a *terrible* mistake!

Admiral Wesson frowned and rested a hand on her forearm. "My dear, are you all right? You've gone suddenly pale." He leaned toward her and smiled reassuringly. "I fear I've upset you with my story, but do not worry. We handed it to those pirates right smartly, and not one of His Majesty's sailors perished!"

A deep breath escaped her, one of irritation at herself for

letting Thomas rattle her to the point that even the old naval officer could see her distress. "Thank heavens for that."

"Yes," Sebastian muttered from the other side of her, also forcibly caught up in the admiral's tale as a result of proximity, since Elizabeth Carlisle had carefully seen to the seating arrangements that put Miranda Hodgkins and the other eligible young ladies as far away from her sons as possible. "Thank heavens that story ended." He reached for his glass of wine. "Happily, that is."

Scowling at her brother's lack of manners, Josie turned toward him—

And caught Thomas's gaze directly. Her breath strangled in her throat at the heat she saw in those blue eyes. *Dear God.* Why was she so helpless over him, this infuriating, impossible, utterly devastating man?

She let him hold her gaze for only a moment, just a few heartbeats that pounded through her ears like a drum corps and drowned out the rest of the world, then she forced her eyes away. No one who happened to be watching them would have suspected anything more than an accidental meeting of gazes. But in that moment Josie remembered every tender word he'd ever spoken to her, every laugh they'd shared, the feel of the fire spreading beneath her skin as she shattered in his arms—just as she sensed the painful onslaught of the void her future would be without him, of the emptiness she'd carry forever inside her heart.

Blinking hard against the sting of her unshed tears, she turned away in her chair, put her back toward him, and fixed a far-too-bright smile onto her face for the admiral.

Tomorrow Thomas would be gone. He'd return to London and the life he wanted in the War Office, thriving among the exclusivity and excitement of the *ton*. In a few weeks, perhaps a few months if she'd made a bigger impression on him than she realistically believed, he would think of her as nothing more than a woman with whom he'd shared an intimacy at a house party. By next year he'd most likely not even remember that.

Lady Royston rose from her chair to signal the end of dinner, and Josie gave a shaking sigh of relief. The men would stay behind in the dining room for at least an hour before rejoining the women, and during that time, while Thomas was trapped with Royston and his cronies, she would pretend a headache and beg her mother to take her home so she would never have to see him again. Because she knew she wouldn't be able to bear it.

Everyone stood, the room suddenly in motion as the ladies moved to excuse themselves and the men shifted to sit closer to Royston at the head of the table and to make passing the port easier. Pockets of conversations flared up as dinner companions shared their last polite banter and friends who had been sitting apart from each other paused to briefly exchange pleasantries. In the shuffle, Josie kept her gaze low and made her way toward the doorway.

A hand closed over her elbow.

"I need to speak with you." The familiar deep voice at her shoulder curled heat down her spine.

She stiffened, her back rigid. "We have nothing more to talk about." With a jerk, she pulled her arm free. "Good night, Lord Chesney."

Then she walked on, her head held high and her gaze firmly focused in front of her despite the shaking in her weakening knees. She forced herself with every ounce of determination she possessed not to give him the satisfaction of glancing back.

Walking on, she headed straight through the drawing room and out the double doors on the other side, then down the hall and through one of the morning rooms, where she opened the French doors leading out onto the side terrace and continued right out into the darkness. Most likely she would have kept right on walking even then if not for the stone balustrade surrounding the terrace, which prevented her from stepping out into the garden and losing herself completely under the cover of night.

Even then she pressed against the balustrade, leaning on her palms and staring out at the dark gardens. She trembled, her elbow still burning from his touch, and inhaled deeply to fill her lungs with the cool night air and calm herself. *Breathe . . .* Tomorrow Thomas would be gone, awake at first light and riding hard for London as soon as the morning mists cleared, as if he'd never arrived in Islingham and stepped into her life at all. *Just breathe . . .*

And while he was riding for London, the life she'd come to know would end, and she'd be locked away, trading herself for John Cooper. Gaol had always been a possibility. From the very first time she'd galloped after a coach, she'd known that, yet even then she'd been willing to give her life for those of the orphans. But that was before she'd met Thomas, before she'd begun to look forward to having a future. Now that her life would never include him, though, would it matter what became of her?

She gave a strangled laugh. Would the constable even believe her?

She'd covered her tracks so well during the past two years that she feared tomorrow would be just as she'd warned Thomas—that no one would think it possible that she could be a highwayman. The daughter of a baron, for goodness' sake! And what proof did she have that she was the highwayman, anyway? None. Even her horse implicated John Cooper, not her. Ironically, the only person who could definitively place blame on her for the crimes was Thomas, and by the time she turned herself in tomorrow, he'd be miles away.

She pressed her hand against her forehead. God, she was pathetic. She couldn't even get herself arrested properly.

Thomas.

The back of her neck tingled as she sensed him step up behind her in the dark shadows like a panther, graceful and silent. And so very dangerous. Without a sound or a touch, he sent her heart racing and the blood coursing hot through her body. He reached around her to place both hands on the balustrade on either side of her, trapping her within his arms and standing close enough that the heat of his body seeped into her back and twined shivers down her spine. She sent up a silent prayer that he couldn't see the way he still affected her. And most likely always would.

"Did you wear that dress for me?" his deep voice purred smoothly over her shoulder, his mouth close to her ear.

"Of course not." A lie. She'd chosen the emerald-green dress specifically with him in mind. With its low neckline and tight bodice that showed off her breasts, it was the most spectacular gown she owned, and with its sleeveless cut and narrow shoulder straps, it was also the one that revealed the most flesh. Wearing it had been childish of her, a fanciful attempt to remind him of how much he'd enjoyed her body and to show him exactly what he'd given up when he chose Royston's ledger over her.

But apparently he *had* noticed, and goose bumps dotted her skin at the thought that even now he still paid attention to her.

"Pity." His breath fanned warmly across her cheek and stirred the tendrils of hair against her face. "Because you look beautiful."

She closed her eyes. "Stop it," she ordered weakly. She held her breath, half fearing he would ignore her chastisement, half fearing he wouldn't.

"My apologies, then." But there was nothing apologetic in the husky tone of his voice. Rather she suspected he knew exactly how much his comment tortured her, devil take him. "Admiral Wesson must be a fascinating dinner partner."

"The admiral is a *true* gentleman." The backhanded insult was sharp, but he deserved it.

"You didn't take your eyes off him all night."

She caught her breath. Was that jealousy? Surely not. "He told exciting stories about his adventures in the Caribbean fighting pirates."

"All lies. Wesson was stationed in Greenwich for most of his career. He's never left European waters."

"How do you kn—" She clamped her mouth shut, realizing with exasperation exactly how he knew.

"My stories, on the other hand, *are* true." He leaned closer, so close that his hard chest brushed tantalizingly against her back. "I really did risk life and limb for England."

"No need to worry. I promise not to tell a soul about you." With a haughty sniff, she shifted away and pressed closer to the balustrade, but immediately he followed, only trapping her more securely. "In fact, I plan on never thinking about you again."

"Pity," he repeated in a hot murmur. "Because I certainly plan on thinking about *you*."

With a cry of vexation, she whirled around in his arms to face him. For a moment he must have thought she'd given in to her desires, because she saw his sensuous lips curl into a self-pleased smile, which only frustrated her more.

"Stop it!" She put her hands against his chest and fiercely shoved.

He stepped back, putting distance between them. His smile faded, but his eyes were just as heated as ever.

So was the ache that sped through her. "I came out here to be alone, so please leave."

But he only folded his arms across his chest and remained firmly in place. "We have to talk."

"There is nothing left between us to discuss."

"There's a mountain left between us," he muttered, risking a second shove by leaning closer. "But that's not why I needed to see you."

Inexplicably, her chest plummeted painfully at his words. He didn't need her; he needed something *from* her. "What do you want?" she demanded angrily, her chest burning with fresh rejection.

The words slipped out before she realized what she was asking. Stupid, stupid girl! His eyes flickered heatedly, and she thought for a moment he might just answer *I want you*, and if he did, *oh God*! She might very well lose the thin string of resolve to which she was clinging and throw herself into his arms.

But, thankfully, he didn't rise to the bait and said instead, "You cannot turn yourself in for the robberies."

"I can, and I will."

"No one will believe you. I've made certain of it."

"How?" She clenched her fists, the familiar doubts rising inside her. She'd made herself vulnerable once by trusting him, and he'd only hurt her. Very deeply. She wouldn't let herself be wounded by him again. "What did you do?"

"Me? Nothing."

Oh, how he made her head spin! "You just said—" She groaned in frustration. "Oh, never mind! Just go back to London tomorrow where you belong, and I'll convince the constable it was me all along."

"With what proof?"

"The cottage. There's plenty of proof there."

"Not anymore."

She stared at him as anguish tightened in her belly. So he'd destroyed everything there that incriminated her, leaving no trace of the robberies. Or of the passion they'd shared. Her heart plummeted. It was as if he were systematically erasing himself from her life, and that realization hurt her so deeply that her breath strangled. She had to swallow hard to clear the knot from her throat to speak. "I have my gang, remember? You'll be gone, but they'll vouch for my involvement. John Cooper will—"

"Listen to me." He took a step closer, his hands again returning to the balustrade on either side of her. He leveled his eyes with hers. "By this time tomorrow, everything will be resolved with the highwayman."

But nothing would be resolved between *them*. He would be far away by then, heading back to his life in London, and she would be here, somehow trying to survive without him. She took a deep breath and resigned herself to that lonely future. "How?"

"I'm setting John Cooper free."

Her eyes widened, her anger vanishing beneath her surprise.

"I'm going to the gaol at midnight to free him. He can hide at the cottage until we find a way to prove he isn't the highwayman."

"I want to help." She reached for his arm, and as her hand closed around the hard muscle beneath his jacket sleeve, heat seeped up her fingers. Her heart skipped. Would she ever be able to touch him again? Ignoring the fresh stab in her hollow chest, she pressed, "What can I do? I know the village. I can—"

"What you can do is go home and stay there until morning. You'll have a solid alibi that you were nowhere near the gaol when Cooper was freed." He paused and his eyes softened. "And I won't have to worry about you getting hurt."

"I want to—"

"*Damnation*, Jo! For once just do as I tell you." He grabbed her shoulders, but instead of shaking her, he closed his fingers around her arms and shifted her closer. "At eleven o'clock I need you to get a headache and ask Robert to take you home. He'll be more than happy to leave with you by then."

"Why?"

"Because I spent all dinner telling Miranda Hodgkins how much he fancies her."

"You didn't!" She gaped at him, not knowing whether to be angry or to laugh with amusement. But the way his blue eyes flickered over her arousingly in the darkness...well, there was nothing amusing about *that*.

"I'll excuse myself shortly after you leave, then sneak out and ride for the village. And you'll be home by then, innocently tucked into bed." His hands slipped slowly down her arms to encircle her waist and draw her against him, the subtle movement anything but innocent.

For one moment she stiffened against the sweet torture of his embrace, not trusting him and certainly not trusting her own weakness for him. She should have been furious at him for destroying her evidence against Royston, for his betrayal of both her and the orphans. But at that moment, surrounded by the protective circle of his arms, all she could think about was how this would be the last time the two of them would be alone together, the last time she would ever be in his arms...With a soft cry, she let herself fall against him, her arms going around him as she rested her head against his chest. Closing her eyes against the rhythm of his heartbeat beneath her cheek, she shivered at the wonderful contact of bodies and the familiar heat and strength of him. Hot tears gathered at her lashes.

"By tomorrow morning," he assured her, his lips resting at her temple, "John Cooper will be free, and you'll be safe."

"And you'll have left for London," she breathed, the painful words barely a sound on her lips as desolation stabbed into her belly.

His shoulders sagged. "This isn't easy," he admitted, gently stroking his knuckles across her cheek. "Having to leave you behind is killing me."

She raised her head and gazed up at him, his handsome face blurry beneath the tears welling in her eyes. "Then why are you doing it?"

"Josephine." Her name tore from him in a hoarse rasp. "What you're asking…" He drew a ragged breath, then shook his head. "There is no future with me."

She nodded knowingly, unable to speak for fear of breaking down. Nothing had changed between them. He'd found a way to save Mr. Cooper but not her heart. Nothing could save that.

"Eleven o'clock," he repeated firmly. "You'll go home, and I'll take care of everything. Trust me." With a last, heart-wrenching kiss, he reluctantly released her and stepped back. "Now go inside before you're missed. I'll be along in a few minutes."

Not trusting herself to speak, she moved away from him to return to the drawing room. But she let herself pause to tearfully glance back one last time before stepping inside and closing the door.

Thomas watched her go, then leaned against the stone balustrade and closed his eyes, taking a quiet moment to gather himself. Even now, under the pressure of the night's pending events and tomorrow's consequences to live through, and knowing what parts he needed all of them to play, he longed for more time alone with her. But that wasn't going to happen.

Dressed all in black and blending into the night, Nathaniel Grey stepped out of the dark shadows of the garden and approached silently to join him. Leaning back against the balustrade beside Thomas, he folded his arms across his chest.

"It's set, then?" Grey asked quietly.

Thomas nodded. "She'll be at the gaol at midnight."

"How can you be certain?"

"Because she never does what I tell her." *Damned woman.* She couldn't even let him slink back to London in peace like a coward. He grimaced. "I suppose you overheard everything."

"Not everything, but enough." He added thoughtfully, "She loves you, you know."

Thomas nodded heavily as he admitted, "I know."

"Which should worry you."

"It does."

"And you love her."

He blew out a hard breath. "Which completely terrifies me."

Shoving himself to his feet, he began to pace, cursing at himself with each step.

Grey's eyes followed him silently back and forth across the terrace. While Thomas didn't know what his brother-in-law thought of the exchange with Josie, his gaze softened as he watched Thomas pace. The two men had been best friends in Spain, brothers born of blood and battle; then Grey married Emily, and they became true brothers. Grey was also the only other person who understood the choice he was being forced to make—his life as an agent or the woman he loved. Grey had chosen Emily. If he did the same, if he chose Josie, would marriage and family be enough compensation for him, too?

But if it wasn't, if he gave up all hope of returning to the War Office and the restlessness and anxiety continued... well, then it would be too late, and he'd have destroyed two lives.

His hand shook with aggravation at his impossible choice as he raked his fingers through his hair. He'd spent years chasing the enemy, and despite several close calls, he'd never once felt as uncertain as he did now. Because of a pretty, green-eyed slip of a woman who both aroused and relaxed him in a way no other female ever had. Nor likely ever would.

"When you met Emily," Thomas bit out, uncomfortable at prying into his brother-in-law's private life with his sister but finding he desperately needed to understand, "how did you know she was special?"

"She shot a gun at me."

He stopped and fully faced Grey, hands on hips. "You are *not* helpful."

"I'm only here for the gaolbreak." Grey shrugged. "You're on your own for the heartbreak."

"Thanks." Thomas grimaced and began pacing again.

Grey watched him for a few moments, then stared down at his hands and quietly admitted, "Marrying Emily was the best thing that ever happened to me, and not a day goes by that I don't thank God for her. Heaven only knows what my life would be without her." He paused, then added solemnly, "You love this woman, Thomas. I can see it in every inch of you, and it's clear as day that she loves you, too. What you need to be asking yourself isn't what makes her the woman with whom you should spend the rest of your life—I think you already know that in your heart. What you should be asking yourself is what your life is going to be like without her."

Thomas shot him a sideways glare. All this talk of Josie had his anxiety rising, his heart pounding— *Damnation!* He didn't need Grey reminding him of what he was giving up by letting her go. For the first time in a year, he wasn't afraid of the darkness or what lurked there. Because of her. She'd brought him a peace and comfort no one else had been able to give, and more—she'd brought him hope and happiness. And yet... "This is my chance to finally get back into the War Office. I'd be a damned fool to let it go."

Grey shook his head regretfully. "You'd be a damned fool to let *her* go."

Thomas wheeled on him. "You think I planned for this? Falling for a woman at the worst possible time?" He sucked in a harsh breath, then expelled it slowly from his lungs in a futile attempt to steady himself. "Being an agent again was the only thing that kept me alive during the past year, that gave me reason to heal and get out of bed every morning. And now, to simply stop wanting that, to give up everything that had any meaning in my life—" He stopped, the words clenching in his throat. "If I give up that, what do I have left to give me purpose?"

Grey's expression softened, his affection for Thomas obvious on his face. "You'll have her," he said quietly. Pushing himself away from the balustrade, he placed a brotherly hand on Thomas's shoulder. "And trust me, that will be more than enough." He held out his hand. "It's time now."

Thomas reached beneath his jacket and placed the bundle of pages in his hand. Then Grey slapped him reassuringly on the back and slipped away into the dark garden. Thomas watched him leave until he faded into the black shadows and completely vanished as if he'd never been there at all.

A burst of male laughter sounded faintly from the dining room and disturbed the quiet darkness. Rubbing the knot of tension at the back of his neck, he paused to listen, and something he couldn't put a name to swept achingly down his spine.

What must it be like to be so carefree and secure as to be able to laugh and drink with a roomful of strangers? He'd never known that kind of ease, and he doubted he ever would. Certainly not if he returned to the War Office. And yet the ability to get drunk in a crowd and find lewd stories amusing was little to lose in comparison to what he'd gained through service to his country. But would his work be enough? In ten years, or twenty, when he was no longer an agent and had inherited a duchy, would the memories be enough to sustain him, when he no longer had anything real to fill the void in his life?

Closing his eyes for a hard moment, he shook his head. *Good God*—twenty years…whom was he fooling? His work wouldn't be enough to fight back the anxiousness he knew would come unbidden tomorrow night, and every lonely night after that, if he wasn't with Josie.

He took a deep breath, knowing what he had to do, and turned toward the house to rejoin the party. In one hour the clock would strike eleven.

And the rest of his life would begin.

CHAPTER TWELVE

~~~~~~

The mantel clock's hands reached midnight.

Standing with a group of men on the other side of the room, idly listening to their heated debate regarding the best birding dogs and not caring one whit, Thomas pretended to ignore the cling-clang of the clock's tiny bells and raised his coffee cup to his lips.

His eyes swept around the room and took in the remaining guests. Most everyone was still there, enjoying the last night of the party and now freely delighting in both Royston's hospitality and each other's company, right down to old Lady Denton, who had cornered Lord Tinsdale with a rant about the tragic dearth of elegant hats on Bond Street this season. He smiled faintly at Miranda Hodgkins, whose spirit hadn't been dampened by Robert's departure with Josie an hour prior and who had turned her attention to Quinton. Someone had struck up a card game, and one of the women played softly on the pianoforte.

But Josie was gone, just as he'd asked her to be. As

eleven o'clock had approached, Josie had played her part well. Her hand pressing to her forehead, her fingers rubbing at her temples—all the signs of a headache coming on gradually so that by the time the clock struck and she claimed to be ill enough that she needed to go home, everyone believed her. Her acting was utterly brilliant, and Thomas was proud of her, more than he had a right to be.

The butler entered the room.

Thomas's eyes followed Greaves as he crossed to Royston and bowed his head apologetically for interrupting as he handed a folded note to his employer, then waited in case the earl wanted him to send a reply.

But Royston waved the man away as he read the note. Then his eyes met Thomas's across the room. A smile spread across his face.

"Chesney!" Royston turned toward the door and motioned for him to follow. "A word with you."

"Of course," he muttered, setting down his coffee and nodding politely to the other guests as he made his way into the front hall after Royston.

"Ha!" Royston gleefully smacked the note with his hand, then held it up for Thomas to see as if it were a trophy. "Have my carriage brought round," he barked at a footman.

"What's the message?" Thomas's attention shifted between the earl's delighted face and the note.

"News from the constable." Instead of simply handing the note over, he slapped it against Thomas's chest and smiled arrogantly. "Cooper has decided to confess."

Thomas frowned and pretended to read the note. "You're going into the village tonight? At this hour?"

"*We're* going," Royston corrected. "I want you there. If Cooper changes his mind, you might have to be…persuasive."

Thomas had no intention of interrogating John Cooper tonight, using harsh measures or not. Yet he nodded slowly. "I'd like to be there when this ends."

Gleefully Royston slapped him on his shoulder, then stalked through the wide front doors when a black carriage pulled up to the steps. Thomas followed slowly after.

The footman shut the carriage door after the two men settled inside. Royston pounded his fist against the roof to signal to the coachman, and the vehicle lurched into motion, rumbling down the drive and into the night.

* * *

The bell of the village church finished striking midnight.

In the dark shadows falling along High Street, dressed in black clothing she'd stolen from Quinn's room, Josie pressed against the wall of the cobbler's shop and watched the gaol. Midnight. Thomas should have been here by now, but the street was quiet and still. She held her breath, waiting, listening intently but hearing nothing, not even the sound of horse hooves against the cobblestones. The minutes ticked on, yet there was no sign of Thomas.

Her heart thumped with worry. Something wasn't right.

She moved away from the shadows and quickly crossed the street, then followed along the fronts of the old buildings to the stone gaol. To her surprise, the door wasn't locked, and it opened with a loud creak. Slipping inside, she closed it behind her and pressed herself back against it to calm her rapid breathing and the pounding of her heart.

Inside, a lantern hanging on a peg dimly lit the little gaol, which also served as the constable's office, the surveyor's office, and the courtroom of the local magistrate. Two stone-

and-bar cells sat side by side in the back of the building. A door closed off the left cell, its top half comprised of thick iron bars, its bottom of a solid sheet of metal, while the door to the cell on the right stood wide open. The main room was empty, with no sign of the constable nor any of his men. Nor of Thomas.

"Mr. Cooper?" she called out in hushed tones. Was she too late? Her heart ached, and she pressed her hand against her chest. Had Thomas already come and gone? Oh God, had she missed her last chance to ever see him again?

A rustle of movement came from behind the cell door, then a shadowy face appeared at the barred window. John Cooper answered, "Aye, miss."

Her throat tightened with both relief and fear. Thomas hadn't been here yet. Something was definitely wrong. "Are you... Did someone... ?" Taking a deep breath, she pushed herself away from the door and stepped carefully across the room. Her body trembled with fear. Chasing after coaches in the dark while hidden safely behind a mask required a completely different sort of courage from boldly sneaking into the gaol itself. She was tempting fate again, and it terrified her. "Where are the constable and his men?"

"Gone a short while ago. A message arrived, an' they all left in a hurry."

"A message?" Could that have been Thomas, some trick to get the men to abandon the building so he could free Mr. Cooper? Yet he wasn't there, and his absence stirred the little hairs on her arms with fear.

"Aye. Then a man arrived—"

Her hands grasped the bars, and she rose up on tiptoe to peer into the cell. Her heart thudded. "He did?"

"Said everything would be set to rights tonight."

Thomas. "Then I haven't missed him," she murmured,

hope warming her chest. One last chance to see him, to talk to him...

Mr. Cooper frowned at her. "Pardon?"

She shook her head. How could she ever explain to him how much Thomas meant to her? Then guilt replaced her relief, and her eyes burned with tears. "Mr. Cooper, I am so sorry about everything. The arrest, the questions—your family must be so upset." She swallowed hard around the growing knot in her throat. "I never wanted this."

"I knew when I agreed to help you what it could mean. I was a lucky one. I got out of that orphanage and found a good place on a farm with a decent family. I know other children weren't so lucky." His lips curled into a determined smile. "Once I learned what you were planning two years ago, miss, nothing could have stopped me from helping you. Like you, I wasn't one of them children the earl put there, but we all have to watch out for each other's backs, don't we?"

"Yes," she whispered, thinking of Thomas's assurances that he would keep her safe and protect her. Yet he was wrong. He couldn't keep her safe from the consequences of her own actions; the time had come to face those. When the constable returned, she planned to confess to all the crimes and take responsibility for every last stolen penny.

"That man left something for you, miss. Said you'd need it tonight."

"What is it?"

"Don't know. He left it there in the other cell."

What on earth did Thomas think she'd need for a gaolbreak? She couldn't imagine, yet curiously she slipped into the adjoining cell and froze. A black book sat on the cot. That couldn't be—it was *impossible*! She'd seen him toss it into the fire, watched it burn to ash...Oh, but she should have known. That man excelled at doing the impossible.

As she reached for it, a loud metal clank reverberated through the stone building. She gasped and pivoted on her heel as the cell door swung shut behind her.

"No!" she cried out fiercely and lunged forward, but she was too late. The door was locked.

A stranger peered inside the shadows of the dark cell at her, then folded his arms and leaned his shoulder easily against the doorframe. "Thank you for your help, Cooper," he called into the adjoining cell.

"My pleasure, sir." Then Mr. Cooper shuffled to the back of his cell, giving them privacy.

"So you're the woman at the heart of all this," he mused, holding her incredulous gaze for a moment before sweeping his eyes over her.

"Who are you?" she demanded as her hands clenched the bars tightly, anger and fear squeezing her chest at the amused gleam in his eyes. This was *not* amusing!

"Colonel Nathaniel Grey." He flashed her an easy grin. "At your service."

She was certain he was attempting to charm her with his smile, just as she was certain many ladies found him to be exactly that—charming. But she'd experienced the warmth of Thomas's true charm, and for her, this man's was nothing but hollow pretense in comparison.

She narrowed her eyes. "Who *are* you?"

"Chesney didn't mention me?" He mocked a wounded look and shook his head with an exaggerated sigh. "Even during a gaolbreak he keeps me from getting all the glory with the ladies."

Thomas. Her heart raced at the mention of his name, and her hands tightened on the bars. "Where is he?"

"Rather busy at the moment, so he sent me to tie up the loose ends in tonight's plan."

"Loose ends?"

He quirked a brow. "You."

"*Me?*" The word popped out as a squeak. "But I'm not even supposed to be here!"

"No, you're exactly where you're supposed to be. Chesney said you were too stubborn to do as you were told." His expression softened. "You'll fit in perfectly with the rest of the Matteson ladies."

The blood drained from her face. This man knew Thomas, but he obviously didn't know him as well as she did if he would suggest something as impossible as her becoming a Matteson lady. "You're mistaken. Lord Chesney and I do not have any sort of understanding. We're only acquaintances."

He chuckled softly, amused at her protest. "No wonder you two are drawn to each other. You lie nearly as well as he does."

"How dare you!" she chastised with as much force as possible given that she was locked behind bars. "I don't know who you are, but I will *not* allow you to slander Lord Chesney. He is a hero who risked his life for his country." She sniffed at him disdainfully, finding him lacking in comparison. "Which I'm certain is far more than can be said for someone like you!"

At that the colonel burst out laughing. "So you're not upset that I accused you of lying, but that I accused Chesney?" He shook his head. "Oh, you two are perfect for each other!"

"I told you—" She swallowed hard as she willed her voice not to tremble. "He and I are only acquaintances."

The colonel leaned toward her until his eyes were level with hers through the bars. "I know who you are, Josephine Carlisle." All the teasing of just moments before had vanished. His expression was solemn, but affection laced his voice. "I know why Thomas came to Lincolnshire. And I know how you two have been spending your time."

Her face flushed hot with mortification. Good heavens, he *knew*!

"From what I know of him, and from all I've seen and heard about you," he told her quietly, "I'm not opposed to you joining the family."

He'd meant to reassure her, but his words only cut deep into her heart. A sigh seeped from her like air from a deflating balloon, and her shoulders slumped heavily. Instead of clenching the bars in anger, she now held them to keep from falling away. "Thomas doesn't want that," she admitted softly, each word tearing from her.

"He doesn't know yet what he wants."

"He knows." Hot tears of utter desolation filled her eyes. "He wants to be with the War Office, and I can't compete with that."

"You don't have to."

With a sad shake of her head, knowing he didn't understand, she took a deep breath. "I'm not important enough for him." She knew the truth. Even if Thomas hadn't wanted to be an agent... "He's going to be a duke, and I'm an or—" She bit off the word and choked out instead, "I'm no one."

"The adopted daughter of a baron, you mean?" he asked gently. "An orphan."

Her eyes shot up to his. There was no harsh judgment on his face and not a trace of pity.

"Trust me." A hint of private amusement gleamed in his eyes. "The Matteson family likes orphans. And you are far from unimportant to him, or I wouldn't be here making certain you're safe."

She desperately wanted to believe that Thomas cared for

her, but if she couldn't trust Thomas to tell her that, how could she trust this stranger?

She pointed at the book on the cot. "And that? Am I supposed to believe that's real? I saw him toss it into the fire. I watched it burn with my own eyes. How am I now supposed to trust either him or you... or that book?"

"As soon as you look at it, you'll understand. You can trust me because Chesney asked me to help you tonight, and I always keep my word. And you can trust him," he assured her quietly, his face softening, "because he loves you."

Her heart thumped so painfully that she pressed her hand against her chest as if she could physically will away the raw pain slicing inside her. No, *impossible*. Thomas didn't love her. If he loved her, he wouldn't have burned the book, and he certainly wouldn't be leaving for London in the morning. And yet she was just foolish enough to hope... "He told you that?"

"Of course not. But he does. He just can't admit it to himself yet."

Closing her eyes against the stinging heat of her unshed tears, she drew a shuddering breath. He was mistaken. Although he seemed to know Thomas well, in this matter she knew him better than anyone, and she knew his heart was still his own, still set on returning to the War Office, no matter the cost.

And the cost was a future with her.

"We're running out of time." He pushed a sack through the bars. "Change into these," he ordered, the concern and gentleness she'd seen in him just moments before replaced by a solemn, businesslike demeanor. "We're due for visitors, and I can't have you so obviously looking as if you were up to nefarious activities tonight. Give me those clothes you're wearing before anyone suspects you might just be a lady bandit after all."

Muttering to him to turn around to give her privacy, she took the sack and retreated to the dark shadows in the rear of the cell. She pulled the muslin dress from the bag, a blue-and-yellow floral print with white lace trim. One of her favorite dresses. She grimaced in irritation. *Of course.*

Thomas must have broken into her home and sneaked into her bedroom to retrieve her clothes, right down to stockings, shoes, and shawl. *That*, she realized, had been the real reason he'd been late to dinner. He hadn't arranged a gaolbreak but a housebreak. She blew out a frustrated breath as she slipped out of the black clothes and into her dress. If Thomas loved her, he certainly had an odd way of showing it.

"I'm finished." With her black clothes inside the sack, she pushed it through the bars. "Here."

"And your pistol." He leveled a hard gaze at her. "Wouldn't want you shooting Chesney before you have the chance to marry him. After all, some things should be left for the honeymoon."

She returned his stare for a moment, her lips parting at his audacity. Then, with a newfound appreciation for his observational skills, which were proving nearly as keen as Thomas's, she lifted her skirt, pulling it up to the end of her stocking and to the small pistol she'd hidden there. To the man's credit, he never looked away from her face.

She handed over the gun.

"Thank you." He tucked the pistol beneath his coat, where she was certain he already carried at least one other pistol, and mumbled to himself, "Never trust a chit with a gun, I always say."

"Never trust a spy, *I* always say," she countered, with a knowing arch of her brow.

At that he hesitated and, without openly acknowledging that she was correct about him, he drawled, "Odd. I always say that the only person you *can* trust is a spy." He shook his head knowingly. "A pretty woman who's too smart for her own good—oh yes, you'll fit perfectly into the Matteson family."

Ignoring the foolish tickle of hope licking at her toes that he might be right, she leaned forward, pressing her face between the bars. "Let me out, please."

"Apologies, but I can't do that. Chesney's orders."

She stared, stunned. "Thomas asked you to lock me up?"

"It's the only way to keep you safe." He gave her a half grin of wry amusement. "Apparently you won't stay where you're told, and we can't have you getting in the way."

Leaving her to fume, he sketched a shallow bow, then tucked the sack beneath his arm and retreated toward the door.

"Miss Carlisle, it was truly a pleasure meeting you. I have a feeling we'll be seeing a lot more of each other in the future." He paused, his hand resting on the door handle. "One more thing. There's a basket of food in the back of your cell. Your alibi for why you're here. You felt terrible that Mr. Cooper had been arrested, so you brought him a basket to comfort him, then stumbled into the cell and accidentally locked yourself inside. After all, you have a reputation for being clumsy." His eyes gleamed mischievously. "Even I heard you fell off your horse in the middle of High Street."

Biting back a sharp curse, knowing the fault was her own for having set herself up like this, she watched him leave.

She sagged against the door. Thomas had ordered her locked up! There was no gaolbreak, and most likely none had ever been planned. The story had been nothing more than an irresistible ruse to get her here so she could be kept out of the way for whatever else he had planned tonight. He'd lied to her, blast him.

But he'd also saved her.

In the morning, when the constable and his men found her locked in the cell, wearing her floral-print dress and waiting with a basket of Cook's biscuits at her feet, no one would believe she could possibly be a highwayman, no matter how much she protested. No one. *Ever.*

By locking her up, Thomas had ensured that she would never be accused of the robberies, but he'd also eliminated any chance he'd had of arresting her and being noticed in London. Yet her chest burned with anguish. Not arresting her because he didn't want to see her hang was a far cry from loving her.

Pressing her hand against her heart, she slumped down onto the cot, and her gaze strayed to the book lying beside her, the ledger that contained all the information she needed to prove Royston guilty. The book with the peculiar list of names, the one Thomas had told her could never leave his room.

She closed her eyes at the stab of pain in her chest. Whatever that list of names meant to him, he'd chosen it over her with a ferocity that had left her trembling. Treating it as if it were some sort of holy book, or secret document, or—

Secret document.

Oh God.

Her throat tightened, and her veins turned to ice. Not just a list of names. Not just a ledger of transacted goods... *Oh God!*

Thomas had known immediately the ramifications of that list, but she'd been so selfish in forcing him to choose between her and the book that she'd been blind to what it truly meant. She thought he'd chosen the list over her, but now... What had she done? What awful choice had she forced him into making?

Her hand shook as she reached for it.

Her tentative fingers picked it up, and she frowned. The back cover was missing, the spine torn down the middle, pages ripped out—

Her heart somersaulted. Thomas hadn't given her the book. He'd cut it in two and given her the front half! She held in her hands the information about Mrs. Potter and the orphanage, all the evidence she needed to link Royston to the orphans. But Thomas had kept the second half for himself, the ledger she was never supposed to have seen and that she now knew put both their lives in danger.

Laughing in pained disbelief as a riot of emotions churned inside her, she turned the book over in her hands. He'd managed to do the impossible after all . . . keep her from being arrested, stop Royston, and prove to the War Office he was ready to return.

But most of all, this half of the book proved that Colonel Grey was right—Thomas loved her. He hadn't said it, but his mad machinations tonight confirmed it.

Yet her hand shook as she swiped at the tears that now rolled freely down her cheeks, and her chest burned with unbearable grief and loss, so much that she could barely breathe through the pain of it. Because for all he'd done tonight, he still hadn't found a way for them to be together.

*   *   *

"It's a shame you came all the way from London for nothing, Chesney," Royston commented in the darkness of the swaying coach as the horses raced toward the village.

Across from him Thomas kept his silence as he casually folded his hands between his knees and relaxed against the squabs.

"The constable beat you to the highwayman, after all, and you did nothing to stop him or hunt him down," he accused coldly. "Might have stayed in London for all the good you did here."

Outside the carriage the night was black. A thick layer of clouds hid the stars and moon, and the scent of rain hung heavy in the air. Thomas's gaze darted out the window at the passing scenery, and he recognized the bend where the road turned to follow the river, flowing along beside them now like a black ribbon sewed tight against the edge of the hard-packed dirt beneath their wheels.

"You know, Chesney," Royston continued, his tone greatly confident, "when I approached you about finding this bandit, I had hopes you were the man I could count on to finish this business. I was assured by several men that you were the man I needed, one who would fulfill his mission and keep his silence. Sadly, they were wrong about you."

Thomas said nothing. Instead he kept his face stoic in the shadows, thankful for the darkness that hid any trace of the hatred he now held for this man who had once been a trusted family friend.

"I should have known you wouldn't be up for the hunt." Royston clucked his tongue softly, as if blaming himself. But Thomas knew full well where the earl was heading, and he let the man continue. "Not after the way you were gunned down last year. Surprised everyone that you lived, thank God."

"Thank Lucifer," Thomas corrected coldly. God had nothing to do with what had happened to him that night.

Royston frowned quizzically but otherwise ignored his comment. "But you didn't come back the same man, did you? I'd heard rumors even then that Chesney had lost his nerve, couldn't hold a gun steady, had lost the thrill of the hunt." He paused to let his words hover in the air between them. "That he'd become completely useless."

Thomas had heard the rumors himself. Worse, he knew them to be true. But that didn't stop his hands from clenching into fists.

"Still, I gave you one last chance to prove yourself, and all you had to do was find a highwayman. One highwayman in a village of less than three hundred people, and you couldn't even do that." Shaking his head, he leaned back against the seat. "I'm certain you understand that I won't be recommending you to the War Office now."

Thomas certainly hoped not, given that Royston was a traitor.

"In fact, I feel obligated to tell Bathurst about the concerns I have regarding your behavior this past sennight." Royston smiled devilishly in the darkness. "After all, we wouldn't want you putting anyone's life at risk."

Josie. The hairs on his arms prickled in warning, and he forced himself to keep his voice even as he asked, "Is that a threat?"

Royston shrugged. "You're returning to London tomorrow a failed hero. And Josephine Carlisle is lovely. *Quite* lovely."

Every ounce of restraint in his body tightened into a ball inside his gut and somehow kept him from lunging across the coach to close his hands around the bastard's throat. "Yes, she is."

"I'd have to be a damned fool not to see you've been plowing her."

Royston was a dead man. At the first opportunity, Thomas would kill him, and the only thing preventing him from doing it now was the very real likelihood that Royston carried a knife up his jacket sleeve.

"You've asked her to perform other dirty deeds for you as well. I found her in my study pretending she'd torn her dress. But you know that, don't you? After all, someone unlocked the door for her. For all I know, you tore the dress yourself before you sent her inside."

His body tensing, ready to spring at the first sign of physical provocation, Thomas carefully kept his silence.

"She might be entertaining on her back, but she's just as incompetent at spying as you are," Royston sneered with a hint of cold delight, "because nothing was missing from my study."

Thomas stared at him darkly. Royston didn't know they'd found the book. The same one he had so carefully replaced after his meeting with Grey and Edward, then stolen a second time from the study and cut in two, right before he'd tardily entered the dining room tonight.

"Whatever it was you sent her after, she didn't find... luckily for her."

Thomas gritted his teeth, so hard his cheek twitched. "Leave her alone," he growled in a low warning.

"I will, you have my word on that. *If* you keep your silence." He shifted in his seat, his hands tugging at his coat sleeves under the pretense of pulling them into place, but Thomas knew he was sliding the hidden knife down toward his palm. "Her fascination with you will fade once you're gone, and there will be no reason to involve her in anything further. But if I hear one whisper about this highwayman and his connection to me, then she *will* pay for your mistakes."

She was already paying for his mistakes, Thomas thought grimly, glancing out the window just long enough to notice that they'd crossed into the cover of the woods.

"She's a pretty little thing, and so spirited." Royston

tugged at his gloves. "But I don't suppose it would take much to break her."

So much more than you realize. Josephine Carlisle was the toughest woman Thomas had ever met.

"Your silence, Chesney," the earl pressed, "in return for the girl's safety."

His eyes remained intently focused on Royston now, but he was alert and aware of every movement and sound around them, from the creak of the carriage as it bounced over a rut in the road to the distant howl of a dog. The night was alive, humming with electricity, but Royston was oblivious to the tension rising around them. And that lack of attention to the details would be his downfall.

"I would do anything to protect her," Thomas assured Royston quietly, and meant every word. He would lay down his life for hers.

Royston smiled, a slow and wicked grin full of arrogance. "I'm glad you're being so reas—"

Gunshots and shouts split the quiet night. The carriage lurched to the side, swaying dangerously onto two wheels and forcing both men to grab for the handholds to keep from being tossed to the floor.

"What's happening?" Royston demanded angrily, pounding his fist against the roof to get the coachman's attention.

"We're being robbed, of course," Thomas answered calmly.

Royston's eyes widened in the darkness. "Impossible! Cooper's locked away in a cell, his horse is being held in the constable's barn."

Thomas said nothing and watched the earl through the shadows, letting the night's events unfold exactly as he'd planned.

The sound of pounding hoofbeats swarmed around them,

more gunshots and shouts. With a yell from the driver, the team pulled to a skidding stop. The carriage creaked and cracked, halting so suddenly it rocked dangerously back and forth on its springs.

Shouted orders for the driver and tiger to move away from the carriage, horses snorting, the sounds of scuffling— through all the noise and confusion, Thomas stared straight at Royston, never taking his eyes off him.

The door opened with a crash as it smacked against the side of the coach. The highwayman leaned down from his horse to point a pistol inside at Royston's chest. "Put up your hands!"

"What is this?" Royston exploded with surprised fury.

"You're being robbed, you nodcock." The highwayman's deep voice rang with annoyance. "So put up your blasted hands!"

Thomas's lips twitched. From the irritated scowl behind the black mask, Edward Westover was clearly not enjoying his part in tonight's events. But as the former colonel of the Scarlet Scoundrels and a well-seasoned veteran of the Peninsular War, he possessed the skilled horsemanship to be a successful highwayman, able to hold up the carriage and lead the constable's men on a chase across the countryside without being caught or shot—

"Hand over your money, goddamn you."

—if not the dashing temperament.

Thomas rolled his eyes. Edward hadn't even bothered to dismount, instead staying straight in the saddle as he tossed the burlap bag at Royston. The earl searched his pockets and withdrew what few valuables he had, dropping into the sack a handful of money, his gold pocket watch, and his signet ring.

The pistol swung toward Thomas. "And now you," Edward demanded gruffly.

"Not me," Thomas muttered quietly, no longer amused by his friend's antics.

"*Especially* you."

With a murderous glare, Thomas reached into his inside jacket pocket and withdrew his money, taking advantage of the distraction to expertly palm a tiny pistol against his large hand. He dropped the money into the sack and casually settled his hand over his thigh, the gun hidden from sight.

Edward shoved the sack into his saddlebag and fastened it securely, then signaled for the three men with him to leave. They spun their horses and dashed off into the woods, vanishing from sight in mere seconds in three different directions. He leaned back in the saddle and holstered his pistol as he glanced around the stretch of dark road, which remained quiet and still. Drumming his fingers on the saddle pommel, he waited impatiently as the seconds ticked by.

"Christ," he muttered, losing all patience. He swung his horse in a tight circle and pointed down the road. "When the constable *finally* arrives, tell him I went that way!"

Then he dug his heels into his horse's side, and the large chestnut gelding leapt into a gallop. The horse's hoofbeats faded into the distance, leaving the stopped carriage in darkness and silence with the bound driver and tiger the only evidence that a robbery had occurred.

As the sound of Edward's horse faded, three riders clamored down the road toward the carriage and pulled up sharply. The constable nearly fell out of his saddle from surprise.

"That way!" Thomas pointed urgently down the road after Edward. "After him!"

"Yes, sir!" The constable spurred his horse and galloped off after his men and straight into the wild goose chase Edward had planned for them, one that would lead them across the countryside and far away from the carriage.

Then Thomas slowly raised his pistol at Royston. "Make any sudden moves, and I'll kill you," he said calmly, noting the flare of surprised fury in the earl's eyes. "We're getting out of this carriage, and you'll send the driver and tiger on into the village while we wait here for the constable to return."

"You'll swing for this, Chesney," he threatened.

His lips curled into a grim smile. "I'll take my chances. Step out of the carriage—and slowly, keeping your hand away from that knife you've got tucked up your sleeve."

With a furious glare, Royston did as ordered and stiffly descended to the ground.

"Untie the driver," Thomas commanded beneath his breath and followed along less than ten feet behind the earl, far enough away that Royston couldn't surprise him with any sudden punches or kicks yet close enough to fire off a kill shot if necessary. There was no way in hell he was letting this traitor escape, certainly not after the way he'd threatened Josie.

Royston freed the driver, then set loose the liveried groom beside him.

"Are you all right, sir?" The tiger's voice shook from the surprise of the robbery, while the driver quickly checked the team and carriage.

"Fine," Royston bit out. His eyes darted murderously toward Thomas, who stood with his hand tucked conspicuously beneath his jacket. "You two drive on into the village."

The two men exchanged puzzled glances at the strange order.

Royston's eyes narrowed on Thomas. "The carriage might be damaged," he lied quickly, and rather expertly,

Thomas noticed. "You two ride into the village and have the blacksmith check it over. Chesney and I will wait here for the constable to return."

"Sir, beggin' yer pardon, I don't think it's safe—"

"Go on!" Royston bellowed.

"Aye, sir." The driver tugged at the brim of his hat, then gestured hurriedly for the tiger to take his position at the rear of the coach. Without questioning his employer further, the man swung up into his seat and set the team forward. They rattled off down the road toward the village, the lamps dimly lighting their way.

"What the hell is going on here?" Royston demanded furiously, wheeling on Thomas. "What are you up to?"

"I'm putting everything to rights tonight." Thomas withdrew the pistol from his jacket and pointed it directly at the earl's chest. "Starting with arresting you for treason."

Royston snorted derisively. "With what proof?"

"The ledger you hid in your study, the one containing the names of British agents you've been selling to the enemy and the recorded amounts of bounty you received for each one you delivered."

As Royston paled at the accusation, a bitter taste rose in Thomas's mouth, and he knew without a doubt the full damage the earl had done to the men listed in that book, to the War Office, and to England. What damage he could have done to him and his family.

"You bastard," Thomas bit out, white-hot fury seething through him. "You listed the price next to each one! Good men died because of your greed."

"Spies," Royston returned. "Not good men."

"My name was on your list. Good God—" The thought sickened him as he forced out, "Our families have been friends for years. Is that why you didn't hand me over?"

Royston stared at him coldly. "I would have, eventually. But you became worthless. A bullet saved you."

With a slight shake of his head, Thomas muttered, "You have no idea." Then he raised two fingers to his lips and gave a shrill whistle.

At his signal four men on horseback, led by Grey on his imposing black horse, surged out of the woods and surrounded them with drawn pistols pointed at Royston. The earl slowly raised his hands.

"You were right, Royston, when you said I didn't come back the same man after the shooting." Thomas leveled his gaze down the barrel of the pistol pointed straight at the man's cold heart. "I came back better."

He cocked back the hammer, the soft click reverberating through the night like cannon fire. Royston shuddered and closed his eyes.

"Grey!" Thomas yelled over his shoulder. "Get him out of here before I kill him."

"Yes, sir," Grey answered firmly, then motioned for his men to come forward and arrest the earl.

Grabbing him roughly by the arms, two of the men pinned Royston against a nearby tree, grinding his face into the rough bark as the third man searched him and pulled the knife from his sleeve. Then they grabbed his wrists and clamped metal shackles around them before tugging him toward the horses and shoving him up onto a saddle. With a pounding of hooves, they were gone, disappearing down the road and into the black night.

Grey tucked his pistol beneath his jacket, retrieving a second pistol and handing it over to Thomas. "That belongs to Miss Carlisle. Give it back to her, will you?"

Thomas grasped it and, with a heaving toss, threw it away toward the black river as hard as he could. It landed out of sight with a dull plop in the cold water, lost forever on the river bottom.

Grey arched a surprised brow.

"I don't like guns," Thomas explained dryly as he tucked his own pistol into his coat pocket, then took a deep breath and exhaled hard to expel the last of the murderous anger inside him.

"Here, catch." Grey tossed him a set of keys.

He easily caught them one-handed. "You'll ride straight through to London, then?"

Grey shook his head. "I don't think the earl's fit enough for that, and I want him delivered alive and in one piece."

Thomas's mouth pressed into a grim line. "So they can torture him and then execute him?"

"Exactly what he deserves. God only knows how many of our men were killed because of him." Grey sent him a hard look. "And he had your name, too, remember. No one comes after my family and gets away with it."

He swung easily up into the saddle. His horse pranced in a circle, eager to be off after the others, but Grey checked him expertly with a firm hand on the reins.

"You'll be staying in Lincolnshire a bit longer, I assume." Grey grinned. "After all, you have that pretty loose end to enjoy tying up."

Thomas ignored the teasing innuendo. He was too preoccupied with that same little hellcat to join in on the joking and simply shook his head. "Only until tomorrow morning. Edward and I will take care of everything here tonight and catch up with you by nightfall tomorrow."

Grey leaned down and extended his hand. "You did well."

He clasped the outstretched hand of this man who had become a true brother to him and acknowledged quietly, "Couldn't have done it without you."

"Damn right." With an arrogant grin and a teasing glint in his eye, Grey drew up straight in the saddle. "Give my best to Miss Carlisle. And tell Westover he makes a damnably poor excuse for a highwayman."

He pressed his heels into the horse's sides, and it reared up onto its hind legs, then plunged forward down the black road at a gallop and out of sight in a matter of seconds. The sound of fading hoofbeats lingered in the night long after he'd vanished.

For a moment Thomas continued to stare through the darkness, letting the silence and stillness of the woods sink beneath his skin. He held his breath and waited for the attack to come, for that fear of the darkness and silence to set his heart racing and his lungs gasping for breath, for that surge of alarm to course through his muscles and leave his body shaking and his stomach sick. The same fear and anxiety that had paralyzed him nearly every night since that evening last year in Mayfair.

He waited…and nothing happened. His heartbeat remained slow and steady, his muscles loose, and with a heavy sigh, he exhaled deeply and began to breathe.

For the first time in over a year, he welcomed the cool air of the night, the silence that let him hear his own heartbeat, and with every pulse, every chill, he felt alive and strong. There was no fear left in the darkness because now the night reminded him only of a pliant and warm body molding against his, a soft voice whispering his name as if he were the only man in the world, a calming touch…and all of it wrapped up into one challenging, stubborn slip of a woman.

Of all the women in the world, he thought with both aggravation and amusement as he untied his horse, which had been left for him in the woods as planned, the one woman who calmed him was the same one who heated his blood.

The one for whom he'd have surrendered his life was the same one he couldn't live without.

The same one, he thought, grimacing as he mounted and set the horse into a canter toward the village, who was currently sitting locked behind bars with nothing to do but think up new ways of tormenting him.

It was time to set her free.

CHAPTER THIRTEEN

The gaol door burst open and slammed back against the wall with a splitting bang.

Startled, Josie jumped up from the cot and raced to the cell door just in time to see her three brothers charge inside, their hands clenched into menacing fists, with the baron and baroness quick on their heels. Behind them, bringing up the rear, bounced Miranda Hodgkins.

"Oh no," Josie groaned, her chest sinking. The last people she wanted to find her like this...

"There she is!" Sebastian pointed toward the cell, and her mother's hands flew to her mouth in horror as she screamed.

"Mama, please!" Josie tried to reassure her, but her outstretched arm through the bars only terrified her mother more. "It's all right. I'm fine."

"Josephine, what on God's earth happened to you?" Her father took her stunned mother by the shoulders and gently handed her to Quinn, who grinned at his sister with unabashed glee and a touch of admiration. Then Papa came

forward and reached a hand through the bars to affectionately cup her face. "Miranda told us we would find you
here."

"Miranda?" Stunned with confusion, Josie looked at the
girl, who absolutely beamed with happiness to find herself
at the center of attention.

"It was Lord Chesney!" Miranda practically squealed,
clasping her hands together at her chest. "He told me in the
drawing room that he trusted me to relay a very important
message about you being here." Her head nodded rapidly in
confirmation. "He asked me to do him a favor . . . a *personal*
favor."

Josie blinked. "He asked *you*, of all people, to—"

"Josephine, why are you here?" her father demanded,
reaching the end of his patience.

Dodging Papa's disapproving scowl, irritation replacing
worry now that he knew she was safe, she lowered her eyes
in humiliation at the idiotic lie she was forced to tell about
herself. "I came to visit Mr. Cooper, and I . . . accidentally
locked myself into the cell."

That stopped them all cold, each of them staring at her
silently. Blinking in wonder. As if she'd just admitted to accidentally setting London on fire.

"You did *what*?" her mother exclaimed incredulously,
batting away Quinn's hand on her arm.

Her shoulders sagged. "I accidentally locked myself into
the cell," she repeated as her cheeks heated with mortification. "I felt terrible that Mr. Cooper had been arrested, so I
went down to the kitchen to fill a basket. I brought it here,
but the constable and his men were away, so I went looking
for a way to put the basket into his cell and accidentally shut
the door on myself." Oh, she felt like the village idiot! "Isn't
that right, Mr. Cooper?"

"Yes, miss, exactly right," John Cooper agreed with her story, which had sounded so much more believable just minutes before when they'd practiced it together.

"That's the food, right there." She pointed in the direction of the basket sitting at the back of the cell, left in plain sight to easily confirm her fake alibi.

"You were looking for a way to give him a basket of food," her father repeated incredulously.

"At midnight," Sebastian added.

Robert put in, "In the adjoining cell—"

"And got yourself locked in!" Quinn finished with a laughing grin, ignoring his mother's orders to shush. Behind him Miranda giggled.

Josie gritted her teeth in embarrassment. If she ever saw him again, she promised herself, Thomas Matteson was going to pay for this. And dearly.

Judging by the suspicious look on her mother's face, however, Elizabeth Carlisle did not believe a word of the story. "We'll discuss this later." She waved her hand in frustration at her husband and oldest son. "Now release her so we can all go home and put this night to bed."

While Sebastian stepped forward to try the barred door, rattling it futilely in his fists, the baron searched through a desk in the center of the small room, hunting for the keys.

"There's nothing here to unlock it," her father mumbled, slamming a drawer closed.

Josie's chest plummeted. Colonel Grey was responsible for that. Of course they wouldn't find any keys, because he'd surely taken them all in case someone came by and tried to let her out before Thomas's plans for the night were over. Oh, how *dearly* he would pay!

"Then we'll get a sledgehammer and bust her out," Robert decided, which caused Quinn to grin even more broadly and rub his hands together gleefully at the prospect of tearing down the wall.

Josie's eyes widened. Apparently there was going to be a gaolbreak tonight after all.

"You are *not* busting down that wall!" their mother exclaimed.

"But it won't take long," Robert assured her. "A few good whacks—"

Quinton interjected, "Just a couple of swings—"

"And we'll have her right out," Sebastian finished.

Her mother imperially arched her brow. "I said no!"

"What the bloody hell!" A cry of surprise split through the loud arguing.

Constable Rivers pushed through the doorway and stared in bewilderment at the four men crowding his gaol.

Then he saw the baroness and, with his face reddening, he snatched his hat from his head and gave her a polite nod. The two men behind him did the same. "Beg yer pardon, my lady."

"Rivers, get my daughter out of there," her father demanded.

The constable glanced over his shoulder toward the cell that should have been empty, saw Josie peering out at him through the bars, and then snapped around to face her, his spine going ramrod-straight. "How in the world...*Miss Carlisle*?"

She nodded from behind the bars with a polite smile. Oh, she was mortified! "Good evening, Mr. Rivers."

"How—how did you— Why are you—" He gaped at her in stunned confusion, opening and closing his mouth in bewilderment like a caught fish.

"She accidentally locked herself into the cell," Miranda piped up helpfully.

Rivers blinked. "You did *what*?"

Her hands covering her face in overwhelming embarrass-ment, Josie sagged against the wall, her cheeks hot and tears stinging at her eyes.

She supposed she deserved this, that this was her due punishment for the past two years of lying and breaking the king's laws. And she now knew exactly why Thomas had wanted her locked up *here*, when he could have just as eas-ily locked her into the cellar at Chestnut Hill, tied her up and left her at the cottage, or found any one of a dozen other places to stash her for the night where he could be assured she wouldn't endanger herself or get in his way during what-ever he'd plotted.

No, she realized as her heart thudded hard with humili-ation. He'd wanted her to be discovered behind bars by her family in order to drive home how much she cared about them and how much they truly loved her. If she was mor-tified that her family had found her like this, presumably behind bars because she'd innocently locked herself in, then how unbearable would the humiliation, scandal, and ruina-tion have been if she'd been placed under arrest for being the highwayman?

And Thomas was right. As she looked at her family now, all of them concerned over her safety, not one of them was willing to leave her here for the night, no matter what they had to do to free her. She had been so wrong to ever doubt her place in their lives or their love for her. A tear rolled down her face as she glanced from her mother to her father with love swelling in her chest, and then she laughed through her tears at her brothers as they still insisted to the constable that the most expeditious way to free her was to knock down the wall. This was her family, now and forever, and finally she believed in her heart that she would have them with her always.

"We could get some gunpowder and blow open the lock," Quinn suggested helpfully.

Josie pressed the back of her hand to her mouth and stifled a tear-filled laugh. Dear God, how much she loved them!

"No gunpowder," her father chastised Quinn. Then he gruffly ordered Rivers, "Release her."

The constable shook himself and started toward the cell, reaching for the ring of keys tied to his belt. "Of course, your lordship."

"I blame you for this, Rivers," her father continued, despite the gentle hand his wife placed on his arm to check his anger. "Why was there no one here tonight on watch?"

"Don't usually keep anyone on watch overnight, sir," Rivers explained, jangling the three keys and trying each one in the lock, frowning when none of them fit. "No need for it."

"But you and your men are all here now."

"Aye." His frown deepening, he went through all the keys again. "We'd gotten a message tonight that the highwayman was going to strike again and rode out to catch him."

"But that's impossible!" Josie squeaked.

"Impossible, all right," John Cooper echoed quickly from his own cell, drawing everyone's attention as he lunged toward the door, his hands folding around the bars as he glared at Rivers, "since you had me locked up for being the highwayman. So either the highwayman didn't rob anyone tonight, or I ain't the highwayman!"

Josie tilted her head as she listened to her old friend, her lips parting suspiciously at the rehearsed tone of his speech. He had known there was going to be a robbery attempt tonight. He'd *known*! And with both of them behind bars, no one would ever be able to place the blame for the robberies on either of them. Their alibis had been literally locked up tight, thanks to Thomas.

The constable's bald head reddened. "There *was* a robbery," he grumbled as he momentarily gave up on her door and stepped over to the adjoining cell to unlock it. "Earl Royston himself."

Josie's hands tightened on the bars. "What?"

"You'd better let me go right now, then," Cooper demanded angrily, his loud voice drowning hers out.

Rivers gritted his teeth as he unlocked the door and swung it open, then stood face-to-face with the tall, lanky farmer. "I still don't think you're innocent in all this, Cooper. You had that horse at your farm."

Josie held her breath, her heart hammering fearfully as she watched the two men stare at each other. She waited for the constable to finally comprehend what events had unfolded tonight, for John Cooper to admit the horse was hers, for the details of the robberies she'd executed so carefully over the past two years to finally be revealed—for her life to end.

"I told you, Rivers," Mr. Cooper insisted, still protecting her. "That horse jumped the fence and ran up to the trough where I feed my own team. The beast was still under the saddle when you found it, weren't it? Think I'm daft enough to ruin a perfectly good saddle and bridle by leaving 'em on a horse in a lot with a farm team?" When the constable obviously didn't believe him, Mr. Cooper tossed up his hands and scowled. "Bah!"

Neither the constable nor his men tried to stop him as he stalked from the gaol, out the door, into the night—

And right past Thomas Matteson as he leaned against the doorway, his arms folded across his chest, curiously watching the scene unfolding before him.

"I think I can explain," he offered casually.

* * *

All at once everyone began to talk at the same time, squawking and quibbling like a flock of chickens, with Althorpe confronting the constable and demanding that his daughter be released immediately, the constable confused because he didn't have the right key, the Carlisle brothers turning on the constable's men, and her mother rolling her eyes sharply at Miranda Hodgkins, who clapped her hands gleefully at all the excitement.

Ignoring the confusion erupting before him, Thomas didn't say a word as his gaze flicked across the room to lock with Josie's. She stood unmoving behind the bars, right where he'd entrusted Grey to place her for safekeeping. But he could also see the confusion flitting across her face as the realization of all that had happened tonight sank through her, right along with all the emotions churning inside her.

"You," she said in stunned wonder, her voice lost beneath the angry bickering rising around them. "You did all this..."

In reply he gave her a slow smile, so damned glad—and utterly relieved—to see her there. Then he pushed himself away from the doorframe and sauntered slowly toward her.

"Chesney!"

The commanding voice bellowed from behind him, cutting through the squabbling between her family and the constable's men and stopping him cold in his steps. Taking a deep breath, he paused for a beat before reluctantly tearing his eyes away from her.

A tall, distinguished man appeared in the doorway, his bushy gray brows drawing together tightly in scowling disapproval beneath a black beaver hat. "You have the situation well out of hand here, I see." The room fell silent at the man's commanding presence. His back was ramrod-straight, his eyes hawkish as they swept around the room before settling on Thomas. "As always."

"Lord Bathurst, sir." Thomas nodded curtly. "You're right on time."

"Your message said one o'clock." He snapped open a gold pocket watch and checked the time, then glanced pointedly at the others as he frowned. "I was under the impression that this was to be a private meeting."

"It will be," he assured the man. Then he bowed his head formally. "Lord Bathurst, Secretary of War and the Colonies, may I present to you Richard Carlisle, Baron Althorpe, and his family."

"Secretary of War?" Josie spoke quietly from behind the bars, then turned away as Thomas's eyes slid in her direction when her father came forward to greet the earl and her mother curtsied deeply.

"Constable Rivers," Thomas continued with a gesture toward the stunned man, who nodded speechlessly at the introduction. "The constable and his men were just about to escort the baron and his family home safely, weren't you, Rivers? After all, there's a highwayman on the loose tonight."

"Aye, sir." Rivers capitulated grudgingly, his feathers ruffled. He clearly didn't like being ordered about inside his own gaol. But he was now outranked to an absurd degree and pointedly reminded of it by the scowl from Lord Bathurst, the most powerful man in the country after the Prince Regent and the prime minister. Then he reddened with embarrassment. "I don't seem to have the key with me to unlock Miss Carlisle."

"*Miss* Carlisle?" Bathurst's bushy brows drew together at the mention of a woman behind bars.

"My daughter, sir." The baron grimaced in her direction.

From the humiliated expression on her face before she turned away, Thomas knew she'd never again embarrass her family like this. *Good.*

Bathurst glanced toward the cell. "Your daughter has been arrested, Althorpe?"

"She accidentally locked herself inside," Miranda informed him quickly.

The secretary's gaze narrowed as it swung suspiciously back to Thomas. "She did, did she?"

"Yes, sir," Thomas answered evenly. "An hour ago."

"Then you'd best let her out."

"Beggin' yer pardon, sir," the constable put in, "but we'll have to send for the blacksmith. I seem to have misplaced the key—"

"Not you. *Him.*" Bathurst's lips tightened irritably as he gestured toward Thomas. "Something tells me Chesney has possession of the key."

On cue Thomas reached into his jacket pocket and held it up. "Rivers, please take the baron and his family home while the secretary and I unlock Miss Carlisle." His order was clear. He wanted them all to leave, and it was not a request.

Althorpe stepped forward. "I am not leaving without my daughter."

"I'll make certain she arrives home safely," Thomas assured him. "I'll escort her to Chestnut Hill myself."

That did not mollify her father. "I will not allow her reputation to—"

"Darling." Elizabeth Carlisle placed her hand gently on her husband's arm, a knowing expression brightening her face as she glanced at Thomas. "It's all right. I'm certain Lord Chesney would never willingly let any harm come to her, neither to her person nor her reputation." Her blue eyes met his, but Thomas was unable to discern if she was forcing a promise from him or giving a warning. "Would you, sir?"

"You have my promise as a gentleman, my lady," he answered solemnly.

His response drew a disgusted grunt from Robert and a heavy sigh from Miranda, but Elizabeth Carlisle gave him a soft smile. When the baron led his wife out of the gaol in grudging acquiescence, the baroness lingered behind to squeeze Thomas's arm in silent approval before stepping out into the night, with all three sons and Miranda trailing after.

When the last of the constable's men left and closed the door, leaving the three of them alone, Thomas shook the secretary's hand. "Thank you for coming, sir. I wasn't certain you would."

"I reckoned I owed you this much."

And Thomas reckoned Bathurst owed him a great deal more for the cold rejection of his attempts during the past year to return to service.

"I have to admit that I am also very curious about what you wrote in your message," he continued, purposefully vague as his eyes darted toward Josie, who watched the two men closely. "I hope it was worth my trouble to come here tonight."

"You won't be disappointed, sir."

Thomas reached beneath his jacket and withdrew the second half of the book. He gave it to Bathurst, then watched silently as the distinguished secretary thumbed through the pages, at first quickly, and then more slowly as page by page the realization of what he was holding in his hands dawned on him. Unable to hide the startled expression registering on his face, he darted his gaze from the book to Thomas, then back to the book. His hands shook.

"Dear God." His voice was low and grim. He blew out a tremulous breath. "Is this what I think it is?"

Thomas answered simply, "Yes."

Bathurst narrowed his eyes at Josie. "If that girl had this—"

"No," Thomas interjected adamantly. "She's only in the cell for safekeeping."

"Then who?" he demanded.

"Simon Royston."

"Royston...*Earl* Royston?" Bushy gray eyes shot up in disbelief. "That's not possible."

"I assure you, sir, it is." His face turned grim. "This accusation will be easily proved, and I think there are others in Parliament and the Regent's cabinet who will find interesting the other activities he's been up to over the past decade as well."

"Where is Royston now?"

"Colonel Grey arrested him and is currently transporting him to London. I'm certain Grey will want to go after whoever gave Royston this information himself." His blue eyes darted toward Josie, but it was impossible in the shadows of the cell to read the expression on her face as he added, "I'll catch up with them tomorrow and be on hand for the questioning, with your permission, sir."

"Of course." Bathurst gave a curt, preoccupied nod, and Thomas knew that was the closest thing to an apology he could ever hope to receive from the secretary for casting him away after the shooting. The War Office wasn't a men's social club, and no quarter was given to those incapable of doing their part, but there was no doubt now that the secretary knew he'd been wrong.

Bathurst lifted the book with a frown. "Where's the other half?"

"There's nothing in it that—"

"I have it!" Josie called out from the cell. She thrust her half of the book out between the bars. "Take it, please."

"Jo, Bathurst doesn't need that," Thomas said quietly. He'd given her that half of the book as evidence against Royston in case his plans for the night went horribly wrong, as her protection if the earl managed to slip through his fingers and get away. But more than that, he'd given it to her as proof that he cared about her and that he would never doubt her again.

She stared at him intently, her eyes filled with a wretchedness that tore at his heart. "But it would be better, though, wouldn't it, to have the whole book? The entire story of everything Royston's done from the very beginning?"

"Royston's being charged with treason," Thomas answered gently. "The evidence against him is too damaging to ever be made public. If you hand over that part of the book, it will be buried with the rest of the evidence. People will know he committed treason, but no one will know how he used the children for his own gains."

"But it will help you return to the War Office." Her voice was nothing more than a soft breath.

He shook his head, his chest tightening. "Josephine, you need to know—"

"Lord Bathurst, will it help if I give you this half, too?" she pressed, turning her gaze on the secretary.

The two men exchanged silent, grim glances, then Bathurst nodded slowly. "Yes, it will."

Thomas bit back a curse as the secretary took the first half of the book from her and mumbled his thanks. He tucked both halves inside his coat, then nodded toward the cell. "Best to take Miss Carlisle home now, Chesney, before her family storms the gaol again and you're forced to explain the truth behind how she came to be locked up tonight."

"Yes, sir." He grimaced and shook Bathurst's hand.

"Miss Carlisle, meeting you was indeed a pleasure." He sketched her a bow before retreating to the door. "Chesney, I'll see you in London in a few days." Just as he stepped outside, he turned to give one last parting look at Thomas. "And welcome back to the War Office."

The door closed behind him.

Thomas glanced toward Josie, but she was gone, retreated into the shadows at the rear of the narrow cell. *Damnation.* He desperately needed to talk to her and explain, but this was not how he wanted the conversation to begin. Taking a deep breath, he unlocked the iron door and swung it open.

She stood at the far end, staring at the wall with her back toward him, one hand on her right hip in a gesture of frustration and anger, but her other hand swiped at her eyes. The small movement nearly undid him.

"Jo," he called softly, his heart breaking that he'd made her cry, tonight of all nights.

She stiffened but didn't face him. "Ironic, isn't it?"

He hesitated. "What is?"

"That you came here to arrest the highwayman but are now setting me free." Her voice choked. "And all the evidence linking Royston to the orphans really is gone forever now."

"You didn't have to give Bathurst your half of the book."

"Yes, I did." She faced him then, and even in the dim light of the lantern and the shadows it cast into the cell, the expression of deep loss on her face cut through him like a knife. "Because you need it to prove how you connected the highwayman to Royston, Royston to the political favors... all the way to that list of names." Her voice choked. "You need it to be a spy again."

He shook his head because she didn't yet understand. "You didn't need to give—"

"Yes, I did," she whispered. Then the words rushed out in a shuddering sigh. "Because I love you."

He froze, every muscle in his body tightening. His heart stopped. Josie loved him, she'd actually said it. *Dear God*...she *loved* him.

When his heart started beating again, the blood coursed through him in shuddering pulses that left him tingling. For the first time since the shooting, he truly felt alive. Because of her. And he knew for certain, then, that the demons and the darkness that had smothered him would never return.

A tear rolled down her cheek. Not bothering to wipe it away, she sank onto the cot. Her body shuddered, her hands white-knuckled as she gripped the edge of the cot beneath her. The sight of her shoulders shaking as she fought back the silent tears pierced his chest.

No, this was definitely *not* how he'd wanted this conversation to begin.

"Josephine." He sat next to her, but when he took her shoulders and drew her against him, she pushed him back.

"Don't," she whispered, and shrank away.

He fought back the urge to grab her and sweep her into his arms, to kiss her senseless and make every last tear disappear. But he would do as she wished and leave her be. For a few minutes. "Tonight isn't what you think." Feeling the overwhelming need to touch her, he slid his hand along the edge of the cot until his fingers brushed warmly against hers. She flinched but didn't pull away. "I did all of this for you, Jo."

"To keep me from being arrested, I know." Her voice hitched in her throat. "But you're leaving for London tomorrow morning."

"Yes," he said solemnly.

"Then I hope—"

"Just as soon as I speak with your father to offer for you in marriage."

Josie stared at him, her lips parting as surprise jolted through her. His handsome face blurred beneath the hot tears welling in her eyes. Oh, heavens, he couldn't have said— certainly couldn't have meant . . . She breathed out, so softly that barely any sound crossed her lips, "*What* did you say?"

"That I love you, too, Josephine Carlisle." He cupped her face in his hand and touched his lips to hers. "And tonight, when I return you to Chestnut Hill, I plan on asking your father for his permission to marry you. And I think your mother will help convince him in my favor." Grinning, he laced his fingers through hers and lifted her hand to his lips to kiss it. "She likes me."

"But—but the War Office," she stammered, just as confused now as she'd been at the start of the conversation when he'd first unlocked the cell door to set her free, when she was convinced he was leaving her behind, condemned to a life without him. "That was the reason you came here, why you sent for Lord Bathurst—you wanted to be an agent again."

"I did want that once." He gently brushed the tear from her cheek. "But now I want you more."

"You want me . . . ," she repeated breathlessly. She blinked as the truth slowly dawned on her. "Everything that happened tonight—the gaolbreak, Colonel Grey, the robbery . . ."

"It was all to keep you safe." He exhaled a long, hard breath. "Even as recently as tonight, I thought leaving you behind was best for both of us, that I could deny my feelings for you and just walk away. You deserve a perfectly safe, normal life, and I was afraid I couldn't give that to you, that I couldn't make you happy."

She smiled through her tears. "You've already made me happ—"

He touched a finger to her lips and silenced her, then lifted a brow. "I practiced this all the way into town, so let me get it out."

She nodded silently against his finger, not daring to utter another word.

"When I met you, I felt healed for the first time since the shooting. I needed that—I needed *you*, Josephine." His finger at her mouth began to caress her lips, and his eyes grew intense as they stared deeply into hers, so deeply that a warm shiver rushed through her. "I still do. And I always will."

Then he sank to one knee in front of her on the stone floor, taking both her hands in his and raising them to his lips to kiss them.

Her eyes widened. "What are you doing?"

"I'm proposing."

"But we're in a gaol—"

"Damnation, Jo." He rolled his eyes in impatient frustration. "I'm trying to be *romantic*. So be quiet and let me do it, all right?"

She nodded, her pulse racing and her breath coming shallow and fast.

He laced his fingers through hers. "I have never met any other woman like you, and I know that I never will again. You are the most challenging, stubborn, determined woman who ever—"

She blinked. "*This* is romantic?"

Except for a twitching of his lips, he ignored her comment and continued, "—who ever graced my life, along with a beauty, kindness, and loyalty beyond measure. I cannot imagine the darkness that would have continued for me if I hadn't met you. But now, with you, I see nothing but a life of happiness and hope ahead of me."

Her throat tightened with emotion. "Thomas," she choked out in a whisper. Tears dropped down her cheeks.

His own voice cracked. "Will you marry me?"

"Yes, I will." She threw her arms around his neck, falling down into his embrace and tumbling onto the floor with him. Her tear-streaked face buried into his shoulder, and she couldn't hold back her sobs of happiness. "Oh yes!"

His arms went around her and pulled her close. Then he kissed her tenderly, with so much desire and love, with so much of his soul, that she trembled.

He shifted away from her just far enough to take her left hand. "With everything that had to be done tonight, I didn't have time to buy you a proper engagement ring, but perhaps this will do until we're in London."

He slipped his gold signet ring tenderly onto her hand, and it dangled huge on her dainty finger. He frowned. One by one, he tried the ring on all her fingers, finally giving up and sliding it onto her thumb.

Laughing with happiness, she cupped his face in her hands and kissed him with all the love she carried inside herself.

This, she thought as he wrapped his arms around her and held her close, *this* was what truly belonging to someone meant. She had her family, and now she had him, and for the first time in her life, she didn't fear the future. She welcomed it.

CHAPTER FOURTEEN

Lady Matteson, Marchioness of Chesney, eventually Duchess of Chatham... *Thomas's wife.*

Josie smiled to herself as she ran the list of names through her mind again. The last one was the best of all.

Too excited to sleep despite all the tiring events of the past few days, she sat curled up in a chair in front of the fire in her bedroom, her legs tucked beneath her and her toes sticking out from under the hem of her night rail. Around her the house slept, dark and quiet, with dawn only a few hours away.

Thomas had brought her safely back to Chestnut Hill as promised, and even now she smiled at the way he'd looked when Papa met them at the front door. This man who was usually so strong, determined, and resolved stood as nervous as a schoolboy as he asked to speak privately with her father. With a reassuring smile at him over her shoulder, she'd been whisked upstairs by Mama, who kept hugging Josie tightly to her bosom and wiping away her tears of happiness.

An hour later—poor man! Papa tortured him for *an hour*—she heard Thomas finally ride off into the night.

Then Papa came to her room and asked her simply, "Do you love this man?"

"With all my heart," she whispered.

"My darling daughter—" His voice cracked with emotion. "Then your marriage has my blessing."

He tenderly kissed her forehead, his eyes glistening, and he led her mother from the room as Mama began to cry even harder.

Her brothers would be told at breakfast, although Josie suspected they already knew. The fact that they hadn't beaten Thomas senseless was definitely a positive sign regarding future family gatherings.

As for her, would the happy tingling in her toes ever stop? Oh, she hoped not! For the entire ride from the village to the house, she'd sat behind him on his horse with her arms tight around him, but she'd felt as if she were flying. She'd never thought she could feel this way about anyone, to want to find a way to wrap him inside not just her arms but also her heart, to hold him close there forever.

In a fortnight she'd be in London. While the details of the marriage contract were being settled, she would meet his family, plan for the wedding, and shop on Bond Street for her trousseau, and her mother had promised her a new wardrobe befitting the fiancée of a marquess.

But she didn't care about any of that. All she cared about was seeing Thomas again.

"Josephine."

The deep voice rained through her and replaced the tingle of excitement in her toes with a different kind of tingle, a different kind of excitement. She scrambled to her feet and faced him, stunned to find him in her room, leaning casually back against the closed door. Her heart leapt into her throat. She hardly dared to believe—

"Thomas," she whispered, smiling happily to herself at the realization that he'd picked the lock on her door to sneak inside her bedroom. That old spy trick . . . *her* spy.

His sapphire eyes moved deliberately over her. "All ready for bed, I see."

His words were a simple statement, surely not meant as a double entendre, but goose bumps sprang up across her bare arms and calves just the same. "Yes."

"Good," he murmured.

Oh, *that* wasn't just a simple statement! The single word trickled through her, heating her from the inside out, and when she licked her suddenly dry lips, she saw his hungry gaze linger at her mouth.

He pushed himself away from the door and stalked toward her. He stopped in front of her, close but not yet touching, and she swallowed, her stomach already beginning to flutter with longing and anticipation. He'd broken into her house, stealing through the darkness to her room—risking his very life if her brothers found out he was there—and she leaned toward him to once again lose herself in his strength and his warmth.

The nearness of him was heady and dizzying, and she drew a deep breath to calm her racing heart. "I thought you'd left for London."

"Soon." He took her chin and lifted it to touch his lips to hers. Gentle, soft, but with enough promise to stir arousal low in her belly. "But I wanted to see you again before I left." His lips caressed the corner of her mouth. "After all, we have a marriage to settle."

Already her heart had begun to race, her mind growing foggy, and his kisses were still light and fluttering, with none of the passion she yearned for. *Yet.* "But I thought you set-tled everything with Papa."

"Not everything."

She stiffened despite the erotic sweep of his tongue be-tween her lips and pulled back just far enough to stare into his eyes. "He told me you'd offered for me, and he ac-cepted." She paused, a stab of fear piercing her. "Have you changed your mind?"

"God, no! You belong with me, Jo. Nothing's stopping that." With a quick peck to her lips, he released her and knelt in front of the fireplace. "But your father isn't you, darling. Your happiness is what matters to me, and I want to settle the marriage agreement with *you*."

A thrill jolted through her. She was important enough to him that he not only wanted to marry her but also wanted to make certain the marriage terms were exactly what she wanted, exactly what would make her happy. As he stirred up the fire and added more coal until it cast a bright light and warmth into the room, she rested her hand on his shoulder.

"Leave that," she ordered softly. His hard muscles quiv-ered beneath her fingertips, and the small reaction thrilled her. She didn't want his attention on the fire—she wanted it completely on her. She wanted him in her arms, kissing her, loving her.

"But we'll need this, I think," he murmured, brushing his hands down his thighs to wipe away the dust, "for what we have to do tonight."

"What do we need to do that involves a fire?" she asked warily. The last time he'd been concerned with a fire, she'd thought he'd destroyed the book, and with it all chances at a future together.

"I told you. We're negotiating our marriage." He stood and shrugged off his jacket, then tossed it carelessly over the chair and deftly removed his waistcoat. "We'll probably want to see each other well when we do it." He voice lowered to a seductive growl. "And I certainly want to see you."

As he stripped his shirt over his head, leaving himself tantalizingly bare from the waist up, she realized he planned on doing far more tonight than discussing their upcoming marriage. Sweet anticipation licked at her toes.

"First." He tossed the shirt aside and bent down to pull off a boot. "When would you like to be married?"

Her eyes drifted shamelessly over him, and she answered a bit huskily, "As soon as possible."

"Good answer." He dropped the boot to the floor and grinned. "How soon?"

"Four months?"

"Two." His heated gaze never leaving hers, he removed the second boot.

"But Mama wants a grand wedding, and I can't cheat her out of the fun she'll have planning for it, all that fussing over details."

"Three?"

She nodded at the compromise, and he dropped the second boot to the floor. Oh, she was beginning to like this marriage negotiation business. A great deal.

He straightened and reached down for the fall on his breeches. "London."

Her gaze shamelessly lowered to his waist and waited for a glimpse of his manhood in the firelight. "What?" she asked thickly. She was trembling now, all of this making her head swim. She marveled that she could understand anything he was saying.

His lips twitched with amusement at her befuddlement, his hand stilling provocatively with his breeches half-unbuttoned. "The wedding will be at St. Paul's." Then he shoved his breeches down and stepped out of them to stand naked in front of her, his body magnificent in the firelight. Hard, sculpted muscles in his shoulders, his chest sprinkled with just a dusting of dark hair that led down to...*oh my*. She swallowed. Even half-erect, he was impressive. And he was all hers, tonight and always. "You'll look so beautiful there in your wedding dress."

If anyone found them together now, he would be a dead man once her brothers finished with him, fiancé or not, and she would be planning a funeral instead of a wedding. But how glad she was that he was willing to risk his life for her tonight. She smiled, far more wickedly than a woman should when discussing a church. "St. Paul's it is, then."

"And you?" He closed the distance between them with a single step and unfastened the half dozen buttons at the neck of her night rail.

"Me?" She closed her eyes as his hands opened her gown, revealing her neck and shoulders, the tops of her breasts beneath. Already her nipples puckered achingly against the soft cotton in expectation of his hands on her, of his body moving deliciously inside hers.

"What demands do you have of this marriage?" He tugged her sleeve down to bare her right breast, and she gasped.

"Babies," she whispered as he tugged down the other sleeve, the night rail falling to her elbows and exposing both breasts to his hungry gaze. "I want a house filled with children."

"Agreed, most definitely." His eyes flashed like sapphires as he pushed the night rail off her arms and let it fall to the floor at her feet. She stood before him completely exposed, now just as bare and vulnerable as he was. "I certainly plan to do everything I can to fulfill that marriage demand. And often."

She shivered as he looked her up and down, his eyes lingering with undisguised desire on her breasts and the patch of curls between her thighs, where even now she'd grown hot, moist, and aching.

"What else can I do for you, Josephine?" He slipped his arms around her and pulled her against him, warm body against warm body, soft curves against hard muscles. "What else can I give you to make you happy?"

Her eyes glistened with tears of happiness. "You."

"Granted." He lowered his head and kissed her, hot and openmouthed. There was no mistaking his desire and need for her. Sweet heavens, he shook with it!

Shoving his hands into her hair and pulling her head back to expose her throat, he moved his mouth down her neck and across her shoulder, nipping and licking and leaving a hot, wet trail across her skin. She bit back a moan. Her fingernails dug into his shoulders as his hands slid down her back to cup her bottom and lift her against him, his penis now fully erect, hot and hard as it pressed into her stomach. He bit her earlobe, and when she gasped at the sweet possessiveness of the bite, he swirled his tongue inside her ear and sent a cascade of fire raining through her.

"I want you, Josephine." His large hands slid around to her hips and brushed up her sides until his hands reached her breasts and captured them against his palms. His fingers spread out possessively across them, and he growled, "Tonight and always."

He rolled her hard nipples between his thumbs and forefingers, and she moaned and arched herself against him. Liquid flames shot from her breasts straight down to the throbbing ache between her legs. Oh, the things this man could do to her with even such a simple touch!

Emboldened by his love for her, she ran her hands down

his chest to the flat of his stomach, then lower still. He sucked in a mouthful of air between his teeth as her hand closed around him and began to stroke. She thrilled with this power she held over him, with the way she was able to make him tremble and lean into her so submissively. He wanted *her*, all of her, and she'd never felt so alive, so feminine, in her life.

He groaned out his pleasure, the words indecipherable in his arousal. She laughed lightly and tightened her grip as she stroked him. He grew impossibly hard in her hand, a rod of steel beneath soft, velvet skin. And every inch belonged to her.

His hooded eyes gazed down at her, dark with arousal and need, as if he could devour her by simply looking. Wanting him to do just that, she devilishly folded both hands around him, and as her palm circled over his enlarged head, made slippery from the droplets of his essence that gathered at his tip, he bit back a groan.

She laughed with happiness, and before she had a chance to stop him, he swept her into his arms and lowered her to the hearthrug in front of the fireplace. His body moved over hers as he kissed her, deeply and longingly, and she wrapped her arms and legs around him to pull him closer into the cradle of her hips, never wanting to let him go.

His hand stroked down between them, and she whimpered in response. She delighted in his touch, in each teasing circle of his fingers, each slow dip into her core, and she wondered again how he could make her feel this heavenly, both this excited and this relaxed at the same time.

"Marry me, Josephine," he urged as he lowered himself into her and sheathed his manhood completely inside her warmth.

"Yes…oh yes." With her arms clenched around his

shoulders, she closed her eyes and rolled her head helplessly against the rug as he stroked inside her, each retreat and deep plunge an exquisite torture.

His lips brushed against her throat. "Come be my wife and live with me forever."

"Yes," she whispered, "I will."

The intensity of his thrusts increased. As he leaned on one forearm over her, he grasped her calf and lifted her leg until her knee was bent between them, seating himself fully against her, shifting the angle of his penetration so he could slide even deeper inside her. With a soft whimper, she dug her fingertips into his shoulders and clung to him, as if she could keep him this close forever.

"I'll protect you," he whispered against her temple as he continued his heated slide in and out of her slick folds, stoking the growing heat licking at her belly. "I will love you, cherish you, and always care for you. There will never be anyone else, not inside my heart nor in my bed." Not pausing in his steady rhythm as he made love to her, he held her gaze in the firelight, his blue eyes flaming and bright. "There will only be you, Josephine."

He dipped his head to brush his lips over her cheeks, kissing away the tears as they fell from her eyes and swallowing her joy.

And then, so softly she barely heard him . . . "I pledge my life to you."

His words flashed through her, his love filling every inch of her. Her body broke around his, not with a passionate cry but with a soft whisper of his name as she buried her face against his chest. The love she carried for him overwhelmed her, and she could barely hold on to him as she seemed to fly away, straight through the ceiling and into the blanket of stars above, carrying him with her in her arms.

He thrust deeply into her, then held his body pressed tight against her as he released himself inside her with a low groan. He poured his life's essence into her and, with that, his soul.

He lay motionless on top of her, and she kept her arms wrapped tightly around his neck and shoulders, their two bodies still joined deliciously together. Slowly their racing hearts calmed, their breathing grew steady, and reluctantly she released her hold on him so he could rest on the rug next to her and pull her into his arms.

She snuggled her naked body close to his and nestled into the hollow between his shoulder and his side, the same side forever marked by the bullet that had nearly claimed his life. The same bullet fate had used to deliver him to her.

"I want to change one of our marriage settlements," she told him as she traced idle circles across the warm skin of his chest with her fingertip.

"As long as it's not the one about having children." He lifted her chin to place a long, languid kiss on her mouth, and when she sighed, she felt him smile against her lips. "After tonight, that one might prove nonnegotiable."

A warmth stirred low in her belly at the possibility that she might have gotten with his child. Thomas's baby inside her! The thought overwhelmed her with sheer happiness. "Actually, I was thinking of a different one."

"Hmm?" His lips brushed across her forehead.

Dawn was coming soon, and he would have to leave, but for now he was completely hers. Without warning she rolled over on top of him, straddling his waist and pinning his shoulders to the floor. She gazed down at him and smiled. "Three months is simply too long to wait."

With a rakish grin, he raised his head to kiss her. "Agreed."

EPILOGUE

Chestnut Hill
May Day 1820

The three men stood shoulder to shoulder at the bottom of the sloping hill and laughed as the women came running toward them, barefoot in the grass beneath their swishing skirts and the children clasping their hands beside them. The afternoon sun shone golden and warm as they raced toward the wide pink ribbon stretched across the bottom of the hill, and around them the scent of honeysuckle and peach blossoms lingered on the late-spring air.

Edward watched Kate lovingly as she plunged down the hill, their three young daughters surrounding her and holding on to her hands and skirts. Her bonnet had fallen away, revealing flame-red hair that burnished in the sun like fire. She caught him watching her across the lawn and smiled at him brilliantly, laughing with happiness and love.

"She's an angel," Grey commented beside him.

Edward shook his head, grinning. "With that hair? She's a devil."

"Not *your* wife, Colonel." He nodded toward Emily as

she brought up the rear, with their four-year-old son running freely beside her and their toddler daughter in her arms. His eyes lit up with love. "Mine."

When the girl cried, Emily stopped to comfort her by rocking her in her arms, completely conceding the race. Immediately Edward's aunt Augusta rose from the tea tables beneath the shading boughs of the nearby chestnut trees and hurried to help her while the boy ran on, diverted from the goal of the ribbon and racing instead toward Grey, who grabbed his son and tossed him up onto his shoulders. When Emily joined them, he kissed her passionately right there in the middle of the May Day games and made her cheeks pinken in a pretty blush.

Halfway down the hill, a blond little girl in a sky-blue dress waved at her three uncles as the Carlisle brothers held the ribbon at the bottom of the hill and urged her toward them.

"Run, Clara!" Thomas cheered his six-year-old adopted daughter.

Her golden ringlets bounced as she slowed into a loping skip and glanced over to send him a bright smile—the same smile she used to consistently escape punishment from her doting father for misbehaving. Behind her Josie waddled as quickly as she could, her hand resting protectively under the large, round baby belly beneath her dress.

Edward's youngest daughter let go of Kate's skirt, and the toddler wobbled unsteadily for a moment, then plopped down in the grass with a scowling look of fierce consternation on her face making her so resemble Edward that a howl of laughter went up from both Thomas and Grey.

Edward ran up the hill and scooped his daughter into his arms, and with the girl giggling with laughter, he carried her down to the finish line and through the ribbon. Then his twin girls ran across the line, jumped onto their papa, and pulled him down to the ground beneath them, all of them laughing happily as they rolled together on the grass. When Kate stood over them, frowning sternly at their behavior, Edward grabbed her hand and pulled her down into the pile with them. Her laughter echoed across the garden.

Thomas watched them all, and his chest swelled—Edward and Kate as they kissed on the grass…Emily and Grey as they held their children in their arms…and his own beautiful, glowing Josie as she fended off well-meaning attempts by Miranda Hodgkins to help her into a chair.

"We made it, Grey," Thomas commented quietly, taking in all the joy and happiness surrounding them, the safe homes the three men had created for themselves and their families far from the madding cries of war, and the love they'd fought so hard to secure for themselves. They had all been wounded, all of them scarred, but the wounds had healed, leaving them stronger than before and ready for the rest of their lives together with the women they loved.

"Yes, we did." Grey rested his hand affectionately on Thomas's shoulder. "We certainly did."

When Edward Westover, Duke of Strathmore, takes possession of his rival's estate, everything that villain held dear—including his lovely daughter—belongs to Edward. Hire a governess, arrange a dowry, and be off on his way. That's Edward's plan. But he's in for the shock of his life. For his new ward is a beautiful, impetuous, and utterly irresistible... woman.

Please see the next page for a preview of

Dukes Are Forever

CHAPTER ONE

London, March 1815

*E*dward Westover stared across the card table at the man he was about to destroy.

The balding, paunchy gambler dabbed at his sweaty forehead with a handkerchief, then tugged at his cravat as if it choked him. The man's gaze lifted to meet his, and a jolt of satisfaction pulsed through him at the fear on the man's face.

Let the bastard be afraid. Let him get exactly what he deserves.

During the past year, Edward had thought of little else than the satisfaction he'd feel when this moment arrived, when he'd finally receive the justice that the English courts had denied him. Nearly every moment since he returned from Spain had been focused on ruining this man's life, and even now, beneath the stoic expression he carefully showed the room, he burned with hatred and a driving need for retribution.

In a matter of seconds, Phillip Benton would lose his last hand, and with that, his life as he knew it would be over. Edward watched the man closely and waited, counting off each heartbeat, and the only outward sign of his anticipation was a slight quickening of his breath. This must be how the devil felt when he took a man's soul, Edward decided, except that Benton had no soul to take.

The dealer turned the last card.

Benton gaped at it, unable to believe he'd lost. As Edward watched him blanch, a flash of satisfaction shot through him.

"The game's finished, Benton." *And so are you.* "Now, I'll take what you owe me." Welcoming the pleasure of the man's destruction, Edward reached for the marker and tossed it to him. "*Everything* you owe."

Benton forced a pacifying smile. "I haven't got it all with me tonight, of course."

Edward glared at him. From his arrogant demeanor, it was clear Benton still had no idea who he was nor realized the tragedy connecting them. But he would learn soon enough, and then Edward planned on making him regret for the rest of his life the actions that brought them together.

Benton motioned the gambling hell manager to the table. "Thompson, I've gotten myself into a spot again." With a forced laugh, Benton's jocular tone belied the desperation of his situation. "Would you assist me with my friend here"—but the scornful glower Edward shot him was far from friendly—"by advancing me enough to pay off my losses?"

Thompson coughed nervously, his eyes darting to Edward. "'Fraid I can't do that."

"Thompson!" he cried incredulously, loud enough that the men at the surrounding tables glanced up. He lowered his voice. "Have I ever failed to repay you? Have I ever forfeited so much as a pence?"

"You've always been a good customer."

Benton beamed. "Hand me a paper, then, and I'll swear out a note. My word's good."

Thompson turned awkwardly toward Edward. "What would you have me do, sir?"

"Why are you asking him?" Benton demanded.

"Because I hold your notes," Edward drawled, taking immense pleasure in the confusion that flashed across the man's face.

Benton snorted. "Thompson holds them."

"I bought them from Thompson," Edward explained, summarizing in a few words the time-consuming work of the past twelve months leading up to this moment, "just as I bought up all your debts. All the credit you owe the merchants, the lease on your rooms, your stable bills, and every pound of your gambling debt in every hell across London."

Benton turned scarlet. "What in God's name is going on here? Thompson!"

The manager shook his head. "You had too many notes, Phillip. You still owe me from last autumn. When I received the offer to purchase your debts—"

"Purchase my debts?" His voice rang loudly through the hell, stopping the play at all the tables. The men paused to stare, and hushed whispers rose throughout the room. "Sir, I demand an explanation!"

"I purchased your debts," Edward answered coldly, hating the man more with each passing heartbeat, "and now I demand repayment on them. *All* of them."

"You cannot demand such a thing."

"The law gives me the right to reclaim them with a fortnight's notice. Consider this your notice." Edward knew the answer, yet he took a perverse pleasure in asking, "Unless you can't pay?"

"Of course, I can pay!" His indignation sounded loud enough that everyone in the room heard it, but as he sank down in his chair, his shoulders sagging, he lowered his voice. "But not in a fortnight."

"Not at all," Edward corrected, relishing in the man's defeat. "Even if you sold every possession you own, you would still be in my debt." *Exactly where the bastard deserves to be.*

Despite the heat of the crowded gambling hell, Benton shivered. He looked at the marker on the table as if staring at his own grave.

"You'd send me to debtor's prison?" Benton's voice strangled in his throat.

Edward had considered doing just that many times during the past year—thrusting him into a cold, windowless prison to let the man rot away in his own filth behind stone walls.

"No." He wanted a public revenge with absolute control of every aspect of the man's life. If he couldn't hang the bastard, he'd at least make the man wish he were dead. There was no mercy in him tonight. That died a year ago with Stephen and Jane. "But I will take your house, all its furnishings, your horse, your clothes..." He venomously bit out each harsh promise and signaled to a distinguished-looking man standing awkwardly by the entrance. "Every last pence."

"I'll be left with nothing." He dabbed at his forehead with the handkerchief, then croaked out a pathetic laugh. "Nothing except my daughter."

"Then I'll take her, too," Edward said with an icy facetiousness. "And every last ribbon on her head."

"Who are you?" Benton demanded again, furious at being publicly humiliated.

The man reached their table. "Yes, Your Grace?"

Benton blinked, then bellowed, "*Your Grace?*"

"This is William Meacham." Edward calmly nodded toward his family's longtime attorney. "He'll inform you of the arrangements."

"Go to hell!" Benton clenched his fists. "I'm not agreeing to anything."

Benton swung his gaze to Meacham, and Edward could see the frantic thoughts spinning through the man's head. He'd seen that same angry desperation on the faces of defeated enemies when the battle was over and the terms of surrender negotiated. How little men changed from battlefield to barroom. And for this man, surrender was unconditional.

He'd give no quarter of any kind to this enemy.

"If you refuse my terms, Benton," Edward promised, "then I *will* throw you into prison."

Benton's face darkened with fury. "You would do that—you would ruin my life?"

"Yes."

"Why?"

"Because you ruined mine."

Benton caught his breath. "Who *are* you?"

"Don't you recognize me?" Edward rose from his chair, drawing up to his full six-foot height. This was the moment he'd planned for during the past year with an almost blind relentlessness, and as he'd expected, with it came a sweet flash of shattering satisfaction. "Edward Westover."

"Westover…" The name struck Benton with a violent shudder. "You're *Colonel Westover*?"

As he stared at Benton, the full force of his hatred and revenge rose in him and vanquished whatever brief satisfaction and pleasure he'd felt only moments earlier. Edward leaned over the table to gaze mercilessly at him. "I am the brother of the man you murdered."

He spun away from the table and stalked through the gambling hell toward the front door, putting the length of the room between them before he strangled Benton with his bare hands. Lost in the wrathful thoughts of his vengeance, he was oblivious to the presence of the man standing in the corner, who had watched tonight's events unfold and fell into step behind him.

His carriage waited at the front entrance, and he climbed inside. The tiger closed the door.

Shutting his eyes, Edward took a deep breath and waited for the peace that should have been his, the relief and happiness at finally making the bastard pay. But it didn't come, and even the flash of exquisite satisfaction he'd felt when Benton realized his identity was now gone. He felt only the same need to destroy Benton that he'd carried for the past year, tempered by the deep emptiness he'd felt since the moment in San Cristobal when he learned of Stephen's death.

The door flung open, and the man who had watched him from the shadows jumped inside. He pounded his fist against the roof, signaling to the coachman to send the team forward into the night.

"Colonel Westover." Thomas Matteson gave a short salute as the carriage lurched into motion. "Interesting evening."

"Captain Matteson." Edward glared at the old friend who had become like a brother to him while fighting together in Spain. And whom he now wanted to throttle for interfering in his life. "Get the hell out."

Ignoring that, Thomas relaxed against the squabs as casually as if he'd been invited into the carriage rather than flinging himself inside.

"We're in London. It's Lord Chesney here, if you don't mind." Thomas flashed a charming grin, the same one that had attracted the hearts of women across the Continent. Edward had lost count of the number of times he'd rescued the man from angry Spanish fathers. "I'm a marquess now, I daresay."

"So I'd heard."

Shortly after the battle at San Cristobal, Thomas's father inherited as Duke of Chatham, which meant this fearless former captain was now Marquess of Chesney and heir to a duchy. Which meant his life was too important to risk in the army. Dying in battle was fine for second sons but never for peers or heirs, a lesson that Edward knew only too well.

"I've proven you wrong." Thomas angled out his long legs. "You said I'd never make anything of myself."

"I said you were reckless and would get yourself killed," he corrected solemnly, unable to keep his concern from his voice. He was afraid his friend might yet prove him right.

"We're both headed to the Lords now." Thomas grinned at him. "Say a prayer for Parliament."

But Edward was in no mood for teasing around tonight, especially given the way fate had thrust the peerage upon both of them. The irony was humorless.

"Where's Grey?" Edward wouldn't have put it past the man not to be outside hanging off the carriage at that very moment.

"Somewhere in England."

Thomas's answer wasn't facetious. After he was wounded in the war, Grey's connections to the underbelly of society made him valuable enough that Lord Bathurst, Secretary of War and the Colonies, insisted he join the War Office. Grey was one of their best agents, and "somewhere in England" was as close as anyone could know.

Edward reached toward the door with the full intent of shoving Thomas out into the night. "I suggest you join him."

The marquess clucked his tongue. "Becoming a duke has

made you rather testy, Colonel. I prefer the man who used to set enemy tents on fire. He was more reasonable."

"You have no idea," he muttered. Then he exhaled a ragged breath, knowing the tenacious man wouldn't leave him alone until he had what he came for. No matter how damnably irritating the trait, Edward couldn't begrudge him. It was the same tenacity that had kept the former captain alive in Spain. "Why are you here?"

"I need your help," Thomas answered solemnly. "I have a friend who needs me to save him from himself."

Edward glared at him through the shadows. He trusted Thomas with his life, but in this, he was overstepping.

"If I wanted your help," he growled, "I would have asked for it a year ago."

"You weren't ready for it then."

Edward gave a derisive snort. "You think I'm ready for it now?"

"I think you're just as bullheaded as you've always been," Thomas answered, affection clear in his voice despite his words, "but I am not going to let you ruin a life without trying to stop you."

"Benton's, you mean."

"Yours."

Edward clenched his teeth, but even that small show of outrage was forced. He wasn't angry at Thomas as much as at what he represented—his old life, the one he'd been forced to leave behind. But that life was gone forever.

"How do you know about my plans for Benton?" he demanded.

"Your aunt Augusta. She asked me to talk you out of this scheme of yours."

"Then you can tell her it's too late," he assured him. "Meacham is settling the agreement now."

"You can still let Benton go." Thomas met Edward's gaze with deep sympathy. "What happened to your brother was unforgivable, and Benton deserved to hang for it. But he didn't. The magistrates let him go, and now you need to let him go, too, before he destroys your life as well."

Edward stared at him blankly, saying nothing.

There was a time when he would have sought out Grey's and Thomas's counsel and most likely taken their advice just as he would have his own brother's, but that was before his world changed. The Colonel Westover whom Thomas had ridden beside in the fires of war was gone. He might as well have died on the battlefield.

"You saved my life, Colonel, many times." Thomas leaned forward, his face intense in the dim shadows cast by the swinging carriage lamps. "And I will not let you ruin your life now."

Edward almost laughed. There was nothing Thomas could do to either stop him or help him. Except… "Can you watch Benton? I need someone I can trust to keep an eye on him until everything is settled."

Apparently realizing it was time to surrender the battle in hopes of eventually winning the war, Thomas grudgingly agreed. "I'll contact Grey to see if he has men to spare. But promise me you'll consider letting Benton go."

The hell I will. Edward held his gaze and lied, "I'll consider it."

But he would never change his mind. Benton was his prisoner now, as surely as if he'd chained him to the walls of Newgate himself. He might be free to come and go as he pleased, but he'd be living in rooms Edward chose for him. His every move would be watched, his every activity and choice would be Edward's to make, and never again would he have so much as a halfpenny to his name. There was nothing that would ever make him set that bastard free when his own brother lay dead in the churchyard.

"Good night, then, Colonel. And give my best to Aunt Augusta." Thomas opened the carriage door and swung outside, to drop away onto the street and disappear into the darkness.

Blowing out an irritated breath, Edward slammed the door shut.

Thomas was wrong. Revenge had proven easy. He didn't have to hang Benton; he didn't even have to give the man enough rope to hang himself. All he'd had to do was follow along behind and pick up the pieces. It had been that simple.

He'd won. He'd attained his revenge and received every capitulation he'd wanted, giving Benton exactly the punishment he deserved—the loss of everything he held dear. At the card table, when Benton realized who he was and what he'd done, an intense satisfaction struck him unlike anything he'd ever experienced before in his life.

But the sensation faded, and quickly, until all that was left was the same emptiness as before. Instead of the happiness and relief he expected, he felt hollow, as if he were missing half his life, with no idea where to find it.

* * *

Katherine Benton pushed back the hood of her cloak as she entered the blacksmith's house, her leather bag gripped tightly in her other hand.

"Forgive us, miss," Mrs. Dobson greeted her, "for fetchin' ye in the midst o' th' night like this."

She smiled reassuringly. "You did the right thing in sending for me."

The worried mother moved the toddler in her arms to the

other hip as another child wailed from somewhere upstairs and two boys chased each other through the rooms. There were now ten children in the small but well-kept house, with Kate delivering the last baby herself.

"Bless ye, miss," Mrs. Dobson sighed gratefully, and for a moment, Kate saw the glisten of fatigued tears in her eyes, "you comin' to help us, an' you wit' all yer own troubles."

Your own troubles. Ignoring the prickle of humiliation, knowing the woman meant well, Kate placed a comforting hand on her arm before Mrs. Dobson could go into detail about those troubles or remind her of how Mr. Dobson had been kind enough to buy her horse last year when she needed money. "Where's Tom?"

She pointed toward the stairs, then shooed away two youngsters at her skirts.

"Would you bring up a kettle of hot water and a mug, please?"

The woman nodded, and Kate hurried upstairs. Tom must have truly been ill tonight to have all the household in such an uproar, the children out of their beds and running wild, from the oldest at fourteen right down to the baby. Stomach trouble, the boy who had been sent to fetch her reported. *Please, God, let it be something I can fix.*

Taking a deep breath to steady herself, she stepped into the little room beneath the eaves that served as the bedroom for all six of the Dobson boys, with the three girls and the baby sharing a room downstairs. A young boy lay scrunched up on the cot in the corner, his father trying uselessly to comfort him as he grasped at his abdomen and groaned in pain.

Kate gently elbowed Mr. Dobson away, set her bag on the edge of the bed and opened it, then looked down at the boy. "Hello, Tom."

"Hello, miss," he returned, forcing the greeting out

through gritted teeth. Sweat beaded on his forehead. His face was pale, and his arms never released their hold over his middle.

She frowned. "James said your stomach hurts."

"Somethin' awful, miss." He swallowed down another groan.

"Show me exactly where."

The boy glanced uncertainly at his father, who nodded his permission, and Tom pushed the blanket down to his hips with one hand while pulling up his nightshirt with the other, baring his little, flat belly.

Kate touched his stomach carefully, starting with his lower left side and working her way across. "Here?"

He shook his head. Moaning, he placed his fingers over a spot high in the middle just under his sternum.

"Here?" Kate pushed into his abdomen, and he cried out. Her eyes narrowed, and from what she knew about this particular boy, she suspected... "Open your mouth for me, Tom."

He opened wide, and when she looked inside, she scowled, all worry inside her vanishing.

Now, she *knew*. "You sneaked out of bed tonight, didn't you?"

His eyes widened—he'd been caught. "Miss?"

"And judging by the pains, I'd guess most likely around midnight. Isn't that so?"

With competing looks of suffering and guilt flitting over his young face, he nodded.

She sat back on the bed and raised a sharp brow. "You got into your papa's tobacco."

He shot a worried glance at his father and moaned. Being caught—and fear of the punishment to come—only made his bellyache even worse.

"Your son has an upset stomach," Kate informed both husband and wife, who had remained in the doorway, the baby still in her arms and a tenacious toddler clinging to her skirts. "He'll be better by morning." She cast a sideways glance at the boy. "And I have a feeling that after tonight, he'll never touch your stash again. Will you, Tom?"

The boy glumly shook his head.

"Good. This should help." She pulled a bottle of white powder from her bag and poured some into the cup Mrs. Dobson handed her when Kate signaled for both it and the kettle. She poured in hot water, then stirred it. "Drink this." When the boy frowned warily into the bubbling mixture, she explained, "It's saleratus. The bubbles will help settle your stomach. Go on—drink it up."

Making a face as if being tortured, Tom gulped it down, then gasped in distaste.

"You'll be better in a few hours." Kate stole a glance at the mother and father, obviously overwhelmed by their brood. "How old are you, Tom—nine or ten?"

"Eleven, miss."

Even better. "Old enough for a job, then. Come visit me at Brambly tomorrow. We could use a boy for the stables."

That was a lie. Brambly had no need of stable boys, because Brambly had no stables. Because Brambly no longer had any horses except for an old swayback no one would take off her hands if she paid them. But she also knew that one less child to worry about would help ease the burden of the Dobson household, even if she wasn't certain how she'd manage to feed one more mouth in hers. But she would. Somehow, she always managed to find a way.

She closed her bag and stood to leave.

"Miss, are ye certain 'bout Tom goin' to work fer ye?" Mrs. Dobson pressed as she followed Kate downstairs. The couple wasn't poor but neither were they wealthy, and although sending Tom to work for Kate meant less money spent on him, more importantly it meant one less child to supervise.

"We could use the extra hands."

From the twitch of the woman's lips, she clearly didn't believe Kate, but she didn't challenge her. "'Twould be a great help, miss. It's always somethin' wi' children, ain't it?"

As if on cue, the baby wailed. The woman sighed and opened the door.

Kate stepped outside into the darkness and cold, not looking forward to the miles she'd have to walk home through the darkness.

"Ye should count yerself fortunate, miss, that ye don't have no children t' constantly scold an' fuss over."

Kate forced her smile not to waver despite the stab of jealousy. No, she had no children of her own and most likely never would. To make the sacrifices necessary to have a husband and family . . . She simply couldn't bring herself to do it.

"Yes." She drew her hood down over her face. "How very fortunate I am."

* * *

Inside his study, Edward poured himself a whiskey. Taking a gasping swallow and welcoming the burn, he turned toward the fireplace, where dying embers still glowed. He jabbed at them with the brass poker until he'd sparked a weak flame, more to physically expel the pent-up frustrations inside him than to stir up a fire. Around him, the town house was dark and quiet, with Aunt Augusta and the servants catching the last few hours of sleep before dawn.

He envied them. He hadn't slept well in over a year. And he knew he wouldn't tonight, either.

He was simply tired. That's why he didn't feel the lasting happiness he'd expected at bringing Benton to justice and why he let Thomas's words prickle him. In the morning, once he'd slept and the success of his revenge settled over him, the joy of vindication would come. He would feel happy then.

Happy? *Christ.* He'd be glad if he could feel anything.

With a curse, he tossed back the remaining whiskey and stared at the fire.

"Your Grace?"

He glanced up as Meacham paused in the doorway. Edward signaled his permission to enter, glad for the man's arrival. The sooner they settled everything regarding Benton's situation, the better.

Meacham nodded politely. The Westover family attorney for nearly thirty years, William Meacham had proven himself time and again to be a superior lawyer and a dedicated employee. Occasionally over the years, even a friend. When Edward's father died and Stephen inherited, with the two brothers just twenty and nineteen, Meacham had been an invaluable advisor, and Edward owed him more gratitude than he could admit or the man would accept.

For all the history between them, however, Meacham would never assume familiarity, and he would never cross any lines of decorum, not even at four in the morning. As the new duke, Edward should have been pleased by the deference paid to him, but it rankled. Since he'd inherited, no one was open and honest with him anymore.

His lips twisted. Apparently, except for Thomas Matteson.

"My apologies for the late hour," Edward said quietly.

"None necessary, Your Grace." Meacham reached inside his coat and withdrew the papers he'd prepared. "Benton agreed to your terms and in exchange signed over all his possessions, just as you demanded. He is bankrupt and in your debt." Then he added quietly, "Congratulations, sir."

Edward glanced at the papers only long enough to make certain Benton's signature crossed the bottom of each, then turned back to the fire.

It was done, then. Phillip Benton was now penniless, his life completely and publicly ruined. He would live in the small room in Cheapside that Edward provided, on a single pound's allowance that Edward gave him, watched at every moment and unable to make a move without permission— he had become a prisoner, or as close to one as he could be without being put into chains. His life had become Edward's to ruin, just as Benton had ruined his.

So why wasn't he happy?

"Thank you, Meacham. We're done for tonight."

The attorney hesitated. "There is one more item, Your Grace."

"What is that?"

"He has a daughter."

Edward frowned into the fire. Benton mentioned a daughter, but he hadn't thought the man was serious. In the months since he'd been having Benton trailed, his investigators hadn't seen nor heard any mention of a child.

He shouldn't be surprised, though, to learn Benton had a daughter who meant so little to him that he never went to see her or contacted her. The bastard had destroyed his own life through gambling, whoring, and drinking, and ruined the girl's life right along with his by denying her the care she deserved. A man like that didn't have the heart to love a child.

Meacham continued cautiously, "He requested that you become her guardian."

"No."

"If I may, sir, I think you should reconsider. Her mother is dead, and now with her father's situation—" A sharp glance from Edward made him censor himself. *Good.* Meacham and Thomas could both keep their bloody opinions about Benton to themselves. "You have your reputation to consid—"

"Damn my reputation," he muttered.

Meacham stiffened. "Your Grace, I do not believe you mean that."

Edward narrowed his eyes on him. This was as close as the man had ever come to overstepping between them, of being so familiar as to attempt to chastise. But Meacham wasn't wrong. Edward couldn't have cared less what happened to his own reputation, but now as the duke, he held the responsibility for the reputation of the Westover family and the title, whether he wanted it or not.

"Sir, you have made it so her father is no longer able to financially support her. Morally, she has become your responsibility. Best to make it legal as well." The attorney added plainly, his expression as paternal as Edward had ever seen it, "If you do not provide for her, and her situation becomes common knowledge, you will become a social pariah."

And Augusta right along with him. His aunt was his only family now, and he would never do anything to hurt her. "Fine." He turned dismissively back to the fire. "Write the contract."

"This is the right decision, sir," Meacham assured him. "It would have been regrettable to you if an innocent had been hurt."

Edward said nothing, not able to summon enough guilt to care. He'd seen hundreds of innocents hurt during the atrocities of war. What was one child's lack of ribbons compared to that?

"Someone should also travel to her home to ensure the suitability of her situation. I'll arrange for one of my assistants to leave next week—"

"No," Edward interrupted. "I'll go."

Meacham paused in surprise. "Pardon?"

"I'll go myself." Not that he truly cared about the little girl's feelings, but a legal clerk swooping down on her and frightening her was the last complication he needed when he wanted everything settled with Benton's situation as quickly and easily as possible. Screaming children and angry nannies would only add to his headaches.

He had another reason for going as well. After the ordeals of the past year, it would do him good to spend a few days alone in the countryside, riding and hunting, far from the family seat at Hartsfield Park and all the memories there. He wanted to go someplace where he could forget, if only for a few days, and where he wouldn't have the constant reminder of Stephen and Jane.

So he would meet the child, determine her living situation was satisfactory, then be on his way. Most likely, he'd be gone by teatime.

"If there's anything else," Edward instructed, "see me in the morning. Good night, Meacham."

"Your Grace." With a shallow bow, Meacham retreated from the study.

Edward refilled his glass and swirled the golden liquid thoughtfully. *So Benton has a daughter.*

Had.

She belonged to him now, as close to being his own

daughter as possible without sharing his blood, and she'd become his responsibility to raise, educate, and eventually marry off when she came of age. Rather, that is, she'd become Meacham's responsibility, as he planned on never directly concerning himself with the child again after his visit to her.

He hadn't planned on this, but now that she was part of the battle's aftermath, the guardianship would only make his revenge that much sweeter. She was a spoil of war he had no intention of ever letting Benton see again.

A daughter's life for a brother's. Fair retribution.

"Strathmore?"

Aunt Augusta appeared in the doorway. Despite the late hour, she held her head regally, every inch of her a countess.

He returned his tired gaze to the fire. *Good God*, he was exhausted... "No, just Edward."

"*Just* Edward?"

He rolled his eyes at the oncoming onslaught from Augusta and her fierce dedication to social position. Childless herself, his widowed aunt raised him and Stephen after their mother died when they were just boys, her duty as the duke's sister to keep them in line and away from scandal. They'd been a handful for her, but she'd corralled them with a stern command and a sharp glance. One of the few people in the world able to reprimand him, she still possessed the ability to shake him with a single look.

Such as the one she now leveled at him. "You are the Duke—"

"It is what I desire tonight." Forced decorum was the last thing he wanted to deal with, all those reminders of how much his life had changed. Tonight, he wanted to be just Edward again. "Please, for tonight, let it be."

She drew up her shoulders in that posture of grudging

surrender she assumed when she knew she'd pressed as far as possible but wouldn't win.

"I apologize for waking you," Edward offered, hoping to mollify her and avoid further argument.

"I heard the door."

"It was Meacham," he told her gently. "You should go back to bed and get a good night's rest. I'll join you for breakfast."

"Do you need anything? Should I call for Huddleston?"

He shook his head. Huddleston was a good valet, always eager to assist and please, but Edward found the attention cloying. He preferred to dress himself, just as he had in Spain despite having an aide-de-camp at his disposal, preferring his privacy. He would gladly do without a man completely if he could, but as a duke, that was impossible, and because Huddleston had been Stephen's valet, Edward kept him on.

"Sleep well, then." As she turned to leave, she rested a hand against his arm.

But he shifted away. He didn't want her motherly concern tonight, preferring to be left alone in his misery. Or it would have been misery, had he been able to feel even that.

Her face softened. "The title does not rest easy on you, does it, Edward?"

With a sag of his shoulders, he looked away, not wanting her to see the grief in his eyes. "It was Stephen's burden to bear, not mine."

"Your brother never considered it a burden. He saw it as his heritage."

"I'm a soldier." He shook his head. "This life was not meant for me."

"But it *is* your life now. Dear boy, you can spend all your time trying to convince yourself that you are still an army colonel, but you are not." A deep sigh escaped her, not of pity or mourning, but one borne of a wish that he could accept his new place as she had. "And you will never be *just* Edward."

With a soft kiss to his cheek, she left the room.

For several moments, Edward simply stared after her, unable to gather enough emotion inside him to be angry or hurt at her words. But he felt nothing. He leaned a tired arm across the mantel, too apathetic even to refill his glass and drink himself into oblivion.

As the second son, he was raised to make his own way in the world, and he had gladly done just that by purchasing an officer's commission when he finished university. On the battlefield, it mattered nothing that his family was one of the most powerful in England. What signified was character. His ability to carry out orders with an unfailing dedication to his men set him apart. And he excelled at it, earning himself four field promotions.

Then, in a cruel twist, fate stripped away all he'd worked so hard to achieve. The moment he inherited, his life as Colonel Westover disappeared, as if he had also died that day in the carriage accident that killed his brother and sister-in-law. He had been forced to step into his brother's life and carry on. As if his own existence up to that point hadn't mattered.

Legally, he was now Duke of Strathmore with titles and properties scattered across England, but he deserved none of it. By rights, he should still be fighting on the Continent, and Stephen should still be alive.

With Jane.

Even now, his chest tightened at the thought of her. The night Edward met her, when she'd entered the ballroom for her debut, he'd been mesmerized. With her dark hair and brown eyes, she wasn't a typical English beauty, but she had a vitality that drew him, a charm that the stiff rules of English society hadn't yet forced from her. He'd somehow managed to secure a waltz, and by the time the orchestra sent up its final flourishes and he whirled her to a stop, laughing in his arms, he was lost, despite knowing she wasn't meant for him.

The daughter of an earl, she was born to be the wife of a peer, and her future—and choice in husbands—had never been her own. And in truth, she'd never made any commitment to him.

Still, he pursued her in that reckless manner he possessed when he was younger, with the devil and his consequences both be damned. But he'd been too young, too inexperienced with women and the world, and far too arrogant to realize there were some things he'd never be able to have. No matter how much he wanted them. And he'd wanted her, not just for an affair but for the rest of his life, yet he never suspected she didn't share the same desires for a future together. So one warm afternoon as they lay tangled in the sheets of an unused guestroom at Hartsfield Park, he told her he loved her.

His eyes pressed shut against the memory. From ten years away, he could hear the sound of her nervous laughter and stunned voice as clearly as if she were still in the room with him…

Love? At least she'd had the decency to cover her mouth with her hand in apologetic shame as she murmured, *Surely, you cannot seriously think that I could ever marry an army officer—oh, Edward, no…* Her wide-eyed disbelief melted into a soft expression of pity. *I thought you understood…*

Apparently, he hadn't understood at all.

One week after that, he left for war, to put as many miles as possible between them, with no intention of ever returning.

And two months later, his brother Stephen, Duke of Strathmore, announced his engagement. To Jane.

Despite the fires of war and his anger at her betrayal in marrying his brother, it took several years to purge her from his mind. He'd led reckless charges into battle and offered to take the place of men of lesser rank in dangerous missions, not because he had a death wish but simply because he no longer cared what became of him, if he lived or died. Eventually, he purged her from his body, too, with a string of nameless women.

All of this he kept from his brother, who had once been his best friend and closest confidant. At first, he was too ashamed to share with Stephen how he'd fallen for a woman he should have realized all along could never be his. Then, when he learned of the engagement, this second, deeper humiliation by the woman who became his sister-in-law changed everything between the two men, and Edward knew he would never be able to tell him. The confidence they'd shared in each other since they were boys had been irrevocably destroyed, costing him not only his heart but also his brother.

The result, he calculated, was a distinguished military career and an immeasurable distrust of women. He would allow himself to enjoy their flirtations and attentions and gladly take whatever pleasures they willingly gave, but he would never again trust one with his heart.

Then, in an instant, his world ended.

Stephen and Jane had gone to London to celebrate the long-awaited news that she was with child. But drunk and angry from a night losing money at cards, Phillip Benton raced his phaeton through the narrow streets, blindly speeding around a corner and into the oncoming carriage. The two teams collided in a mangle of wood and metal, blood and